PENGUIN MODERN CLASSICS

TALES FROM THE UNDERWORLD

Hans Fallada was born Rudolf Wilhelm Adolf Ditzen in 1893 in Greifswald, north-east Germany, and took his pen-name from a Brothers Grimm fairy tale. He spent a number of years in prison and in psychiatric care, yet produced some of the most significant German novels of the twentieth century, including *Little Man, What Now?*, *Iron Gustav*, *Once a Jailbird*, *A Small Circus*, *The Drinker* and *Alone in Berlin*, the last of which was only published in English for the first time in 2009, to near-universal acclaim. He also wrote many remarkable short stories, the best of which are collected in *Tales from the Underworld*. Fallada died in Berlin in 1947.

Iron Gustav, *Once a Jailbird*, *A Small Circus* and *Alone in Berlin* are all published in Penguin Modern Classics.

Michael Hofmann is the author of several books of poems and the translator of many modern and contemporary German authors. Penguin publishes his translations of Fallada's *Alone in Berlin* and *A Small Circus*, Kafka's *Amerika* and *Metamorphosis and Other Stories*, Ernst Jünger's *Storm of Steel*, Irmgard Keun's *Child of All Nations* and Jakob Wassermann's *My First Wife*.

Jenny Williams is Professor Emeritus at Dublin City University and is the author of *More Lives than One: A Biography of Hans Fallada*, which is published by Penguin.

HANS FALLADA

Tales from the Underworld

Selected Shorter Fiction

Edited and Translated by MICHAEL HOFMANN

Foreword by JENNY WILLIAMS

PENGUIN BOOKS

PENGUIN CLASSICS

Published by the Penguin Group
Penguin Books Ltd, 80 Strand, London WC2R ORL, England
Penguin Group (USA) Inc., 375 Hudson Street, New York, New York 10014, USA
Penguin Group (Canada), 90 Eglinton Avenue East, Suite 700, Toronto, Ontario, Canada M4P 2Y3
(a division of Pearson Penguin Canada Inc.)
Penguin Ireland, 25 St Stephen's Green, Dublin 2, Ireland (a division of Penguin Books Ltd)
Penguin Group (Australia), 707 Collins Street, Melbourne, Victoria 3008, Australia
(a division of Pearson Australia Group Pty Ltd)
Penguin Books India Pvt Ltd, 11 Community Centre, Panchsheel Park, New Delhi – 110 017, India
Penguin Group (NZ), 67 Apollo Drive, Rosedale, Auckland 0632, New Zealand
(a division of Pearson New Zealand Ltd)
Penguin Books (South Africa) (Pty) Ltd, Block D, Rosebank Office Park,
181 Jan Smuts Avenue, Parktown North, Gauteng 2193, South Africa

Penguin Books Ltd, Registered Offices: 80 Strand, London WC2R ORL, England

www.penguin.com

First published in Great Britain by Penguin Classics 2014
001

Copyright © Aufbau Verlag GmbH & Co. KG, Berlin, 2009
(First published in 1991, edited by Günter Caspar)
Selection and translation copyright © Michael Hofmann, 2014
'Short Treatise on the Joys of Morphinism' and 'Three Years of Life'
first translation copyright © Michael Hofmann, 2011
Foreword copyright © Jenny Williams, 2014
All rights reserved

The moral right of the copyright holder, the translator and the introducer has been asserted

Set in 11/13pt Dante MT Std
Typeset by Jouve (UK), Milton Keynes
Printed in England by Clays Ltd, St Ives plc

Except in the United States of America, this book is sold subject
to the condition that it shall not, by way of trade or otherwise, be lent,
re-sold, hired out, or otherwise circulated without the publisher's
prior consent in any form of binding or cover other than that in
which it is published and without a similar condition including this
condition being imposed on the subsequent purchaser

ISBN: 978-0-141-39285-1

www.greenpenguin.co.uk

MIX
Paper from
responsible sources
FSC   FSC™ C018179
www.fsc.org

Penguin Books is committed to a sustainable
future for our business, our readers and our planet.
This book is made from Forest Stewardship
Council™ certified paper.

Contents

Foreword   vii

The Wedding Ring   1

Passion   15

Tales from the Underworld   31

Farmers in the Revenue Office   40

Kubsch and His Allotment   44

Mother Lives on Her Pension   48

A Burglar's Dreams Are of His Cell   51

Why Do You Wear a Cheap Watch?   54

On the Lam   57

I Get a Job   70

A Bad Night   83

The Open Door   93

War Monument or Urinal?   99

Happiness and Woe   109

With Measuring Tape and Watering Can   117

The Lucky Beggar   130

Just Like Thirty Years Ago   137

Fifty Marks and a Merry Christmas   141

The Good Pasture on the Right   161

The Missing Greenfinches   170

Food and Grub   184

The Good Meadow   190

Calendar Stories   201

The Returning Soldier   217

The Old Flame   226

Short Treatise on the Joys of Morphinism   234

Three Years of Life   253

Svenda, a Dream Fragment; *or*, My Worries   280

Looking for My Father   285

Note on Sources   303

Foreword

Hans Fallada wrote some ninety short stories during his lifetime. This anthology opens with the first story Fallada published, 'The Wedding Ring', which appeared in August 1925. It also includes one of his last stories, 'The Old Flame', which was published in November 1946, three months before his death.

Looking back on his career as a writer, Fallada declared in a radio broadcast in 1946 that 'everything in my life ends up in my books'. This statement applies not only to his novels but also to his shorter fiction, for the themes of the stories in this volume are drawn to a large extent from the turbulent life of Rudolf Ditzen (1893–1947), the man behind the pen-name Hans Fallada.

Ditzen's experience of working on the estates of the landed gentry in central and eastern Germany during the years 1913 to 1925 forms the basis of stories such as 'The Open Door' and 'Food and Grub'. It was his addiction to morphine and experimentation with cocaine during and immediately after the First World War that lends such an air of authenticity to the account of drug addiction in 'A Short Treatise on the Joys of Morphinism'. Unable to sustain such an expensive habit on the modest income of a steward, Ditzen was twice imprisoned for embezzlement in the 1920s. In prison he became acquainted with the lives of petty criminals and this encounter provided the material for 'Tales from the Underworld' and 'Three Years of Life', as well as 'Looking for My Father'.

Ditzen's struggle to find work after leaving prison in 1928 is reflected in 'I Get a Job'. He eventually found employment as a journalist in Neumünster in Schleswig–Holstein. 'War Monument or Urinal?' is based on his experience of the politics of a small town in Germany at the end of the 1920s, and 'Fifty Marks and a Merry Christmas' contains echoes of his first Christmas as a married man in 1929.

January 1930 saw Ditzen in Berlin, where the publisher of his first two novels, Ernst Rowohlt, had offered him a job in his reviews department. It was here that he witnessed the effects of the Great Depression on the lives of ordinary people in the city, such as the woman in 'Mother Lives on Her Pension' and the salesmen in the two stories 'With Measuring Tape and Watering Can' and 'The Lucky Beggar'.

In the autumn of 1933, Ditzen and his family moved to the remote village of Carwitz in the Mecklenburg Lake District, some eighty miles north of Berlin, in an attempt to escape the political and social turmoil that attended the Nazis' rise to power in the capital. 'The Good Pasture on the Right', which Fallada regarded as one of his best short stories, is set close to Carwitz and reflects the author's observation of the problems facing small farmers in the area.

'Svenda, a Dream Fragment' was composed in a Nazi psychiatric prison in the autumn of 1944. It forms part of the Prison Diary that Ditzen wrote in an almost indecipherable hand and managed to smuggle out under his shirt. The entry for 1 October opens with this story and it is clearly based on the previous night's dream. Its subtitle, 'My Worries', reflects the crisis in which he found himself. His first marriage had ended in divorce in the summer of 1944. Alcoholism and depression had taken a heavy toll on his health, and he had been incarcerated for observation and with no date for release in a Nazi institution that practised sterilization and euthanasia. The mysterious figure of Svenda bears some resemblance to his second wife, Ulla, whom he had met earlier that year. The description of the ruins of Berlin is based on his first-hand experience of walking through the city in February 1944, when he was undergoing treatment for depression.

'The Returning Soldier' deals with a common problem in the

aftermath of war and also refers to the Democratic Land Reform, which expropriated the large estates of the former landowners and redistributed the land among small farmers. This proved to be a very popular measure in the Soviet Zone of Occupation in 1946. Kurt Karwe in 'The Good Meadow' benefits directly from this policy and feels that 'life was just beginning for him' as a result.

Fallada's shorter fiction often relates in fascinating ways to the author's longer prose works. There are stories in this volume that are partially or completely recycled in later novels. The closing scene in 'A Burglar's Dreams Are of His Cell' (1931) anticipates Kufalt's return to prison in *Once a Jailbird* (1934), and chapter six of the novel contains an echo of the 'funny money' scene in 'A Visit to Jemmy-Max's' (1928). 'The Open Door' (1932) appears in a shortened form in *Once We Had a Child* (1934), where it is the newly wed Elise Gäntschow who suffers from her tyrannical husband's obsession with closing doors. Fallada incorporates the material of 'A Bad Night' (1931) into *Wolf Among Wolves* (1937).

In one case a story offers a glimpse of an early work that has not survived. 'Passion' is based on *Ria. A Short Novel*, which Rowohlt's editor Franz Hessel rejected in 1923. Two years later Fallada reworked the material into the short story 'Passion' and sent it to a rival publisher, who seems to have rejected this version, too, for it was not published until some twenty years after the author's death.

'Happiness and Woe' provides an insight into the creative process that produced the bestselling *Little Man – What Now?* (1932). The story represents an earlier and radically different version of an episode towards the end of the novel when the unemployed protagonist and his family are living illegally in an allotment on the outskirts of Berlin. A comparison of the two versions shows that Fallada chose a more conventional ending for the novel, a choice that was to contribute significantly to its success.

Although Fallada frequently insisted that he preferred the scope offered by a novel to the constraints of shorter prose works, he nevertheless continued to write shorter fiction. Following the publication of his first two novels, *Young Goedeschal* (1920) and *Anton and Gerda* (1923), his early short stories were part of a strategy to establish himself as a writer. After the success of *A Small Circus* (1931) and, particularly, *Little Man – What Now?*, he was inundated by requests for stories from a range of newspapers, magazines and literary journals.

However, as the Nazi Party began to tighten its grip on cultural life in Germany, the outlets for Fallada's short stories gradually disappeared. In the meantime, Rudolf Ditzen had discovered, like Kurt Karwe in 'The Good Meadow', that 'children are the only real riches in this life'. The stories that he invented to entertain his children gave him the idea for his first volume of children's stories. Published in 1936, this consisted of seven stories, including 'The Missing Greenfinches'. A second volume of children's stories followed in 1938. During the war years Fallada published two short works of young adult fiction, and while in prison in 1944 he wrote a story about Fridolin the badger for his eleven-year-old daughter, Lore. Children's stories allowed the author to create a world in which justice reigns and good generally triumphs over evil. In 'The Missing Greenfinches', young Thomas is brought up to respect all living creatures and to reject the cynical doctrine of 'might is right'. In the fictional world of children's literature, Fallada was able to make the kind of plea for humanity that could no longer be made in the public arena in Germany.

In the immediate post-war period, Ditzen and his second wife found themselves in the Soviet sector of Berlin. Here they received support from the cultural authorities that in 1945 were keen to enlist all non-Nazi writers and artists in the construction of a new Germany. Ditzen had not survived the war unscathed, for both he and especially his wife were heavily addicted to morphine. He spent the last seventeen months of his life in poor health, moving between clinics, hospitals and home among the rubble and chaos of post-war Berlin. The daily newspapers in the

Soviet sector paid extremely well and provided a most welcome source of income. This no doubt accounts for the fact that Fallada published twelve short stories as well as other short prose works, in addition to the two novels *The Nightmare* (1946) and *Alone in Berlin* (1947), between December 1945 and his death in February 1947. Given the speed at which the later stories were written, it is not surprising that some are of little literary merit, the rehashing of the Ria story in 'The Old Flame' being a prime example.

The fables and morality tales of the 'Calendar Stories' (1946) marked a new departure for Fallada. Here he draws on a tradition that originated in the religious stories incorporated in the folk calendars of sixteenth-century Germany. This type of edifying tale gradually developed into a short story sub-genre in its own right, as illustrated by Johann Peter Hebel's *The Treasure Chest* of 1811. Fallada concludes each of his nine 'Calendar Stories' with an explicit moral, in which he gives expression to his humanist principles.

Fallada's short stories attracted attention outside Germany during his lifetime. In the autumn of 1932, a Mr G. E. Halliday from the Curtis Brown literary agency in London approached Rowohlt for permission to translate some of Fallada's shorter fiction. Between 1933 and 1936 a number of stories appeared in newspapers and magazines in England. In January 1936, Halliday's translation of 'Fifty Marks and a Merry Christmas' appeared under the title 'Wishing is Free' in *The Argosy*, a magazine devoted to short stories. This story even made its way across the Atlantic to the USA, where it was included in a reader for students of German in 1937. The following year the Oxford University Press included 'I Get a Job' in its *Modern German Short Stories*, where the title was translated as 'I Find Work'. In this anthology Fallada found himself in the company of Thomas Mann, Ricarda Huch, Franz Kafka and Arthur Schnitzler, among others. The inclusion of Fallada's short story in this prestigious volume was evidence of Fallada's standing as a German writer in the English-speaking world at the time. It was also an indication that not everyone shared the author's reservations about his shorter fiction. In January 1939, the London publisher Robert Hale announced his intention to buy the translation rights to Fallada's second volume of children's stories. The outbreak of the Second World War put paid to such plans, however, and it has taken a further seventy-four years for the first collection of Fallada's short stories to appear in English.

The stories in this volume are populated with characters close to Fallada's heart: the ordinary man and woman in the street who bear the brunt of economic and political crises, the victims of the criminal justice system, the weak and the powerless, who are trapped in situations from which they cannot escape, as well as the children who bear the hope for the future. Fallada's acute observation of the human condition finds expression in a particularly concentrated way in the shorter fiction form. And through it all flows the author's commitment to human decency and his unflagging belief in the power of the human spirit. Or, as he put it in his sixth 'Calendar Story': 'victories won by force are not lasting. Lasting victories are only obtained by love and patience and common sense.'

Jenny Williams, 2013

The Wedding Ring
(1925)*

1

The women troop out to the field where they're going to lift potatoes. It's late autumn, there's been a light freeze overnight. Frost sparkles in the low sun. They're cold, but they walk slowly, and at the back of the line dawdles foreman Wrede, with his hands stuffed into his pockets.

He listens with half an ear to the women's chatter, he's had a bad night, his debts kept him awake. But all his thinking didn't help: it's only a small sum, thirty or forty marks, but he's damned if he knows how to lay his hands on it. Now, if he was a steward! It's ridiculously easy to make a few hundredweight of rye vanish without anyone being any the wiser. But as a foreman . . . what a hopeless life! He yawns; spits.

The line has reached the potato field. The tops are brownish-black and sodden, the ground is claggy and wet. Wrede assigns them to their respective rows, of course there's some backchat from the women, he ignores it, sits down on the wagon thill. The first flash of a mattock in the sun, then things quieten down and work begins. Slowly the stooped figures make their way over the ground.

Wrede pats his pocket for his tobacco pouch, but he's left it at home. A sullen rage stirs in him against this life, so grim, so monotonously bleak, a rage looking for a way out. He tramps off after the labourers. Where he spots a potato overlooked, he swears, but it's no release, his rage continues to boil.

He has to go back to the box cart, the first baskets are being

---

* The dates in brackets are those of the stories' composition. See Note on Sources.

emptied, he has tokens to give out. He stands on the thill and checks that the baskets are properly full. He'll show them who's boss all right, no one's going to get a token for anything less than a brimming basket. Why should they all be merry as grigs when he's out of sorts?

And now here's the Utesch woman. Another one of those bitches: thinks just because she's pretty and married young, she's exempt. He's slipped her potato tokens once or twice on the sly, but she's not to think she can make a monkey out of him. Anyway, she's in love with her man.

You couldn't say her basket was full, not with the best will in the world. He looks thoughtfully at the tubers rolling around at the bottom of her almost empty basket, looks at the woman standing on tiptoe, her basket held way over her head, and his eye fixes on her hand, jammed between basket and box, earth on it, but for a labourer's slender and shapely.

Something glints among the rolling potatoes. Wrede moves, is about to say something. Then bites his tongue. The woman takes back her empty basket, he gives her a token, she walks off.

He stands there quite still, his face suddenly feels hot, his brow is creased – is he thinking about something, very hard? Suddenly he yells, jumps into the box like a maniac, stands there with his feet among the potatoes and yells: 'Which of you has put stones in with her potatoes?'

He bends down, hurls clods of earth and potatoes out into the field; all the time his hands are groping feverishly. The harvesters are laughing, he hears scraps of mockery from one to another: 'He's really lost it this time.' – 'His missus must have had a headache.' – 'What a bastard, all he can do is torment people, he needs a mattock in his brain.'

Wrede climbs out of the box. Again, he shouts: 'If I catch anyone dropping stones in here, she's out of a job, you hear!'

But even that is an effort. He feels very hot, his heart is overbrimming. He knows very well he's going to have to keep this up all morning, if he's not to incur suspicion. He needs to go on scolding – even though he can now pay his debt.

He can pay his debt!

2

The day's over. Martha Utesch is in her kitchen, stirring barley mash for her pigs. She dunks her arms up to the elbows in the warm mass, to feel for any intact potatoes and break them up. The creamy mixture feels soothing. A vague feeling of emptiness comes up in her, an unspecific sense of things being somehow altered; slowly she pulls her right arm out of the swill and looks at it. It's gloved in a thick layer of creamy white. Almost reluctantly she takes out her other hand to help, takes it out of the bucket, her left hand brushes over her right wrist. She watches. Then across the back of her hand, which emerges a soft pink from the dripping swill. Then her knuckles . . . 'I don't believe it,' she breathes. And then she screams. She covers her face with her hands, she can no longer see, she plunges forward.

The carpenter's plane in the workshop suddenly stops. Utesch opens the door and asks: 'Did you call, Martha?'

Slowly she turns her face to her husband, and she is far away when she says: 'No. It wasn't anything. It was just the swill was too hot, and I scalded myself.'

He stands in the doorway, looking. The light of the oil lamp gives her hair a golden sheen, and the delicate pink of her face deepens to red. 'Really, Willem, it wasn't anything,' she says again, and she gets up, grabs the buckets and runs to the two pigs in the sty. She empties the swill into their trough, and they start slobbering and smacking right away.

I must have lost it grubbing in the earth, she thinks. There's no point in looking for it, it could be anywhere, I will have pressed it into the earth with my knees, and it's well and truly buried. What can I do? There's a chance it might surface later when we turn the ground, but who would ever see a little thing like that? What am I going to do?

She picks up her buckets, turns to the door, puts them down again.

Willem must never know. He wouldn't believe the ring was in the ground somewhere. The shepherd in Zülkenhagen had said a charm over the ring, and that was what had cured Willem of his jealousy. 'As long as you wear the ring, you're mine. If someone else finds it, you'll be his. Never take it off, not even for a second.' He believes in that. Just as well it's in the ground somewhere, maybe I'd believe in it too otherwise.

Her face looks still more downcast.

I'll have to get a new one made. It won't be easy. The price of the gold, and then a goldsmith to work on it, discreetly. It was hand-crafted . . .

She's back in the kitchen. The plane is making its whining noise again next door. She picks up the hatchet and starts chopping kindling. The plane stops. Wilhelm asks: 'Are you chopping wood now?'

'It's all sopping wet,' she says. 'Bloody awful weather.' And the hatchet again.

How clumsy Martha's being, thinks Utesch. She's not normally this clumsy. And he sees a hand, reddening, reddening. Blood everywhere.

'I cut myself,' says Martha, looking white. With trembling mouth she looks at her hand, which is a mess of blood.

He leaps over to her. 'Why start chopping wood at night? Couldn't I do that?'

'Leave me alone! Leave me alone!' she screams, and runs to the bedroom. 'I can bandage it.'

Then they are sitting over supper. Wilhelm keeps staring at her hand, which is thickly bandaged. 'You won't be digging any more potatoes with that. Too bad, we could have used the money.' Then, after a while: 'What about the ring? Did you take it off?'

4

Martha laughs. 'No, that's on! I won't be taking that off any time soon. That's on. Here, feel!' And she guides his fingers over the thick bandage.

3

The Utesches are asleep. Frau Utesch was wandering through the rooms of a dream, led by someone she couldn't see, someone she was afraid of. Suddenly her guide was gone, she sensed he wasn't there any more, she was all alone in a purple void, and her fear grew.

All at once she heard a voice calling, wild, random cries into space. The world assembled itself. In the red light of dawn the first mattock flashing among the sodden potato tops, and there was Wrede standing on the cart, grumbling and shouting and bellyaching away.

Martha was awake. 'He's got the ring! It's him!' she whispered, and she listened out into the night, to check that she couldn't hear him shouting. Silence. But the dark silence seemed to swell and swell, the silence called and called.

Martha Utesch got up, she stopped at the door to listen to her husband asleep, and again on the silent village street, and then she made her way up to the big house.

'He's got the ring! It's him!'

Strange walking through the starless night. The telegraph wires are humming and humming away at one tuneless melody. The wind rustles through the turning leaves, and the words rustle: 'He's got the ring! It's him!' Someone is walking ahead of her, she can't see him but even so he's leading her, and she's afraid of him.

Suddenly she sees the old shepherd from Zülkenhagen again. He is charming the ring, he cups his old, bent, liver-spotted hand over hers. 'This ring owns your body. As long as you keep it, you will keep yourself. Give it up, and you give yourself up.'

And again night, and the humming wires in the blackness.

4

Wrede isn't sleeping either. He has cleaned the ring and inspected the mark, and he's thinking how best to sell his lucky find. To send it to a friend would be too risky, the post office madams are all too nosy, and everything would be found out. And to go into town, even if he had the day off, would be too expensive.

At any rate, it's his now. He flashes the beam of his torch over it, and the reddish gold flashes mildly, he hits the ring against the marble top of the nightstand and listens enraptured to the bright *ching!* that only gold makes.

He too begins to dream. These few grammes of gold to the value of thirty or forty marks seem to open the doors to all the world. He pictures himself far away, in Berlin, bowling up to the best hotel, the porter wishing him a good afternoon, sir, and the waiters all bowing. He is standing in his hotel room, his luggage piled up in front of him, the soft leather armchairs and sofas draped with exquisite, colourful dresses, a barman is mixing drinks, the room is like an aviary, full of twittering women's voices and laughter. Someone knocks.

Someone knocks . . .

Wrede gives a start. He drops the ring, it rolls away, rolls and rolls, curls to a stop somewhere in the dark. One more sound, then none. 'Who is it?' A rap on the window. 'I said, who is it?' Nothing. He is afraid. Could it be the police already? In a shaky voice he asks: 'Is it you, steward? Is one of the animals not well?'

A faint voice calls back: 'It's me.'

He stands there listening. Suddenly he understands, he yanks open the window and yells: 'What do you mean it's me? Who's me? Everyone's me! Stuff and bloody nonsense.'

The quavering voice: 'Give me back my ring, Herr Wrede. Please.'

'Who's that? Is that Marie? Girl, leave me alone. It's not May time. Not even the cats are courting now.'

'Please will you give me my ring back, Herr Wrede.'

'Well, well, it's Martha Utesch! Now, Martha, does your Wilhelm know you go knocking on strange men's windows in the middle of the night?'

'Give me my ring back. There'll be trouble otherwise, Herr Wrede.'

'Well, if you must, Martha. Hop up, one leg on the sill. I'll pull you up. Don't be shy.'

His sweating fingers reach for her face, he can feel it, her warm shoulder, her breast. 'Come on, Martha!'

Silence. A long silence. Then very quietly: 'All right, I will, if you promise to give me back my ring, Herr Wrede.'

Then a silence from him, and finally a rather deliberate blustering: 'Ah, give over. Either you will or you won't. I'm going to shut the window now.'

'I'll buy the ring off you. I'll give you fifty marks for it.'

Swiftly: 'Have you got it on you, fifty marks?'

'Only twenty. I'll bring you the rest next week.'

'Let's have it.'

'First the ring.'

'Give it here!'

'There . . .'

He feels the banknote, and takes it. He laughs. 'Crazy bloody women! They're even paying me now! Whatever next.'

The window clatters down. Despairing walk home through the night.

5

By the time the night was over, Wrede had decided to make it all a dream. If anyone asked, he would deny all knowledge. He thought about what had happened, and what was certain was that the woman wasn't a tough nut, she was butter-soft. And butter wants churning. Why sell a ring he might as well hang onto? Let her pay and pay!

Even so, it bothered him not to see Martha Utesch with the others on the potato field. Why had she stayed home? Had she spoken to her husband? Or was she afraid? Whichever, he was determined not to loosen his hold. If she didn't come to him, he would go to her, the nights were long enough and dark enough. The flash of the ring would be enough to get anything he wanted out of her.

He listened out. The potato-diggers were talking about Martha Utesch too. They knew why she wasn't there. She had been out at night, her husband had woken up and found the bed beside him empty. There had been a noisy quarrel between the woman coming home and the man, and if the neighbours hadn't exactly heard what words were exchanged, they were more than happy to make them up. What was sure was that the man had realized that his wife was going with young Nagel. She hadn't been willing to admit where she'd been, but she couldn't pull the wool over the eyes of her besotted husband any more. After all, hadn't young Nagel been spoony on her before the wedding? Utesch just needed to give her a right old seeing-to, but of course men were far too soft nowadays. A proper thrashing, that would have taken care of things.

Wrede too regretted that there had been no beating. Even if the husband would have only softened up his wife for him. The more difficult the circumstances, the higher the price he would get for the ring. In fact, he wasn't at all sure that if he did give it to someone, it would be to the wife. Perhaps the husband would make the better purchaser. Couldn't he have got it from Nagel, say, who had found it on the ground? And then once you had the money you called it quits, and skedaddled. Let everyone else beat their brains out, it wasn't hard to see that the one who copped it in the end would be the woman anyway.

Next to the desire for money, and a lot of it, it was a desire to be avenged on the woman that drove Wrede on. He felt the softness of her shoulder again, she had hesitated about coming to him. Even the high price of the ring seemed to her – reflexively – like a small price compared to her revulsion for him. And the fact that he saw such a nocturnal visit as nothing out of the ordinary made him indignant about such a fuss. Martha – what was Martha Utesch anyway? Was she too good? Or he not good enough? Let her sweat it out.

That evening he pressed his face against the lit-up panes of the carpenter's house. Through the lace curtains he could see a lonely shape sitting there motionless. Was it her? Was she on her own? Or was it the carpenter? And she on her way out to the estate again?

A hand tapped him on the shoulder. 'If it's Utesch you're wanting, Foreman, he's in the pub. But he's probably pretty far gone by now.'

Wrede jumped. The person speaking to him was the saddle-maker Hinz, the village radio as he was known. 'Yes, I'm looking for Utesch, I've got a job for him to do. Far gone, you say. Well, I'll see, maybe it will be possible to speak a reasonable word with him. He's not normally a drinker, is he?'

The saddle-maker trotted along beside him. The story apparently had a new twist. The carpenter had wanted to take the ring away from his wife because she had brought disgrace to it, it wouldn't come off, and he had cut it off using a carving knife. The woman's screams had been something to hear. She had bandaged up her hand. No one knew what was going to happen next. Things weren't over yet.

Even though the invention in the story was plain to hear, Wrede was a little spooked. He could imagine her screaming. Her voice, when she asked him for the return of her ring, had been hesitant, timid, small. Now she was screaming. And the ring, always the ring. Even in that tissue of lies, its traitorous gleam. For a moment he was overcome by a false sympathy for the woman. He thought of turning back, giving her the ring for nothing. But he couldn't do that, not with Hinz walking along beside him. The old gossip walked with him all the way to the bar.

6

The bar was dark and all but empty. The grumpy landlord was wiping beertaps with a towel at one end of the bar, later he took himself off. In a corner, barely lit by a weak bulb, a solitary customer sat with a bottle of corn brandy, his head in his hands, motionless: Wilhelm Utesch.

'I've just been round to your house, Master. Wanted to know if you had time tomorrow to come up to the estate. We've got something for you to look at.'

'Time? Time? I've got all the time in the world.' The red eyes looked up, saw the bottle. Awkwardly Utesch poured himself another glass, looked across the table, made a pouring motion, stopped. 'Will you have one yourself?'

'I won't say no. Hey, Päplow, a glass for me.' Wrede took the bottle, helped himself. 'Well, cheers, long necks for our children.' They drank. Straight away Wrede refilled his glass.

The drunk sat quietly, fixing the chequered tablecloth. Finally, he began: 'Well, 's late to be still out. Young people nowadays . . .' He whistled, his mouth twisted into a miserable smile. He spoke hastily, unclearly, leaning across the table to the other man: 'I'll tell you this much, foreman, you can't blame them for it. What's there to keep them. But once a man's married, then I say: enough!' He cracked his knuckles.

Wrede said: 'Absolutely. Workhorses belong in the stable when the day's done, not out on the meadow.'

'I agree with you there, right enough,' said Utesch in sudden animation. 'That's gospel to me.' He collapsed into himself again.

'Let's have another!'

Wrede poured himself another glass.

The drunk whispered: 'But when a woman's married, and goes out at night and comes home, and you ask her where she's been, and she just smiles at you, then that's betrayal, foreman! That's what I'd call betrayal and adultery.'

He stopped, as though he'd frightened himself, his look alert and fixed on the man opposite. 'You know everything, Foreman. Of course you know everything. Only I know nothing.' And very slowly now: 'Where did my wife go, I'm asking you, Foreman, where did my wife go at two in the blessed morning?'

'I don't know, Master. I don't listen to people's chit-chat.'

'You know. Everyone knows. If only somebody would tell me . . .' He stopped pensively, his face was lit up by an idea. 'Let's drink!' – 'And another.'

'It's not too much for you?'

'How could it be too much, young man? I've already polished off a bottle by myself, and I can drink another without getting drunk. So, let's drink!'

'Fine by me,' said Wrede, and drank, while it dawned on him that the carpenter had the ridiculous idea of getting him drunk, and making him talk.

But then he was off again. 'The last evening, she cut her hand with the hatchet, chopping wood. Blood flowed over the ring. What's the significance of that? I'd need to know what that signified. And I don't know anything.'

Then the foreman thought of something. He reached into his waistcoat pocket. He pulled his hand out. 'Let's have another.'

And the carpenter echoed: 'Another!'

They drank. 'Where was my wife, Foreman?'

'I don't know, Master.'

'You don't know. How could you know. No one knows. Every man's on his own. And every man does everything for hisself.' Utesch staggered to his feet, slowly and gropingly he walked to the door, stopped. 'I'll be back in a jiffy.' And he walked out.

Wrede took a look around: the bar was gloomy and deserted. A late fly took off with some élan, buzzed for a while and stopped. Wrede took the ring out of his pocket and looked at it cupped in the hollow of his hand. It was broad and heavy, made from fine old ducat gold, beaten with a thousand hammer taps, for a man who still believes there's a meaning in things.

Wrede took an end of string out of his pocket. He tied it to the ring, tied the other end to a waistcoat button and put the ring back in his pocket. He got up and walked around. When Utesch came back, he was sitting down again.

The night air had made the carpenter even drunker. He was barely able to find his chair and sit on it, and could no longer speak, only babble. Wrede poured.

'It's a clear night, Master. D'you think there'll be a frost?'

And the echo: 'there'll be a frost!'

'Let's drink,' said Wrede.

'Less drink,' said the other, and didn't move.

Then Wrede reached into his pocket. He placed the ring on the edge of the table, and his hands some way away from it. 'Let's drink, Master,' he said again, and he knocked over his glass. It struck the bottle. The dull eyes sought to find what had caused the noise. Instantly, he was awake. He saw the little gleaming round, the unmistakable pledge to him of all troth. Drunk as he was, the carpenter lurched across the table. Everything fell over. The ring on its string jumped back inside Wrede's jacket. There was nothing to look at.

'What's come over you, Utesch?' yelled Wrede. 'Are you out of your mind?'

'The ring,' breathed the man quietly, 'that was the ring.'

'What ring are you talking about? Where has it gone?'

The carpenter stood in front of him. He was still in a state of shock. He looked piercingly at Wrede. 'The ring. I saw it, on the edge of the table. You've got it. I'm telling you, it's on you.' He took Wrede by the scruff, but was pushed away, hard.

'You're babbling. What would I be doing with your bloody ring.'

The carpenter caught himself, pulled himself upright. Stammering, he said: 'You've got it! Everyone's got the ring. Only she doesn't.' He stood there, musing. Suddenly he yelled out: 'Now I know: she doesn't have it.'

Utesch ran over to the door, pulled it open and disappeared into the night. Suddenly alarmed, Wrede shouted across the village square: 'Master, come back. You'll get your ring.'

Silence. No one came. No one heard.

7

It's dark and quiet in the room, nothing stirs, no moonlight comes in through the broken panes, because the moon has not yet risen. Some darker patch of darkness is leaning against the wall, listening for sounds from inside, quickly pulls back.

A sudden noise, someone comes running. He crashes into the garden fence, gropes for the gate, finds it open, hurries up the garden path, tries the front door. It's locked, and won't give. For a while Wrede stands there, thinking. Then he goes to the window to rap on it, knocks against a pane, which breaks in a thousand jingling pieces. He gets a start, stands there listening, listening to the room, where nothing stirs. A long, stubborn silence seems to be coming from the room, something sticky and malignant.

He takes the plunge. Softly he calls out: 'Utesch!' Nothing. And another time: 'Master Utesch!' Nothing at all. Only a little stir of wind in the rustling autumn leaves.

Another time, in fear, he calls out: 'Martha! Martha Utesch!' and he falls to his knees as a hand is laid on his shoulder, and a voice whispers: 'Be quiet! Ssh! Can't you hear?'

With his knees in the cool garden loam, under the mysterious hand, he listens, and he has a sense of something moaning inside the house, a series of brief moans.

Suddenly he gets it. 'The plane! Is that Utesch in the workshop?'

The other: 'He's probably making her coffin.' And with a terrible curiosity: 'Do you think he killed her?'

Wrede gets up. 'Listen, Hinz. Run for the nightwatchman as fast as you can. I'll stay here and make sure Utesch doesn't try and make a break for it.'

The other hesitates.

'Go on, run!'

Hinz disappears, he's gone, dissolved in the dark.

Slowly Wrede approaches the window. Gropes. One half is open. He leans into the room, a match flares.

He sees . . . he sees . . . something white, all alone, stretched out, something no more able to grasp, something slack that would like to grasp but can't. Oh my God, it's a hand! A severed hand!

And further, a dark form swathed under a cloth, a viscous pool . . . the match goes out.

Wrede reaches into his pocket and throws the ring into the dark room, he hears it go *ching!*, with the soft, bright sound that only gold makes.

Then Wrede plunges into the night, into the silence of the fields, where the only noise is the wind, or from time to time the rustle of a small beast. No humans. Where there is silence, long silence.

And now here come lights, and people, and the police.

Passion
(1925)

1

He walked in, and Ria understood right away that she was wrong, and her father right, to invite this junior scribbler, as she contemptuously called him, into the house to keep them company on some of his solitary evenings.

He bowed to her mother and kissed her hand, he spoke a few quick, smiling words to her father, and now he was in front of her, their hands brushed against each other, their eyes met. She looked down in a strange confusion, and when she looked up again the others were talking, something to do with the farm workers, of course, and of course he was of the same opinion as her father.

Somehow Ria felt disappointed, and while confusion and embarrassment compacted into a sort of irritation in her, she studied the speaker beside her, thought his shaved, beardless head looked ridiculously small, his form too thin and lanky and his hands and knuckles exaggeratedly bony, and with a pout she mouthed her words: 'Junior scribbler!'

He happened to be looking across at her, and the eyes behind the large spectacles were creased with mirth, so that it was obvious he had understood her. He hitched his shoulder and went on talking to her father about eviction orders that might be served upon obstinate workers, and suddenly his voice and choice of words seemed to be suffused with a puzzling ambivalence: he was saying one thing and meaning something else, and this something else was for her, and perhaps for all those who were without shelter and work, but above all for her. She didn't understand.

Later on they faced each other over the chessboard. He played quickly, lightly, with impetuousness and abruptness, so that she never could guess what he was planning. Before she moved, he said: 'If you do that, you'll be checkmate,' and she felt his foot alongside hers. He was pressing himself against her, quite unmistakably, she could feel the warmth of his leg against her calf, and a blush mantled her cheek.

Confused, she asked: 'Excuse me, what should I not do?' and pulled her foot away.

'This,' he said, made the move she had been going to make, and caught her foot between his two. He looked at her full on; his eyes were cold, cruel, knowing, and they frightened her.

'I'm too tired to play,' she said, knocking over some of the figures on the board. A few rolled to the floor, and he stooped to pick them up. His hand grasped her leg.

Never had anyone touched her so shamelessly. She was angry now, half-aloud she said: 'You stop that or I'll tell my parents.'

'Perhaps you'd like *me* to tell them?' he retorted, and made a move in the direction of her mother and father, who were laying patiences.

She looked at him, and once again she had the sense he had said something completely different, way beyond the sound of his actual words, a deeper, hidden meaning beyond the words, something that concerned her and perhaps the whole of life, its doubtfulness, its uncertainty, its transitoriness.

She raised her hands in protest, and dropped them. 'Mama, Herr Martens wants to say good night,' was all she said.

2

For a long time Ria lay awake in her girl's bed. Now that he was far off, now that his eyes, his hand and his smile were no longer working on her, her fury grew. What did he take her for, to treat her so outrageously? Some sort of prostitute? Never ever had a man dared to look at her that way, or touch her like that. She thought of the kisses she had once – and only once – permitted a friend of her brother's, after a dance. Those kisses had been mild and childish compared to the way this man eyed her up, touched her, trampled all over her.

She had grown up in the country, she had watched animals, she knew the village girls had their beaux, and an illegitimate child was neither a rarity nor a mystery. But that was village girls! Did he take her for one of them? She, the daughter of an estate owner, letting herself be treated in such a way by a simple secretary of her father's!

She would tell him! Never again would he permit himself to flutter his eyes at her like that. She would sort him out, by herself, without her parents, she would go to his office and tell him in plain terms that his days here in Baumgarten were numbered, should he ever again . . .

Waking up in the morning, she put off her resolution. But when her father clambered into his hunting wagon after lunch, and her mother went upstairs for her nap, she suddenly saw herself crossing the farm. She was hesitating at his door, and knocking, and his 'Come' summoned her.

He wasn't alone. It hadn't occurred to her that she might find him with someone else. He was standing by the window, smoking, with the village schoolmaster, and he didn't turn his head to see who it was, just said, 'Well?' and there was no answer, and after a time he turned to her, still standing in the doorway.

There was no trace of confusion, he didn't appear in the least surprised. 'What can I do for you, miss?'

He took a step or two towards her, didn't take her hand, only bowed to her.

'I need a couple of bills of lading,' she said.

He went to a cupboard. 'What kind would you like? Express or ordinary?'

She hesitated, she was ill at ease. Was this the same man as last night? After a bow the schoolmaster had turned away, he had his back to her, and was looking out of the window.

'Oh, just give me one of each!' she called out impatiently. All this felt so ridiculous, so shameful, so wrong.

'There you are,' he said, and gave them to her and looked at her. She took them, was about to go, and he asked gently and innocently: 'Just so you have the complete set, wouldn't you like one for livestock as well?'

She felt her fury return, and looked at him. And in the same instant saw that she was lost, that nothing could stifle her laughter, and already it burst out of her and, crumpling the lading bills in her hand, she called out, through her laughter: 'The complete set!'

He laughed too, and she heard his voice say: 'Be gone now, pedant. Take yourself off somewhere else.'

The door closed, and they were alone together and in silence. The last traces of smiles slipped out of their faces, and with trembling voice she said: 'How can you send Wille packing like that? What will he think of us?'

He leaned forward and whispered into her ear: 'You silly little girl.' She flinched and took several paces back from him, murmured beseechingly: 'Don't touch me! Don't you dare touch me! I won't have you touching me!'

His arm was wrapped around her, his lips brushed hers, under their pressure her mouth opened. 'Oh, darling,' she whispered.

3

They met wherever they could, in various places, behind the greenhouses, in the arboretum, on the farm, in the store, by day and at night in the park. Once they thought they saw Ria's father away in the distance, and fled through waterlogged alders and willows to stop breathless in a potato field, through whose blackish-brown autumnal tops a hunting dog was stalking. Often it was just for the exchange of a rushed word or two, their hands brushed against each other in passing, their eyes hailed each other, but again and again there were hours in which his kisses overwhelmed her, left her breathless, his hand travelled . . . She freed herself from his embrace, for the hundredth time she repeated that no man would have her without promising her marriage.

He was beside her, telling her about the women who had passed through his life; he sent them smiles, he saluted their memory. They moved on, vanished. Others came, and her pride was outraged at being one of a long series. He smiled, he measured out the brief duration of passion in the length of a life, he held his hand aloft, he was touchingly proud that not one of all these women had broken with him in anger, and suddenly the laughing happiness of his words had a dim, dry smell of rose petals tied up in packets of letters. A vague sadness caught her, the man at her side was never out for this one particular moment, but all the others too, never to love just her but all her predecessors just as much, and those that would come after. She reached for his hand, to persuade herself that he was here now, at least physically, and dropped it discouraged, thinking how little meaning this flesh had.

And then the fresh onslaught of his kisses.

4

One night he knocked on her door.

He was standing outside, demanding to be let in, not asking, no, demanding. Trembling, she listened for sounds from her parents' bedroom, asked him through the door how he had managed to get into the locked house, begged him to go away.

Then she thought she caught a sound downstairs, she unlocked the door, he crept in and took her in his arms. She fought him off with the crazed fear of a maiden, scolded him, screamed that she would hate him for ever and ever.

And a moment came when the world seemed to stand still, everything listened and held its breath, and she felt herself sinking and sinking. Suddenly she was drifting, adrift on a blissful, festive stream of life: so many bannerets, so much happy waving of green twigs, purple tents and joyous birds. She threw her arms around him, pulled him down to her, and the least thing had its meaning now, and the long waiting and resisting and torment – all had their meaning.

After that they met every night. He would come late to the back door, where she was waiting, she would lead him by the hand up the dark staircase, in stockinged feet, then there was the sweet white brightness of her girl's room, and the festivities began. Often they would stop and listen to the house, follow the footfall of a servant girl who seemed to hang about for ever outside Ria's door, and then they would breathe a sigh of relief and look into the glowing, happy face of the other.

Lying together, her head pillowed on his arm, they would tell each other stories. He opened the expanses of his varied life, with cities and foreign lands, he had travelled on board ship, he had known poverty and then become rich again, before finally longing for rest, finding *her* in this little backwater.

She asked questions, she let nothing go. Hadn't she seen all his various testimonials before he was taken on, and personally advised her father to take him? Hadn't he – as she had too – lived all his life in the country?

He just smiled, suddenly the streets were full of endless columns of automobiles, they made their way through them, took refuge in a quiet restaurant, music struck up, exotically beautiful women dancing, and a gaudily clad Negro paced solemnly up and down with a marshal's baton.

Ria felt fear for the man who was lying beside her, something was not quite right. Who was he really? And she saw the deep, contented peace in his features, she understood that he had suffered for this love as much as she had; how could the rough suitor of yore, the pitiless exploiter, the lover of so many women have become so altered? He was a happy child, and his love was so new to him, it was as though he had never loved before. There was nothing in him of any yesterday or tomorrow; to make her happy today was as far as his thinking went.

Each time they parted they promised to forbear the next night, to allow the other to sleep, and then she would lie awake full of desire for him, till at last, at midnight, a pebble would strike her window, and she hurried downstairs to let him in, every night, for two whole weeks.

5

A telegram came for him, he had to go to Berlin. He asked her father for the day off, they met up as they did every night, they didn't sleep, but the day after next he would be back. Hidden behind the curtain she watched his carriage drive past, she agitated the white material, and saw the happy delight on his face.

In those days she rested deeply. When she awoke, something lightsome had blown through her featureless dreams, a taste of some sun-dappled summer's day filled her mouth, her whole form swayed and danced.

The carriage came back empty from the station. Had he missed his train? One or two days passed in anguished expectation, her father began to get anxious, had Martens met with some accident perhaps? No news, nothing, not a line, not a word of him.

She remembered exactly the morning hour when her father came to the breakfast table, looking pale and stooped. It was raining outside, a fine rain slanted across the windows when her father told her the rural constable had asked after Martens. There was a possibility that he was a notorious swindler, with a warrant out for his arrest, who had gone to ground in the country with them. The mystery was how he managed to time his departure to the very day the authorities planned to nab him. It was all a little up in the air: perhaps his staying away was a matter of chance, a similarity in the names, the descriptions.

'I never trusted him,' Ria said quickly, and it was possible she spoke the truth. The man she loved had remained a stranger to her, the one who fulfilled her being had come from some other, richer world which he had only wanted to show to her, never would she set foot on its lighter roads.

She wasn't even angry with him. It was just the way he had to do things, and not easy for him at that, just as it was her way to remain in a life of constancy and silence and quiet work.

No, she was angry with him. Not for leaving her, for being a confidence trickster, what was there to be angry about there? But sneaking away from her without a word, not trusting her, that was wormwood, and that rankled.

Then there was a telegram from him, from a small southern city, he wasn't coming back, the keys would be returned in a separate envelope. They arrived, and now the familiar office, the very thought of which made her gasp a little, was occupied by an auditor, going through the books.

It turned out that the book-keeping had been exemplary right up until a fortnight before the man's flight; thereafter there was nothing, no entries, receipts randomly stuffed in different drawers, the complete cessation of any work. Chaos.

When her father, shaking with rage, told her this, Ria had to turn away and smile to herself. How alike they were! Hadn't she too put off every kind of work for two weeks, with happiness floating on the crest of the crystalline wave, on the lookout for fertile shores?

But even now it was uncertain whether he was a bounder in love or purely and simply a lover. Funds might have been embezzled or not, it wasn't possible to say for sure. And once again she was angry with him that this too was left uncertain; perhaps he was honest, perhaps a thief, she would never know.

When the embezzler's belongings were to be bundled up – her

father persisted in referring to him as that – she insisted on going along. For the first time she entered his room – there on the wash-table was the nailbrush he had just put down – all the many little bottles caused her father to snort with derision. Then the suitcases snapped shut, the things were carried up to the attic and his successor moved in.

And now the grey monotony of uneventful country living resumed in which she had formerly been so contented. Before he had come, before there had been any happiness. She counted the hours, she looked intently at each new day, and none promised even a minute of the bliss she had enjoyed; the winds blew to no end, the sun shone for nothing. Gladly she would have forgotten herself, but there was no man in reach who might have plausibly offered her such forgetting; his successor was fat and had a limp and sniffed incessantly.

The dreariness of it all!

6

Then there was a letter from him. She held it in her hand, uncomprehending, the possession of the little paper rectangle caused her to blush, as though he himself leaned down over her and pressed his mouth to hers.

He was writing from some faraway city. She read what he wrote, and the signature, she sat there, had she read anything, had he put his name to anything? Very good, he was thinking of her. And what else? He was missing her. And then? Not a word about why he had gone, not a word about what he was doing now. She pushed the letter away, she wouldn't write back, she hid it in a mass of her old papers, she would dig it up years hence, and barely remember who it was from.

She read it again and again. A rigid toughness came over her, a determination to understand him, and gradually it dawned on her that perhaps he wasn't disguising himself, omitting things, lying. Flight, swindling, theft – these were all the hallmarks of his outer life, but their life together was love. What else could they possibly have shared, what else did they want to know of one another?

Life was monotony, but on a glorious beach somewhere he was building the glittering tent of their love in all its gaudiness, and everyday matters were kept out.

She wrote to him. He wrote back. She wrote. Immaterial things, just as he did. She was mistaken in him, he was just like everyone else. He wrote. She wrote. He stopped writing.

7

One dark winter evening a man came towards her on the avenue, walked right up to her, she panicked, he laid his hand on her shoulder. It was he.

They held each other, breathless with happiness they looked into one another's eyes. 'I can't believe it's you.' – 'I love you so much.'

All the intervening things were forgotten. Shuddering, her body remembered the grip of his hand, her lips tasted his much-missed mouth, she felt at peace against his chest.

'It's really you!' And: 'Wait here. Once things are quiet in the village, I'll come and get you.'

She went away from him, turned round, ran back into his arms. Her eyes sparkled with all the purple of the long-set winter sun. Slowly, with a clumsy modesty the trees seemed to sag, and then he was kneeling over her, rubbing her forehead with snow. 'It's joy,' she said, 'you've been too long away.'

Greedily he stared at her face, which was the loveliest face in the world, it seemed to have got paler and narrower, and the eyes sparkled in a mild, sad joy as before.

She walked away from him. She came back for him. She locked

him up in her room, he stayed there for days and nights, she took her place at table as ever, she went with her mother to visit the sick, maybe someone happened to knock on the door and he, half-asleep, happened to call out 'Come in.'

She didn't ask him any questions, there was nothing to ask, he was there. And yet everything felt different to before. In those two weeks it would only have taken the consent of her father, and everything would have ended in the traditional way.

Now she knew deep down that this was and would remain impossible, their love could only exist away from everyone and against everyone, it had become that fairy tale that was probably the thing he had always wanted.

Brighter, purer and more lambent was the flame of their love as it rose towards heaven. They held each other faster because, as they well understood, every hour could be their last. Time and again they caught one another up, one slid away into exhaustion, the other roused him with a look, and the seeking, imploring look started everything up again. They knew no fatigue, sleep meant forgetting, and forgetting was death, pressed up against one another, feeling the surging breath like a wave, a softly veiled brightness. Then the look again. And then love.

8

One night she had been out and was late coming home, she unlocked the door and found him gone. Her first instinct was to think she had made a mistake. Had she failed to lock the door when she went? No, no, he was gone, without a note, without a last embrace.

She sat down on the side of the bed, her bed that still bore the impress of his body. This was the end, she had always known it would come, now she had to be brave. She had had a dream of an intensity very few people experienced. She had had a matchless lover who had been all hers, who had never spoken a cross word to her or made a disrespectful remark. His love was youthful and new, and now he was gone before it could age.

What was she doing sitting there? She jumped up. Perhaps he's at the far end of the avenue, waiting for me. Perhaps he had to run away again. Always on the run. My poor darling.

She looked for him all night. The shuffling through snow, in the small circle lit by her torch, kept her heart distracted. Once, she thought she came upon his traces, then she lost them again, among others'. This endless looking, the constant chance that he might turn up at any moment and throw his arms around her, exhausted. When she turned back to go home it was clear to her that she was leaving him behind. But later on, waking from deep, dreamless sleep, she knew that he was there, and she here, and everything was over.

Later she noticed some money was missing. With a joyful lurch she thanked him for not desecrating their love by turning to her for money, all that had been kept outside. All there was between them was love and love alone . . .

Or did he hope she might disdain the thief so as more easily to live without the lover? He was way beyond the reach of rejection. She breathed, she lived, she loved, those were all unquestioning functions, did she stop to ask herself whether to breathe or not?

He was probably having a hard time. He would have to struggle, and just as his love had been extreme, his life probably was as well. Other women were bound to intrude, but because his love would always be new with every one of them they didn't take anything away from her. To her, he would always remain the one he had been.

Later still it was discovered that his things were gone. The attic had been broken into and his suitcases were gone, constables came to look for whoever must have helped the thief with horse and cart. She was left with the irksome feeling of having wandered around following false trails on that snowy night, while he was long gone in a swift conveyance; left with the irritation of not knowing whether he had come back for her love, or just to pick up his things.

She saw him, hardly out of her embrace, slinking around in the dark attic, trying locks, filing keys. She saw him gauging the depth of her exhaustion, rootling around in her things, taking a print of her keys – and, smiling, he turned the unchanged face of his love upon the incensed woman.

Perhaps he had never loved her at all.

9

The rings subside that a stone makes in water, and so experience fades. The days passed and made weeks, the weeks turned into months, and when Ria invoked her memory of the man who had been her lover, she found it harder and harder to remind herself of his face, his gestures, the way he spoke. Already she was confusing him with others. Perhaps the only reason she thought he was exceptional was because he was the first man in her life? Perhaps any other man would have had the effect on her that he did?

She looked around, her movements that had become slow and slothful tautened; she agreed to leave the estate, to go to a seaside spa with her parents. He surely wouldn't come again, and if he missed her this time, that was his loss.

In the little harbour town they had a couple of hours to wait for their ferry. They strolled over grass-grown cobbles, looked up at brick gables, walked round churches and tried to remember what they had learned of Gothic and Romanesque at school, they took in every dress and hat, and in this way they also – bored and half-abstracted – took in a strange vehicle, large, blue, loaded with wood, pulled by ten or a dozen fellows on belts. Two uniformed men gave them a sabre-jangling escort.

'Convicts doing road work,' explained her father.

'Father!' she exclaimed. 'Look, Father!'

There he was, standing next to the shaft, quite unmistakable in spite of the ugly gear. Under the round convict's cap his pale, shattered face, his shoulder leaning into the strap and, shooting a furtive look at the escort, he felt for a cigarette end, picked it up as he walked, shoved it into his mouth.

She caught his eye and he, looking at her standing on the pavement, made a quick movement, as if to flee, and his cold, knowing look admitted everything to her, that this was now his life, that this too was his life, and that he had always reckoned on it being so.

'Father!' she exclaimed. 'Father!'

'You're right, that does look like Martens,' he said in surprise.

10

She was waiting, now she was waiting for him again, there was nothing for him to do but return to her as soon as he was at liberty again. Months went into a year, and then another: not a squeak from him. It was as though she had cried out into space and was waiting and waiting for a reply. None came.

She spun a tissue of lies and secretly went back to the town, she saw the blue cart with the convicts but she didn't see him. She plucked up all her courage, she went to the prison and asked after Martens. There'd never been anyone there by that name, she heard. She didn't try again.

So where was he? Was he on the way up or the way down? Was it conceivable that, while she was leading her same unvarying life, he was in danger, fleeing, cheating, swindling, being captured and always, always suffering indescribably for her, and thinking of her?

One day, one hour, she held a letter from him in her hand. She read it and she knew: now everything really was over. She had never experienced him as so wretchedly small. He asked for her hand, they should run away together, the hot words on paper that were intended to make her blood wild were the product of a cold, calculating brain. He hadn't been thinking of her at all, he had only her money in mind.

The last nonsensical step of a man facing suicide, she thought, and scrunched up his letter. She never read it again, she forgot it.

11

She married. She lived quietly and happily at the side of her husband, she had children. She had interests and pursuits, she had money, she no longer knew anything about the girl she had once been.

On the street once, over her shoulder, a voice said: 'Ria.'

She spun round, it was the same old youthful face as before, laughing with the knowledge of a love that was always there and always would be.

They walked together, talking only of those early days, when they had played chess together, when he had crept up to her room at night. Their voices trembled. A full, obliterating summer opened before them, there were still purple tents standing by the glittering sea, far, far away from all known life. Their hands reached for each other. 'We do love each other!' – 'We do love each other!'

They met many times, this wasn't an adventure, it was their life. Husband and children were husk, this was heart and core.

He disappeared, he came back. He turned up on her doorstep begging for a bowl of soup, he walked past her with a smile, she saw him dancing in operettas, her speeding car flung dust in his face as he was breaking stones.

He was everywhere and nowhere, here and there, up and down. She no longer forgot him, she knew she never would. He was everything she had lived for, nothing else had any meaning.

She grew very old and very patient. One day she saw her youngest daughter in the park with a man. She walked on by, they didn't see her. Her heart spun in turmoil. It was him, young, odd, captivating, as he had been in her early days, now with her daughter.

She wanted to make a fuss, then she smiled. And there was everything in that smile: understanding and forgiveness, forgetting and love, and the long, long duration of their passion.

Tales from the Underworld
(1928)

My Friend the Crook

I met him in the fourth-class waiting room past midnight, in the wee small hours. He had a newspaper on his lap, full of cigarette ends. Every end was carefully broken open, and the tobacco emptied into a tin. He was doing well, the tin was almost full.

Otherwise, things weren't so hot for him. He didn't have a penny piece in his pocket, and he hadn't eaten anything all day. If he remembered correctly, he had been hungry for a while now.

'Can't be helped. No one has money these days, so crooks like me are up against it. Not that I'm planning anything. I'm only a week out of clink. Mind you, if I had five hundred marks . . . I have an idea—'

All the time he spoke, no one escaped his rapid observation. He saw them all, sized them up like a hunter his quarry. 'That fat bespectacled feller with the walrus moustache, he's a cop. Well, my papers are okay. Those guys are so full of themselves! As if I'd come to a place like this if they were looking for me. But he's after someone . . .'

We looked at the man propping up the bar with a half-pint in front of him. I thought he might be a chef or a glazier or something, chewing the fat with the chilly barmaid. 'He's looking for someone,' muttered Otsche, the crook, 'and it's a greenhorn, otherwise he wouldn't be putting himself on show like that.'

What was it he wanted five hundred marks for?

'Three hundred would do, at a pinch. I don't mind telling you, you won't steal it. Something I've done once before, as it happens, in Frankfurt. A small ad in the paper: "Lost: one silver-handled

31

riding crop. If found, kindly return to Frau Masoch, Schulgasse 3." '
He looked at me expectantly.

'So—?' I asked uncomprehendingly.

'A spanking,' he said laconically. 'The bell never stopped ringing. All of them crème de la crème, with fat wallets. You'd be
surprised at the demand there is for it.'

He laughed. Whatever people wanted, there was money to be
made from it. His job was to scope out the market. 'But of course
we had to shut up shop after a couple of days, before the cops got
wind of it.'

The plainclothesman at the bar was still quipping away. 'Wonder who it is? No one local, I'll be bound, I know them all.'

And again: 'But you have to look the part. Let me tell you
something: your fizzog doesn't matter, just so long as your trousers are pressed and your hands are manicured. And then of
course you need to speak proper, which isn't so easy for some of
us. Then people will trust you. You tell them you're a doctor, and
you pronounce di-a-ther-mi-a and ar-te-ri-o-scle-ro-sis without
stumbling, and show their wives you're kind-hearted if something
happens to go wrong, then you can leave your wallet behind,
they'll be happy to treat you.

'But the plainclothesman over there's making me nervous. I
wouldn't worry so, if it was me he was after.' He scanned the room.
The dim bulbs were wreathed in cigarette smoke. The rumpled,
sleepy clientele were lost in dreams. 'Who can it be?' He had another
look around, then whistled through his teeth. 'It's a she! That's why
I didn't get it first time. See the little girl in the corner with her head
on her arms pretending to sleep? She's no more asleep than I am!
She's got her foot on a little valise, that's where the loot is!'

'Are you sure, Otsche? He's not even looking at her.'

'Yeah, but there's a mirror behind the bar where he can over-
look that whole corner. Hang on a mo.' He had rolled himself a
cigarette, now he strolled, hands in pockets, to a table where a
couple of depressed-looking workers were sitting over their cof-

fee. He got himself a light, started a conversation and moved back and forth, keeping himself between the mirror and the girl. The fellow at the bar took a step to the right, and the crook followed suit, a step to the left didn't get any better results, so the walrus moustache paid up and went over to a fruit machine from where he enjoyed unrestricted vision.

A couple of minutes later Otsche was back. 'You were right,' I said. 'He is after her, and she knows it. Just now, when you blocked his view, she took a look at the door to maybe make a dash for it.'

'Maybe she does know. What's certain is that she's a goner. There's no helping her.' His cheerfulness was gone and he was chomping agitatedly on his roll-up.

'You're upset, aren't you, Otsche, you'd like to try and help her.'

'You're damned right I would!' he spluttered. 'I know, you're a gent, so you've no idea how mad the likes of us gets when he sees a plainclothesman and thinks of interrogations and trials and choky. I've been out for a week, and if I get involved now I'll be in for a year or two at least. No, I'm going to keep my hands clean, I won't touch anything for the next three months.'

He fell silent and looked over at the girl. She seemed to be asleep, and the policeman was walking up and down like someone waiting for a train.

'Not that I'm scared, mind you. But these high-minded episodes always go wrong. If I was stupid enough to start something here so that he had to nab me and the little miss could fly away, what's in it for me? She doesn't even know who I am, and if she did, well, no woman waits two years for a man behind bars. Don't come to me with women.'

'But I'm not asking you to do anything, Otsche. I think it's very sensible of you to keep your nose clean.'

'Baloney!' he retorted. 'All you know is from thrillers, so of course you believe in honour among thieves. Crap! Nothing makes a writer happier than when a crime has been brilliantly cleared up by a fancy-dan detective, and the crook's behind bars. But where's the fun in that for us? It's not much of a return for me, for my bit of chivalry. Two years' hard. Is that what you've got in mind for me?'

He had been getting increasingly wrought up. The sleepy souls at the adjacent tables were turning to see what the trouble was.

'Calm yourself, Otsche,' I said. 'I don't want anything of the sort. Keep your nose clean, and—'

'There!' he said. 'Here we go. Another plainclothes cop.'

A tall, fair-haired, clean-shaven man was standing next to the glazier, and they were both staring openly at the girl. She sat there, face turned to the wall, valise within easy reach.

'We don't need to sit and watch this, Otsche,' I said. 'Come on. We'll find somewhere that's open, and I'll buy you dinner.'

'I'll tell you what you can do with your fucking dinner,' he yelled. 'You can shove it!'

The two detectives turned to us.

'Calm down,' I tried to placate him. 'People are staring.' I put my hand on his shoulder, to try and induce him to leave.

'Don't you touch me!' he wailed. 'Don't you fucking touch me . . .'

The glazier took a great leap over in our direction. It was too late. Everything went red, then black. The last thing I remember is a sense that I was falling.

It must have been a fabulous punch, technically perfect: I only came round in the emergency ward. And it took a long time for my poor brain to grasp that my good friend Otsche had signed me up for a minor role in his drama. I had played my part in covering an otherwise hopeless retreat, and the girl with the hot gems in her valise had got away.

And Otsche too, who wasn't so entirely innocent of girl or jewels as he claimed to be, Otsche too was gone. 'You know, in the ensuing confusion,' the still-sweating glazier told me.

It's all fair enough. And, to be perfectly honest, I'm quite happy not to have to confront Otsche in some courtroom in my present state. I think he'd find me upsettingly ugly.

A Visit to Jemmy-Max's

In a careless hour once I lent my friend, Jemmy-Max, an out-of-work burglar, the sum of seventy-five Reichsmarks. Ever since then, I have taken it upon myself to apply to him every Friday night for partial repayment. Because, through some inscrutable quirk of circumstance, Jemmy-Max has been in work for the past few weeks, he is a hard-working locksmith and takes home sixty marks a week. Or do they ever get there?

After barking my shins on some damned flight of stairs in the harbour quarter and by my ensuing yells widely alerting all the denizens as to a stranger's presence in their ward, I have taken to simply turning up at Max's. The house lacks such basic amenities as gas, doorbell or electric light. Locks seem to have been dispensed with for the opposite reason, their imperfections and inadequacies being all too widely understood.

Max is sitting at a table by the light of an oil lamp, shaving. I put on my winningest smile. 'I just came by to see you, old son. How are you off these days? You know I really need at least ten marks.'

Max looks at me glumly. 'Rock bottom, Doctor.'

'But Max, that can't be, you've trousered your week's wages this lunchtime.' I flatter him: 'Go on, be sensible, otherwise you'll never get out of debt.'

'Have you any idea of the extent of my obligations!' He waxes elegiac. 'In my old housebreaking days, I always used to pay my debts right away. But ever since I've gone straight, I can't be that irresponsible any more.'

'Sixty marks is a fair chunk of change,' I say dreamily. 'There's nothing for it, you've got to spit up at least ten. You've got earnings on the side and all.'

'When I'm straight, I'm straight. I won't do any more jobs.'

'*You* don't need to do anything, Max.'

'You mean my old lady, going on the game at the patriotic monument? It's no good, I'm telling you. I'd have thought by the first of the month at least that line of business might have perked up, there's usually some players on the first, but Jesus! Poor woman out on her feet all day long in this weather, and no one comes across.'

'Business gone soft?'

'The girl's willing, I tell you. She's not sitting around in cafés, spending her money. But if the punters can't . . . !'

Max is all down in the dumps. No travelling salesman could be more dejected about the state of the textile industry than Max about his pavement princess. 'I bought her new stockings and combinations, nothing's any good.'

'Now, Max,' I say soothingly, because I'm feeling his pain, 'I didn't know things were quite this bad for you. What do you say we leave it till next Friday?'

Jemmy-Max has finished shaving and is reaching for his jacket. The wallet he pulls out seems strangely swollen to me. He opens it, and as he thumbs through the banknotes, his face is beaming.

I am astounded. Green fifties, brown twenties, lots and lots of them. 'Max, where does all this dosh come from? That must be well over a thousand!'

'A thousand? I doubt it.'

'Well, look.' I pull out my own, rather leaner wallet, produce his IOU. 'Here, Max, why don't we clear this up on the spot.'

Max's beam widens. 'Oh, Doctor, Doctor. You don't get it, do you. Can't you tell this is all funny money?'

'Funny money?' I ask in bewilderment.

'Sure. Funny money!' he echoes. 'Natch. Take a look. I've combed all the coin dealers and numismatists in Hamburg to get this load together. It's all Inflation money.'

I thumb through the notes. Now that he's told me, I notice

something. These brown twenties do look a shade different to our current ones, these green fifties aren't just exactly what the Reichsbank presses into your hot little hands nowadays, but I'll admit, I wouldn't have detected it.

'Nor do thousands of other people neither!' he says, well pleased. 'You just need to have a good eye for when you can chance it. And if you fall for it, you've been swindled by someone. Of course, I never go out with more than one at a time, this is my supply. Can I tempt you, Doctor?'

'I think I'll wait, Max, if it's all one to you,' I say. 'There's no great hurry. I couldn't fool anyone if I were trying to foist one of those funny fifties on them.'

Max grinned with cheerful contempt. 'You're just a solid citizen, aren't you. I'd like to know what you'd do in a strange city without a penny, and not knowing anyone. You'd probably go straight to the lost and found and report yourself missing. Well, take comfort, not everyone can crack it. What about it, then? Coming out with me tonight? One of these notes is burning a hole in my pocket.'

Max is quite right, I'm just a timid, honest citizen, and so I found I had other engagements for that evening.

But I've noticed that every Friday since, I check and double-check any notes that come into my hands. I am terrified lest I get one of Max's *billets-doux*, and am left sitting on it. You see, he's just as inflexible as the Reichsbank: he doesn't change funny money.

Dear Lotte Zielesch

Dear Lotte Zielesch,

A day or two back in your column in the 8 Uhr-Abendblatt you were pleased to talk about the expenses we housebreakers incurred on the job, and shed a tear about our sorry prospects.

Lotte, you're quite right! But this in your shell-like, authoress, we have an old saying: the best break-ins are done with an iron, and not with dynamite.

What good is it to me if I blow a grade-A safe and find a bit of loose change! I don't make my expenses, and the next day I get a bad press. Much more useful than dynamite is reliable information as to where you might find money poorly secured, like on pay day, at a racecourse, or after a dividend pay-out. But information like that is about as plentiful as virgins nowadays.

And should you ever make your way to a police exhibition, then you'll see that history-making jobs were not done with shop-quality tools, but with a crowbar and a couple of home-made wire jemmies; if there is explosive involved, then it's likely to be the home-made variety, and filled into tin cans. If that was the rule – simple tools and good information and a reputable fence financing the operation – then who wouldn't become a housebreaker!

And while I'm on, let me tell you that the honest-to-goodness break-in is facing extinction. I know lots of lads who are specialists in breaking and entering, and they are forced to go on the state, just because the work can't feed a man these days. Money's so short, and when you turn up at your fence's with half a rack of mink coats, what are you offered for the goods? Chickenfeed!

Now, if we'd come into the world with velvet paws! Pocket work is a different business. But unfortunately my hands are too clumsy for it, and I'm too old to learn. And so a man in his prime is put on starvation wages, doing little cheap jobs, and the pride of the profession suffers. I mean, what would the other lads say if one of us was forced into a racket like begging with menaces or wound up in jug? All the respect you'd accrued in twenty years, certificated by our system of justice, would be shot to pieces. I'd have to be ashamed if I met a policeman!

Well, any road, I want to thank you, Lotte, for putting in a word for our difficult occupation in these trying times. If there's anything I can do for you (a nice necklace or what have you) just say the word to

Your Jemmy-Max

Farmers in the Revenue Office
(1931)

When a townie, a trader, a craftsman, or (as we like to say) an entrepreneur has a problem with the Revenue, then he sits himself down and writes his declaration or his petition or his complaint — at any rate he writes something. Farmers have never been great ones for writing, though, and the proliferation of authorities during the 14–18 War and after has done little to cure them of their aversion. I had a boss in the country once, a very respectable landowner and quite literate, who issued a strong edict against taking up a pen on a Friday. 'Writing is the source of all evil,' he would proclaim. 'Did you ever meet anyone who did well from writing on a Friday?' I couldn't say I had. 'You see!' he crowed and, just in case, locked up the ink bottle and typewriter. 'Time was, it was only labourers that wrote.'

This landowner received a visit from a Revenue official who wanted to repay some excess tax. (These things do happen, it was long ago.) But it was a Friday, and it wasn't possible to get anyone to sign anything. Saturday was pay day, and the Revenue office was a long way away, money was short, but a signature — absolutely not! 'If I were you, I'd get off my land sharpish,' said my boss menacingly. 'You've got a nasty pencil thingummy behind your ear, and it makes me ill to so much as look at it. I don't think any good will come of that.'

There are two worlds, and when they collide you get fire and brimstone. And things don't always pass off so smoothly as on this next occasion, when the lord of a hundred acres sold his motor plough, bought during the Inflation. He had put an ad for it in the local rag, the motor plough was sold, the money went where last year's snow goes, and then there was a letter from the Revenue (which is an avid reader of the local press): 'We note there is no mention in your annual accounts of proceeds from the sale of the advertised motor plough, etc. etc.' – 'Put it with the other stuff,' said my boss. I put it on what he was pleased to call the dung heap. Time passed, and a further letter came from the Revenue: '1. We ask you for immediate response to our query of the nth inst. regarding tax due on the sale of your *motor* plough. 2. In case of deferral, we request reasons.' – 'Just write this,' said my boss: 'To the Tax Office in Altholm. Firstly. I have never owned a *steam* plough. Secondly, see firstly. Yours faithfully . . .' The Revenue didn't get in touch again.

But these teasing arabesques are in a minority: the man was a landowner and had a sense of humour; more usually when a small farmer sees the official letterhead, he panics. Total incompetents proceed like the Rügen farmer who drove up with a load of cabbages – took them down ten miles of rough track too, wouldn't you know it – and offered to pay his taxes in kind, in the form of his cabbages. 'The wholesaler offers me sixty pfennigs, but the local paper says the official rate is one-ten. You're not telling me you're not official!' The taxman can talk with the tongue of an angel, but the farmer won't get his head around it. The man sat there in the Revenue office, and every half-hour or so he heaved a sigh and improved his offer. By the time the office closed, he was down to sixty-five pfennigs. It was a fair price and they were excellent cabbages, but no one would play ball and he was baffled – baffled and furious.

Another story comes to mind – this from the time of the Inflation – of a landowner buying his wife a silver fox. Unfortunately his book-keeper had entered the acquisition under 'livestock'. Then when the time came for doing the inventory, they were an animal short in the stables. It had to be there, it was down on paper as an acquisition, and the owner was suspected of having sold the horse cash down – till the silver fox came out of the wardrobe and the receipt was produced from the file.

Today's farmers don't have it easy, not at all, but I almost think the bailiffs have a harder time of it. I'm not thinking about over-work, and making your way from farm to farm over rough tracks, and negotiating the savage dogs, the hostile faces, the muttered threats. He's just a public official, he doesn't set the taxes he has to collect, he doesn't know how they're calculated and why they are calculated as they are. All he has to do is seize and impound. And in the end, to auction off.

I once attended an auction like that, and I'll never forget it. It was a tiny farm, just about fifty acres, and a lot of bidders had come out. There was the auctioneer, and there were his assist-ants, and everything was all set to begin. But there was a group of farmers standing in the corner, not so very many, but it was probably the entire village. They stood there quietly, some way off, on a little rise. The first lot was called, it was a cart. And the first bid was called. And in the same moment as the little crofter, ten villages away, called out his 'Twenty marks' there was a sort of grumble, or groan, like a distant roll of thunder. The farmers stood there quite still, they didn't move their lips, and you can groan without opening your mouth.

There were rural constables on the farm, there were many more bidders and interested parties than farmers, and there were in fact two or three more shy bids, but after a while there weren't any more. The cart was knocked down, just for the sake of a price having been achieved, but the successful bidder had sud-denly disappeared, vanished, not there. The auction was a failure. The farm was of course sold after all, the stock was shipped out here and there to other areas, and the mortgage-holder was left owning the farm.

But I can still see the farmers standing there, grumbling with mouths closed.

I think of this as an ongoing war as I write this, and whenever it comes to be read. It isn't easy to lose a farm that has been in the family for generations, nor is it easy to drive someone away from such a farm when they haven't done anything. Both are difficult, and if you're asked whose fault it is – always the question, who's really to blame? – then you can only answer in the words of Theodor Fontane, 'well, that's a wide field'.

Kubsch and His Allotment
(1931)

In the beginning, all land was farm land, arable land. Plough and scythe went over it in everlasting alternation. Then speculators came and they saw that the land was good land, even by their lights, and that there were woods and lakes nearby. An estate agent moved into the old manor house, and posts went up in the middle of fields with signs that read: Plot 85/86 or road B13.

Kubsch was a small employee at Bergmann's or Pintsch's, on two hundred and twenty gross. Twenty-four years old. Things at home were tight. His girl worked in administration somewhere, and if they pooled their savings, it came to sixteen hundred marks, which wasn't bad for a start. They saw the land, they saw the cheerful-looking summer houses, they saw the first green leaves, they were brave. It meant his commute to work was ninety minutes, and things might occasionally get a little lonely for the intending Frau Kubsch. But they would be together within their own four walls, not at the mercy of ill-tempered relatives, snatching little stolen kisses in the corners of pubs and entrances of houses.

One Sunday morning Kubsch went into the office, and bought allotment 368, and paid eighty marks down. That in effect was their wedding. Minnie said proudly, 'See!' Whatever was still to come, registry office and church, was more for the relatives, who liked to make a fuss.

If a person insists on living out in the wilderness, the first and most important thing is to lick it into shape, so that he can feel at ease there. Kubsch had to enclose his little portion of the planet, Minnie insisted on it, the estate agents demanded it, it was an imperative to him too. The second thing was a summer house to live in, but it wasn't to be an ordinary summer house, but one of those dinky wooden huts, with a little bedroom, a little kitchenette and a little balconette. The house came, grew and flourished; if you put a deckchair out on the veranda, you had your feet in the open; when Kubsch wanted to help with the washing-up he would stand outside the kitchen window and Minnie passed the plates out to him, there was no room for him in the kitchen. And the third thing needed was a well. They were lucky: just twenty feet down the well-digger struck groundwater. For an outlay of just a hundred and twenty marks they had a lovely green well with pure, natural water, not the artificial stuff that comes in pipes.

They toured their demesne; it was early summer or late spring. Thank God the little house couldn't accommodate much in the way of furniture, it was full already. Then again, their wallets were empty, the sixteen hundred were gone; now they had to start work.

It's remarkable what can be squeezed out of two hundred and twenty a month when there's a will. Kubsch trotted off in his good suit every morning at a quarter to seven and was back home at a quarter past six, when he changed into his oldest clothes and got to work. Weeds were ripped out, potatoes hurriedly laid out, cabbages and tomatoes planted, parsley sown, strawberries planted.

Kubsch had to learn on the job. He had no neighbours to turn to for advice, even though neighbours eventuated. One was the well-to-do Herr Knopp, who drove out on Saturdays in his small automobile. He paid a gardener to do his garden, and his house was built from brick. Their other neighbour was good with his hands, but he was far too mean to give them any tips, and such things as he did tell them were usually wrong. Kubsch would squinny over the fence to see what this neighbour was doing; sometimes it turned out well, sometimes not so well. But Minnie was dear in offering help, when she wasn't missing all her girlfriends from the office who she used to have such lovely gossips with. If things got too bad they would lock up the garden for two or three days, and spend a few nights on the sofas or floors of friends. And when they then returned to their summer house it seemed all the more lovely, fresh, clean and peaceful.

Autumn came, and they dug up their potatoes, and the garden became damp, gloomy and dead. Their neighbours moved back into the city. They stayed, there was a by-law that permitted people to winter in their summer houses, and where else could they have gone anyway? Things got very lonesome for Minnie. Kubsch did overtime, and only got home at eight or nine at night. 'Just wait, you'll be surprised how soon winter's over,' he promised. 'Wait till you see how beautiful the spring is here.'

Spring came, and it was beautiful. They had fruit trees, half a dozen each of cherry, apple, pear and plum. The gooseberries and currants flowered like mad. Of their thousand square yards, at most three hundred were unplanted, and they planned to take them into cultivation next year. Everything was so much nicer than it had been their first year. Kubsch got the hang of napping on the train, and never missed his stop. And he would go on working in the garden till he couldn't see the hand in front of his face.

The next winter, admittedly, was bad. It seemed not to want to end; spring simply refused to come. And then there were pay cuts, and even short-time working. He was expected to put eight hundred marks into a road fund because they were going to asphalt their track, as well as the usual taxes and fees; sometimes they just sat there and looked at each other. By mid-March they were out of coal, and no possibility of buying more. Just enough for Minnie to cook by. Kubsch came home with accounts of polar explorations from the library, and they read about Mikkelsen and Nansen, and pretended to be two polar explorers in their tent.

Finally, at the beginning of May, spring arrived, if hesitantly. Slowly, painfully slowly, the buds thickened and burst, first the currants then the gooseberries. And, long after they had greened, finally the trees. Now, today, everything is in flower *chez* Kubsch, twenty-four fruit trees in full bloom. He has put in so many potatoes they'll be able to sell the surplus; he will trade with the coal merchant.

Sometimes, for a quarter of an hour in the evening, he takes Minnie on a walk around their garden. There isn't really a conversation as such, because he keeps stumbling upon new things to show her. 'Look, the parsley's sprouting at last. Well, well.' He straightens up and surveys his estate. 'Everything comes good, you just need to wait for it sometimes. I'm not worried.'

And then Minnie takes him by the hand.

Mother Lives on Her Pension
(1931)

She is seventy-six years old, withered from a hard-working life, with a little bird's head her loose skin bunches and bags over. Her voice has grown lighter and higher in the last decade, and she screams because she can't judge volume any more: her deaf ears no longer pick up anything.

Even though she has seven surviving children she lives with strangers, who have rented her the attic for four marks a month. She gets a pension of thirty-five marks, 'more than enough' to live off, only the winters feel terribly long, and coal is unafford-able. She doesn't calculate by marks and pfennigs, but by the price of a loaf. When her pension is reduced by two marks, she says: 'Just imagine, that's four loaves of bread! Four whole loaves!'

Bread has always been the cornerstone of her existence; every-thing has always revolved around bread. She knows better than anyone else what it is: bread – and she knows what it is to be without it. There were times when it came easily and willingly into her house and was never finished, there was always another slice to be cut from it. And there were other times when she could only see the gleaming brown loaves in the windows of bakers' shops; everything was topsy-turvy and the children fret-ful. She managed to get through those times, she can no longer say how. Bread returned, not suddenly but gradually, and there was again enough to go round.

Then they invented a wonderful substance called margarine, which was so much better than beet syrup or the plum mush of yore. Yes, the world was making progress, poor people were no worse off, they muddled along, God only knew how.

She was never really envious of the rich – and rich for her began

48

a long way down. Shop windows, dresses, fur coats, bright, happy, attractive women with soft, snow-white hands – that was another world, remote and unattainable, it was nothing to do with her. Her fingers, yellowish and rough like the claws of a bird, are crooked now, she can no longer straighten them. For the whole of an endless life they were always grasping some utensil, the handle of a tool, the handle of a paring knife. How many thousands of tonnes of potatoes she must have peeled in the course of her life!

And she is still at it today, day after day, month after month. At eight in the morning she slips out of her garret, walks ten blocks to the restaurant of her son. She sits there until noon, peeling potatoes and washing up, and in return she gets a meal. Her daughter-in-law is loath to give it to her, the old woman doesn't deserve it for the work she does. But here it's as well that she's deaf and doesn't hear the griping and cursing. Her son's place is going well, he has an Opel, he is well fed and contented, often a little tipsy. 'You leave Mama alone,' he says, 'she's got an appetite like a sparrow anyway.' She feels grateful to him, never having heard the proverb, 'Who gives bread to their children and later falls upon hard times has no one to blame but themselves.' She is glad her children have come to something.

None of the others want to know. If she visits, she's sat down in a corner or told to go away. 'Mother has her pension.' But the seventh, the one she never thought much of – because of course she had her favourites – the seventh is the best of them. She hasn't seen him now for twenty years – or is it thirty? – but he still sends her postal orders from time to time. Five marks, or ten. She puts them by. They'll give her a wonderful send-off that way. A good boy, even if she never cared for him much.

At least once a month, she takes the long trip out to the grave-yard to visit her old feller. He's been dead eleven years, but she still tells him everything, shares her life with him. On visiting days she begs her neighbours for a couple of flowers. They tease her: she's to convey the regards of Frau Rohwedder, is that right, or Toni Menzel. As if! She wouldn't even tell him the flowers were a present, he's to think she bought them for him. Men don't need to know everything. She doesn't feel sad, she doesn't cry, with her light chirruping child's voice she tells him stories. Why should she be sad? Her children have grown up, she has a roof over her head and bread. Is there any more you can ask for from this life?

A Burglar's Dreams Are of His Cell
(1931)

He has two years of penitentiary behind him in Hamburg, and five more in Prussia, and the bottom line is that he doesn't much care for the Prussians. Their penal system is rubbish, a well-behaved convict doesn't even get to enjoy a kickabout, you have to crawl to obtain such privileges. When he goes to work now he always takes a map with him, so as to make damned well certain he doesn't do a job somewhere in Prussian-administered Altona instead of Hamburg. Each time he passes the Nobis Gate on the Reeperbahn, he reminds himself: 'Commit a murder here, it's fifteen years; one more step, and it's off with your block.'

When you see him, he's bound to make a decent impression on you. He's polished and polite, because in the course of his life he's had to negotiate many difficult situations. He's a sharp dresser, because he mustn't arouse suspicion by looking shabby. He has strikingly dextrous hands, quick hands, clever hands, he needs those for his line of work. He's alert, how else would he ever have got to be thirty in that line of work, with only seven of them spent behind bars. He is, if called upon to be so, brutal: caution and regard aren't much help when it comes to cracking safes.

He has two passions, and two only. And that's his strength: most people have more. One is breaking and entering, he's done that from when he was a nipper. Even today he thrills to the memory of first cutting a window pane with a diamond at thirteen, climbing in and standing in his uncle's bedroom, listening to the easy rhythm of his sleep, and fumbling for the dresser and taking his wallet. It was an impressive show of nerve for a thirteen-year-old. Sure, it got him a place in a young offenders' centre, but that wasn't so bad, and he learned lots of useful things while he was there.

Today he disdains such crimes of opportunity, he doesn't mind taking up to six months patiently scoping out a job. Ideally he works alone, use a leg man and you always end up as the mug. He's popular with his fences, they give him sweetheart deals, up to twenty per cent of the value of an item: he's yet to shop one of them.

His second passion is women: an inclination, admittedly, he shares with most of his sex. Only that he won't stick to just one. The girls on the Reeperbahn and the harbour district all know him. He's never seen, or tried to find, other girls. He can't be doing with the fuss. He needs women, but they're all the same to him, he doesn't distinguish between them. They're all stupid, all money-hungry, untrustworthy, loose-mouthed, only good for one thing. He's like a Muslim in that regard; he would laugh if you tried to tell him women were more than flesh.

He reserves his hatred for the cops, but even more for traitors in his own ranks. If he happens to run into one the world goes red, he will knock him down on the street, bite and kick and rip his ear off, smash his nose, till he comes to his senses in some station holding pen – his senses, yes, but never remorse. He's big on professional ethics: don't attempt stupid jobs, do good work, cover your fence come what may, don't shop anyone or anything. He's a reliable fellow till it comes to divvying up the goods, where his watchword is: get more than your fair share. Afterwards, everything is sorted out. He's a sworn enemy to the respectable world.

And so he goes through life, almost silent in the human crush, with little sense of participating in its needs and joys. But sometimes, in his off hours, when the police are on his tail, when he doesn't have an hour to himself day or night, or when he's just simply blue, he rides out to Ohlsdorf and tours the prisons at Fuhlsbüttel. He looks up at the barred windows and dreams of being inside again. In there is quiet, sleep without fear, regular meals, his own sort. Behind those lit-up windows he's worked in the carpentry shop and made roll-top desks, nice, demanding work, and not without its little touch of irony.

Finally he goes home to the big city, which has no home for him. Enemy to all, enemy to himself, with the dream in his heart of a barren cell.

Why Do You Wear a Cheap Watch?
(1931)

My father's a watch-maker – that's right, my old man has a watch shop, I could say he's awash in watches, and that's not just a way of speech – but I, his only son, wear a nickel watch that cost two eighty-five, chain included, with a one-year guarantee. I bought it for myself, and not at my father's shop either.

My friends ask me: Why do you wear a nickel watch? Are you down to that?

I could answer them: Hush, friends! Times are hard, it's a struggle for everyone. Or I could say: I'm giving the two-eighty-five mechanism a try-out. I may be a law student, but watches are in my blood, I'm studying this mechanism for my father.

No, I hate diplomatic lies! I tell them: The reason I'm wearing this nickel watch is because my father is mean, stingy, selfish. He doesn't have a gold watch for his only son, he deals in watches, he doesn't give them away, that's what he's like. That's what I tell them, and it's true.

My friends say: Oh dear, poor lad, with such a stingy father.

But then I ask them: Don't you think my father's behaviour is correct?

It was my big day: I had passed my school exams. Since I don't have any children yet myself, I can be frank: it was a mediocre pass, I just about scraped through. When I come to have my own children, then I'll say to them that I passed with distinction, the education ministry sent an official specifically to congratulate me, he shook me by the hand, tears of emotion welled up in his eyes: Young man, that was the best exam ever taken in these cloistered halls . . .

So, no, for the time being anyway it was a moderate exam, but my father went ahead and gave me a gold watch. It wasn't from his shop, no it was an heirloom from an unpleasant and happily long-deceased godfather, who used to call me 'little monkey' and 'howler' by turns.

Perhaps his dislike of me had transferred itself to the watch, which didn't accompany me so much as keep its distance from me. My friend Kloß keeps a sailing boat on the Wannsee. We sail out, we bathe from the boat; our clothes are left on deck.

I've had enough of swimming, I want to get back in the boat, I pull myself up the side, the boat tips and all our things glide into the water. Kloß was there, and we fished everything out of the water, only my gold graduation watch had plummeted fifty feet straight to the bottom.

My father is a tidy man, my father is a methodical man, it's an occupational disease with him. It's not possible to tell him that the watch I inherited from my godfather wound up in the drink. No, we were in the public baths, and from the water we saw someone going through our things. We swam back as fast as we could, and gave chase, but he got away.

'Hmm,' went my father. He let things rest for a week, then he gave me a gold watch from his shop, a Glashütte, flat as an oyster, gorgeous.

That watch and I got along, it was the most dependable of watches, it never let me down.

Nor was it easily parted from me . . . This time it wasn't Kloß, it was Kipferling with whom I went on a trip to Munich. Munich is a fine city, there are many things to do there; both Kipferling and I ended up wiring our parents for travel money home. By the time we were actually ready to leave, our travel money had melted away.

We had only one object of value: my Glashütte watch. Kipferling set off with it, I begged him only to pawn it so that I could redeem it once we were back in Berlin; nothing doing, he came back with the watch, it was outright sale or nothing. So we took the plunge.

All the way home I was racking my brain for a plausible story to tell my father. But my imagination had seized up, I couldn't think of one. Finally I was left with a thief on Munich station, heaving crowds, suddenly my watch was gone. Those international pickpockets . . .

My father remarked, a trifle dryly: 'Well, you'd be the best judge of that, son.' I thought it didn't sound very nice. I was left waiting quite a long time for my next watch. In fact, I had to help get it; I was always late for everything, every appointment, the theatre – what could I do, without a watch . . .

Finally, I got one. It wasn't so flat, but it had two lids, and a loud tick. It was what we call in the trade a potato – reliable, gold, nothing spectacular, but in the end we are at the mercy of the feelings of our makers, and I was reasonably happy with it.

Well, so I go to play tennis, I play tennis, I get dressed afterwards, and what do you know? Eh? Yes, my watch has disappeared! Imagine my despair! My dependable potato – gone!

So now imagine my situation: what do I tell the old man? Yes, what do I tell him? Go on, tell me, give me a way out . . . That older generation is so suspicious!

Well, the upshot is that ever since then I've worn a two-eighty-five nickel watch, with a one-year guarantee.

I tell everyone perfectly truthfully that my father's stingy. Or do you think he's behaved well?

He simply won't believe that my watch was stolen. Won't believe it. Now you say something!

On the Lam
(1931)

How Sänftlein came to be called Sänftlein, he can no longer recall. In the files of a series of German prosecution authorities he appears under divers other names, but that doesn't concern us. Sänftlein doesn't accord with the general picture of notorious villains that you get from reading thrillers. He has watery-blue, earnest eyes, a pear-shaped head, a thatch of blond hair, a clumsy, puppyish sort of body; he looks like a good boy.

Our interview took place in a prison yard, he and I were both wearing blue. Sänftlein was unimpressed with the professionalism of one or two of our fellow inmates: 'Those are occasional workers. They were unlucky. Their hands slipped.'

I said I thought there were a couple of gifted characters among them.

Sänftlein was all contempt. 'Them? Gifted? Well, maybe by your lights. I'd like to see them get by without clothes, in winter, in an unknown city, without a penny piece, hunger in their bellies and the cops on their tail. Because that's when you sort the wheat from the chaff.'

I asked him what he would do in such a situation. And he told me what he had done, and I remembered it, I even wrote it down.

In Hamburg they'd given me eight years, now I had a court appointment in Kassel, for begging while armed. My only chance was to give the whole occasion a miss.

I had two cellmates, one was solid, the other was a crooked bank employee, not our sort at all. I broke off a piece of iron fitting from the bed frame and bent it so that it would lie snug and flat against my hipbone. Then we knocked a leg off the stool,

I needed a lever. White-collar boy was leaned on not to tell and the guard searching us was half-asleep, I got the stuff on the train with me, no bother.

Our express stopped in every cow-village. We weren't due in Kassel until ten o'clock. After four was the best time to do a bunk because it would be dark. It was cold outside, just above freezing, with occasional flurries of snow. White-collar kept himself to himself, which was fine, so long as he didn't squeal. I felt perfectly calm, I knew my plan would work.

A little before five o'clock we stopped somewhere for a really long time. I got undressed, took out crowbar and stool leg, and was in shirt, trousers and socks. By the time the train got moving again I had knocked the glass pane out of the window without making a sound.

The goddamned first bar made me break out in a sweat, I didn't have room to insert my crowbar. There were a couple of loud cracks. We could hear the cops chatting in the corridor, but they didn't hear us.

Once the first bar was gone the others were a doddle. In five minutes I had the window clear, and I was half-hanging outside. The wind howled, and it was dark and perishing. I was just on my way back inside when I could feel the train starting to slow down, in the distance I could see the lights of the next station.

We could hardly pull into the station with the window bars smashed to buggery and the glass gone, so my mind was made up for me. I swung back inside the apartment, called out: 'Station ahead, I'm off!' and went out the window again, feet first this time. For a moment I hung by my left hand, the wind bit my face like crazy, the lights were zooming up frighteningly fast, and I threw myself to the right as hard as I could, so as not to land under the wheels.

The train screeched past me with rattle and spatter of gravel and there I was, lying on the sharp ballast on the adjacent track. When I got up my bones were all right, but my trousers were hanging off me in shreds, blood was running down my legs, and in some places there was no skin left.

Up ahead I could hear shouting, the train stopped, shadowy figures were running here and there. I made haste to get off the rails. I tripped over a signal wire, rolled down an embankment and wound up in a ditch with ice and water. It burned like fury, it took my breath away.

Before I was even up, I saw them running up above, the cops. There were even two of them along the rim of the ditch, so I kept quiet, even though the ice mush was warping me so that I thought I'd never get up again.

Once they were passed, I got to my feet. I was as bent as a pistol, and the first hundred paces took me about an hour. Shirt and trousers were turned to ice, and were scraping off what skin I had left. After a while though I couldn't feel anything, and ran along as in a dream.

I had promised myself not to touch anything in the first village by way of clothes or food. There were people everywhere, and lights on in the windows, so I went cross-country until I hit a road, which I turned down.

It was maybe nine o'clock when I saw the next village under a hangnail of moon. But the houses were all tight, and the lousy farmers weren't asleep yet, so I slunk around for a while without finding anything I could use. In the end, I just went on.

I was tired, and starting to feel cold again. I felt as though my feet, which had lost the last shred of sock long ago, were swelling up by the minute. I didn't want to know.

Finally I came to a nice, remote farmhouse, just right for someone in my pickle. The dwelling had a light on. There weren't no curtains, so I could see the farmer and his wife sitting there, him smoking, her sewing. I didn't want to do anything chancy, so I thought I'd wait for them to hit the sack. I stood at the window for ever, every fifteen minutes or so she would say something, and he wouldn't even reply. Farmers, I ask you!

I was trying to keep my hands a bit warm. My fingers were warped like pincers, I tried straightening them out by force, shoved them in my mouth, nothing doing. I was as stiff as a board. That's why everything went wrong. When I pushed in the window frame it fell into the room, there was noise, dogs barking, a light went on in another window – I had to move off.

I was furious, I can tell you, I ran off, God knows how long for. Ideally, I would have fallen down and died, but I didn't want to do the filth the favour of handing myself in like that.

At about midnight I came to another hamlet, and this time it was do or die, that was clear. In the first farm I came to the coach house was open, I crept inside, but couldn't find a thing. For a while I lay in the coach under the apron, and dozed off. But the cold had me awake again in no time.

Behind a wall, I could hear the sound of cows chained up. There was a padlock, but I only had to tap it twice with a stone and it opened. I hung it on the lock as if someone had left it there, and pulled the door to quietly after me.

Stepping into dark, warm air felt like a lit-up Christmas tree with presents to a small boy. I took just a couple of steps, and then I dropped blindly into the straw between two cows. They didn't mind me, and as I burrowed myself further in, I felt like crying from sheer happiness.

I lay there for five minutes, gradually absorbing the warmth into my body, then the pain started. I pressed my fist and straw in my mouth so as not to cry out loud. My hands and feet were being sliced with knives, my peeled thighs burned like fury. I rubbed cowshit on them. That helped for a while, but then the pain started again.

Somehow, I got through the night. As it got light, I crept up the ladder into the hayloft. At least there was no wind there, and it felt a little bit warm. Then the women came along to milk. Their voices and the plashing of the milk got me excited after the long stretch in prison. But finally I used them to get to sleep to. By afternoon, I crept down and was able to have a meal of milk, beets and bran, which did me good.

From the pattern of activity and snatches of overheard conversation, I had learned that the stables and the stable lads' room were directly adjacent to the cowshed. Now it all depended on whether they all went over to supper in the main house at the same time, or if one stayed behind to watch the horses. When the doors slammed, I was already halfway down the ladder. There was no one in the cowshed or stables. There was even a light left in the lads' room, an ordinary candle, and lots of stuff hanging from hooks on the wall.

I thought I heard someone crossing the farmyard, I was much more agitated than I ever got outside for a big heist. I put both arms round a big bundle of stuff, and tore it off the hook with a jerk. The tabs burst, and I'm pretty sure I took a few hooks as well. I shot out into the dark farmyard, ran behind the barn, dropped the lot on a potato pit and listened out. Nothing.

I had a vague idea of what I had grabbed, and I got togged up. Two shirts, two pairs of underpants, a thick knitted jerkin, a woollen waistcoat, a jacket and a pair of corduroys. I doubled in bulk, and I left a lot more stuff lying there. Only no cap, no socks and no shoes. I wondered if I shouldn't go back inside, but I didn't have the balls, I preferred to leave it till the next village.

It was bitter to have to march through snow with bare, bleeding feet, but I soon remedied the situation. I filched a pair of clogs from an outbuilding. I also got a cap when I ran into a workman on the road a little after ten at night. I played drunk, barged into him and knocked the cap off his head with my arm. Then I put my foot down on it, and pretended not to know. The fellow was unbelievably obstinate, he stood there for half an hour asking me to get off his cap, but as a drunk I wasn't obliged to understand a word he said. Finally he pushed off, chuntering to himself. I was keen on his socks and shoes too, but that would have had the police on my tracks in no time; this was just a drunk from the next village playing up.

I walked all night and the better part of the next day, with a lot of hunger in my belly. In all my pockets there wasn't a coin, or crumb of tobacco. That told me a lot about country living.

Finally I got to Kassel. First hanging round the waiting rooms, but there was the sour smell of cops, so I got out and walked the streets. I didn't know a sod in Kassel or of any sort of opening, but I needed to do a job, and right away, that was clear. I walked through a snowy park with no one out and about, then some streets of villas, then a working-class quarter.

I found myself behind a cart; it would stop every now and again and boxes were unloaded from it. If they were too big the coach-man would help the delivery boy, and they would carry the boxes into the houses together.

I picked out an item, not too big, something that looked like it might be valuable, just to get the ball rolling. I walked up and lifted it while the two guys were in the nearest house, and I took it up an entrance. There was a flight of steps to the basement; I went down and parked myself outside the door.

Now it was a question of whether the fellows would realize right away there was something missing or not. Half an hour passed, and nothing stirred. So I set off with my package. I walked through the working-class district, then the streets with the villas. As I went, I speculated what might be in the box. It was a lot lighter than I thought, at the most fifty or sixty pounds. So long as it's not booze, I thought. Because then I would get drunk on my empty stomach, and they would nab me, that was for sure.

In the park it was quiet and dark, it was snowing, and no sign of anyone. I dropped the box off in a bush. It was fastened with a metal band, and bloody hard to open. I needed to use one of my clogs as hammer and chisel, and of course I wrecked the sole.

I was pretty tense when I finally reached under the lid, but it was all right: bottles. I pocketed a couple and went over to the next lamp post. Dralle's birch hair-restorer! I'd known worse, but there wasn't going to be much money in this for me. As I was filling my pockets, I noticed that there was some other stuff in the box as well, cartons of soap and scent, little gift packages for Christmas. I took a few samples of those, slipped into my ruined clog and set off again.

I found a working-class barber. The shop was already shut, but I rang the upstairs bell and asked the woman if I could speak to the gaffer. I wanted a shave. She let me in, I guess I really did look like I wanted a shave.

I saw right away that I'd come to the right guy, a little yellow-looking fellow who wouldn't look a gift horse in the mouth. I didn't say anything about wanting a shave any more, I just pulled my samples out of my pockets and asked him if he could use any of my stuff. The woman stood by, just looking at me: she'd seen right away that one of my clogs was busted.

First he was cagey enough, and said a few odds and ends of things didn't interest him. I said I might know where to get some more. He gave me five marks, and said he'd stay open till I got back, and he lent me a rucksack so I didn't have to haul that chest through the streets at night.

Everything passed off smoothly, I got another sixty marks and a shave. The woman gave me dinner and, without my saying a word, a pair of her old man's shoes.

Then I found a bar where there was music and girls and a few of the right sort. I managed to stay off the booze. I shacked up with a little blonde, who gave me a shirt and collar and tie from her pimp.

But in the night, the pain in my feet got going again. I stuck it out for two days, but then I went to a doctor. He said he'd never seen anything like it. He cut off four of my toes, but then it didn't hurt any more, and I had plenty of dough, and a good set of prostheses.

I asked Sänftlein how long he had lasted.

He grinned sheepishly. 'Three weeks and they arrested me again. It was grim.'

What had happened?

'It's public education! There's too many things they don't tell you!' he yelled in a fury. 'I mean, did you know that smoked salmon doesn't do well at sub-zero temperatures?'

Not as such. But then it didn't come as a total shock to me either.

'All that thinking . . . thinking . . . In the end it's the stupid ones who are smart. Anyway, it's on account of my ignorance that they picked me up.'

'Go on, Sänftlein, do tell,' I said.

And he did.

In the long run, Kassel was too small a town for my line of work, I didn't really fancy trying to mount a big job there. So I just turned one or two little things, until I had enough cash in hand, and I went back to Hamburg, where I was familiar with the market.

Remember, I had been in the pen for three years. It was all change. My old pals were gone, and the youngsters looked like bleeding amateurs to me. They liked having money, but they weren't prepared to do anything to get it. Finally, I'd got together three who looked dependable to me.

It was a hard winter. I wasn't able to scope things out myself, the police in Hamburg knew me, because I'd once had a pop at one of them; so I had to send my lads out instead. All the schemes they came up with were rubbish, either far too difficult for beginners like them, or else no hope of decent reward.

Finally they came across a big salmon-smoking operation, very light security. They made a song and dance about the price of salmon, and I couldn't keep saying no, so we went ahead with it. It was a lousy night, I had a bad feeling right away, the lads were bickering, they hadn't even lined up anyone to fence the stuff. By and by I was in a towering rage.

We got into the yard where the smoke shop was; one man kept watch outside.

Then we're standing in front of the door, and what do you know, my master criminals have left the jemmies at home. We're standing there like a clueless bunch of idiots, a simple lock and no jemmy! My gang are at each other's throats again, about who's to blame; I bawl them out, I give them a proper carpeting, I didn't care if anyone heard. Then I say: 'Give up? Forget it!' and I take a crowbar and proceed to smash in the door panels. That was loud, the sound echoed all over the yard, sometimes I stopped and thought, this isn't going to end well. But nothing stirred.

By now my merry men were long gone. Pressure dropping like a stone, storm imminent. I made a nice big hole, after all I needed to leave by it with a couple of suitcases, and I climbed in. It took me five minutes to unhook and pack a couple of hundredweight of salmon, and head off home. No sign of the others.

The whole time I was wondering what to do with the suitcases. I didn't want them at home. I end up stashing them two streets away on a building site. It was nice and quiet, fifteen below, the brickies would all be lounging at home with the missus.

In bed at night with my blonde I'm thinking and thinking: what am I going to do with the stuff? A fence who doesn't know me puts the frighteners on me and fobs me off with ten marks; the ones that do know me are all behind bars or in the Bahamas. Ach, I think, just risk it. I need money, what use is this rotten life? In the morning I check out the prices in the shops, then I go to my building site, pack a case with sixty pounds or so of the stuff, get into a nice suit, and totter off.

So I walk into a delicatessen, ask to talk to the boss; he won't even see me: no thanks, no interest. The next one has enough salmon to last him the whole year, and so it goes on, up and down the scale, a great product I've got, I don't even need to open my little case.

Finally, I think, you're wasting your time with these small fry, think big. The department stores sell the stuff too. Right. Specials. Seasonal goods, bulk buyers, now we're cooking with gas. What have you got with you? Let's see. Very nice fish. Looks good. Let's sample it, shall we?

Takes a knife, hacks off a piece, tries it, looks at me. 'Oh dear, sir, this has got frost damage.'

'Oh?' I say. 'The fish has got frost damage? You must be joking.'

'The fish has got frost damage. It's all soft.'

'Soft, you say?' I ask. 'Well, it's reflected in the price.'

'No,' says the man, 'you don't get it. This is a write-off. Mr So-and-so, would you show the gentleman one of our salmon.'

We wait, the fellow brings the salmon. 'You see, it's firm under the knife, whereas yours cuts up soft.'

He starts sawing away; hello, I think, there'll be nothing left.

'Now let's wait a moment longer,' he says. 'There's still ice in your fish. Once that's melted away, you'll see how soft your fish is then, I tell you it'll be like a pudding.'

'I'm afraid I can't wait just now,' I say. 'I need to go . . .'

'You can go here,' he says. 'Use the staff toilets. I just want to save you from losses.'

'You do,' I say. 'I have the utmost belief that you do, Mr Salesman. But if you knew there's a price on my head of three thousand, then you'd understand I can't be all that patient.'

And so saying, I pull my friend halfway out of my pocket, and look at him. He turns pale, and all the other fellows look at me too, but none of them does a thing.

I walk out backwards, saying: 'Hang onto that fish, Mr Salesman, I think it is a bit soft. Let me make you a present of it for your bravery for wanting to get one over on me.'

And with that I'm outside, and down the steps and across the yard, and on the pavement. I take a carriage and then a car, and then I take a little ride out in the countryside, and in the evening I go back to my place, and as I pass the building site, I think: There's my salmon! When the builders see that in the springtime, they'll think someone started a maggot farm.

The next morning, it's just getting light, and I'm thinking I'm hearing some whispering. My door had a translucent glass panel, and the corridor behind it was in light, so I had a good view of a couple of heads with pork pie hats. So they're onto you, I think. Well, the door's locked, I think, and by the time you're inside, I'll be into my trousers and out the window.

I'm just wondering whether to wake my little bird first, when I see the handle turn. You turn away, I think to myself, you can turn that for a long time when – words fail me – the door opens. Did I forget to lock it? I tell you, in those days my head was all over the place.

So the two coppers are in the room, with their little friends out. One of them – the copper, not the friend – even looked familiar.

'You're up early, gents,' I say. 'Don't frighten my little bird, if you don't mind.'

'No tricks,' they say. 'We know you. One move, and we'll shoot you full of holes. We're not going to stand there and let you shoot us.'

'Peace,' I say. 'You're talking to a naked man. Now be nice and let the girl out, she's nothing to do with anything.'

She was lying beside me trembling and teeth chattering.

'You get up,' he said to me. 'Stand in the middle of the room. Fräulein, get out of here.'

The little one goes, not even dressed, things over her arm, in her slip. She was so afraid it was funny.

'You surely won't mind me getting dressed, Inspector,' I say.

'Stay where you are. If you try anything, I'd love to let you have it, you know because of whom.'

I knew they were thinking of the cop I'd shot. One of them handed me my things, one at a time. Once he'd checked the garment over, he tossed it to me. There was nothing I could do, his buddy kept his pistol in my face, while my own was on the bedside table, under the bowl.

So I slowly got dressed, me chatting to them pleasantly all the while, so they didn't start to think I was going to try anything. But while I got dressed I took half a step and then another and then another half in the direction of the window, while the arm of the cop with the gun was getting tired, and he was pointing it mostly at the ground.

'All done,' he says.

'Just my toothbrush,' I say and reach for the basin.

'Stop!' he yells, but I fire twice, and then crash backwards through the window. They will have thought, second floor and all that, no chance, but under my window was a veranda roof.

I crash through the glass; they're banging away, but far too high because I'm not hanging around. Already I'm skittering down the veranda. There's another blue in the courtyard; I shoot on sight, he waddles away trying to open his holster, and I'm halfway across the yard.

I was seeing red. I was in a mean mood. I run out through the entrance to the street, gun in hand. There's a woman standing in the entrance; she flattens herself against the wall when she sees me and goes deathly pale. I won't have been a pretty sight either, bleeding from my encounter with the window, revolver in my paw.

There's more on the street. 'Get lost, you sons of bitches!' I yell, and fire. They're running and I'm running, up the street and round the corner, along the next street. I'm hoping to disappear in the crowd, but everyone seems to melt away, and the street is empty ahead of me. And if I turn around, I see them coming after me, a thick black mass with a thousand white faces, and shooting.

I think it's time to lose the cannon, and only hold it tighter. I think there's bushes in the park, but the bushes are bare, around me everything looks emptier, what am I running for? I think.

Go into a building, I think, up the stairs, across the rooftops, to get them off my tail, and I turn into an entrance.

As I look around, I'm standing in a bank, large room one single door, which is the one I've just come through. I start yelling:

'Everybody out! Get out of here!' And they stream past me out the door, and outside they're standing in a big circle, the other side of the square, all in black and no one daring to come any nearer. The last one past me was a pale lardy guy who was trying to run lightly past me when he tripped over an umbrella-holder and lay there flat on the floor, his mouth popping like a fish's. I fired once more, that was my last shot, and he crawled out of the door, and I was on my own.

So there I was with all my talent and the empty pistol and nowhere to go. In the tills there was masses of money, more money than I'd seen in my life. But I wasn't interested, nothing interested me, I had to think about them all running from me, and me standing there. The girl had run off too.

Outside there was a ringing, fire engines, I thought, is there a fire somewhere? And it came in through the window, a jet of water, God knows how many atmospheres of pressure. I lay flat on the floor, it splattered all over me, I felt as though I had broken all the bones in my body. I couldn't move one finger.

So I lay there for a while, and they went on squirting their hose at me, and after a time the cops walked in, and they picked me up.

I Get a Job
(1932)

1

As autumn came on, the city filled with unemployed, prices climbed ever higher, and our prospects of making a few marks got ever smaller. Willi and I decided to try the provinces: we settled on Altholm. There was a timber factory there where Willi had once done piecework, nailing crates. He had earned good money at the time, and he liked to think back on it, he hoped to maybe get something like that again. It wasn't so simple for me, I wasn't up to such physical work, but we thought I could find something there too, with luck.

We sent our things on ahead of us in a basket as registered freight, and walked the hundred miles. It was a fine, windy, sunny autumn, it did us good to be out of doors and not think about work the whole time. Food cost us practically nothing: there were plenty of apples on the trees, and Willi was able to cadge bread from the country bakers. We always timed our entrance so that there was a woman in the shop, then Willi would go in and stand behind her. He had a funny way of looking at women with his round, seal-like head, that made them laugh, and they gave him whatever he wanted. We never begged for money, we were both fine for clothes, in our nice blue suits, and I had a mac on top, and Willi had his anorak.

You do all right on apples and bread, it was probably six months since we'd had regular hot meals and we felt pretty good. At night we slept in farmers' straw for ten pfennigs or so. Before we went off to sleep, they would always go through our pockets for matches and cigarettes. Then they would give us them back the next morning; once one of them even made us a present of a couple of cigars.

So we made it to Altholm in six or seven days, and found a room with a leather-worker on Starenstraße for six marks a week. There was a table and a chair and a bed, which we had to share, but the nights were drawing in, so that wasn't all bad. Willi was in luck, on our third day he got a job at his old timber factory. This time he was nailing nesting boxes for chickens, piecework again, and brought home twenty-five or even thirty marks. It was a little factory with untrained workers and non-union pay rates. We knew it was wrong to fall in with an operation like that, but we had been hungry for too long to be picky.

2

Jobs I could do were never advertised, but I ran around town a lot, and tried to see what I might possibly do. If I happened to see a queue of people in a shop, I would go in and ask if I could lend a hand. Sometimes I'd get packing work for an hour or so, and would come home with fifty pfennigs. Early doors, I would hang around the station a lot, because when people are travelling somewhere they are more liable to spend money, and occasionally I would get a suitcase to carry, or something like that. Only a uniformed porter spotted me and chased me, scolding me for a blackleg. He called me all sorts of other names, strike-breaker, scab, welfare cheat, and from then on, every time he saw me from a distance he would start shouting. I had to try and avoid being seen by him, so I stopped going to the station.

My main responsibility was looking after Willi. In the morning I would get up first, make him some coffee and cut him some bread, and then wake him. When he was away in the factory I would tidy the room and wash our clothes, then I would go out and look for work. I had to be back at three, to cook his supper.

Now that he was working again, he wanted hot meals and meat. I stuck to our old diet: bread and marge and a herring at lunch-time, but sometimes it got damned hard frying his meat for him, and I would help myself to a little of it. He would almost always notice, he had an uncanny sense of what half a pound felt like and looked like. And then we would fall out and argue.

It seemed we argued more than we used to in times when neither of us was working. Of course that all stemmed from his feeling that he was the breadwinner, and that gave him licence to find fault and criticize me. Once or twice he would come home drunk on Friday, and then the bed would be too small for both of us, and he would throw me out. I was annoyed with him and irked by my own lack of success at getting work, so I would talk back, and we would sometimes go at it for hours.

The thing that annoyed him the most was that I had a habit of wearing stiff collars. He was like a kid about it, he couldn't see that I'd never pick up an office job if I wasn't wearing a stiff collar. According to him, you should only wear a collar on Sundays; to run around wearing one on weekdays was just vanity. I couldn't starch and iron my collars myself, and he resented giving me money for it. I would steal it from his pocket when he was drunk, but he would notice later, when I put on a fresh collar, and then our ding-dong would start again.

Once, I was completely out of them and I borrowed his Sunday collar. I really thought I was going to get a job that day. Well, that didn't happen, instead I was caught in the rain, and blow me if that evening he didn't want to take a girl out and found his collar sodden. He fell into a temper, we shouted at each other, and he threw me out of the room. He was fed up with me, he said, I should go and get a place of my own if I could. In the end the leather-worker put me up in his room, I slept on the sofa, and he and his wife shared the bed.

The next morning I made Willi's coffee, same as always, and he didn't say anything, there was silence between us. As he was walking out the door he stopped and said, I might try with a minister, there was someone in his factory who had been helped to his job by a priest. Then he went. That was his way of being conciliatory, because I couldn't really be angry with him. It's not easy being back in work and keeping someone else going who doesn't really mean anything to you.

3

I got the addresses of local ministers from the paper. There were two papers in the town, a big one and a little one. I had only been to the big one once, and they were all full of themselves and snapped at me for wanting some information. They were friendly at the little one, always had time for a chat, and gave me what advice they had. There were five ministers in the town, and I spent the whole of one day going round all of them and putting my case. They listened to me amiably enough, asked me the odd question, but basically they all struck me as people who were used to worse misery than mine. Then they tried to get rid of me as quickly as possible. No one knew of a job for me.

Willi was nice about it when I told him of my failure, he even took me to the cinema by way of consolation; to show how grateful I was, I took my collar off when we went. Going to sleep that night, he said I should try the Catholic priest tomorrow, the Catholics were where the influence was. I didn't want to argue with him, so I agreed to try, and got the address. Once again, the managing editor of the paper couldn't have been kinder, I had to tell him about the Lutheran ministers and promise to report back to him on what happened with the Catholic priest.

Anyway, I was received by a nun or whatever she was, I couldn't see much of her face under the big white bonnet, and after a while the priest came along. He was a big, well-built man with white hair, soft-spoken and slow in his speech, probably a farmer's son from the coast, where they are apt to be strong and silent. He listened to me for a long time, you could see he understood what it felt like to be out of work for four years, and desperate. Finally he said: 'I'll give you a letter for the manager of the leather factory. I'm not saying it'll help. But I'll give it to you.' He sat down and started writing, once he looked up and asked: 'You wouldn't be of the faith, now, would you?' I had discussed with Willi the necessity of lying on that point, but I couldn't help being truthful when he looked at me. He just said 'that's fine' and went on writing.

I delivered the letter to the manager's flat and was asked to present myself the next day. When I came, the maid gave me thirty pfennigs and asked me not to call again. I stood there on the steps feeling pretty woebegone. When she was back in the kitchen, I pushed the thirty pfennigs through the slit in the door and ran down the steps while the coins jingled in the box.

4

I went to my friend on the paper and told him my story. He said he had expected nothing else, and why didn't I go round to his place and help his wife move some furniture. She was spring-cleaning, and I gave her no end of help, beating the carpets and scrubbing and waxing the floor – and in the evening my friend came home, and I was to eat with them. He said he had had a word with the proprietor, and he was happy to have me go out on a subscription round. I didn't even ask about the terms, I just said yes right away, that was how happy I was to hear that. I was told I would be given a pad of receipts with subscriptions for the month. The first month's I could go ahead and cash, and that would be my commission. It was one-fifty a time. It was a good idea to start with the master craftsmen, because each week the paper carried an article by the union syndic on craft-related questions. I should tell the wives that the serials in the *Chronicle* were acknowledged to be superior to those in the *News*. I should take care to read the current serialization. Then I should also bear in mind that anyone who subscribed in the middle of the month would get the paper delivered absolutely free for the rest of that month. That all sounded very good to me, and I went home feeling very enthused, and bursting to tell Willi all about it. At first he was pissed off with me because I hadn't made him any lunch, but finally he came round to the idea, and reckoned I would probably make a ton of money.

Early the next morning I went round to my paper, the *Chronicle*, to get hold of the addresses of craftsmen. It was still too early to set out, the managing editor reckoned I'd best not bother anyone before nine-thirty. So I sat down and read the article by the union syndic, which I thought was very boring, and then a bit of the serial, which was set in very exclusive circles. At half past nine I set off.

My heart was beating as I stood in front of the first address I'd been given. Before ringing the bell, I waited for it to settle down, but it kept getting louder. I rang, and a girl opened the door. Might I speak to master painter Bierla? 'Come in,' and, 'Papa, here's someone to see you.' I was shown into a large room where a nice elderly lady was sitting at a table, chopping cabbage. The master was standing by the window in conversation with another gentleman. 'Good morning,' and how could he help. I bowed politely, to his wife as well, and the visitor. 'Good morning,' and how I represented the *Chronicle*, and had come to ask whether Herr Bierla might care to subscribe to our newspaper, perhaps on a trial basis initially. I had thought up a proper little spiel about how 'we' represented the interests of trades and crafts, that craftsmen needed to stick together in these difficult times, and then there was the syndic and his magisterial essays, and finally, with a glance at his wife, our celebrated serials.

Suddenly my talk was over, I didn't know what else to say, no one spoke, and there was silence. It was so quiet that I started up again, but lost my way, stammered and ground to a halt. Then the woman at the table piped up: 'We could try it, dear,' to which he, 'What does it cost to take the *Chronicle*?' Now I had to talk again, there were the free deliveries to your doorstep, the first month's subscription was gratis, I filled in the little form and gave it to the master, who sent me off with it to his wife. He was back in conversation with his guest. I got my money, one mark fifty for five minutes of talking! When I left I crossed the road to look at the house from the other side. It was a good house, a practical house, I liked it. It was well maintained, with a master painter you expected that attention to detail, in the ground floor there was a shop, Johanssen, tobacconist. For an instant I had the notion of chatting to Johanssen but I decided to stick to my plan, and stay with craftsmen. I took one last look at the house and went on.

The next master craftsman wasn't home, nor his wife. The one after had a bone to pick with the syndic, who was a smart alec who took a lot of money from the guilds and had done precious little with it. The one after was very glad I had come because he had always wanted to subscribe to the *Chronicle*. The *News* had completely misreported it when he had been called upon to pay a fine just because an apprentice of his happened to do a couple of hours of overtime. And so it went on. Sometimes I had to traipse right the way across the town, the sun was still shining brightly, but the last leaves were falling from the trees.

At half past one it felt like time to knock off. I was feeling a bit stale and mechanical, and anyway I was cutting into people's lunchtime. In four hours I had managed to recruit six new subscribers from the twenty-one I had paid calls on, and I had nine marks in my pocket. 'Not a bad start,' said the managing editor when I presented him with the addresses of his new readers, so that they would get tomorrow's edition. Then I got something to eat, cooked and fried, but for myself as well. When Willi arrived everything was ready, and he shared in my pleasure. 'You'll be raking in sixty marks a week! My, oh my!' We made ambitious plans, then we tidied up and went to the cinema together.

5

The second day wasn't as good as the first, and the third was a lot worse than the second. I understood that I had had my best day, and that there would be no repeat. It wasn't that I'd been through the painters, and after them the smiths, and then the bakers, who were a totally different class of people. It was that I had lost my élan, and was doing it by rote. You need to be a born seller to go after the fiftieth potential customer with the same zeal as the first. You need to believe in what you're saying, or at the very least make it seem as though you did. When I was told: We've been reading the *News* for ten years, and the *News* is better than the *Chronicle*, why should we change? – then, in my heart of hearts I had to admit they were right. My riposte was abject. In fact, I couldn't understand what would possess someone to take the *Chronicle* anyway. The *News* was always four, or eight, or even twelve pages longer, their four-column layout looked much livelier than our three-. They had as many personals and three times as many business ads as we did. They had a clean look, because they were properly set, whereas we for the most part were matrixed in Berlin. Over time I got to have an eye for all these things, from various people's complaints. When I took it up with the managing editor later, he would often get angry: 'Just remember, if we were the *News*, our subscription drive wouldn't consist of you.'

I no longer made twenty-one calls a day, sometimes there were ten, sometimes just three. If I suffered two rebuffs first thing, I wouldn't feel like going on. I would spend ages walking up and down outside a blacksmith's, they were hammering away inside, the fire cast a red glow through the windows, then finally I would pull myself together and go in. The master was cutting the frog out of a horse's hoof and testing the fit of a shoe, a couple of journeymen were making ready to wrap an iron rim on a cartwheel. I stood in the doorway and waited. I had learned this, it was best not to disturb people while working. While I stood there and watched the fire throwing sparks and listened to the hiss of the bellows, I heard that they were talking about me. ''S nothing,' said one of the journeymen to the master. 'Just another time-waster.' – 'Goes strutting about instead of working,' declared the other. And the apprentice called shrilly: 'Buy my buttons and braces and safety pins! Come buy, come buy!' Then things went quiet again, the journeymen were busy with their wheel, the master was knocking the horseshoe into shape on the anvil. The apprentice was holding it fast with a pair of tongs. The coachman had picked up the leg of his horse so that the hoof was pressed right up against its thigh. They were all of them working, they all had a living they were making. I thought that I too had once gone to a nice clean office at a certain time and done nice clean work. Now I was running around making a nuisance of myself. On the first day of my subscription round I had done it, I walked into the room of the master painter like a chatty earl, an envoy from the fourth estate, but I was no longer able to perform the part with any conviction. Now I felt like a little travelling salesman trying to talk people into something they didn't want.

Behind me the door opened, and someone walked in. I took a look at him: it was another traveller. He put his little case down beside him, called out a hearty 'Good morning!' and looked hard at me, to see if I was from the other lot. I shook my head to indicate I wasn't. The journeymen started scolding again: 'Let them stand there, Master, till we've got a full dozen, then send them all away at once. It's too bad!' The master walked over to us: 'All right, what do you want?' After three words he interrupted me: 'Subscribe, because you're on the side of labour? Have you got them to lower taxes? Your syndic, don't make me laugh! He's best mates with the Treasurer in Town Hall. No. That's enough. Not another word. Thank you!' He turned to the newcomer: 'And what do you want?'

If I had two such experiences in succession, I often wouldn't feel like seeing anyone else at all, and would just walk in the park for hours. I would dream of finding money, vast sums of money. I walked around with my eyes to the ground scanning the paths, but I never found anything beyond a handkerchief and the occasional button. There were many days when I brought home no money at all. Willi had reverted to his previous snippiness.

A perennial hope of mine was a master baker on Lohstedter Straße. He never quite ruled out the possibility, and said: 'Come by again. I'd like to think about it.' And when I came the next time, he needed to think about it some more. He would always greet me with a cordial handshake, and say: 'Well, young man, have you come up with a clinching reason why I should take out a subscription to the *Chronicle*? Because those I have aren't quite sufficient. Almost, but not quite.' Then I would try and bring up something or other. It took a very long time before I understood that I was one of his court jesters, to whom he looked for a pastime. I'm sure he had a lot of them contributing to his amusement, there were enough of us running around town.

Most people didn't welcome being called on by so many travellers; for the majority we were a pest. Sometimes, on entering a house I would hear the next ring, I would hear my predecessor speaking, sometimes lively and hortatory, sometimes humbly hand-wringing. Then I would wait for my colleague to come down, and we would walk together a ways, and let off steam. Everyone grumbled, it didn't matter whether they were fancy-dans travelling with vacuum cleaners or carried a box with sticking plasters and spare buttons. We grumbled about how badly we were treated, and then after a while we admitted that 'actually' the people were right, there were too many of us running around, in particular some who were just scouting out opportunities for break-ins.

It always felt especially bitter to me to be taken for one of these last. I had rung and stood patiently outside the door, and after a while I heard a scuffed footfall, and an eye appeared at the peephole.

It always looked very dark with a lot of white, and you could never tell whether it was a man's eye or a woman's. So there you stood for what felt like a very long time, being looked at, and then the peephole would shut with a little clack, and the scuffed footfall would go away again. Or the door would open, but the chain stayed in front of it, and you started talking through the crack, and suddenly when you were halfway through your sentence the door would shut in your face, and you stood there, choking on the half-done sentence, before slinking back down the stairs.

Sometimes I had the feeling that all these humiliations were collecting in my chest, and I was never going to get rid of them and one day they would crush me. I understood better and better that almost every traveller would one day blow up, go drumming his fists and yelling at a particularly unpleasant locked door, or abusing a rude housewife. I understood it very well, but I still thought it wouldn't happen to me, since it all struck me as being just temporary: in the end I would get to sit in a clean, well-lighted office again.

6

Then my day also came.

I had got on to master tailors. One of these was a woman, a Fräulein Kehding. The managing editor on the *Chronicle* had warned me: 'She's not a woman, she's a devil. She's the nastiest piece of work in the whole of Altholm. I'd give her a miss if I were you.' Well, I did go to her, if only because it was a change from so many men.

From the steps you walked straight into the tailor's workshop. Something had just happened, because one of the seamstresses was in floods of tears, and the others sat around looking awkward and not knowing how to behave. Fräulein Kehding was pacing up and down, and only stopped her scolding when she noticed me standing there. 'And what do you want?' she asked, but not unkindly. In fact, she disappointed me by looking rather decent for a devil, with a long, straight nose, bright eyes and a fresh complexion. While I was saying my piece, she stood there with her hands behind her, looking at me. She was actually one of the easier ones to talk to, she listened and put in the odd word herself: 'Oh, does our syndic write for your pages?' – 'Absolutely, the crafts must hold together.'

When I was done, I had secured a new subscriber. Everything had gone unbelievably smoothly, and I was writing out the receipt. Fräulein Kehding stood a little to one side; while writing I looked across to the sewing machines, to the girl who had been crying. She was a pretty thing and, blinking back her tears, she smiled at me. I smiled back.

Then I heard a sort of hissing sound next to me, a suppressed cry of rage, and I looked up at the mistress. She was white with fury, presumably she was incensed that I had smiled at one of her girls. Carefully I held out the receipt to her. 'One mark fifty, if you please.'

She took the receipt and looked at it. 'You call this a receipt?' she said. 'Anyone can get hold of those.'

'Those are *Chronicle* receipts,' I said. 'That's the way they are.'

'Are they indeed?' she asked mockingly, and getting going a bit. 'You get them made out, and you cheat people of their money, and there's no newspaper at the end of it. Where's your ID?'

'I don't have an ID, these receipts are my ID.'

'Where's your commercial agent's certificate then?' she screamed – she was screaming by now. 'You must have a commercial agent's certificate to go in people's houses like that.' I had none, I didn't know whether I needed one or not. 'You're a swindler!' she screamed. 'But you're not going to fool me. Elfriede, run and get Sergeant Schmidt. We have a swindler here.' The girl who had been crying got up timorously and walked over to the door.

I said, 'Fräulein, here is my book of receipts, the counterfoils, there are the names of other tailors.'

'Will you get moving, Elfriede!' she screamed. 'Shall I chase you?! Is that what you want, for this wretched man to make a clean getaway!' The girl ran out and I started to feel flustered.

'Fräulein,' I said, 'will you give me back my book of receipts. I don't want your money. Let me go.'

'Not likely!' she cried. 'So you can run off, eh? Toni, lock the door.'

'Fräulein,' I cried. 'You're being mean. I know why you're doing it. Because I smiled at one of your girls. You want to make all the pretty ones cry, because you haven't got a man.'

We got into a shouting match, Sergeant Schmidt didn't understand what it was about, but he hauled me off to the station just in case. As I sat there on the bunk, I sobered up quickly enough. I regretted that I'd got so heated. My job was recruiting subscribers, not smiling at girls, and the Kehding woman was more right than wrong.

7

After the police had made a few enquiries, they let me go. I walked slowly over to the *Chronicle*, feeling pretty wretched. I wasn't surprised to find the 'mistress' had been in to complain about me. 'Enough,' said the managing editor. 'She'll turn the whole small business community against us if I let you go on. You shouldn't have gone there anyway. I told you not to.'

He gave me five marks, he was and remained a decent guy. When I got back to Starenstraße, Willi wasn't home yet. The mere thought of his reproaches made me shudder. I threw my things in my suitcase and left them with the landlady. I would write for them in the fullness of time. Then I walked out of the house, out of the town, onto the high road. It was the second week of December, light frost, a bit of snow. I had nine marks left. I would go to the city, and try and find something there.

A Bad Night
(1931)

Wrede walked into my room and asked crossly: 'Why are you still here? It's past eight o'clock.'

I helped myself to another piece of bread and butter. 'People don't go thieving that early. There's still too many lights on in the village.'

'If the lieutenant sees you're not gone yet,' said Wrede, 'he'll make a stink.'

'The girl's just brought me my supper.'

'I need you to be on time!' he screamed at me. 'You leave at eight o'clock. It's half past. If you don't do exactly what I say, I'll have you out on your ear.'

'Just mind you don't get thrown out yourself,' I said viciously.

Wrede walked out and slammed the door. I went on eating my bread. When I was finished eating, I got the pistol out of the dresser and wiped and greased it. I was just finished doing that when Wrede came back. 'All right. I'm on my way!' I said hurriedly, and pulled on my watchman's fur.

But this time he was all friendly. 'What have you got there?' he asked. 'My word, it's a cavalry pistol! Where did you get that from?'

'I got it from the coachman,' I said. 'He brought it back from the war. There's a hundred and fifty round of ammunition to go with it too.'

'What did you pay him for it?'

'Twenty thousand.'

'Twenty thousand marks!' he cried. 'That's not even forty pounds of rye. It's under a dollar. I reckon you got the best of that one.' I laughed. 'You know what,' he suddenly said, 'sell it to me. You've got your nice little Ortgies, what do you need that heavy old thing for? I'll give you forty thousand for it.'

'No chance,' I said. 'I wouldn't sell it to you for four hundred thousand.'

Wrede had a think. 'All right. I'll give you half a mill,' he said solemnly.

I caught my breath. 'Right away?' I asked.

'Right away,' he said.

Half a million; if I went into town bright and early tomorrow morning, I could buy myself a pair of shoes and a suit. And I could use them. I looked pretty shabby. 'It's a deal,' I said.

'Okay,' he said. 'I'll get the money.'

I heard him go into the office. He could be as careful as he liked, the safe door creaked when he shut it. Handy, I thought. Well, why should I care where he got the money from. I was selling it legally. I got the ammunition out of the dresser, put it on the table, filled the magazine, clicked it in and locked it.

Wrede came back and gave me the dough. 'There,' he said, 'count it.' He was in a bad mood again. 'Count it so you don't come wailing to me tomorrow that I didn't give it to you.' He was fiddling around with the pistol on the other side of the table from me.

'I expect it's right,' I said. 'Seeing as it's not your money, it'll be right.'

He looked up at me. 'Tell me what you mean by that! Tell me right away what you mean!'

'I don't mean anything by it!' I laughed. 'Because you always have the correct change, that's what I mean. How would I get change for a fifty-thousand-mark note? No one would change it.'

'Fucker!' he said.

Suddenly I realized he'd been drinking. A wave of schnapps breath wafted over the table. 'Wrede!' I called. 'That pistol's loaded, be careful. With the lever like that, the safety catch is off.'

'It's on!' he cried furiously. 'If you see the "S" it's on.'

'Baloney,' I said. 'When the little lever's over the "S" the safety is on. Now it's off.'

'Baloney?' he yelled. 'Who are you saying baloney to? I'll give you baloney. The safety's on. I'll prove it.' He raised the pistol and aimed it at me.

'Don't be stupid,' I yelled. 'It's off!' I threw myself to the side. The shot rang around the little room like a thunderbolt, it passed over my head. I ran to the window. It passed through the curtain and the glass, and must have buried itself in the barn wall opposite.

I stood by the window for a moment, breathing hard. I heard people cursing from the farmyard, but no one came in. They were used to our antics. In our cups, we sometimes aimed at the office from our room. I wasn't afraid that Wrede would shoot a second time.

When I was perfectly calm again, I turned round. Wrede was standing by the table, the pistol still in his hand, white as a sheet. I picked up my Ortgies, stuck it in the pocket of my fur, and went out without a word. He could stay there for ever if he liked, I didn't care.

Outside it was cold, dark and windy, the snow hadn't come yet. I crossed the yard, the cowshed was already dark, but there was a light on in the stables. In front of the big house was the boss's car; Siebert the chauffeur was running up and down, trying to keep warm.

'Where are you off to then?' I asked.

'They're going to the theatre. Madam isn't ready. What was that shooting about?'

'Wasn't me. It was Wrede. Just a shot.'

'The way you two carry on, I'm surprised you're alive.'

'Quality's built to last.'

'Yes, and weeds never die.'

The lieutenant came out with his wife. She was in her fur, with a silk scarf over her hair. She clumped down the steps in her big galoshes, with the lieutenant holding her arm so she didn't fall. Her throat looked very white.

The boss and Siebert wrapped her under the rugs. The boss told him to drive like blazes so that they made it by the interval at least. I would have loved to go along, instead of keeping watch for the whole long, cold night. The whole drive smelled of Madam's perfume.

Then the lieutenant called out to me: 'And you keep a better watch. Last night two potato clamps were open. Let's go, Siebert!' And the car hummed off.

I headed slowly in the other direction, towards the woods, to the fields. It was completely dark, and the wind whistled across the bare fields. I kept to the middle of the path and tried to see into the shadows of the trees. Every twenty paces or so I would switch on the bull's-eye and lit a piece of my way, as well as I could.

It was nine o'clock now. I had to run around here all night, till six in the morning, watching for thieves, and I felt desperate. Wrede was definitely not going to relieve me tonight, I had provoked him too much. Two clamps open, the lieutenant said. Let him stand watch out here. You couldn't do a bloody thing about it.

'Halloo! Halloo!' It was Maison the old gamekeeper, whom I'd brushed with my light. He came tottering along, when we met we both stopped. He was a couple of feet from me, and in spite of that I could hardly see him.

'Is that you, Maison?' I asked.

'Yes. Are you going out now? Bloody weather.'

'Yes, it's getting colder.'

'Yes. The rye's perishing in the ground. There could be snow. Mind yourself,' he said. 'In section seventy-three I found a heap of potatoes covered over with fir twigs. Thieves will have put them aside for later. Go and have a look.'

'I'm buggered if I'm going into the woods alone on a night like this,' I exploded. 'If I turn on the light, then I give them something to aim at, and if I go in the dark I don't see a sausage, and will just get one over the head.'

'Is Wrede not coming?'

'I'm not sure.'

'Listen,' Maison creaked confidentially in his old man's voice in the dark. 'Wrede talks ill of you in the village. Have you two had a falling-out?'

'Not especially. What do you mean, talks ill of me? What does he say?'

'Well, his money. He says there's some missing from petty cash, that kind of thing.'

'So?'

'Well. You know!'

'Let me tell you something,' I said, and I suddenly felt angry. 'I don't give a shit about Wrede and his gossip. If there's something wrong with his balances, then you need to ask the publican and his girlfriend how much he spends there every night. And then take a look in his wardrobe and see how many suits he's got hanging there. And ask around in Stettin how he paid for his motorbike.'

'I'm only saying what he said. I didn't say I believed him.'

'Yeah, but you pass it on. Good night, Maison, I suggest you go to the office and tell Wrede everything I've just said. And then you can tell him from me that the next time he takes a pot-shot at me, to expect one back, you got that? He'll understand. G'night!'

He trotted off, muttering to himself. Let him mutter, I'd had it up to here. Wrede was the big man, he let them all drink on his tab, and they did, as if they believed he could pay for them all out of his piddling Inflation-era wages. And they crawled to him, just as he crawled to the lieutenant, whose ear he had. I did guard duty at night, and come the end of the month my wage wasn't enough for new soles for my shoes. But now I had some money, and if Wrede cut up rough with me tonight, then I was out of here, I'd go someplace else, and let them see how they could keep the hungry people of Stettin out of their potatoes.

Not that I could do anything about it myself either. Two potato clamps open, yes, why not. They lay there in the dark like endlessly long, slightly darker animals, a regiment of long earthworks, each of them two hundred and fifty yards long, five feet high, about thirty of them, twenty-eight thousand hundredweight of potatoes packed in with straw and earth to protect them from the cold. Well, plenty of people walked the ten miles from Stettin with their sacks and their handcarts to get potatoes cheap in these dear times. How was anyone going to catch them? The bit of field where the clamps were abutted the wood on two sides. It was out of the wood that they came. And then they scrabbled at the clamps' ends like moles. If you walked down the long sides, they played hide and seek with you. Usually you didn't see them, or at most a couple of fleeting shadows.

But the next morning, when the lieutenant came, he could see where they'd been all right. Because here was one open clamp and there another. And the worst of it wasn't the three or four hundredweight that had been taken, it was that frost could penetrate the open clamps. The frozen potatoes mouldered away, and the mould spread and ate its way right through the whole clamp, and in the end, come spring, you were left with a stinking heap of mould that was good for compost and nothing much else.

Could I do anything about it? No, I could not. I walked up and down, I was a conscientious worker, and in the end I was shouted at.

I felt depressed that night on guard, furious with Wrede, the gamekeeper, the lieutenant. But I wasn't quite as hopelessly sad as I was sometimes, there was a bit of gristle in my rage. I had half a million marks in my pocket, that was a bit of freedom. While I walked and from time to time flashed the bull's-eye, I thought about what I might do with the money. And when I had got through it, I would get more. I would find it lying in a railway compartment, and buy myself more stuff. And in the end, I would get myself enough to fit out my own flat.

Once I'd done that, it was past midnight. I got under the trees in the lee of the wind, unpacked my sandwiches and began to eat. Now the scene with Wrede was bugging me again. It was possible he'd shot at me on purpose, but most likely he was just drunk, and hadn't been sure about the safety catch. I shouldn't have said that stuff to the gamekeeper. I wondered what I could say to get out of it tomorrow, when Wrede asked, because the gamekeeper was certain to blab . . .

I lost my train of thought because I heard a sound. I stood perfectly still and now I could hear it clearly, repeated and dull: someone was going at the frozen clamp with a mattock. It was maybe six or seven clamps away from me, at the head end facing the open field, a crazy place to start, seeing as if you tried at the woods end, you could always duck under the trees if I happened to come looking.

I took a decent pull of the pint of corn brandy I got every night, took the pistol with the catch off in one hand and the bull's-eye lantern in the other, and set off. The hacking was very obvious. I was making good headway, and not making too much noise either, of course you can't get across frozen plough land like parquet. The banging was ever closer. I was pretty close to it now, just past one more clamp, and the fellow was ten feet away. I would dazzle him with the lantern.

I listen out for the next hack. But there's silence. I think it's just time feeling slow, in a moment he'll get going again. But he doesn't. Has he heard me coming?

I make my move. I take three paces round the clamp and switch the lantern on. Nothing! Am I drunk? No sign of anything. Someone's just been hacking away for the past five minutes at least, and the clamp is perfectly intact. What's going on? No sign. It was here – but what?

More banging. At the other end of the clamp this time, two

hundred yards away, the head end, into the woods. I'm not drunk, am I? Some funny business here. Ach, sod it, I'll go home. Something stinks. After all it's my own bones I'm risking, no thanks, not me.

And yet I follow the clamp very slowly to the other end and the trees. Knocking, then louder knocking, closer and clearer; I stop every twenty paces or so and listen out. Then I notice my heart beating as well. I can still turn back, there's another fifty yards to go. The knocking. The bloody dark. Oh Jesus, I'm scared. Still knocking. Ten yards.

Silence. I listen. Silence. Then I slowly take the last few steps, someone has been chopping at the clamp for the last ten minutes, and there's nothing whatsoever to see. The clamp is all bright and clean and intact.

It was more instinct than a sound: I drop the lantern and leap aside as far as I can. The shot thunders, echoes back from the woods. I run. I recognize the report. I'm running for my life. Another bang. It's mad to run the length of the clamp, I'm an easy target. I throw myself against one of the walls. Here he comes running, I can see his shadow advancing, another shot, the muzzle flash lights his face, he shoots again. He runs past me, thinks I'm still ahead of him.

I press myself against the wall of the clamp, he hasn't seen me, he shoots once more, thirty yards away from me. Then silence returns.

I don't move, I feel frozen, suddenly I have the fear I haven't had all night. Again I see the muzzle flash light up his pale, contorted face, contorted by drink, by hatred. But it's not really him I'm frightened of, it's this life, this perspectiveless dirty muddle that suddenly scares me. These nocturnal walks looking for poor petty thieves, these mad drinking bouts, these stupid shooting games, these loud-mouthed superiors, the hustle for a few banknotes that, no sooner are you holding them in your hand than they're worthless – no, I can't be doing with any more of any of that.

The footsteps return. The first moment will decide everything. I peel away from the shade, I say: 'Good morning, Herr Wrede!' and step right up to him. He makes a movement, but I quickly say: 'That was you shooting, wasn't it? Were there thieves? Did you hit any?'

He doesn't say anything. I try again. 'I want to get away from here, Wrede. You've got to help me. I want to leave right away. I've had it here. Won't you help me?'

He says: 'Let's go back.' He clears his throat. We set off.

I say: 'Will you help me?'

For a while he doesn't say anything, then he says: 'What do you think you would do?'

'I'd go to a friend. I can stay with him till I find a new job.'

'And what would you tell the lieutenant?'

'What would I say? I've gone, I wouldn't tell him anything.'

'All right,' he says. 'I'll write you a testimonial about your time here.'

'Thanks, Wrede,' I say.

'You sure you won't say anything?' he asks after another pause. 'Not to anyone?'

'Why would I?' I say. 'If you'll write me a letter.'

'Word of honour?'

'Word of honour,' I say. His hand feels for mine, we shake on it.

We're back at the farm. 'Get packed up,' he says. 'I'll harness up the gig with Senna. I'll run you down myself.'

'Thanks, Wrede,' I say again.

Finally, he's standing by the train, I have my head out of the window. He says: 'I wish you all the best. You'll land a new job.' He looks at the stationmaster with the red cap. 'I won't give you any more money. You've got enough. You'd only get into trouble otherwise.' He is perfectly serious.

Suddenly I ask him: 'Hey, Wrede, how did you do that with the potato clamps, you chopped at them, but they looked perfectly intact?'

He doesn't bat an eyelid. 'I hit them with the flat of a plank,' he says. 'Just hit them. You know?'

'God, I'm thick!' I say.

'Yes,' he says.

The train pulls out. He's standing on the platform, watching me go. Once, briefly, he waves. Then I don't see him any more. I never saw him again, and wonder sometimes what became of him. He was a short, stout guy, he looked just like a dim little farmer.

The Open Door
(1932)

Lini and Max Johannsen got married in early December. He was an old bachelor – round about thirty-five – who had terrorized his farm for many years. He was not a gentle person, and marriage wasn't his idea either. She was ten years younger, mild and blue-eyed, and so besotted with her Max that she had prevailed on him. In the end they had both said their 'I do's in front of the altar, and concluded the union that . . . etc. etc.

The first differences emerged shortly before Christmas. He had pulled a suit out of the wardrobe, and in the process knocked down one of her dresses. She had scolded him. Whereupon he had thrown all her dresses out of the wardrobe. 'Just because we're married, doesn't mean we share a wardrobe.'

She thought he was terribly mean. And that was just the beginning.

Christmas wasn't Max Johannsen's thing at all. He sat around at home, not able to yell at anyone or do anything. He had to keep eating and drinking and smoking, and had his wife in his sights all day long. He noticed she went into his room and said something to him. She left the door open, he got up and shut it. They spoke. She left. The door was open. He closed it. He noticed.

As established, he was unoccupied. If it hadn't been Christmas, maybe nothing would have happened. As it was, he said: 'Lini, shut the door, will you.'

He said: 'The door's open, Lini.'

He asked her: 'Please will you shut the door after you, Lini.'

He reckoned: 'You must have had sacks outside your door at home.'

She was in a wonderful mood. She burst into his room, eager to tell him something. He looked from his room across the drawing room and the yard to her kitchen. He said: 'The door's open again, Lini.'

She said: 'Oh, sorry!' and rushed back to her turkey. Of course the door stood ajar.

At heart, Max Johannsen was a patient soul: you can't work with animals and not be patient. The second phase of his campaign regarding doors was to warn Lini: 'Lini, you must close the door after you.'

'Lini, there'll be trouble if you don't close the door.'

'For Christ's sake, you've left the bloody door open again!'

Lini said: 'Sorry,' and then either shut the door, or forgot to.

On Christmas Eve, Johannsen said threateningly: 'Lini, if you don't start shutting a few doors around here, I'll have to teach you to, and you won't like that.'

'But I do shut the doors, Max,' she said in puzzlement, 'almost always.' Went out, and left it open.

That night Johannsen woke up. There was a cold draught around his shoulders, and the door was open. Quietly he called out: 'Lini?' but Lini was gone. Johannsen stood up, shivering, and closed the door. He lay there waiting. Lini came back to bed. Johannsen felt the chill round his shoulders again. He waited a while, then got up and shut the door.

The next morning at five he had a meeting with Stachoviak in the cowshed. Stachoviak was a young fellow from Galicia, eighteen or nineteen, no oil painting. A clink of silver, Stachoviak grinned.

At six, Frau Johannsen got up. She emerged from her bedroom and got a shock. There was a person standing there. The person grinned, said 'Good morning, Madka,' and then he closed the bedroom door. Frau Johannsen went into the kitchen. Stachoviak went into the kitchen. She had left the door open, he closed it. Frau Johannsen said something hasty and agitated to Stachoviak, but maybe his German wasn't good enough. He laughed. Frau Johannsen said very loudly: 'Out! Get out, Stachoviak!' and pointed to the kitchen door. Stachoviak went over to the door, tried the handle and nodded approvingly: the door was closed.

Lini gets an idea, she plunges out into the yard, and calls her husband. Stachoviak dashes after her, closing the doors. Herr Johannsen has ridden out into the fields.

Max is back for lunch. He sits at one end of the table, his wife at the other. In between are the inspector and his assistant, the steward and the housekeeper-cook. Behind Frau Johannsen stands Stachoviak. Frau Johannsen notices the salt is missing. She dashes into the kitchen, shutting the doors. Stachoviak dashes after her.

The assistant gets a laughing fit, Johannsen asks tetchily: 'Something the matter, Herr Kaliebe?' Frau Johannsen returns more slowly bearing salt, Stachoviak in her wake. No one speaks at lunch.

The couple's conversation afterwards is short. Max is adamant. 'Asking you politely didn't produce the required effect, so we have to do it this way.'

'I think it's cruel.'

'Maybe, but so long as it helps.'

'How long is it going to go on for?'

'Till I'm convinced it's done the trick.'

'All right. But you'll see . . .'

What he is to see is not spelled out. At any rate, behind the door stands Stachoviak.

Then the farmyard witnesses the spectacle as well: wherever Frau Johannsen shows up, Stachoviak is in attendance. Lini is grim, restrained, quiet, she doesn't seem to be aware of the presence of the cowhand. The farm is all too aware of him. She needs to see to her hens. Stachoviak sees with her. She sees to the calves. Stachoviak too. Oh dear, Wandlitz is a bit primitive . . . in the yard, between stable and barn are two green-painted hutments with little heart-shaped cut-outs in their doors, Frau Johannsen is only human. Well, Stachoviak stands guard, even though this is one door she certainly remembers to close.

It's evening. It's night. It's morning. A second morning with Stachoviak. The debate between the couple is very lively today, and there is a new development: Frau Johannsen gives Stachoviak a slap! And how! Whereupon Johannsen calls the youth into his office. More silver changes hands . . . and the door-closer is fortified against further slaps.

The crisis is on the third day. Frau Johannsen is in the farmyard, a coach comes up the drive, visitors! Frau Johannsen dashes along, Stachoviak dashes after. It's Frau Bendler from the neighbouring estate of Varnkewitz . . . It's so embarrassing, they walk into the house together, with Stachoviak following after. As they cross the gravel and the drawing room, Lini keeps making sounds and gestures, as though shooing away a hen, but Stachoviak will not be shooed away. What must Frau Bendler think!

Well, the women have a long chat together. When the maid comes in with a tray of refreshments, they see Stachu politely closing the door after her. Well, that opens her heart. The women laugh and cry, they whisper and then they laugh again: they are closeted together for a long time. Finally Johannsen joins them, and accepts an invitation to see in the New Year with the Bendlers . . . It's a great honour, and seems to have done him some good . . . He hums and whistles to himself all evening, and the next morning, Stachoviak is back with his oxen.

So it's too bad that the young wife can't make it on New Year's Eve! It's their first party together, and she can't come! She's sick. No, she isn't upset, she's very nice about it: she insists that he go on his own. Finally he goes.

Ah, New Year's Eve at Varnkewitz is something else! What a dinner! The charming ladies! The wines! The brandies! The cigars! And everyone is so nice to him. They drink his health. They keep refilling his glass. They need to comfort him, newly married and already a grass-widower . . . Such a delightful lady, too! Well, drink, brother, drink!

Did Johannsen even make it to the midnight hour? He no longer knows. There's only one thing he remembers for sure: Wacker came driving up in his dog cart, Wacker his good old coachman, Wacker* like his name. Johannsen tries to get in, but the steps on those dog carts are deuced steep, and he doesn't make it. He laughs and takes a little run-up, he still doesn't make it. The other gentlemen laugh with him. Finally two take him under the arms. They heave him up. He's up and in, but . . . no sooner in than out again, he passes through it, like a cannon ball.

The gentlemen are covered in confusion . . . is he hurt? They help him up again, swing him up, Oh Lord, there's the handle, I've got to hold on. Out again! No, this can't be. Another wagon drives up, this one laden with straw. They lay him down on it gently, and he's asleep right away. They could harness a pair of cows to it and he wouldn't notice. But they're not like that, they take oxen.

It's night when Johannsen wakes up, feeling very ill. And with the clear-sightedness that comes with a royal hangover, he knows: they have made a fool of him, it wasn't for nothing that they kept toasting him . . . and propelling him through his dog cart. The only thing they meant was that he had a charming wife. Such a gentle little creature, and he such a barbarian and uncouth . . .

He lies there for a while, it's perfectly dark. Is this his bed? . . . He's not undressed . . . There's someone snoring . . . Oh my God, he feels so ill!

'Lini?' he asks softly. Silence.

'Lini?' this time a little louder.

'Lini, darling?' he feels in her direction.

He feels stubble. A rough voice asks: 'Panje?'

---

* The English equivalent would be 'Doughty'.

It gets light. Stachoviak is leaning over him. 'Do you want a drink, Panje?'

He is with Stachu, in Stachu's bed.

What else is left to say? Max Johannsen went quietly and gently across the farmyard to his house. He sits down in his room, and has a long think. He's left alone, because it was New Year's Day, then Lini came into the room.

He's had time to think. Time for him to wish her a Happy New Year, and he meant 'new', rather more than most conventional well-wishers.

War Monument or Urinal?
(1932)

Report from a German Provincial Town in 1931

Like all stories – not just stories from small provincial towns –
this one starts with nothing at all, and like all stories it comes to
be enormous – especially for small provincial towns.

Pumm, a young unemployed schoolteacher, who earned a
few shillings on the side as a reporter for the Social Democratic
Volksstimme – this Pumm was stood up one fine Sunday afternoon by his girl of the time, and was dawdling a little aimlessly
across the market square of his home town of Neustadt. At
the end of the market on a wooden platform stood Sergeant
Schlieker, directing the traffic, which was distinctly lively today.
All the vehicular traffic from Hamburg to the Baltic resorts
goes through Neustadt. Perhaps that was why, behind Sergeant
Schlieker, a second sergeant by the name of Weiß had been put
there, with a notebook.

'What are you doing up there?' asked Pumm. 'Are you a speed
trap, Weiß?'

'Nonsense,' wheezed Weiß. 'We're not short of money. I'm
compiling statistics.'

'What are you doing? Statesmanship?'

'Statistics,' the policeman Weiß loftily corrected the schoolmaster. 'Statistics, Herr Pumm. Your comrade Mayor Wendel wants
to know how many cars come through Neustadt on a Sunday.'

'Whatever for?' asked Pumm. 'You can tell me. There's a cigar
in it for you too.'

'I've no idea, Pumm. Honest. No idea.'

Pumm reflected, asked what the score was so far, exclaimed,

'That many,' and stopped, to help him count. Till midnight. Sometimes they took turns so the other could get a drink, but most of the time they stayed there together and kept a most scrupulous and exact count.

As I say, that's how it all began.

The next day, in the *Volksstimme* the local news page came with a long lead from their special correspondent, more or less as follows: 'Between six in the morning and midnight, no fewer than 13,764 cars drove through our beautiful town. Enquiries at the hostelries on the market square established that just 11 (eleven!) visitors stopped in Neustadt. That's a rate of less than one in a thousand! . . . We present these figures to our generally so proactive traffic spokesman, Mayor Wendel. Something must be done, some attraction must be created here to make this extraordinary stream of moneyed visitors from the city useful to our town . . . We suggest the erecting of a modern petrol station on the market square.'

The article appeared at one in the afternoon on Monday. Officer Wrede spent the rest of Monday looking for Herr Pumm. The population of Neustadt is forty thousand, so it should be possible to track down a single individual. It was seven o'clock when Wrede finally nailed Herr Pumm in Gotthold's café. Gotthold's is renowned for its pastries and its back room. Herr Gotthold, who serves his customers personally, never enters the back room unasked, and even then he clears his throat loudly.

Pumm was there, converting the fee for his article into coffee, cake and dalliance. He was making amends for the lost Sunday.

'The mayor wants to see you,' said Officer Wrede.

'Yeah, yeah,' said Pumm in a bate. 'Stop staring like that, man, it's a girl! Don't tell me you haven't seen one before?!'

'I'm to take you there, Herr Pumm,' said Wrede, continuing to stare stonily at the lady's legs. 'I've been looking for you since three o'clock.'

'If you say one more word—!' yelled Pumm, and then recovered his self-possession. 'What do you say to a drink.'

'I thought you'd never ask,' said Wrede.

The mayor was still in his office at a quarter past seven.

'Something about an article you've written, Comrade Pumm.'

'Yes?' asked Pumm.

'You shouldn't have written that article, Comrade Pumm.'

'No?' asked Pumm.

'That article has caused some bad blood. The publicans and restaurateurs on the market place resent the imputation that they can't attract customers from the big city.'

'But—' began Pumm.

'You should have raised it with me first, Comrade,' said the mayor earnestly.

'But, Mr Mayor,' began Pumm pleadingly, because what was at stake now was more than an article, it was his future in Neustadt. 'I've often written pieces for the *Volksstimme* . . .'

'I know,' said the mayor, 'I know. But this one's different. This is an idea!'

'An idea?'

'The thing with the petrol station, yes. A new idea. You can't release something just like that. No one knows what to say, and everyone has to take a position. Have you no idea of the chaos you've created!'

In the end Pumm went home, profoundly shaken. He had promised the mayor – and shaken hands on it – not to have any ideas without permission, no new ones at any rate.

But such a private agreement was unable to halt the march of events. Things happened, for instance this:

In the Neustadt *General-Anzeiger* a statement appeared from the restaurateurs' and publicans' guild, indignantly repudiating the notion that their utterly contemporary bars and restaurants were unable to attract the motorists of Hamburg. The *General-Anzeiger* itself in an editorial begged leave to question the accuracy of the quoted statistics.

The apothecaries Maltzahn and Raps and the bicycle-seller

Behrens, who kept petrol tanks on the public pavement on the approaches to the market place, objected that the town, their own landlord, was proposing to put them out of business by commissioning a large petrol station.

Derop and Shell, businesses hitherto unknown in Neustadt, put in bids for the running of the petrol station.

Ilona Linde, a worker in Maison's stocking factory, had a lot to endure from her parents and co-workers, to do with Gotthold-related gossip. (The drink hadn't silenced Wrede's mouth.) Was it true that she had fastened her stays in the presence of Officer Wrede?

As far as Pumm was concerned, he lost his little sideline at the *Volksstimme*. 'Your wretched column landed me in so much hot water!' scolded the editor, Kaliebe.

The official policy towards the large petrol station was silence. But the odd publican and restaurateur thought to himself: 13,764 cars . . . I could use the trade! But . . . is anything else possible after that decision? Presumably not, but someone else . . .

Silence. Till Puttbreese, the builder who walked off with the contracts to almost all the buildings that were put to tender in the town, brought in a bid to the Economic and Traffic Subcommittee to petition the council through the town's traffic spokesman, whether a new petrol station wouldn't in fact positively boost the amount of traffic in the town. Think of the sums the town might hope to gain from issuing a lease!

Mayor Wendel, as Chairman of the Economic and Traffic Subcommittee, invited Mayor Wendel, in his capacity as traffic spokesman, to work out a proposal to be submitted to the full council and the committees . . . Carried unanimously!

Carried unanimously! 'Commitment to Petrol Station on Market Place' blared the *Volksstimme*. 'Town Hall Bosses Accept Our Suggestion of New Petrol Station' boasted the *General-Anzeiger*.

Pumm was allowed to write for the *Volksstimme* again. 'That was just a storm in a teacup,' said editor Kaliebe.

Pumm had a meeting with the mayor. 'Perhaps a temporary

supply teaching post at the gymnasium. We'll see,' said the mayor. 'Your proposal is not bad. Though of course I had something in mind along those very lines when I commissioned the survey in the first place.'

The municipal board of works was given the task of elaborating the specifications for the garage. The situation was as follows: town surveyor Blöcker was Stahlhelm,* if not worse. At any rate he had voted in the plebiscite in favour of abolishing the council. On the other hand, one had to concede that the market place, divided by Grotenstraße, fell into two halves. In one half is the town's sole public convenience, built in 1926, with a loan from the community. Cost at the time was 21,000 marks. In the other half is the 1870–71 Franco-Prussian War memorial. Cast-iron railings (Gothic) over six foot high, four red slabs of polished granite, then a few grey and black tumbled cubes of granite, with bronze eagles, a few stray artillery pieces, all decked with laurel, and on top of the lot a man with a cast-iron flag on a broken iron spike.

'So as to guarantee,' thus surveyor Blöcker's preliminary report, 'so as to guarantee unimpeded access to the planned petrol station, either the public conveniences in the northern half of the market place would have to be levelled, or the war memorial in the southern half. Before I submit the final plans, I request a decision from the town planning authority.'

'That's the dilemma,' said Mayor Wendel.

Playing possum didn't help, progress had to be made. By a canny indiscretion on the part of the mayor the preliminary report of the planning authority landed in the office of the *General-Anzeiger*, which positioned itself as follows: 'Here we have yet more proof, if proof were needed, of the chronic lack of

---

* A veterans' organization, the largest of the right-wing paramilitary groupings that sprang up after the First World War and bedevilled the Weimar Republic throughout its brief existence. In 1934 it was assimilated by the Nazis into the SA (Sturm Abteilung, the paramilitary force of the Nazi Party).

forward thinking on the part of our Red administration. If the convenience – the vastly expensive pet project of the Social Democrats – had been put up at the northern end of the market place, instead of slap bang in the middle of it, there would be no threat now to the generous traffic plan. Relocating the memorial to our forefathers, a source of inspiration and quiet solace to so many of our citizens in these times of national humiliation, is of course out of the question.'

The *Volksstimme* was silent.

However, the cinema-owner Hermann Heiß walked into the offices of the *General-Anzeiger* with a reader's letter: 'Why not in the field of honour?' The writer, fired by local patriotism, suggested moving the 1870–71 monument to the military cemetery in the town park. 'That is the place for it, among the fallen of the Great War!' With gritted teeth the board of the *General-Anzeiger* printed this letter from one of their steadiest advertisers, even though they saw through the move: Heiß was a Reichsbanner* man.

The following day, the *Volksstimme* printed a brief but forceful piece in which they made the surprisingly fair-minded and practical suggestion their own: 'Put the monument in the marble orchard!'

The *General-Anzeiger* responded with an announcement, first, that they took no editorial responsibility for the contents of their letters page. 'Herr Heiß has come forward with an interesting proposal; however, it doesn't seem to us that the terms of the issue are sufficiently clear for us to come down on one side or the other. We therefore took the decision to widen and deepen the debate by inviting Town Medical Officer Sernau to publish his views.' And Sernau: 'Are we trampling our cultural inheritance underfoot?' – 'Absolutely, we're dragging anything and everything that reminds us of a time we were rich and powerful

---

* The 'Reichsbanner Schwarz-Rot-Gold' ('Black, Red, Gold Banner of the Reich') was a Social Democratic paramilitary force formed during the Weimar Republic in 1924.

out of sight! Let's wallow in our humiliation! Instead of a heroic monument, a great stumbling block, that's us all over! I suggest Mayor Wendel first ensure that the paths to the heroes' resting place are made passable in wet weather! The suggestion that recently appeared in these pages, masquerading as a reader's letter, will cause every true German's blood to boil! Are we to hide all memory of our victories? Wouldn't that just suit certain gentlemen nicely! Never!!!'

At the heroes' monument a much-regarded wreath with red, white and black ribbon appeared: 'Loyal unto Death!' Meanwhile, at the toilet's little cottage, there was an answering inscription, 'Red Front Lives'.

The people of the town racked their brains: who was responsible for the hard-to-remove inscription? The Communists? Or the Nazis? The Stahlhelm? Or the Socialists? They were all capable of having done it. No, none of them! Yes, the Communists! They're not too stupid! Yes, I suppose you're right there.

The next plenary session was unusually well attended. Substantial issues were on the agenda: a new one-and-a-half-million sewage plant, Christmas money for the unemployed, the sale of four town properties, the long-awaited licensing of a bus line to Mellen – none of them aroused any interest. What's happening with the petrol station? You mean the big fume-ument!

Every party sent its chief orator to do battle. The German Nationalists were against. The German People's Party, against. The Reich Economic Party,* divided: a free vote for party members. The German Democrats, ditto. Centre Party, not represented. Socialists, yes. Communists: oh, can't you just feed the people. The vote: eleven in favour of the petrol station, five against. All others abstained.

Outcry: swindle! Fisticuffs round the table. Keenly observed

---

* In this spectrum of Weimar politics, this is the right-of-centre 'Reichswirtschaftspartei' or 'Reichspartei des deutschen Mittelstandes'.

difference of opinion between Town Medical Officer Sernau and cinema-proprietor Heiß.

'We know your sort, fraternity members!'

'Corroding our daughters' morals with your decadent big-city productions!'

'Don't presume to lecture me about morals, Medical Councillor!'

'You have no idea!'

Anyway, the result was that the petrol station was approved in principle, the town planning office was invited to submit blueprints for the site around the present heroes' monument. Then a delay, a very long delay. Finally the blueprints started to come in. The removal of the heroes' monument will cost 3,200 marks, the construction of a petrol station 42,375 marks. War, war in the trenches.

Once again, Pumm is *persona non grata* at his newspaper, and Ilona is sure now that she's up the spout. The mayor will not receive Pumm, who feels which way the wind's blowing, and promptly joins the Nazi Party.

The architect Hennies submits an alternative proposal, total costs (including the resiting of the monument) 17,000 marks.

Furious quarrel between surveyor Blöcker and Hennies.

One of the eagles on the monument loses a wing, and the following night the face of the flag-bearer is given a coating of red lead paint.

From that point on the monument has to be placed under police guard every night. That makes one hour of service more per man jack. The monument is cleaned off, the eagle wing is lost for ever, but its feet are still there for the Stahlhelm association to hold a celebration. That evening there are violent clashes between Stahlhelm and Communists, Reichsbanner and Nazis. Cause for the newest surge of bad feeling is the sight of the Nazis' newest recruit: Herr Pumm. 'Turncoat!' – 'Stinkers!' – 'Give him one in the chops!' Someone does, end result: three serious injuries, one fatality. The President thereupon (at the town's expense) orders a hundred special constables to Neustadt, since the local force had shown itself not up to the task of keeping the peace. The mayor gets a carpeting. The *General-Anzeiger* comes out with an (unsigned) article: 'What happens when someone approaches the mayor with an idea.'

The town is simmering, Neustadt is at boiling point.

A thing once begun needs to be continued; an avalanche ends only when the snow has reached the bottom. Further meeting of the committee heads: surveyor Blöcker presents his estimate, code word 'petroleum delivery point', 42,375 plus 3,200 marks. Estimate from the architect Hennies, code word 'modern': 17,000 marks. With the votes of the Social Democrats, the German Democrats, part of the Economic Party and the Communists (*sic!* observes the *General-Anzeiger*), Hennies' estimate gets the nod.

The building of the petrol station is a done deal.

Shouting. Jeering. More shouting.

Factory-owner Maison (German Nationalist) rises and on behalf of his party requests the following rider: 'The town government stipulates that the petrol station is to be built in such a way that every major petrol company is equally represented. Reasoning: it's unfair to give any one firm an effective monopoly on petrol sales in our town. Also it would fail of its purpose to maximize the custom from all the big city motorists, who are known to favour different marques. The petrol station should be built so that five or six firms are able to offer and supply their products equitably and side by side.'

Mayor Wendel loses it. 'But gentlemen, that's impossible. I appeal to your common sense! The only way a firm would be interested is if it had the petrol station to itself.'

Maison: 'I thank the mayor for the compliment. Abuse like that doesn't do much to support his argument. My experience as an entrepreneur tells me this can be done easily. I envisage something very attractive: a row of six or eight cabins with their various company inscriptions. Six or eight pump attendants, and we've found jobs for six or eight of our unemployed.'

Shouting, jeering, abuse, or rather eloquence. A vote is taken.

Maison's rider is carried by seven votes. The equitable petrol station monument is at hand. The architect Hennies gets to his feet at the press conference. 'In view of these proposed changes, my estimate of the costs no longer applies.'

The Medical Officer begs to know what Herr Hennies is doing at the press conference. The mayor doesn't know, Herr Hennies walks out.

Amid the general tumult, senior councillor Comrade Platau gets to speak. 'Gentlemen!' he calls out. 'Gentlemen!' He gets a measure of silence, because Platau is of good standing with the Right as well, having traded in his arm for an Iron Cross. 'Gentlemen, I don't think it's right to leave this matter hanging. Now, on the one hand we've agreed to have a petrol station—'

'A fume-ument!'

'Actually, I quite like the smell of petrol. On the one hand, we've agreed to build it, on the other hand it's to be fitted out for six or eight suppliers. And that way we won't find anyone to lease it.'

'Quite right!'

'Under those circumstances, I suggest we table the following resolution: a petrol station will not be built. That way, we'll save costs to our town, we get rid of an apple of discord and we preserve the character of our beautiful market place. That strikes me as a positive outcome. Gentlemen, I move—!'

General surprise. Serious, pensive expressions. Formally speaking, the motion has of course not been properly presented, but no one opposes going to an immediate vote.

Tension. Breathless silence. More tension.

Result: unanimous (unanimous!) acceptance. Full-spectrum unity: no great petrol station! Beaming faces. Peace breaks out all over Neustadt.

A gravely discredited Herr Pumm walks out on both his home town and a bonny little baby boy. He is resolved never to have another idea as long as he lives.

Happiness and Woe
(1932)

At six o'clock, still dark, the man got home from stealing wood. He lit a lantern and split the logs so that, in case a policeman came looking for wood thieves, he would find nothing incriminating. While he worked, he could hear the others in the allotment huts around variously chopping and sawing; they always went out in groups of four or five, so that the forester thought better of meddling with them.

When the man was finished with his work, he went into his summer house. It was now seven o'clock, and starting to get light. His wife was asleep, but his son was awake, sitting up in his cot, going 'Pepp-Pepp' and 'Memm-Memm' by turns. The man gently laid his hand on his wife's shoulder and said, 'Seven o'clock, Elise.' She took a lot of waking, she had been washing clothes all day yesterday. Today she was going out again.

'Can I put the boy with you just for a minute?' he asked, and she murmured sleepily. The boy was very cheerful, and laughed when his father picked him up, and set him down next to his mother. Then he saw the alarm clock, called 'Tick-Tick' and reached for it. His father gave it to the boy. He sat there playing beside his mother, while the man lit the fire, put on coffee and warmed up milk for the boy.

A while later, they were breakfasting together, the boy wasn't eating. 'We'll have to try and get some good butter for the boy,' said the man.

The woman said: 'I've got another two days of laundry to do this week, that'll bring in twenty marks.'

'And I'm getting twenty-five in unemployment money. I'll buy half a pound of butter.'

'Yes,' said the woman, 'it's better for him than margarine. Perhaps teething'll be easier for him then.'

'We still owe for the rent.'

'Yes, take care of it when you're in town today.'

'I will,' said the man.

The boy was cheerful; he was sitting on the ground, tearing a newspaper in tiny pieces, all the while saying 'Pi', which meant picture, and hence all other printed matter. Just before eight, the woman got ready to go out.

'Will you be running late today?' he asked. 'Because I have to go to the labour exchange. I won't be back before six.'

'I'll try and be back by five,' said the woman. 'Maybe he'll have a long sleep.'

'I hope so,' said the man. 'It's always a wretched feeling leaving him on his own so long.'

'I know,' said the woman. 'But what else can we do?' And then she went.

The man tidied up the room, and hung the bedding in the open window to air. He did the dishes and peeled potatoes and scraped carrots for lunch. The boy ran around and pressed his face against the featherbeds. Then the man said: 'Noni's gone. Where's Noni?' and the boy looked up and crowed in triumph. He ran to his father and buried his face against his legs. After a while, the man said: 'All right, Noni. That'll do, little man.' And the boy ran off to play again.

When the housework was done, the man dressed the boy for going out, he put a white woollen cap on him, and dressed him in coat and shoes. Then the boy climbed into his little white cart and the pair set off. There was nothing left to do in the garden, it was early winter, the earth had been turned, and the strawberry plants buried in straw. They trundled along between the houses. Only a very few were still inhabited, whoever could afford the extra rent was wintering in the city. After a while they reached the nice, smooth asphalt road, and the man stopped the cart, unbuckled the strap and said, 'You can get out and push now, Noni.' The boy looked at his father with a cheerful smile, poked one leg out of the cart, blinked and pulled it back in. 'Come on, Noni, let's be having you,' said the father. The boy put a leg out, and pulled it in again. It was a game he liked to play with his father, a little tease he had thought up all by himself. 'Then I'll go on by myself,' said the father, and walked off, leaving son and cart behind. Straight away the boy scrambled out and excitedly called: 'Pepp-Pepp!' The man turned, the boy pointed to his leather braces, he had a keen sense of order, and they looked untidy hanging out, and his father had to tie them up and put them inside the cart.

Now the child was pushing the cart; at times he walked quickly, even breaking into a trot, and then he would stop and watch a dog, and go 'Wow-wow' to it. The father had to go 'Wow-wow' too, the boy repeated it until his father had confirmed it. If he saw chickens, he would say: 'Cheep-cheep!' and his father would say, 'Yes, Noni, those are little chicks and ducks.' That too would satisfy the boy even though he couldn't say the words yet, he was only eighteen months.

The boy then discovered the tensioning wire of a telegraph pole, which consisted of five or six individual strands that were a little slack. He was able to push a finger in between them, and did so time and again. His father called him repeatedly, and kept on walking, but Noni was unwilling to leave his wire. Then the father stopped behind a hedge, and when the boy saw that his father was gone, he ran down the road after him. At that the father poked his head out from behind the corner, and when the boy saw that his father was still there, he spun round and ran back to his wire.

By the time he finally tired of his game, his father had gone much farther, he really was a very long way off, to the boy it seemed too far. He set off after him, but the father was not thinking about his boy any more, and was walking slowly on. The boy stopped, looked along the road, cried 'Pepp-Pepp!' then took hold of his cap and pulled it down over his whole face. The father turned round when the boy called, and there was his son with his cap covering his face, totally blind. He tottered a few steps this way and that, always close to tripping and falling. The father raced to reach him in time, his heart was pounding, he thought: eighteen months, and he's come up with this all by himself. Blinds himself so that I have to come and get him. He pulled the cap off his son's face, and the boy beamed at him. 'You're a silly-billy, aren't you, Noni, what a silly-billy!' The father kept saying it, he had tears of emotion in his eyes.

A little after noon, the father had washed and changed his son, given him his lunch, had something to eat himself and put him to bed. 'Good night, Noni, good night,' said the father, and stepped behind the wardrobe, so that the boy couldn't see him. Now it needed Noni to drop off quickly, because the man had to be at the labour exchange at three, to be given his benefit. The man waited perfectly still, the boy burbled away a little more, then he tried calling or luring him: 'Pepp-Pepp!' but the father didn't stir. And only then did Noni go to sleep.

The man locked the summer house, hid the keys for his wife and set off into the city. He had a good two hours' walk to the labour exchange; officially they were still registered in the city, he hadn't been given permission to live anywhere outside. It was always a worry to leave the boy on his own for so long, but there was no other way. The man walked very fast, he often repeated that he had to buy butter and bananas, which the boy called 'Na' and which were only five pfennigs on the fruit carts in the city, whereas out here they took you for fifteen. Then the rent was due, fifteen marks, but his wife would pick up twenty, so they would get through the week in good shape. Even so, it was hard going, only three months ago they had cleared three hundred marks a month, before he had lost his job.

He collected his unemployment money, and went to the man

they rented the summer house from. But he wasn't in, and wasn't expected back till seven. The man decided to try again later, and walked back down the street. He did his shopping, and because he was near Friedrichstraße, he went there, to take a look at the shops and the crowds of people. He walked slowly back and forth, he had come here a lot earlier, before he was married. There hadn't been so many girls standing on the corners then. He looked at them now, a few looked really good, but most of them were hopeless. He was accosted regularly. Then he would blink his eyes shut and smile and slowly shake his head.

Darkness fell, the lamps came on, the lights in the shop windows looked horribly garish. There was music in all the cafés. The man felt very downcast, he found it harder and harder to shake his head when propositioned. What's the matter with me? he asked restlessly. Is it because I'm so far out of things, because everything is so hopeless that makes me so sad? He kept walking up and down Friedrichstraße, from Leipziger Straße to the station, it was getting late. Once he trotted after a girl in a green hat for quite a long way, but she avoided looking at him or wasn't interested, because he had such an angry and scared expression. Finally, he forgot about her in a huff, and walked into a café. The café was dismal and empty, he sat down and ordered a beer and a cognac. What am I doing? he asked himself. Do I want to sleep with a girl like that? No, I don't. So what is it? I could have been home long ago, and I haven't paid the rent either. And now it's too late for that.

It was past nine o'clock. The man paid, to his alarm the bill came to two marks forty. The alcohol affected him powerfully; as he left, he had formed a new resolve: if I'm not accosted now, on the way to the station, I'm going to go straight home. And if I am . . . He didn't know what he would do.

He wasn't accosted, and he got on the train. He had to change at Schlesischer Bahnhof, and there between platforms he was seized by his old restlessness, he walked out of the station, and up the nearest street. A girl asked him: 'Come with me, darling?'

He stopped and said: 'You can come and have a drink with me, until my train goes.'

'I can't do that,' she said. 'I need to earn money, dearie.'

'I'll give you three marks, go on,' he said, and she pushed her arm through his.

In the bar they sat facing each other, and drank Curaçao, which tasted like petrol. He asked the girl if she had a kid, but she said she hadn't. He was disappointed, he wanted to talk to her about children. As it was, they talked about the hard times, two weeks ago she had taken a pair of shoes to be mended, they were going to cost her one mark eighty; but each time she thought she had the money together, rent and food claimed their share. He told her about the job he used to have, back when life was good, and then about his wife, and then – after all – about their son.

After a long time they got up to catch the last train, but they ended up just going to another bar instead. He had to be with her, to tell her things. They drank quite a lot, he gave her three marks, and then another three marks later. Sometime after midnight he was out of money, and they went out onto the street. 'Now I'm going to take you home with me, and give you some coffee,' he said to the girl.

'Yes, and your wife is going to throw me out,' she said.

'She won't throw you out, she'll make you coffee. And you'll get another five marks if you come.'

The girl pushed her arm through his, and they set off. He kept talking, so that she wouldn't notice how far it was. Sometimes she would stop and not want to go on. Then he would tempt her with the five marks. He was talkative and in a good mood, and all the time the sadness was growing in him.

A long time later, they got to the summer house colony. 'This is where I live,' he told the girl.

'Better let me go,' said the girl. 'Your wife will kick up. Give me the five marks and let me go.'

'The money's inside,' he said.

They knocked. Elise opened quickly. She was in her dressing gown, her cheeks were rosy from sleep, and she looked very adorable. The girl was nothing compared to her. 'Will you make us some coffee,' said the man. 'She kept me company all the way here.'

The woman shook hands with the girl and said: 'Have a seat. A long walk like that, I don't know another man in the world who could have talked you into that.'

The girl said a little sheepishly: 'Yes, it was a long way, I suppose.'

The woman lit the fire and put on water to boil. She got some cups and sugar. 'I need the milk for my little boy,' she said.

'That's all right, Elise, we'll take it without milk,' he said. 'Will you give the girl five marks, I promised her.'

The woman looked at her husband for a moment, he closed his eyes, and nodded slowly to her to indicate his complete loyalty to her. Elise took five marks from her purse and gave them to the girl. 'Thank you very much,' said the girl. 'Now I can go and reclaim my shoes tomorrow.'

The man took the girl by the hand and said, 'I want to show you my little boy.' They went into the corner where the cot was. The child was fast asleep. His long, fine, blond hair was tangled up, he had his fist pressed against his red cheek and his mouth was half-open.

'Now I can tell you,' said the girl. 'I've got a kid too, her name's Gerda, and she's three years old.'

'You see,' said the man. 'My boy's just eighteen months. He's very cheerful.'

After they had drunk their coffee, the girl said: 'I don't want to bother you any more.'

'Don't you want to wait for it to get a bit light?' asked the woman.

'Who's going to bother me,' said the girl. 'No, I'll go now.' The man walked her to the garden gate.

When he came back, his wife had cleared away the cups and was back in bed. The man undressed in silence. After a while he asked: 'What are we going to do for money?'

'Did you pay the rent?' she asked back.

'No,' he said.

They didn't speak for a while, then the woman said: 'We'll get by somehow. We'll just have to be very careful over the next few weeks.'

'Yes,' said the man. 'It was like an illness. I don't know what came over me.'

'No,' she said, 'I know. You just need to remember that things won't ever get really bad. You know: Noni.'

'Yes,' he said. 'Of course. I think it's just because everything's so hopeless.'

'I know,' said the woman. 'You don't need to explain. And now try and get some sleep. You've got the boy all day. I'm laundering again.'

'Yes,' he said. 'Well, good night.'

'Good night,' she said, and turned the light off.

With Measuring Tape and Watering Can
(1932)

From the Life of Menswear Section
Manager Franz Einenkel

When Franz Einenkel, head of the menswear section in Haarklein & Co.'s department store, awoke early during the summer months – and, with business so poor, he usually woke early – he would think about the cat.

He had many things he could have thought about: the unpaid mortgage instalments on the house, his shrinking salary, Gerda's bronchial catarrh – 'the doctors out here don't know anything' – wretched Herr Mamlock on his staff; but, no, Einenkel thought about the cat.

In the twin bed next to his, Lotte was calmly and deeply asleep; in the room next door, which opened off theirs, Gerda and Ruth were still silently asleep, the maroon rayon curtains were already aglow in the light . . . So it would be another fine day without rain, Einenkel would have to water the vegetables at least, the water bill this summer was bound to be horrendous – but what the heck, it was barely five o'clock, and maybe the old Muthesius baggage was already up, and had let her tom-cat Peter out the back door, and the sandbox . . .

But let's back up a bit: Grünheide, where Einenkel was paying off his own summer house in a row of fifty, Grünheide had heavy, claggy soil: a mix of loam and clay. And little Ruthie had turned two this year, so she had to have a sandbox to play in. Einenkel had ordered two loads of fine, clean, white sand (at a cost of forty marks) from three miles away, and had built a wonderful sandbox, with a ledge around it for baking cakes, and the Einenkels' visitors (though not Ruthie) loved playing there – until the old Muthesius cat started . . .

Well, it wasn't quite five, and the sun was shining beautifully, it would do him good to loaf in bed and doze a little, there were seventy-three unsold blue trench coats in stock, he had to think about that, but now he had just thought about the potatoes . . .

With a sigh, Einenkel lowered his legs over the side of his bed. Lotte murmured: 'Are you getting up already, Franz?' and went straight back to sleep. In blue striped pyjamas, bare feet in red slippers, Einenkel slipped down into the cellar.

What in God's name had the woman done with the potatoes? They were supposed to be in the second crate on the right, the first was for Ruthie's carrots, carrots are supposed to be terribly good for children, and luckily Ruthie ate hers with a passion – no, no potatoes. He had lectured Lotte endlessly on the importance of organization, in his menswear department he could find any suit, any coat blindfolded, but she didn't get it! They had been married for twelve years and she didn't get it, the potatoes were in a big cardboard box that had no business in the cellar, potatoes belonged in the attic, the cellar was much too damp – he would have to kick up another fuss, and he was so exhausted from the difficulties at work!

He gathered up six or eight good-sized potatoes and climbed, quietly groaning to himself, back up to the kitchen. He lined up the potatoes on the kitchen window sill, the window was opened, the garden lay squarely in Herr Einenkel's field of vision. He stands there, waiting for the cat, that blasted Muthesius woman's blasted tom, whom he suspects of doing his business in little Ruthie's pristine sandbox – well, the garden is before him. He loves his garden, all spread out before him with its bushes and trees, and soft green grass – 'I gave it nitrogen, it came up beautifully, the best lawn in the settlement' – and its flowers and vegetable patch.

But he has no eyes for it, the morning wind is just enough to shake the branches, they dance a little, all he sees is the yellow square of the sandbox, the potatoes are ranked in front of him, he will fling them at the creature: whatever his old lady says, there's no other way. Small, thick-waisted, full of worries, he stands there, life should be perfect, he really does what he can, he is peaceable, methodical, but everything seems to go wrong. He buys a house on the instalment plan, and promptly gets two pay cuts; he is a stickler for order, and Lotte thinks he's a silly pedant; they had welcomed Gerda into the family, and now nine years later Ruthie pops up and they practically had to start over – why does life have to be so difficult!

He has asked the widow Muthesius politely, he has written to her, he has gone to the police about her, or rather her old tom-cat, Peter, nothing did any good; and now he's standing and shivering behind a battery of eight missiles, perhaps he should buy a small revolver . . .

Well, the sparrows are twittering, the starlings are all over the cherry tree, he would like to scare them off, but if he did that, maybe the cat would take fright. At six the maid Rosa starts to stir in her room, she mustn't find him here like this, and he's just going up when something dappled hurries through the garden: Peter. He charges out of the back door with angry cries, he despatches his potatoes, two gardens away old Muthesius can be heard telling her schoolteacher daughter: 'And he claims to be a civilized human being!' Herr Einenkel withdraws, he can't even remonstrate; if he thinks about it properly it wasn't an insult, it was a failure pure and simple – this is going to be one of those days.

An hour later, and Ruthie anyway is having a whale of a time. Her parents are seated at two sides of the breakfast table, at the third is Gerda, and Pappi is trying to learn from Gerda what her French homework was. But on the fourth side of the table, on the settle, stands Ruthie, her mug of milk in front of her and a roll in her hand. 'Now eat up, Ruthie,' says Einenkel.

'Pappi – you,' says the little creature, and holds the roll in his direction.

'No, Ruthie, you must eat it.'

'Pappi – you!'

Einenkel gives in and takes a bite. The sun is streaming through the windows, the lace curtains are still white from their recent spring-cleaning. Ruthie is a little bundle of joy; it seems that Gerda has prepared herself thoroughly for school. Light skitters in the golden tea, and pings little reflections on the ceiling. Everything's right, we did the right thing when we left the Bleibtreustraße flat, even if the house is a drain on our finances . . . But in another two years we'll be over the worst, and then maybe we can think of buying a small car on the never-never, admittedly we'll first have to build a garage for it, with a proper laundry room, but there's always something else to take care of first.

'Will you leave me a little money, Franz?' asks Frau Einenkel sweetly.

He makes a movement. And: 'Off to school, Gerda, it's time!' And calls out: 'Rosa, Rosa, will you take the little one to her sandbox!'

'But Ruthie hasn't eaten her breakfast yet!'

'She needs to learn to do things at the proper time, then. Goddamnit, she can't spend two hours over breakfast every day! Why are you out of money again? It's the twenty-second for Christ's sake!'

Talk, argy-bargy, back and forth. Finally he gives her twenty marks. 'But mind that lasts you!' Of course it won't, this is how it's been for twelve years. She simply will not get it. Lotte doesn't get it. Two Sundays with five visitors are enough to knock her budget for six. No forward planning. 'Imagine if I ran my summer ulsters the way you do your housekeeping . . .'

She lets him talk, she says 'Yes.' Of course she's not listening, he knows her face well enough to tell she's thinking about some frippery like a tablecloth, when she already has three or four.

Suddenly something occurs to him. Rather magnificently, he says: 'Perhaps the grey lined summer coats will be in. I tell you, Lotte, Berlin hasn't seen the like! That'll be a coup! At twenty-three fifty they'll walk out of the shop!'

He beams, he is ecstatic, he describes the material and the cut. Suddenly his mien darkens. 'So long as Herr Krebs doesn't make trouble! He's rumoured to want to slap twenty-five per cent warehousing on each item. Then the coats would be priced at over twenty-five. And it's so important nowadays to have them under, where no one's got any money!'

Finally, getting up: 'Well, I'd better catch my train. Give Ruthie a kiss from her Papa. And don't spend those twenty marks right away! Bye!'

As is his custom, he falls into a gentle jog-trot as soon as the door is closed behind him. From No. 17, Herr Wrede falls in with him. 'Morning!'

'Good morning to you! King of a day, isn't it?'

'Yes, splendid!'

'But we'll have to sprinkle again today, is your water bill as high as ours?'

'No, my wife is a little miracle-worker. She always uses the bathwater to soak the clothes in.'

Herr Einenkel is a little put out. 'My wife is very clever as well. She'll make you lunch from leftovers: absolutely delicious!'

'There's never anything left over in our household!'

Neither knows how much the other makes, though each believes it's less than himself.

'I'm thinking of acquiring an automobile. Nothing swanky, just a nice little runabout.'

'Oh, you're not! What are you going to do for a garage? You've just got a little handkerchief garden anyway!'

Then a sudden cry from Herr Wrede: 'Oh, Herr Einenkel, I knew there was something I had to tell you! The Dingeldeys are having to leave, they've missed three payments.'

'You don't say! But I always said it was bound to happen!'

'They over-extended themselves: vacuum cleaner, carpets, furniture, and they left themselves no money for the house, naïve isn't the word for it!'

The Dingeldeys keep them busy halfway to the city. Other gentlemen have joined them in the compartment, gentlemen who did not reside in 'Waldheim' as they did, but these gentlemen join in the conversation anyway, that Dingeldey must be a strange fellow, totally unreliable, on a perfectly ordinary workday he just goes out for a walk, it's not a holiday and he stays at home, 'don't feel like it today,' I mean, I ask you!

'That's what our republic is lacking these days: a sense of duty!'

'That's absolutely right, Herr Einenkel, if everyone chipped in . . .'

'Why, then we wouldn't have any unemployment!'

'You know, we had a broken window, you couldn't see it from the front, we could have left it, no probs. But I tell my wife anyway: have someone come and fix it, I'll manage, I want everyone to have work . . .'

'Would one of you gentlemen have a light?'

Deathly silence.

Then Herr Einenkel sacrifices his cigar: 'Please, Fräulein!'

In this second-class compartment (you need to have a season ticket to travel second, everyone of any standing in the settlement travels second-class) – in this second-class compartment a girl travelled unnoticed among five men, the daily commuters ignored her in their conversation: the Dingeldeys, work creation schemes . . .

Now she's sitting there, smoking. Very nicely dressed, looks like a million dollars – now, if one were in constant company of something like that, those feet, a flash of leg like that can drive a man insane . . .

'Have you been to the theatre at all lately?'

'You were going on holiday too, weren't you? There's nothing like the sea, the proper sea. To me it's become a sort of annual necessity . . .'

'In Friedrichstraße I saw an original oil painting, it must have been twenty square feet, it was first-rate, and not even all that pricey!'

The girl sits there, smoking. She looks out of the window at the countryside flashing past, sun, shade, fields, green trees . . .

The gentlemen talk slowly and pompously, they avoid the word 'beauty', they're not even thinking about it, but they have a different range of conversational topics than before. The girl smokes, once upon a time, I was young and hopeful . . . I remember reading a book . . . it was quite inspiring . . . 'I'll be damned if I don't go to the cinema later this week! A man shouldn't let himself grow rusty.'

At half past eight on the dot, Herr Einenkel strides into the menswear department of Haarklein & Co. He's not the type to go sniffing round the whole department to check whether his sales staff of five and the three trainees are all present. He goes over to his desk and gets out the order books and does some sums, and in between times he looks around. Of course, Heller takes care to walk past his desk, do a little bow and bid him a good morning. That's really not called for, Heller is and remains a poor salesman, even though Einenkel isn't averse to the odd bit of buttering-up. The trainees are giving the whole department a little brush-up, everything's in order, just Mamlock—

'Now, Herr Mamlock,' says Herr Einenkel perfectly pleasantly at eight fifty-five, 'I'm getting a little fed up with your lack of punctuality. If you can't manage to keep time . . .'

Mamlock simply looks at Herr Einenkel. Who, with a little more feeling, continues: 'It's irresponsible of you! You must have some decency in your bones! Eight fifty-five is not the same as eight-thirty! I don't know what goes on in that head of yours!'

Mamlock doesn't appear to be thinking at all, he is simply

looking. With bitterness, Einenkel thinks of the instalment payments on his house, which have to be punctual to the minute. 'You are sloppy!' he shouts. 'In a word, I will suggest your dismissal to Herr Liepmann! I cannot and will not work with people like you!'

Mamlock hasn't said a word. Mamlock has gone down into the stock room. If he's banking on being the best salesman on my staff—! Herr Einenkel tosses the books this way and that impetuously. How can he be expected to do his sums! In these times, when everything's so sticky, Mamlock's drawing two hundred and ten marks, but has he ever stopped to think how many sales he needs to make to justify that sort of salary! Who buys . . . Turnover is way down!

And suddenly Herr Einenkel is smiling, he has it on good authority that his department is outperforming all the others at Haarklein. Now bring on the grey ulsters! That's his coup, the bit of luck he's missed of late, he's going to be selling them hand over fist! Oh dear, oh dear, so long as the manufacturer's stock matches the original design!

He's standing behind his desk, smiling, dreaming of sales reports that will floor Herr Krebs. Herr Haarklein, Haarklein the great, will come and tell him in person: 'You've really got your section in order, Einenkel, your section is doing first-class work!'

And while he's daydreaming like this, the usual morning expectation comes over him, a light, not disagreeable tingling in his spine. Nine-thirteen; at this time yesterday, the first customer was already making a purchase. And then the quiet fear: what if no one comes before ten, eleven, twelve?

'It can't be made up,' he mutters to himself, even as the first customer shows up. Hesse's onto him. Good. Hesse won't let anyone down, Hesse's the man. And the next customer. And the next. The place is filling up, all his sellers are engaged, are selling, no flops yet, no customer's walked out, so far, no: 'I'll go home and think about it.'

Herr Einenkel is everywhere, he takes on the hard cases himself, intervenes with a mild reproach: 'But Herr Heller, you should show the gentleman our tracksuits! We have all the latest models!'

And: 'That coat suits you so well! Really dazzling! Wouldn't you say, Herr Mamlock?'

And he's off to the till, six hundred and ten taken in already, that's quite outstanding for half past eleven. Oh, happiness! People come, you sell them something, a few make difficulties. Why does that portly gentleman insist on a jacket with angled pockets? 'But of course we'll adjust it for you, sir. I completely understand' (absurd) – and he's with Mamlock again, saying almost casually: 'Well, no need to worry just yet, Mamlock, but a little more punctuality wouldn't hurt, eh?'

'Herr Einenkel to see Herr Krebs, please!'

Oh my God, the coats are in, the grey coats. Krebs will get an earful from me if he prices them at a penny over twenty-five marks, Einenkel will make such a fuss, he's prepared to take it all the way up to Haarklein . . .

But it turned out there was nothing to fuss about. You see, Frau Krebs still isn't feeling any better, how unfortunate, Herr Einenkel is terribly sorry, perhaps they would both like to come out and visit him sometime, his own wife would be only too glad to see them, they have a place in the country, and the air is so healthy . . .

'Of course I see, my dear Herr Krebs, I understand, of course I do, but a ready reckoner like you who understands his business absolutely . . . Tied by directives from above? But Herr Krebs, that can't be! Not a man like you! You can do what you please . . .'

Herr Einenkel softens him up for fully an hour, then he goes. The coats will arrive in the menswear section tomorrow, splendid coats, exactly the cut of the prototype, and – they're going on sale at twenty-four ninety! They will take out advertisements, he can imagine everyone, all his customers, their rooms, the whole city – they see the ads, they come and they buy. If he could sing – if he could sing at work – then he would sing now. His wife Lotte does when sometimes, after a spring rain, the sweet peas open, row upon row of them, all pale green; each time something does its stuff, she bursts into song. Einenkel doesn't have a word for it, nor does he waste much time trying to think of one; the word is happiness. Three hundred grey ulsters at twenty-four ninety: that's happiness. Woe is the instalments on the house and the blasted cat, but this here is happiness!

But of course it's not possible to be gone for an hour, and everything in the menswear section stay the way it's meant to be. Between the clothes-stands Herr Einenkel runs into a pale, spotty youth – 'I've been standing around for an hour! Do you employ any sales assistants at all! No, thanks, I've had enough. I imagine you just do as you please here . . .'

The youth has a tantrum, Herr Einenkel handles him in person, but it remains a blank: spotty face refuses to calm down. Afterwards, once he's left, having bought nothing, Herr Einenkel has a wobbly himself, it's the quiet time of lunch, no customers are in sight, he can afford to have a little shout. Mamlock, Hesse, Heller, Ziebarth, Zeddies and the trainees, every man jack of them, all get an earful, and how! Herr Einenkel runs up and down, dripping with sweat, he's red-faced, roaring, not even the shelving has been properly dusted, and then he goes for his lunch.

The section-leaders have got their own table in the canteen, it came about sort of by accident. Sure, there are some real sh-1-ts among them, but of course it would undermine their authority if they were to sit with the sales personnel.

Thanks be to God that in spite of his most enjoyable rant, which if the day and the heavens had seen fit would have gone on for ever and ever, he still collars the good seat with the view of the salesgirls' table. And there she is again, the charming, delicate little wagtail of a thing from ladies' hats. Shyly Herr Einenkel looks at her three or four times. He has to have those looks; the success or failure of a day depends sheerly on whether they come off, or whether he's got his back to her. It is not related whether Fräulein Bild knows of Herr Einenkel's existence or not; certainly she doesn't know what part she has to play in his dreams.

Oh, if he'd only run into that little brunette, say, fifteen years ago! Lotte's not so bad, but Lotte's the day-to-day. If he could unobtrusively get hold of her address, he would send her a fabulous bouquet tomorrow, roses or lilacs, anonymously, of course, just to perk her up.

And he hears himself saying: 'Yes, I had a bit of a rant – you probably heard it. You need to take those salespeople down every so often, they get so full of themselves! Tell me, gents, didn't we ever have to work when we were young?'

And now we get all those stories of olden days, before salespeople were given Sundays off: those Sundays when you were forever having to pull the blinds up and down, adjust the awnings, switch the window display lighting off and on.

'I had a boss in Rogasen . . .'

And: 'Do you remember Lehmann? We all used to call him "loco Lehmann", for a while he was on the road for Hübsch & Niedlich?'

It's four-fifteen before Herr Einenkel is back in his section. He's missed nothing, though, the sheen of the day is gone, it's a long, dreary, disappointing afternoon with four failures and a tiny take. Herr Einenkel stands behind his desk. First he took a hand and drove on, now he stands there looking pale and sad, he'll be left with seventy-three trench coats on his books, and then what? He's a bad manager, it's mean of him to have a go at the staff, he's no better than anyone . . .

He sighs deeply and passes slowly up and down between the rows of clothes, he won't be home till quarter to nine, Ruthie will be asleep, Gerda probably as well. Lotte says the birds are singing so beautifully in the garden at the moment, by the time he comes it's dark and they're all quiet.

At one stand he sees Krieblich the trainee, a timid, apprehensive

lad. ('That boy will never make a salesman, he's got no balls!')
Now he's pale as a sheet, holding onto a couple of coats, reeling.

'For goodness' sake, Krieblich, what's the matter?'

The boy is incapable of an answer, or else he's frightened
again. He would even have fallen over, perhaps taking the
clothes-stand with him, if Einenkel hadn't supported him. 'Easy,
boy, easy, you must be ill . . . Mamlock, will you take over the section, I'm taking Krieblich to the infirmary . . .'

Oh, what a good father has become of stern, irascible Herr
Einenkel! 'Come along, lad, just hold onto me. Two more steps.
Come on, it's getting better, and you'll be able to have a nice
lie-down when we get there.'

The examination isn't complicated: the cause is undernourish-
ment. To put it simply, the boy is faint with hunger. They don't
get anything to eat, they're work-experience, and the lad earns
basically nothing.

An agitated Herr Einenkel runs back and forth. 'Not to have
enough to eat! That's not on, something is going to have to be
done about that. Just hang in there, Krieblich, lad . . .'

Herr Einenkel takes the trainee home, he pays the taxi himself
and tips the driver, it's a little more than he can afford, but that's
the way he is . . . 'And of course there'll be help. We have a sort
of fund at Haarklein & Co. I'll see to it first thing tomorrow. Not
to have enough to eat is awful . . . !'

Now it's not worth going back to the store, so Herr Einenkel
gets home a couple of trains earlier than usual. Ruthie is standing
in the tub, screeching and splashing to her heart's content. She
throws the sponge at Papa. What joy to be there for that, and
while she's eating her bread and milk; then kisses at bedtime, big
wavey-wavey, little wavey-wavey, it's as good as Sunday.

And while Lotte, with Rosa's help, is getting supper ready, he
takes Gerda round the garden, and has a nice, serious talk with
her. It's still, a little breeze stirs the treetops. Goodness, the
girl has things on her mind. There are all these stars in the

sky; does Papa believe that anyone lives on them? Yes? Is it possible? And did God make people there as well, and did He send His son Jesus to all of them? Really? Every one of them?!

Einenkel is moved and bewildered, he takes the little grubby hand in his. 'Well, to tell you the truth, I don't know either, Gerda. It would be awful, wouldn't it? Let's just hope the people there are better . . .'

He sits at her bedside for a moment, and she gives him a spontaneous kiss, it occurs to him she hasn't done that for months. All those things you miss through work and the store and his worries about paying down the house . . . Well, of course, that's just the way it is, but it's still funny . . . the thing with the stars, he's never really thought about them like that. The problems a girl like that has! Perhaps he should have told her about his coats going for twenty-four ninety, that might have pleased her, and it might have lightened her heart too.

But then it's all over again, and as soon as he's sitting down to supper he feels terribly tired. 'I'm going to go to bed now,' he says to Lotte, and he wonders whether to tell her of his voluntary decision to give her another twenty marks to see her through the rest of the month. But he'd rather put it off till tomorrow morning. Let's see how I feel then!

And as he drops off to sleep, everything gets muddled up in his head: the girl on the train with the shapely knees and his new consignment of ulsters to look forward to. Fräulein Bild with her silken doe's legs and famished Krieblich. He'll have to get up early tomorrow on account of the cat, but he's definitely going to buy himself a pistol now, straight after the first of the month, the stars and Gerda, and hopefully Mamlock will be punctual tomorrow, so he won't have to get angry with him straight away.

And then, as he falls asleep, he says a kind of night prayer, not really in words, but a vague yearning to the effect of: dear God, please let the take be good tomorrow! Dear God!

Enough! Asleep! No more!

The Lucky Beggar
(1932)

His rise had been slow and difficult, year by year, trainee, third-class salesman, second-class salesman, first-class salesman. He was thirty-eight when he became head of section, at the end of twenty-two years of smiles, flexibility, stifled abuse, bowing and scraping and being kicked in the teeth. His fall was as fast as you like: notice at the earliest possible date. 'It's the times, Herr Möcke . . . You understand . . . We need to tighten our belts, and your expensive supervisor's salary, Herr Möcke . . .'

He wouldn't have been able to tell you how he made it home. But there was the little house in the sun, a proper little rental home in the garden suburb, one thousand down payment to the co-op and sixty-five marks per month. The roses in the front garden stood there like little dolls, he had bought them himself, planted them, tended them, the windows flashed like mirrors, the curtains moved just a little. Herr Möcke woke up when he saw it, then he heaved a sigh and went in to tell Linni the news.

They were luckier than tens of thousands of others, the Möckes. They had no children, and the furnishings had been paid off a year ago, more. Also, Möcke would be quickly re-employed, perhaps as a first-class salesman, certainly second-, he was known in the trade and he was no slouch. Then came the day he was let go, the last pay day, and Kunze the head of personnel said: 'Now, Möcke, goodbye but not farewell. I hope we'll see each other very soon.'

Possibly that was just an expression meant to console, but equally possible that it meant something. Three days later, when Möcke went to collect his unemployment along with another gentleman from the settlement, he was convinced there was something behind it. His colleague Wrede had always been a nasty piece of work.

'You know, Herr Möcke,' said the other gentleman, 'do you think I'm still paying my rent? Am I hell! I'm just paying down my co-op money. A thousand marks means I have a long time here yet.'

'My situation is different,' said Möcke carefully. 'I have fallen victim to a regrettable intrigue. But the matter is about to be resolved. Our head of personnel has given me assurances . . .'

'Oh, so you think you'll find work again, do you?' said the other. 'Everyone thinks that. You're pushing forty, you'll never get another job as long as you live. It's just obvious. Think about it, you cost almost twice as much to employ as a nineteen-year-old.'

'Certain promises have been made me . . .' Herr Möcke persisted.

Then he's in with the grey tide of the unemployed, washing past the counters, he's in there for weeks and months. It's very hard to keep yourself apart from such a tide. Herr Möcke feels nothing less than obliged to, he has been made certain promises. Herr Kunze will be writing to him any day now. In the meantime, they are tightening their belts. Ninety-six marks of unemployment benefit, sixty-five marks in rent, but he has to keep it up, he mustn't do anything to harm his reputation, so that, when Herr Kunze comes to make his checks . . .

Linni has been hearing about Herr Kunze for four months now, Linni doesn't have to join the grey tide of the unemployed twice a week at the office where they teach her husband to hope, Linni just says: 'Pah, your Kunze's never going to write to you . . .'

Möcke gives Linni a look and he leaves the room, he goes downstairs into the garden, and he stands there and looks around: a damp, autumnal garden is a fairly dismal kind of place, a grey sky, a rough wind, dismal. Linni's right, thinks Möcke. Kunze really could have written. And, ten minutes later: I know, I'll write to Kunze!

A big decision, a heroic decision but, all in all, Columbus's egg. That evening Herr Möcke sits down and writes to Herr Kunze, to ask him for an appointment. As he is leaving the house the next morning with the fateful letter, the doorbell happens to ring, Möcke opens without looking to see who's there – and he sees a beggar.

It's like this: earlier, when Möcke still had his job, he would often open the door to beggars, and when the man went through his spiel about being out of work and out of luck, Herr Möcke would reply curtly: 'Sorry, mate, I'm out of work myself.' Then, when he actually did lose his job, he would lie awake at night, thinking: I should never have said that. It's my own fault. It's not just that nasty piece of work Wrede, I brought it on myself with my foolish talk. Since that time, the Möckes have stopped opening the door to beggars. They look through the peephole to see who's rung the bell.

This time, though, with his thoughts on his letter, Herr Möcke didn't check. The beggar is standing in front of him, and the beggar says: 'Good morning, doctor, sir, just a small consideration.'

Herr Möcke looks at the beggar, the beggar is a big, strongly built man with strong bones, he has a pale, smooth face with a little blond moustache, but above all he has quick, intense eyes. Herr Möcke stands there with his important letter in his hands, he's sent so many beggars packing in his time . . .

'Just a few pennies, doctor,' says the man. 'I'll bring you luck. I've already brought luck to lots of fellows.' Herr Möcke reaches into his pocket. 'I'll spit on your door three times, to make the spit run.'

'There's no need to do that,' says Herr Möcke, but he gives the man ten pfennigs anyway.

The man spits on the door three times, and it runs. 'You see, doctor, you're in luck. But your wife's not to wipe it off. I'll come back and ask how it's going,' says the man, and heads off to the next bell. On his way to the post office, Möcke shakes his head vigorously about so much prejudice in the population. But at least it can't hurt. And he drops his letter in the bag.

Once such a letter has been mailed, the sender may sometimes feel lighter, certain veils have been lifted. What actually had Kunze said to him? Nothing, consolation, soft soap – on the way to the labour exchange, everything looks different again. Well, Möcke waits, but he's not really waiting, in between times he remembers the spitting beggar and he shakes his head again.

Well, at the end of five days of waiting, Möcke gets his letter: Kunze would be pleased to see his old friend Möcke in such and such a café at such and such a time. And now behold Möcke in his garden! Speaking to Linni! Opening the door to the beggar on the day of the rendezvous! Yes, it's exactly on that day that the beggar pays his return visit.

'Well, doctor,' he says. 'How are we doing now? Did it help or did it help?'

Herr Möcke smiles a thin smile, it's all nonsense of course, it's the most primitive superstition, but he replies with a smile that he's about to find out this afternoon if it worked or not.

'So what about it?' asks the man with the strong bones. 'Would you like me to spit again?'

Möcke looks at the man, he mustn't allow himself to be overly compromised. 'If you reckon it'll do any good. I wouldn't mind.'

'That'll be a mark, then, doctor,' he says. 'The last time was a kind of introductory offer. My spit always helps.'

Now Herr Möcke gets angry. 'You want a mark, when I'm on the dole! You're crazy! I won't even entertain it. Get away from my door.'

Möcke goes back into his garden, he puts straw on his roses on account of the frost, to give himself something to do. He keeps sighing. Perhaps it was over-hasty of him, the man would probably have done it for fifty pfennigs . . .

Now then, a trip into the city, a café, these things don't come cheap, and it turns out Kunze just wanted a chinwag with his old mucker and a chance to pour out his heart, things at work are so bad these days! But of course he's thinking of Möcke, tomorrow morning he'll take soundings, first-class salesman, why on earth not, he'll write as soon as there's an opening . . .

Möcke waits. There are no immediate openings, the thing is taking its time. Sometimes, when he goes for a walk, he runs into the big, raw-boned beggar. Herr Möcke walks past him, looking straight ahead. Perhaps the fellow spoiled everything with his absurd demand of one mark, who knows in this world.

The labour exchange. Picking up his dole money. The ever-rising tide. Oh, how stoutly his Pharisaic heart resists: I am not like these others, I have prospects, Kunze will write. Kunze doesn't write. And finally Herr Möcke goes to a meeting of the unemployed, one might as well lend an ear. And it does him good to hear what demands they are putting forward. Herr Möcke smiles, he knows better, these things aren't about to happen any time soon, but it does him good in his heart just to hear them being voiced.

Next to Herr Möcke sits the big, raw-boned beggar, and in his benign mood Herr Möcke says to him: 'Fancy running into you here, when you're meant to be so lucky.'

'Of course I'm here,' says the beggar, 'that's the whole point. If I was lucky for myself, I would hardly be lucky for others now, would I?'

Herr Möcke sits there, stunned, the man's right really. And then after a while he asks him: 'You haven't been by for a long time, what about it?'

The man replies curtly: 'This isn't a spitting job any more, you've messed that up for yourself.'

Möcke doesn't speak, Möcke broods, sometimes he listens to what the speaker on the platform is saying, but the demands don't really rejoice him any more, he has a feeling as though his last chance has just, so to speak, gone begging. The beggar is merely silent.

Now, afterwards, after the meeting, they do get into conversation again. Was there nothing he could do any more? The doctor is waiting for a letter, but he's been waiting for a long time. No, the beggar can't help, Möcke's lost his chance, but he does know of a woman: she'll get you your letter! A little back and forth, whispers, up the road, down the road, she can do it, she's fabulous, she's done this for one fellow and that for another. Would he have a picture of his man Kunze, by any chance? No, well, it can be done without. She can do everything!

'Expense?'

The beggar looks at him. 'You're running away again, doctor, aren't you? Do you think a woman with gifts like that'd come cheap?'

No, no, Herr Möcke's not running anywhere, he will listen to the beggar's conditions perfectly calmly. He can always say no.

Of course he can. Well, because it's the doctor, and because the doctor's out of work, something in the vicinity of fifty marks, and if that isn't cheap . . .

Now Möcke has stalked off again, he didn't even say no. And he's waiting again, same as before, and going to the labour exchange, and when spring comes round he leaves the 'unemployed' desk and goes over to 'crisis' because if they didn't come through with a few marks, then he'd be forced to follow his friend's example and stop paying rent.

And after Möcke has waited and pondered and resisted for long enough, he goes into the city again. He stands by the employees' entrance to his old business, and waits for Herr Kunze to come out. Oh, what a nice surprise, to see old Möcke again! He's been thinking about him such a lot, once or twice things were almost at the point, but each time there was a problem, but maybe in the next couple of weeks . . .

Möcke goes home, his head is reeling, he knows that things were almost at the point, but there was a problem. He knows what it was, too: the first time it was one mark, the second it was fifty.

Möcke takes fifty marks of his last, his very last iron reserve, and walks the streets, looking for his beggar. He spends four days looking for him. Things need doing in the garden, Linni's cross with him, but Möcke's only got one thing in his head, and it even pursues him into his dreams: how to get fifty marks to the beggar.

Because then, then everything will come out! He sees the store again, the clean, well-lighted place, the waxed floors, the merchandise on the shelves, the customers streaming in, he bows, he makes a sale – my, isn't life sweet!

On the fifth day, Möcke runs into his beggar. He is confused, nervous, he can't even speak properly. 'Here,' he says. 'For that woman,' he says. 'You know what I need,' he says. 'Work . . . !'

Day after day Herr Möcke stands behind the dining room curtains. From there he can keep an eye on the steps, it could be an express letter, or a telegram. From morning till night he stands there waiting, at night he jumps up: 'Wasn't that someone at the door just now, Linni?'

But Linni doesn't say anything, she's crying, crying her eyes out. While Möcke waits and waits and waits . . .

Just Like Thirty Years Ago
(1932)

Back when Gotthold fell in love with her, Tini was a dark blonde, slender slip of a girl. She was fresh out of Thuringia, and was serving customers at her relatives' restaurant, somewhere in the north of Berlin. She had coiled braids over her ears, she liked to laugh, and for some reason she was nice to Gotthold.

Gotthold was the son of an ambitious schoolmaster, but in spite of considerable physical and intellectual prompting, he never got past fifth grade. So he had been shunted off into the banking business. In disfavour with his father, he sat at the current accounts window, and thought bitterly of those who got on in life, who were more gifted and laughed more.

Today, after thirty years of marriage, Tini knows that Gotthold never 'truly' loved her. He only wanted to take her away from the others, and keep her laughter and her cheerfulness for himself. At the time, he was a dazzling match for a poor waitress who didn't even speak proper German, today . . .

Today . . . Well, at fifty and fifty-three respectively they're pretty much through with their lives. Their two children, a boy and a girl, are married off. His ambition to make it to branch manager has remained unfulfilled. In the course of the latest wave of rationalizations, they gave Gotthold early retirement. There they are sitting in a little house in the suburbs, with a bit of garden . . . They have their small, dependable pension guaranteed as long as they live . . . And aside from that, what have they got?

He has become yellow and wrinkled, has Gotthold. With his scraggy little yellow bird's head he spends all day pottering around at home or in the garden. He's forever wiping something, nailing something, polishing something.

'How did the sideboard get that scratch, Tini?' he wheezes. 'It wasn't there yesterday, and it's there today. What did you do?'

He wipes, he gets some furniture polish and heats up the wax. He never reads a book, but he's always on Tini's case about something. 'Where did you leave the little red vase with the white angel that the Hempels gave us for our wedding? I was thinking about it last night. I haven't seen it for ten years.'

'It broke,' says Tini. Or she says nothing at all. She's grown fat, her feet are killing her, but even at the end of thirty years she still tries to be gentle. She keeps trying. She rushes through her household like a wind in a hurry. In fact, she has hardly anything to do; the children have left home, but what she does do she wants to do quickly. 'Quick, Gotthold, hurry! The Wredes have already planted their strawberries. Run to the nursery.'

'Why should I? You run!'

'They'll be laughing all over their faces, if we're last to put our strawberries into the ground. But have it your way.'

He fiddles with his azalea, pinches off a diseased-looking leaf. Examines it to check that it actually was diseased. 'I bet you knocked into my azalea too.' No reply. 'All right, then at least tell me how many strawberry plants we need. You never give me proper information.'

Her daughter's written: she's seen a fur coat . . . only four hundred marks . . . she's wanted one for so long . . . could Mother not help? It would be soooo nice! They get three hundred marks pension, her son-in-law makes seven hundred . . . But of course she will help. Letters like that are sent care of the neighbours. Her husband mustn't see them, he mustn't notice anything at all. If she's a diligent housewife, she can save fifty marks of the housekeeping money without her husband noticing. She also needs to go to the doctor again, her leg is giving her such gyp . . . She's sure she's ruptured a vein. That makes him happy, he doesn't mind shelling out forty or sixty marks for something like that.

'You see,' he says. 'Does it hurt? I always told you . . . not to run around so much. Does it really hurt?'

It makes him happy when she's in pain or upset. Their son didn't write on her birthday. 'You see! I told you so. You always stood up for the worthless so-and-so, and the result is he's got no respect for you now. He's right too, now he's a court official and you can't even speak proper German.'

His little yellow head bobs around on his narrow shoulders. He laughs. 'Do you remember the time I wanted to slap his cheeky face, it was Christmas of 1909, and you got in the way, and I slapped you? See!'

He laughs again, then he potters off into the village. Secretly he goes to a café and he stuffs his face with cake. It's his passion, but it's not good for him: his gall bladder screams. At nights she gets up and makes him compresses. 'Hotter!' he screams. 'Hotter! It's because you don't know how to cook properly.'

'I'm sure you must have had some cake again, Gotthold.'

'How can you claim something like that?'

'Don't shout so, Gotthold, the neighbours . . .'

'That's why I am shouting. I want them all to know about the kind of wife I have. The woman can't even speak proper German.'

Five years, ten years, twenty years, thirty years . . . How many more? Thirty more years? His father lived to be really old. Sometimes she succumbs to despair, then she locks herself away and has a cry. At least she's safe from him there. Then he comes and rattles the door. 'What are you doing, locking yourself away? Since when have you locked the door against me? Are you keeping secrets from me? Who wants money from you? Those leeches!'

'It's nothing, Gotthold. I just felt a bit sick.'

'A bit sick? You see. Didn't I tell you not to eat gherkins at night? They never agree with me.'

Yes, she's in despair . . . but for ten minutes at a time . . . half an hour at the most. She's just remembered the last time they were together, her daughter-in-law was wearing such an ugly jumper, she'll knit her a pretty one, buy some wool, get going on it, eight hours a day for one week, her eyes are hurting . . .

'Are they really hurting you? I told you . . .' But if it's done, it has to be done quickly. She's already looking forward to her daughter-in-law's pleasure. Finished, off to the post office, mailed it. She waits for three days, a week, three weeks, then at last there's a postcard: 'Best wishes from the wonderful Baltic. Helga. Hans. PS. The jumper is really nice.'

But she's on to something else by then. She's remembered something. They've got the little spare room for visitors, though of course they never have any visitors. She's going to put Gotthold's bed in there, and keep her bedroom for herself. For thirty years she hasn't had a single night to herself.

Of course he'll never agree to it. She lies awake for nights, thinking. There is her sister in Lüneburg. She'll have to send Gotthold an urgent invitation. What about some financial advice? After all, he is the banker in the family. She'll have to keep him there for two or three days.

In the meantime she'll get a man in to help her move the furniture. She'll do it in such a way that he won't be able to move it back unaided. He will swear and scold and rant, but he'll never hire anyone to help him, he's too stingy. In fact, it probably won't even occur to him. First she'll leave the door open between the two rooms, then half-open, then closed, and finally locked. Oh my God, she'll be able to sleep alone, like she did thirty years ago. She dreams and fantasizes. Please God, let it come to pass. Then at least she'll have her nights to herself, just like thirty years ago . . .

Fifty Marks and a Merry Christmas
(1932)

We were newlyweds, Itzenplitz and me, and basically we had nothing. If you're young and newly married and very much in love, then it doesn't really matter that much if you've 'basically got nothing'. Of course, we each had our occasional moments of wistfulness, but then the other one would laugh and say: 'It doesn't need to be right away. We've got all the time in the world . . .' And then the little wistful pang was over.

But then I remember a conversation we had in the park once, when Itzenplitz sighed and said: 'If only we didn't have to count our pennies the whole time!'

I wasn't quite sure where this was going. 'Yes, and?' I asked. 'What then?'

'Then I would buy myself something,' said Itzenplitz dreamily.

'And what might you like to buy yourself?'

Itzenplitz hunted around. She really had to think for quite some time before she said: 'Well, for instance a pair of nice warm slippers.'

'Surely not!' I said, astonished at the imagination of my wife Elisabeth (which had become Ibeth, and then somehow Itzenplitz). Because we were conducting this conversation in the middle of summer, the sun was smiting, and as far as I was concerned I couldn't imagine anything much beyond a cool shandy and a cigarette.

Our Christmas wish-list was the product of this summer conversation. 'You know, Mumm,' Itzenplitz said, and she rubbed hard at her long and pointy nose, 'we should start keeping a record of every wish we think of. Because later on, at Christmas time, everything gets a bit frantic, and we might end up giving each other silly presents we didn't really want.'

So I tore off a piece of paper from my subscription pad and we wrote down our first Christmas wishes: 'A pair of warm slippers for Itzenplitz,' and below that, because we meant to be rigorously fair, I added, after much frowning thought: 'And a good book for Mumm!' Mumm is me. 'Fine,' said Itzenplitz, and stared at the list with such holy fervour as though a pair of slippers and a book might straight away emerge from the paper.

Our wish-list grew through summer into late autumn, and the first damp snow and the earliest Christmas decorations, grew and grew . . . 'It doesn't matter that there's such a lot on it,' Itzenplitz comforted me. 'That means we'll have a choice. In fact, all it is is a sort of menu. Just before Christmas, we'll cut out everything impossible, but for now we can still wish.' She thought for a moment and said: 'I can wish for whatever I want, can't I, Mumm?'

'Of course,' I replied, unthinkingly.

'Good,' she said, and started writing, and after a while I saw: 'Blue silk evening dress (floor-length).' She looked at me challengingly.

'Well, really, Itzenplitz,' I said.

'You said I could wish for whatever I wanted.'

'That's true,' I said, and I wrote: 'And a four-valve wireless set' – and then gave her the challenging look back. And then we got into a forceful and ingenious debate as to which was more urgently needed, the evening dress or the wireless – when all the time we both knew perfectly well that there was no chance of either for at least five years.

But all that happened much, much later, for now we're still in the park, it's summer and we've just committed our first wishes to paper. I've already had occasion to refer to Itzenplitz's nose a couple of times – her 'duck's beak' I sometimes called it. Well, she uses it to sniff around, and further to it she has the quickest, dartingest eyes in the world. She's forever lighting on something, and so at this moment too she cried: 'Oh, look! Oh, Mumm, it's our first ten-pfennig piece towards Christmas!' And she nudged it with the tip of her toe.

'For Christmas?' I asked, picking it up. 'I think I'll just go and get myself three cigarettes for it in the kiosk.'

'Give it here! It's going in our Christmas collection tin.'

Lots of novelties here. 'Since when have you got a collection tin?' I asked. 'I've never seen you with it.'

'I'll find one, you—! Just give me a chance to look.' And she scanned the trees, as though there was one hanging there somewhere.

'Why don't we do it this way,' I suggested. 'We'll think about what we want to spend at Christmas, let's say fifty marks . . . There's six more pay days till Christmas, let's say we put aside eight marks each time, no, eight marks fifty. And now I think I'll go and get those cigarettes.'

'Those ten pfennigs are mine! And as for what you just said, I don't think I've ever heard so much nonsense. We're going to go about it completely differently . . .'

'Oh, you don't say! Well, spit it out!'

'When we come back from a trip on Sundays, you know, and we're dog-tired and we want to take the tram, then we'll save the fifty pfennigs, and walk, and the harder it is, the more determined we'll be . . .'

'I bet!' I mocked.

'And when you're dying for a shandy, and I'm dying for a cup of cocoa, and when we both feel like a joint of meat on Sunday instead of sour lentils the whole time – oh, you're such a silly boy! I'm not going to speak to you for three days, and I'm certainly not going to be seen on the street with you . . . !'

And with that she turned on her heel and shot off, and I slowly tramped after her. Later on, when we got into the city streets, she was walking on one side of the road, and I on the other, as though we had nothing to do with each other. And each time a clump of fat Sunday burghers came along, I would tease her by calling out: 'Psst, Fräulein! Hey, Fräulein, I want to tell you something!' The burghers stared and stared at her, and she blushed beet-red and tossed her head crossly this way and that.

But then she did suddenly come running over the road to me, because she had remembered that we had an empty can of condensed milk, with two holes in to pour through, and if I just punched a slit across the top with my chisel, we'd have us a perfect savings tin. Even the make of the condensed milk was 'Glücksklee'* . . .

'Wonderful,' I mocked. 'I wonder what money looks like once it's been marinating for six months in milk dregs!' Then she was gone again, and I was back to 'Psst, Fräulein!' She was ready to blow a gasket.

But then *I* remembered something, and I raced across the road to her and yelled: 'Listen, there's something we both forgot about, which is my fifty marks bonus!' First, she wanted to slap me down again, and had already begun with who was ever going to give an idiot like me a bonus, but then we stopped to think about it seriously, and we got to wondering if there would even be any bonuses this year, with the economy going so badly and all, but maybe so, yes, almost certainly, and we came to the conclusion: 'Let's behave as though there won't be. But wouldn't it be lovely if there was . . . !'

Now I still need to tell you why we turned every penny over and what we were actually living on, and what sort of prospects we actually had of me getting a bonus. It's not so easy to say what sort of job I had, and today I shake my head when I think of it, and it's far from clear to me (not so very much later) how I managed to combine all my multifarious activities. Anyway, in the mornings from seven o'clock onwards, I was on the staff of the

* Four-leafed clover.

local rag, and was responsible for half the local news, while sitting opposite me was the editor Pressbold, who filled the rest of the paper with the help of pictures, matrixes, letters to the editor, the wireless programme and a distinctly ropy typewriter. For that I was paid eighty marks a month, and that was all the regular, dependable income we had. Once that was done, though, I would set off on subscription and advertising drives (walks, actually), for which I was paid a bonus of one Reichsmark twenty-five per subscriber, and ten per cent of any advertisement. In addition, I had the collecting of a voluntary supplemental insurance (three per cent of the contributions) and the gathering of membership fees for a gymnastic association (five pfennigs per man and month). And, last and least, I was also secretary of the economic and traffic association, but for that I just had the honour and expenses and the somewhat nebulous prospect of the gentlemen helping me out, if there was ever anything they could do for me.

So I wasn't short of work, and the dismal part was that all my activities put together barely made me enough money to keep Itzenplitz and me alive – 'acquisitions' was a term not known to us. Sometimes I would get home drained and wretched, from running around half the day, ringing on fifty doorbells and earning less than half a mark. Today I am firmly convinced (even if she still won't agree) that the only reason Itzenplitz was so full of schemes and wheezes was to excite my imagination and get me thinking about other things.

It must have been in autumn, damp fogs and rotten moods in my case, and our Christmas box still hadn't taken on any firm shape, that I got home one day and found Itzenplitz with a kitchen knife in one hand and a briquette sawn through lengthwise in the other.

'What on earth are you doing now?' I asked in astonishment, because she was intent on hollowing out the half-briquette with the tip of her knife. The other half lay in front of her on the table.

'Be quiet, Mumm!' she whispered secretively. 'There are bad

people everywhere.' And she pointed with her knife at the papered-over door behind which lived our neighbour, whom we had dubbed Klaus Störtebeker, after the celebrated corsair.

'All right, what is it?' And then I heard, in her best conspiratorial voice, how she had cut the briquette in half, and wanted to hollow it out, and carve a slit in it, and glue the whole thing back together again, and conceal it among the other briquettes. Her eyes sparkled with cunning and secrecy, and her long nose was twitching away more than ever . . . 'And you're completely bonkers!' I said. 'And anyway, as for Christmas, Heber said there's absolutely no chance of a bonus being paid, the boss is soooo because the paper is going badly . . .'

'All right,' she said, 'just tell me everything in order, so I know who gets the briquette thrown at them on Christmas Eve.'

I've already said how our editor was a Herr Pressbold. He was a fine gentleman, grumpy, grouchy and getting fatter all the time, who had nothing to say however much he said. All the say was from Herr Heber, who ran accounts and had the ear of the great chief. We little Indians only got to see the great chief twice a year or so, because he liked to roll around the countryside in his Mercedes, where he had a sawmill here and a little provincial paper there, and here a tenement house and there a little country estate.

But his right-hand man in the office, as already stated, was Herr Heber, a lanky, bony, dusty figures man, whom I'd mentioned the matter of Christmas bonus and fifty marks to without getting an answer, in fact he'd asked me if I'd suffered a touch of early frost this year, and did I have the faintest notion of what it meant to be working in a loss-making enterprise, and it would be no thanks to me if the whole shebang wasn't wound up in the New Year.

The worst thing was that Pressbold, on whose support I'd been counting, was tooting out of the same horn, and even complaining about my absurd notions, I should be glad not to be turfed out, and would be advised not to irk the great chief. And while they were both having a go at me, I thought the whole loss-making business and the worries of the great chieftain didn't matter a damn to me, because I could see my wish-list being consigned to the four winds, and the warm slippers and the evening dress and the good book and the Christmas duck were all gone to the kibosh.

Yes, the Christmas duck gives me the opportunity to introduce a new character (mentioned just in passing once already) in my account: the neighbour behind the papered-over door, our so-called Klaus Störtebeker. We never found out Störtebeker's real name, but he lived in the north-facing attic, while we had the south-facing one. He was really dark-looking, with bristly black hair, wild black sparkling eyes and a scruffy black beard. In the town, and especially with the police, he was known and feared as a drinker and a brawler. On the side, he worked as a stoker in the local power station. We lived almost on top of each other; when he turned over in bed, we knew about it, and I suppose he will have heard the odd noise from us as well.

The thing with the duck for instance he definitely heard. That was a Christmas debate between us. In her family and in mine the traditional Christmas fare (or fowl) had been the goose, but we agreed that a twelve-pound goose ('if it's any less, it's just skin and bone') was a bit much for the two of us. So a duck was what we wanted, the octavo version instead of the full folio, only where to buy it, and how much . . . ?

At that moment there was a raucous yell from Störtebeker's room, and a moment later a fist battered against the door. As wild in appearance as any jungle creature, but straight out of bed and roaring drunk, we saw Störtebeker in our doorway, dressed only in shirt and trousers, which he held up with his free hand. 'I'll get yerz yer Christmas bird,' Störtebeker gruffed, and he leered at us.

We were first alarmed, and then embarrassed. Itzenplitz rubbed her nose and muttered something about 'very kind' and 'terribly generous' and I attempted to get out of it by saying we weren't completely sure whether we were in the market for a goose, or a turkey or . . .

'Fools!' yelled Störtebeker, and slammed the door so hard the plaster rained down from the ceiling.

But he can't have been too offended by our foolishness because, while not repeating his offer of a duck directly, when he ran into Itzenplitz outside, trying to nail a Christmas tree support from a couple of planks, he took them away from her, and said: 'I'll take care of it. I've got a planed piece of wood by the stove. Christmas present to yerz. Make a great base.'

But I'm getting ahead of myself again, we were still talking about the bonus. My first attempt was rebuffed, and as a sort of consolation we undertook a financial check-up, to see what we had actually managed to put aside since our decision to save for Christmas. It wasn't an easy matter, since Itzenplitz had a complicated system of funds: housekeeping money, pocket money, Mumm's spending money, coal money, acquisitions money, rent money and Christmas money. And since in almost all these boxes and chests, according to our financial state, there was deep ebb, the bit of money we did have tended to go like a badger from one to another, and it wasn't easy to see where what little went.

Itzenplitz rubbed her reddening nose many times, disposed here and disposed there, took away (mostly), added on (not much), all the while I stood by the stove, making sarcastic comments. Finally, it was established that in the three months of its existence, our Christmas fund had soared to seven marks eighty-five pfennigs, provided the briquettes lasted us till the first. If they didn't, then two-fifty would have to revert to the coal fund.

We exchanged looks . . . But misfortunes rarely come singly, and so it was that in that moment of penury, Itzenplitz's brain turned first to her mother-in-law, and then to Tutti and Hänschen, her niece and nephew. 'I've always given something to Mama and the little ones for Christmas. I've got to, Mumm!'

'Go ahead, by all means . . . but maybe you could tell me in a word, how?'

Itzenplitz didn't, but she did something inspired instead: she came to pick me up from work at the paper, and beguiled that old stick-in-the-mud of a Heber with conversation. I can still see him, with his long, curmudgeonly horse face, but with a real patch of red on the cheeks, leaning on the barrier in despatch, listening to Itzenplitz on the one cane chair, Itzenplitz in kid gloves and white blouse with red polka dots and pleated skirt and cheap and cheerful summer coat. And she was jabbering away nineteen to the dozen, a yackfest, a gossip. She gave him what he craved, she fed his desiccated old bachelor heart with gossip, she made things up non-stop, a name would fall and she came up with the most outrageous stories. She gossiped about people she'd never met, affianced them, broke them up again, it was a whirl and a gas, she populated the world with children, killed off elderly aunts, why, the cook for the Paradeisers—!

And a sparkle came into Heber's dead fish-eyes, his bony fist came down on the partition. 'I always supposed that was the case! No, who would have thought it possible!' And gently, almost imperceptibly, she quit the terrain of amours for that of money, the expensive new curtains at Spieckermann's, how could they afford something like that, she certainly couldn't, and Lesegangs were having difficulties as well, but thank God things at the paper seemed to be pretty robust, no wonder, given the quality of the management. 'And we're counting on you putting in a word for us with the boss, Herr Heber, regarding the Christmas bonus, you can do it, I know you can . . .'

She sat there, drained, but in her eyes there was a halo of zeal and rapture and beseeching – and I couldn't help it, I crept around behind her, and gave her a quick shoulder-rub to indicate my approval. But that dull old stick of a Heber of course wasn't the least bit moved, he coughed like a sheep and, raising his voice and with a look at me, explained that of course he fully understood what was going on, and a trap needed to be baited, but we wouldn't catch him out like that, and whoever wanted to get an earful was welcome to take his case directly to the boss, not that he would recommend it!

It was a comprehensive humiliation. With wretched stammerings we slunk out of despatch, and I felt dreadfully sorry for Itzenplitz. For at least five minutes she didn't say a word, just sniffled away to herself, that's how crushed she was.

But regardless of the scene just passed and the poor prospects of a bonus and the usual pre-Christmas gloom, it managed to snow for the first time that year, on 13 December. It was a proper dry, cold snow that fell on frozen ground and lay there, and of course we couldn't help ourselves, we ran out into the blizzard.

My God, the little old town! The gaslights made almost no impact on the falling snow, and on our own street the people ran around like pallid ghosts. But then when we got to Breite Straße, everything was splendidly lit up by the shop windows. And the first (electric) Christmas lights were on, and we pressed our faces against the glass and talked about this and pointed to that. 'Look, wouldn't that be perfect for us!' (I think about ninety-seven per cent of what we saw would have been perfect for us.)

And then there was Harland's good old delicatessen, and we were picked up by a wave of exuberance, and we went in and bought half a pound of hazelnuts and half a pound of filberts and half a pound of Brazil nuts. 'Just for a little bit of a Christmassy feeling at home. We don't need a nutcracker, we can just open them in the door jamb.' And then we got to Ranft's bookshop, and there something wonderful met our eyes: *Buddenbrooks* for just two eighty-five . . . 'Look, Itzenplitz, I'm sure they cost twelve marks originally, and now they're going for just two eighty-five, that's a saving of nine marks fifteen . . . And I'm sure to be able to pick up some Christmas advertising!' So we bought the *Buddenbrooks*, and then we came to Hänel's department store and went in just to see what they might have for Mother and

Tutti and Hänschen, and we bought Mother a pair of very warm black gloves (five marks fifty), and Tutti got a lovely big rubber ball for one mark, and lucky Hänschen got a roller (one mark ninety-five). And we were still on our wave, and I can still see Itzenplitz in the throng of shoppers standing in front of a mirror, and trying out a little lace collar on her coat with such an earnest and blissful expression on her face (such blissful earnestness!): 'And you're going to get me something for Christmas too, aren't you, Mummchen, and maybe the collar won't be there later – isn't it dear?'

It was still snowing as we wandered home arm in arm, her hand in the pocket of my overcoat entwined with mine, and we were festooned with parcels, just like any real Christmas shoppers. And we felt incredibly happy, and for sure the advertisers would take out space . . .

But while Itzenplitz was frying the potatoes for our supper, I, a tidy, almost pedantically inclined sort of fellow, unpacked the parcels, and put all our purchases together, and then I popped all the packing paper in our little cooking stove that we called the Tiger, and it did full justice to its name. We were so happy and cheerful with our fried potatoes, and suddenly Itzenplitz jumped up and said: 'Don't be cross, Mumm, but I've just got to try on that sweet little collar again!'

That was fine, but – where was the collar? We looked and looked . . .

'Oh, golly, you can't have burned it along with the wrapping paper!'

'How could I have done that if we didn't even buy it . . .'

But she pulled the stove door open, and stared and stared at the embers ('it was so dear!'), while I set off and barged into the department store that was just closing, and terrorized tired salespeople, and walked slowly, slowly home . . . And then we slunk around quiet and glum and wary of each other until it was bedtime . . .

But there's always another morning, and you wake up, and the snow's twinkling and dazzling away under a clear blue winter sky. And the world is short one lace collar.

'Just wait, darling, we're going to buy ourselves stacks of collars in our lives . . .'

'It would happen to us, we're made of money, so we can send as many three-mark collars up the chimney as we like!'

But now it was the 14th, and fourteen is twice my lucky number, and whether I got into work especially early or the old cleaning lady was running late, either way she was still there, old Frau Lenz, a real battleaxe with a face like one too, who had brought up nine children, I can't imagine how, and all of them preferred to keep their old mother working for them than raising a finger for themselves.

Old Frau Lenz told me in her spluttery voice how she had been given a big chocolate Santa Claus from the chocolate department at Hesse's, where she also worked – 'almost two feet high, probably hollow inside, but my grandchildren would have loved it! And I put it on the sideboard, and every day I'm happy to see it, and today as I'm dusting at home, I pick it up and if that wretched Friedel my youngest hasn't started eating the back of that Santa Claus, so there's just a little bit of his front side left . . . She'd propped him up against a vase, to keep him from falling over . . .' She wheezed, spluttered, snorted with fury. 'But wait, when I get my twenty marks Christmas money from Heber, she won't get a single penny of it, even if she bangs on at me all week, so she won't go to the dance . . .'

To which I replied that my understanding was that there wasn't going to be any bonus money from Heber this year. And then old Frau Lenz, a barrel of gunpowder, a volcano, how she spluttered and spat! 'Oh, I'll show him, old misery guts! He'll wish he'd never been born! No money for Christmas? Oh, leave it out, Herr Mumm! The boss won't forgo one single glass of schnapps, with this so-called miserable economy! The old sot! And always the little people! Isn't he just going to catch it!'

And Heber caught it. There she stood, old Frau Lenz, scruffy and dingy and wrinkled and frightful to behold, and she let fly . . . The racket even drew Pressbold out of his hole, and, strange to relate, that same Pressbold who had left me high and dry, now that it was Frau Lenz who was laying into them, started to provide a chorus for her remarks: 'I don't think it's right either, Heber . . .' And: 'I think Frau Lenz has got a point . . .'

Until Heber, white with rage, had had all he could take: 'Right, get out of here, the lot of you! Do I decide who gets paid a bonus here? You're mad, all of you! But you wait, Mumm, I know you're stirring things up, you're to blame for all this . . .' I didn't hang around to hear any more. Another defeat. The outlook was dim . . .

My report on our first Christmas together would be incomplete if I failed to mention children. When Itzenplitz and I talked about earlier Christmases in our lives, then it was always the festivities of our childhoods that were brought back to life. In time, they had rather merged into one, but no Christmas trees ever sparkled like the Christmas trees of yore – and I could tell Itzenplitz in detail about the time I got the puppet theatre, and then, a couple of years later, the lead figures for the Robinson Crusoe set . . .

'It only really makes sense with children. I think we'll be a bit lonely just the two of us . . .' And Itzenplitz would look slowly about her, into the corners where the shadows lurked . . .

And then we did get a child, just before Christmas. It was the 18th, the snow had given way to dirty slush, horrid piercing damp and dull, cloying fogs, days that refused to brighten. On one of those afternoons that were neither day nor night, we heard a little wailing outside the door of our flat that sounded almost like a child crying, and when Itzenplitz opened the door, there was something huddled on the doorstep half-dead with cold and damp: a cat, a small grey and white cat.

I didn't get to see the addition to our household till a couple of hours later, when I got home from one of my subscription walks. She was already warmed up and half-kempt, but there was no question that this little grey-white creature with a black mark over half its face was a real alley cat . . . 'Holy-Moly,' said Itzenplitz. 'She's our little Holy-Moly . . .'

There was no gainsaying that, she was spending the night on our sofa, and in the morning Itzenplitz would try and get hold of an old margarine crate from the shopkeeper, and some scraps of material for Holy-Moly (though such scraps were in short supply in as recent a household as ours) – well, and in short we had our child, and wouldn't be quite so much all on our own as we thought.

I woke up in the night, though, it must have been quite late, because the electric light was on, and a white shape stood perfectly still in its nightgown. 'Itzenplitz,' I called out. 'Come back to bed, you'll only catch cold . . .' She indicated she wouldn't return right away, and shortly after I got up and stood there beside her.

'Look,' she whispered. 'Look at that!' The little cat was awake. She wiped her head with her forearms, then put out a rosy pink tongue, and yawned and stretched. Itzenplitz watched with fascination. With two of her fingers she stroked the cat behind the ears.

'Holy-Moly,' she whispered. 'Our very own Holy-Moly . . .'

She looked at me.

A man doesn't forget that kind of thing. It was my Christmas and Easter and Whitsun and all the other red-letter days rolled into one.

After the 18th it was the 19th, and so the days went on, and money remained scarce, and the newspaper advertising line didn't keep what it promised, and our prospects were bleak. On the night of the 22nd, Itzenplitz began to enquire again whether Heber wasn't showing some signs of maybe, and perhaps if he wasn't, then whether I shouldn't go and beard the big chief myself, and things couldn't be allowed to just go on like this, someone should just tell us, one way or the other . . .

On the 23rd, I slunk around Heber like a bridegroom round his young bride, but he didn't betray any sign of anything at all, and was just as bony and fishy as he always was. And on the night of the 23rd, Itzenplitz and I had our first real quarrel, because I hadn't said anything, and also because Holy-Moly had savaged our African violets, which we had been given by Frau Pressbold, so that there was not one left, and also Störtebeker had once again failed to deliver the Christmas tree support, and instead put Itzenplitz off with 'tomorrow'.

And tomorrow duly came, 24 December, Christmas Eve, and it looked like an ordinary, foggy, grey winter day, neither cold nor warm. At ten o'clock Heber went in to see the boss, and I sat and waited for him to come out, and while I waited I wrote some nonsense about the Christmas film showing in the Olympia, which was half-decent. Heber came out, looking just as fishy and bony as ever, and sat down on his chair, and said to me gruffly: 'Mumm, you have to go over to Ladewig's beds right away. He claims he ordered a quarter-page ad, and you billed him for a half. It seems you're forever making these kinds of blunders . . .'

And as I trotted off, I kept thinking: poor Itzenplitz . . . poor Itzenplitz . . . I felt completely crushed, we had five marks left, but I hadn't ever really believed I was going to get this bonus. If you need something really desperately, you never get it.When I got to Ladewig's it turned out that of course I was right, and in the end Ladewig remembered, and was decent enough to admit it. Then I dawdled back to the newspaper and told Heber, who said: 'Well, didn't I tell you. And those are the kind of people who try and set up in business . . . By the way, sign this receipt will you, I managed to talk the boss round after all . . .'

Initially I felt I was blacking out, my head was in a total spin. And then everything brightened, looked somehow dazzling, and I felt like grabbing hold of the old haddock and giving him a smacker on each bony cheek. And then I grabbed the fifty-mark note, and called: 'One minute, Herr Heber . . .' and I sprinted, money in hand, down Breite Straße into Neuhäuser, across the church square, along Reepschläger Passage into Stadtrat-Hempelstraße, and I charged up the stairs and burst into our flat like a typhoon, and slammed the money down on the table, and yelled: 'Make a list, Itzenplitz! And come get me at two!' And I gave her a kiss and I turned on my heel, and I was back downstairs again and in a trice I was back at the paper, and that ornamental carp of a Heber couldn't have got over his initial astonishment at my disappearance, because he was still mouthing away to himself: 'I wish for one hour on Sunday I could be as stupid as you are all your life!'

Then two o'clock came round, and Heber was gone, and she arrived. And this was the note she gave me, our final version, which she presented:

1. for eating:
1 duck	5.00	
red cabbage	0.50	
apples	0.60	
nuts	2.00	
figs, dates, raisins, etc.	3.00	
sundries	<u>5.00</u>	16.10

2. for the tree:
our tree	1.00	
one doz. candles	0.60	
candle-holders	0.75	
tinsel	0.50	
sparklers	<u>0.25</u>	3.10

3. for Holy-Moly:
1 bucket of fresh sand	0.25	
1 herring	<u>0.15</u>	0.40

4. for Mumm:
1 pr gloves	4.00	
cigarettes	2.00	

```
    1 shirt................................................... 4.00
    1 tie..................................................... 2.00
    something else .................................... 2.00      14.00

5.  for Itzenplitz:
    1 lottery ticket..................................... 1.00
    1 pr scissors ........................................ 2.50
    1 collar (lace) ...................................... 3.00
    1 shawl................................................ 6.00
    1 shampoo and cut............................... 2.00      14.50


    Our Christmas:.................................................  48.10
```

'I know,' said Itzenplitz, going like a train, because Heber was back from lunch at four, and we had to have finished our shopping by then, 'I know. It's an awful lot of money to spend on food, but the duck will last us at least four days, and Christmas only comes round once a year. And I need a decent pair of scissors for my sewing, I really can't go on using my nail scissors. And the prices are pretty up-to-date, and we'll have seven marks left to keep us going till the first, which is one mark per day, which is plenty. I have to have sparklers for the tree, and I'm sorry I rate fifty pfennigs more than you, I suppose I could always forget about the lottery ticket, but I think you need to have something to hope for at Christmas as well, even though I'm sure we won't win anything—'

'What's the "something else"?' I broke in.

'Oh, Mumm, that's just a little tiny thing I've got up my sleeve for you!'

'Well then I want two marks for "something else" too,' I said gruffly.

'Oh dear, then we'll be down to five marks, and what if the gas man comes, and then I'm all of two-fifty ahead of you! And it's really not necessary, I'm so happy about our Christmas!'

'But I insist,' I insisted.

And then Itzenplitz went and got old Frau Lenz, who promised to hold the fort till four o'clock, and a pretty good stand-in she made too. Anyway, who on earth was going to call on the afternoon of the 24th?

We raced off anyway, and of course all the prices were a bit off, my shirt cost seven marks, so we forgot about the tie, and we found gloves that were one mark less. Itzenplitz found a lovely shawl in red and white and blue in a sort of crinkly silky stuff. And we found a collar that was exactly the match of the one we'd burned! The duck in Harland's high-class delicatessen weighed four and a quarter pounds and came to five marks forty-five, but that was some duck!

Of course we didn't manage everything by four, but we agreed that I was to run back to the paper so Heber didn't find me gone, and at half past four I was to ask him to let me go early. In the meantime, Itzenplitz was going to get her shampoo and cut, and afterwards we would finish the shopping together.

I was back at the paper at five to four, and lo and behold, Frau Lenz had taken in an engagement announcement for nine marks eighty (was there nothing the woman couldn't do), and when Heber came in, I nagged him till he forked out my ninety-eight pfennigs commission. He couldn't believe I needed money again only minutes after getting my bonus, but I must say he honoured the true festive spirit when he gave me a whole mark.

A little after five he did finally let me go, and I raced round to Steinmetzstrasße, and I found poor Unger at home, who had cancelled his engagement just three weeks before and had asked for his presents back, and was in an awful state. We came to terms, and I bought the little gold chain with the aquamarine pendant for three marks down (two marks of 'something else' and one of engagement royalty), plus fifteen weekly instalments of one mark, payable from 1 January.

Now if I'd expected to find Itzenplitz waiting for me outside the hairdresser's, I was wrong. It seemed all the girls and women in the world were set on getting their hair done today. But I wasn't annoyed, in spite of standing around with wet feet, when she came out with her hair a mob of corkscrew curls and little ringlets, and we plunged straight back into the Christmas shopping, me with the aquamarine pendant in my pocket over my heart.

Then we were home again, and it had been dark for ages, and I was handed the bucket, and I raced off again to the building materials for sand, and the manager was not happy to be faced with such a major order at a quarter to seven. When I got home, Itzenplitz was in despair. Störtebeker still hadn't come round with his tree support, even though we could hear him fossicking around next door so he was at least home.

Hand in hand we crept across the landing and knocked on his door, heard him tossing and turning, heard snores, and opened the door: there was a lit candle in one empty bottle, while Klaus Störtebeker seemed to have passed out halfway through another. We were very much afraid of him, but we crept into his room like a couple of Red Indians, looking for the base. There wasn't much there, and certainly no sign of the base. With typical female obstinacy Itzenplitz was just pulling open a drawer, when there was a groan from the bed: 'What're you doing, you young pups . . . base for your Christmas tree? Tomorrow, thassa promise!' And he was off again.

At five to seven I was running into town again, and at Günther's hardware store they were out of Christmas tree bases, and at Mamlock's the shutters clattered down in my face.

At ten past seven I was home, empty-handed, and there, upright in a sand bucket – in fact, not to put too fine a point on it, in Holy-Moly's bucket of cat sand – sumptuously draped with a white tablecloth, stood our little sparkling and gleaming tree.

Wonderful, beautiful Christmas – and blow me if old Itzenplitz didn't start blubbing like a baby when I gave her her aquamarine pendant. 'It's so much nicer than what I've got for you.' Though

I have to say, the lighter was lovely too. Then we stood there and watched as Holy-Moly laid into her herring, with plenty of cracking of bones and lugging and pulling this way and that, and then Itzenplitz said so quietly I could hardly hear her: 'We'll have more than Holy-Moly next year.'

The Good Pasture on the Right
(1934)

It was on Thursday that Father got the registered letter. It took him quite a long time to open it and read it, and I could see how agitated he was. Then he sat there for a long time with his fingers clutched at his hair, staring at the letter as though he couldn't understand what it said.

'What's in your letter, Father?' asked Mother.

Father didn't answer. Then we went out into the fields as usual. We were ploughing some dung into the potatoes, but he didn't say a thing all day. He had the letter in his jacket pocket, and so far as I could see he didn't take it out once: he had probably understood what was in it by now.

We ate dinner as usual, and supper too, the only difference being that Father was maybe even quieter than usual. I had my eyes on him, but there was no sign of anything being different. After supper, I went into the byre to see if the cows were thirsty, and Father came with me. He watched silently while Blösch, our best cow, put away almost three buckets of water. When he saw that, he sighed and said: 'I wonder how we're going to get our animals through the winter this time.'

'There's plenty of fodder for them on the Kruselin meadow,' I said.

'That's true enough,' said Father. 'Will you come with me?'

I went with him. We walked through the village. At the Fingers' house I saw the farmer and his wife standing on the stoop, talking about something with Stark the wheelwright, but by the time we got level with them they disappeared. It might have been coincidence, but it didn't seem so to me. Something was amiss, I felt it more and more keenly.

At the Kleinschmidts' I looked around for Martha, but she kept out of sight. I hardly ever see Martha on the street, she's always busy doing something inside, even when it's quite late. They're just cottars, the Kleinschmidts, not farmers like ourselves, or the Fingers, but I go round there a lot just the same, I've got a soft spot for Martha.

When we were through the village and coming up to the wood, Father kept going, and then I knew we were going to the Kruselin meadow. And when I thought about the registered letter coming in the morning, and the Fingers avoiding us on the street just now, then I knew quite a bit about what was going on, even if Father hadn't said a word. I never would have thought the Fingers capable of something like that. The Kruselin meadow is theirs, but we've leased it from them pretty much since for ever. Not with contract and money and so forth, but we look after it, we turn it over and fertilize it, make sure the drainage ditches stay open, and we mow it. And half of what we cut is ours in return for our labour, and half is the Fingers' because they own it. We put up a fence around it to keep out deer. We need the meadow for our farm, without it we could never get our cows through the winter, if we didn't have hay from the 'Kruselin meadow right'. The Fingers don't need the meadow, they've got the 'Kruselin meadow left', and they get so much hay, they even sell it on. That's why it's so mean of the Fingers, and with the registered letter and all, when they live five houses away. But I know how these things go, and Father knew it too.

We stood on the edge of the wood looking at the meadow. It was already fairly dark, and there was a ground fog, but we knew the meadow, so we knew what good fodder grew on it. We had no need to look at it more closely, but of course it was good to be looking at it at all. That was why Father had taken me along to go and see it.

'Oh, dear,' said Father. 'So is this really for the last time?'

'Surely not,' I said.

'I don't know what we're going to do for feed,' said Father, ignoring me. 'We'll have to slaughter at least half the cattle. But we can't do that either, because then we won't have enough dung.'

'Is it supposed to happen right away?' I asked.

'Yes, before the first mowing. It's because we've got nothing in writing, so they don't have to worry about giving us notice or anything. I should have had some written agreement, but of course that never occurs to you.'

'It didn't to me either,' I agreed.

Then we walked down from the wood's edge to the meadow after all. It smelled fresh, a really good meadow, with lovely wild flowers in it, the animals love the hay from it. It was a shame to lose a meadow like that. We would never be able to cope, the farm would never be the same.

'Mind, I'm not leaning on you, Jochen,' said Father.

'No, no,' I agreed.

'It's just a question of whether you can bring yourself to do it.'

'I don't think I can,' I said.

'Is it on account of Martha?'

'As well,' I admitted. I hadn't discussed her with Father, because she's just a cottar's daughter. Some things you don't do. 'But I think, even without Martha, Ella isn't right for me.'

'It's up to you,' said Father. 'But just bear in mind you've got plenty of work to keep you busy all your days, and at night you'll both be tired. You don't have to spend that much time together.'

'Maybe not,' I said.

Then we went home. It had got completely dark, Father was walking ahead of me, once or twice he heaved a deep sigh. I felt sorry for him, he's getting on, and he put an awful lot of work into the farm. He really made a go of it, but if the good Kruselin meadow right were to go, then it was all for nothing. You can't buy meadowland around here. We do what we can with serra-dilla, but if it's a dry year and the serradilla fails, then we've got nowt. No, it was an awful blow, but however sorry I felt for him there was nothing I could do to get him out of it.

In front of the pub, Father stopped. 'You feel like dropping in for a bit, Jochen?'

'Me?' I asked. 'With you?'

'No, not tonight. But perhaps you ought to go. Here's two marks for you.'

'It won't do any good, Father,' I said. But I didn't want to be disobliging, and so I went in. There was only Strasen in there – the fisherman – and the landlord. They were talking about what a dry spring it was turning out to be. It really wasn't what I wanted to talk about at all, I had to keep thinking about the meadow and the serradilla on the dunes with no rain, but I kept my end up. And I was putting it away. It was about ten o'clock when I got up and paid. There was no change from two marks, I'd had eight shorts, a beer and a cigar. I was pretty raddled, but it didn't help; I wasn't about to do what Father wanted me to do.

I didn't go home, I went the back way to the Kleinschmidts' and climbed over their fence. All the lights were out, and I rapped on Martha's window.

She was there in a trice. I said: 'Can you come out for a bit?' and she came right away.

Martha is fully a head shorter than me, but I like her a lot. She has lovely ash-blonde hair, and not a new-fangled bob, but plaits. And then she has dark eyebrows and brown eyes, and her cheeks are always red; however much she does in the house, she never looks pale. She's the best worker in the village, and her work is never shoddy, not ever.

I told her all about it, and she listened to me calmly; it was as though she already knew everything. And of course she did – there's no secrets in a village. She did know everything.

We walked for a bit, and then we came to a stop, she was listening very quietly. Then we walked some more, till we were standing by the lake, and the water was plashing quietly among the rushes, and I was desperate for her to say something. I told her in no uncertain terms that I wasn't going to do it, and that I would never lay a hand on Ella, but she didn't say a word. I felt all the wind was taken out of my sails.

I talked a bit more, but I saw there was no point, and then I stopped. We were sitting down on a rock, very close together, and suddenly I noticed she was crying. I'd never seen her cry before. First I tried to talk to her, then I just took her in my arms. She was wonderful to hold, she made you feel you were everything in the world to her, not just a silly farmer's lad, but everything she wanted. We had never held each other like that, and then one thing led . . .

The following Sunday we went to see the Fingers, Father, Mother and me. They were expecting us, maybe Mother had said we were coming, anyway everything seemed to have been sorted out, I didn't need to say anything. There wasn't any more talk of the Kruselin meadow being taken away. Afterwards, all six of us went to look at the animals, Ella too, and we went to stand in front of the pigs, our parents contrived to leave us alone.

We were both there by the edge of the trough, looking over the low wall into the sty. The sow had farrowed overnight, there were ten little ones, and Ella reckoned they wouldn't all pull through. While she was saying that, the old folks went off, and I saw we were alone. It didn't feel good to be alone with her, but that didn't matter, I was going to have to be alone with her an awful lot over the next thirty or forty years. Ella's not a bad-looking piece, big and strong with breasts on her. She works hard too, but I knew from school how cold and greedy she can be, and a tongue on her; not a good word for anyone, not even her own parents.

When we saw we were alone, we stood for a while very still on the edge of the trough, watching the sow suckling her piglets. After a bit I noticed Ella pushing her arm closer to mine, and a bit later she was pressing against my shoulder. Then I kissed her. Kissing her wasn't so bad, she had a nice full mouth and seemed to like it, she pressed herself against me harder. Then suddenly I could tell by her quick breathing that she was really keen on me, and that she was desperate to have me – and with that everything suddenly felt really awful, and I had to let go of her.

She could tell right away what was going on, and for a long time she just stood there looking at me. But I didn't dare look up at her till she asked me: 'I suppose you're thinking about Martha?'

With that, I had to look at her, and I saw she wasn't looking at me angrily or hungrily, but just unhappily that she had done something to hurt me. And so what I replied was: 'No, I'm not.' But I didn't feel really sorry for her either.

'Do you think you'll ever be really fond of me?' she asked, then.

I thought of pretending I hadn't heard, because she did ask in a very quiet voice, but I went ahead and said: 'Yes. Sure I will,' and then we walked out of the pigsty together, and for the rest of that day we were apart.

The Fingers were in a hurry with the banns, and only a week later it was all settled. I expect tongues were wagging all over the village, but I didn't pay them any mind. I didn't care about Ella either: whenever I had to go past their house, I took care to be looking the other way. But I didn't go around to Martha's either, for many weeks I didn't see her at all. I discovered I liked being all on my own.

It was a difficult time, and I didn't know what to do with myself. I suppose I felt happiest in the bar. I let Father do the work, and I went in there in the mornings to drink. There was no one around, the landlord's wife put out beer and spirits for me, the landlord was up in the fields. The flies hummed and buzzed, and there were always little puddles of beer and schnapps on the wooden tables. I felt at home there; previously, I'd never gone there much, it didn't feel right. I couldn't say if I did a lot of thinking in all the time I was sitting there alone. I don't think I did,

I just sat there and drank, and felt empty and somehow scorched inside.

The first few times, Father or Mother would come to the pub and get me if I was gone for too long. Father was extremely gentle with me, he never spoke to me in anger, even though he was sure to be ashamed that his son was now known to be a drunkard. Mother was more inclined to rebuke me. Nor did Father make me cut hay on the Kruselin meadow either. He could appreciate that I didn't want to set eyes on it. He actually hired someone to work on it in my stead. But when I asked Father one time whether I couldn't take off somewhere for good, after the honeymoon, after all we had the meadow, he shook his head and said no. No, I couldn't do that.

After a few weeks had passed – the wedding was coming ever closer – I could see that there was no getting round it: I was going to have to see Martha again. But she didn't seem to be around anywhere, and finally I heard the landlord saying that she had left the village, and was working as a chambermaid in a hotel in town. I took some money, and went into town. I got in pretty late, and so I wasn't able to see her that night. But in the morning she opened my door because I had rung three times for room service, as it said on the card – and there she was, and this time she looked as white as the paint on the ceiling.

She was slumped against the door jamb, and after a while she said: 'Oh, dear Jochen,' with the tears pouring down her cheeks.

I said hello, and I held out my hand, and we stood there like that for quite a while, hand in hand, and I could feel the spasms in my chest and in my throat, and if I'd been able to, I think I'd have cried as well. But I couldn't.

We stood there for a long time, and we heard the bells going off all over the hotel lots of times, but she didn't move. What did we care. Finally she whispered: 'Oh, Jochen, you shouldn't have done that, you shouldn't have followed me here,' and I pulled her to me.

And then I forgot everything else, everything but her dark brown eyes and her dark eyebrows and her lovely silky hair, and I loved her so much because she was so pretty, and I was so angry with her because she had agreed that the Kruselin meadow had to be, just like Father was always saying. I pulled her closer and closer to me, when with a jerk she freed herself.

'You're getting married in two weeks,' she said. 'You think I'm the kind of girl you can see before or after, whenever it suits you?'

'Just this once—' I started to implore, but she stopped listening. And when I went on, and started bothering her and pawing her, and the hotel bell kept going out on the landing, then she got angry. I could see a change come over her eyes, how they glittered, and her lips were pressed together tight, and she struck me. 'You're a drunk,' she said. 'It's the drink that wants me, not you.'

'I won't drink any more, Martha!' I said, but then I caught another blow in the face. It's a long time since anyone's hit me, not since I was at school, and with a fist, flush in the face. I almost hit her back because I saw the red mist, but she slipped away and ran out of the room.

She didn't come back, and I sat in front of the window for a long time, feeling that everything was busted and could never be fixed, neither in me and with my face and everything, and if we'd turned our backs on the Kruselin meadow now, that wouldn't have made anything better either. Not with Martha.

Finally I rang for the waiter and ordered a bottle of cognac, and then I asked him if I could have my room cleaned. He sent Martha up, and she had to clean the room under my watching eyes, while I sat by the window, drinking the cognac and watching. She didn't look up once, and when she was done I said, 'Thank you,' and put down a mark. But she left it there.

I felt like staying on for a couple of days and watching her silently, but that night I suddenly had a change of plan, and I went home, and got married a fortnight later. My marriage didn't turn out so bad, because Ella's frightened of me. I don't drink any more either.

But sometimes the old yen comes over me, and then I go looking for Martha, and though she keeps moving on, I always manage to find her in the end. I stand somewhere near her, and look at her. We've never said a word to each other, but I know she's not angry with me any more. Sometimes when she's not wanted in the kitchen, she goes out into the town where she's working. Then she sits down on a bench, and I sit down on another bench, and sometimes we look at each other. There'll never be a girl I'll care for as much as her. Then after an hour or two, she'll get up to go home. She enters a stone house, and she turns round and waves to me through the window. But she's careful only to do it when the door's closed between us. She understands how difficult things are for me.

Then, when she's gone, I get on the train home. That's right, home.

The Kruselin meadow is a right good meadow, and without it we couldn't have kept the farm going. But I don't really understand, and now that I've written it all down, I still don't understand. I always thought I must have left something out, so it didn't make sense, but I haven't left anything out. It's more than a person can understand. The miller is supposed to have called me a lily-livered coward, and I expect he's right, but I still don't see what else I could have done. We have four children, and I kept on hoping one would turn out like Martha. But they're all like Ella, and so I prefer to be on my own. Father's pretty broken-down these days.

The writing hasn't done me any good, so I suppose I'll have to get the train again tomorrow and try and see her. I've decided that when I get to be fifty, I'll talk to her once more. I draw a bit of comfort from that, but even so it's a long way off, what with my being thirty-two now. Good night!

The Missing Greenfinches
(1935)

In the Rogges' garden stood a line of twelve bushes, alternating gooseberries and currants. Their stout trunks were three feet high, and they were topped by pretty, well-pruned, dark-green crowns, so dense that there was no harvested bush that didn't still have the odd overlooked berry or sweet cluster for little Tommy in its interior.

It was Liebrecht the farmhand who discovered that the currant bush closest to the house had a further secret. The whole village, and of course everyone on the farm, knew why the Rogges didn't keep a cat. So Liebrecht thought nothing of barging into the farmer's study and bringing him out into the garden.

'What do we have here?' asked Rogge, carefully parting the twigs – while Tommy tugged at his father's trouser legs, begging: 'Papa! Papa! Me too!'

'I see,' said his father, and his voice sounded very grave and contented. 'A nesting pair of greenfinches! You must admit they would never have settled here, Liebrecht, if we had kept a cat . . . It's birds or cats, that's the way of the world, and I for my part would rather have birds in my garden. All right, Tommy, you can have a look now.'

He picked the little boy up in one arm, and with the other parted the twigs for him. There perched in his nest sat the little bird with the pretty yellow-green back and the ash-grey neck. He had his wings out beside him like little fans, edged in lemon yellow, and he pressed his little head down against the side of the nest, because it must have felt shocking to him in his sun-dappled green fastness to see two big round white moon faces, a big moon and a little one . . .

'Papa!' exclaimed Tommy, and the little bird pressed itself still harder into its nest, and a pale grey membrane seemed to flicker rapidly across the shining black eyes . . .

'And you have to be very quiet,' the father said, 'otherwise he'll fly away and never come back. Now, I'd say you've seen enough.'

And he set the boy back down on the ground.

'But why would he fly away, Papa? We won't hurt him!'

'Greenfinches are always nervous, Tommy, because they're so small and frail. If you throw your hat up in the air, it'll think it's a hawk, and hide.'

'Will you throw your hat up in the air, Papa?'

'Honestly, Tom, do you want to scare him off? He's keeping the eggs warm. And they'll hatch into little baby greenfinches, and they'll eat the charlock seeds in our oats, so our little grey horse will get nice pure oats to eat.'

'Papa, will you let me see the eggs, I want to see them.'

'Not now, Tom,' said his father. 'We mustn't scare the little bird. But I'll tell you something: sometimes the mama finch has to fly away to find something to eat for herself. Then you should stand here on the path and keep this bush in view. When she comes flying out, I want you to call me, and I'll pick you up, and we can both look at the eggs.'

'You won't even need to pick me up, Papa, I'll get my stool and see all by myself!'

The father was afraid for the little nursery in his currant bush. 'Now, Tom,' he said gravely. 'You must not do that under any circumstances, don't look in there by yourself. I want you to call Mama first, or Herr Liebrecht or Herr Schulz. I don't want you to look in there alone, otherwise you'll scare away them away, and we won't get any little ones . . .'

'Yes, and then the grey will get bad oats . . . I understand, Papa.'

'So, is that a promise, Tom?'

'You can leave me now, Papa. I'll stand here and keep watch.'

His father disappeared behind the bushes, but he didn't go far. His young son was standing on the sandy path in the bright sunshine, looking across at the little bush. I wonder how this will turn out, the father asked himself anxiously. How long will he keep it up?

His son stood there perfectly immobile, like a wall, with sun and shadow in his face. The father waited. He fancied a cigar, but thought he wasn't far enough away. He knew his son had sharp hearing that would pick up the scrape of a match, and a keen nose for cigar smoke.

Thomas made a mark with his foot on the path, and then he stood still again. His father thought his patience was unnatural, and began to get bored. The sun shone on the garden, a light breeze got up and stirred the leaves, then stopped, and there was silence again. It was so quiet that you could hear the clang of a hoe striking a stone in the potato field behind the house.

In the pleasant warmth, he must have dropped off, because the next time he looked, there was no Tom on the garden path any more. Instead the boy was under the currant bush – tapping the trunk with his finger.

Thomas! He wanted to call out, but felt ashamed of his snooping. No, he didn't call out, he took a step or two back. I've asked him to do something he can't possibly do, he thought, upset with himself.

The boy went on tapping. The grown-up, torn between solicitude for the birds and pedagogy, went round the corner, lit a cigar and, clearing his throat, approached his son.

'Papa,' he was greeted, not at all awkward, unlike his spying father. 'I keep knocking, and each time the little bird answers me "Cheep, cheep". Does that mean I can come in?'

'Well, let's take a look, shall we,' said Herr Rogge, now reconciled to his fate. 'But I want that to be all for today, all right, Thomas?'

'Pick me up,' said the boy, when – whoosh! – the greenfinch shot out of the shrubbery with an angry cheeping.

'You see, we did bother it too much,' said the father in concern, and then both looked at the nest. Six little eggs, pale blue with little pink dots, lay there.

'Oh, Papa!' said Tommy, enraptured.

'Yes, that's right,' said his father, just as thrilled. 'How lovely they look, don't they? Once they've hatched into little baby finches . . .'

There was a 'Cheep! Cheep!'

'See, there she is!' exclaimed Herr Rogge. And there on the weeping willow, plaintively, insistently cheeping, sat the little greenfinch, looking at the pair of them with her darting black eyes. 'We should take that as a sign to go and stop bothering her. Come on, Tom.'

No sooner had they taken their first steps away, than something shot past them, slid in between the closely clustered twigs, and was gone!

'Sweet little Mama finch!' enthused the boy, a little disingenuously, as his father thought. 'When are the babies going to be born? Will it be today? How can you tell which is the Mama and which is the Papa? Where is the Papa anyway?'

The father led the boy by the hand into his study, and looked at books and pictures with him, first of finches, and then of all sorts of other birds, and then at trains, cars and aeroplanes, until the greenfinch phase was over, and the boy could be allowed to go out into the garden again unsupervised – wanting to build a motorway in his sandbox, with a multi-storey garage.

Yes, he had pulled it off. The little pair of bird parents could do their business in the next days and weeks without fear of disruption from cats or children. Father and son did indeed go to visit the nest in the currant bush from time to time, and look and whisper. But the initial and worst danger was past. The mother and father birds became familiar with the two visitors – the two full moons – and no more did they press their heads down anxiously against the parapet of the nest when they loomed. Instead they waited – at the most with an irritated cheep – for the two lightless heavenly bodies to vanish, or even, on an urgent feeding mission, flew straight past them, to the greedily gaping, begging cluster of beaks.

Yes, the shells were broken and had been tossed over the edge. Pitiful, hideous, scrawny, yellow-skinned shapes with black speckles had crawled out of them. Thomas couldn't believe that they would ever turn into anything as trim and lovely as their greenfinch parents. They were hungry, their indefatigable parents brought them little seeds to eat, and they grew.

Space in the nest got tight. When father or mother arrived with feed in their beaks, then the little ones would barge each other aside with their little stumps of wings on the parapet of the nest, so that the humans worried lest they knock each other into the terrifying abyss.

'Soon they'll be fledged and fly away, Tommy,' said Herr Rogge happily. Sure, it was a small, even a slightly ridiculous joy, but what life can be altogether bad that offers such joys in the course of an after-breakfast walk?

'When will they fly away, Papa? Today?' Thomas asked impatiently.

'We don't know. Today or tomorrow or the day after – we just have to bide our time.'

Together they walked back to the house, Herr Rogge returned to his work, and Thomas thinking he might go into the village to see if he couldn't find someone to play cars with.

Three hours later, at noon, Herr Rogge made his usual rounds of the farm, garden and fields. In the stables he ran into Herr Schulz, and the two of them exchanged a few words about the pigs, whose appetite seemed to have returned at last.

'There's nothing to beat fishmeal, eh!'

'But six weeks before slaughtering, they have to be taken off it.'

'Else the bacon will be yellow . . .'

'And taste oily.'

'That's right,' affirmed Herr Rogge, and went out onto the sunny garden path. It was a glorious day, the sky was a deep blue, the leaves a deep green, the flowers all sorts of other deep colours. Over the fields to the right of him and ahead of him, the larks were singing and mafficking away, a pair of coots were chasing and splashing each other on the lake, the midday smoke climbed peacefully from all the village chimneys over on the opposite side.

Peaceful . . .

A pitiful 'Cheep, cheep!' came from the direction of the weeping willow.

Under the currant bush stood the little three-legged stool that Thomas liked to use in his games . . . Herr Rogge parted the twigs carefully . . .

Peaceful . . .

The little clumps of foliage looked strangely empty to him . . . bare twigs . . . no sign of a nest . . . all gone . . . nothing . . .

'Cheep, cheep!' went the mother finch.

Herr Rogge's heart was beating hard. It's not possible, he thought. Thomas wouldn't do anything like that . . .

He looked down at the ground. No trace, no dropped feather, no helpless chick, no sign of the homely nest . . .

Grief and rage in his heart, Herr Rogge started to run. So meaningless . . . he thought. Perhaps as early as tomorrow they might have been fledged . . . Twenty-four hours – and fate has other ideas! Fate?!

Herr Rogge ran. Yes, there was a tragedy, a stain, a disgrace. He was running, but it wasn't from running that his face was red, and his hands damp with sweat . . .

Thomas wasn't in his sandbox. He wasn't on the lake. He wasn't in the stable. But he was sitting on his swing, swinging with another boy – wasn't that Walter Rehberg from the village?

'Look, Papa, see what we—'

He broke off, alarmed by the expression on his father's face, and his own contorted itself – with fear.

His father stopped the swing, lifted his son onto the ground, knelt down in front of him – he ignored Walter Rehberg: 'Thomas, what happened to the finches?'

With trembling hands he gripped his son, and looked at him in fear and dread. 'Thomas?!'

The boy's face twisted, he started crying, he was bawling . . .

'Thomas!' the father beseeched him. 'Stop wailing. I won't hurt you. Just tell me: where are our little birds? The green-finches?'

The answer came out in fits and bursts, between sobs and cries, barely comprehensible. 'I didn't throw them in the water.'

The father let go his son, suddenly his agitation was passed. He could see clearly, as in a dream, where you watch the full spectrum of your personal terrors in a condition of helplessness – clearly see the awful hand reaching for the nest where the sixfold help-lessness was slowly growing into life . . . Painfully loudly he heard the terrified 'Cheep, cheep!' of the bereft parents . . . He saw the quick jog trot to the lake with the little pier jutting out into it . . .

He was there as well, in his mind's eye, running along with them . . .

And then the nest was shaken out, and one after the other they tumbled out, perhaps cheeping still, but for sure the parents filled the air with their lamentations . . . There were plenty of people in the house and the farm, but no one there to prevent the tragedy . . .

But surely tragedy was something else, six worthless birds . . . Herr Rogge knew from books: bird's-nesting was a popular pursuit. He was just being sentimental, and that was the truth.

Little Thomas was yelling for all he was worth, because he had got going, and it was a useful measure in case his father planned to chastise him . . . But in his heart the thing his parents had tried to prevent had now come about: the rapine of helplessness, the brute, destructive lesson of the power of the stronger . . .

'It wasn't me!' wailed the five-year-old.

Herr Rogge looked up. The other lad, the big twelve- or fourteen-year-old (just then he seemed to Herr Rogge to be vastly old, completely irresponsible and utterly corrupt), stood there, grinning.

'Did you throw them in the water?' asked Herr Rogge.

'Yeah!' said Walter Rehberg.

'But why in the world? What possessed you?' demanded Herr Rogge in a reversion to his initial agitation.

'Just because,' said the boy obtusely. 'Stupid bloody birds.'

Herr Rogge took a deep breath. He took his beloved son by the hand and shouted 'Murderer!' in the other boy's face. He took a few steps away with Thomas, then turned round: 'Don't you ever show your face on my land! And I forbid you to play with my son. I'm going to tell your father, and tell your teacher! You deserve a whipping! Now, get out of my sight!'

Herr Rogge fell into an exhausted silence. Grinning sheepishly, understanding nothing, young Rehberg sloped off round the corner of the stables.

Hand in hand, father and son returned to the garden. The sobs that shook the little chest had settled, as had the rage in the bigger chest. The father was left with a sensation of melancholy and grief, of which he tried to convey something to his son by taking him to the orphaned spot in the currant bush. Make him understand, by showing him the void in his own life, the end of the joyful mission of setting out to peek into the bush first thing each morning, to watch the comings and goings of the finches . . .

'Oh, Papa, but they were about to fly away anyway!'

A little crossly, Herr Rogge took Thomas by the hand again, and walked him down to the lake. The seed of mischief needed to be dug up before it could put down any roots. Then, standing on the pier, looking out over the surface of the water, he tried to make his son understand how pitiful the fate of the little drowned things was, how they would never be able to fly, never peck at

weeds in the fields and garden, never sing their happy little
song . . .

He brought his son to a rueful, heart-rending weeping, a weeping that seemed not to want to stop, and that was punctuated by
cries of: 'Please, Papa, bring them back! I want the greenfinches
to come back . . .'

The education of children to little human beings is no easy
matter. Herr Rogge couldn't have borne it if his son had slipped
past this little cataclysm in cold oblivion. But when he was lying
in his bed that night, next to the bed of his wife Dete, both of
them still reading, and the child suddenly started to cry in his
sleep, and they ran over to him, and were unable to comfort him,
and 'It's just a bad dream! Naughty, naughty birds!' Well, that
didn't seem to be quite the thing either.

And when Dete asked him mildly: 'Are you quite sure you didn't
overdo it a bit, Zips?' Then it was all Herr Rogge could do to answer
soberly: 'Maybe I did. Yes, I'm afraid I probably did. But what
should I have done? You can't just let things like that go on.'

'At any rate, Thomas would never have thrown the little nest-
lings in the water,' said Dete with conviction. 'And you can't
look to a five-year-old for emotional maturity, my dear thirty-
five-year-old!'

'Yes, I'm foolish, I know,' said Zips ruefully. 'For once in my life
I'd really like to know what other people do in a situation like
this.'

'That's a nice conundrum for you to fall asleep over,' said Dete
with a laugh. 'Because now we're going to turn the lights off. If
I'm not completely mistaken, we'll be in for a rough old day
tomorrow with our Tommy, and all kinds of complaints and
squabbles. And that makes it all the more important that we both
get a decent night's sleep.'

And with that, the lights went out, and the Rogges went to
sleep, because I don't suppose Herr Rogge pursued the question,
'What do other people do?' with any very great persistence.

The night was followed by the day, and then by many other days, and late spring became summer and then autumn. Thomas played and gambolled through the year, and in the evenings he was so tired that hardly a 'bad' dream ever came to disturb his childish sleep. No one could tell whether he ever thought about the greenfinches or not, he certainly didn't raise the subject. But then nor did the others remind him of them, instructions to that effect were given out the very next morning. The only factor not in the Rogges' control, that 'horrible brute' Walter Rehberg, was no longer seen in their son's circle of friends – perhaps Herr Rogge's absurd shout of 'murderer' had made an impression on him after all.

The pears ripened and the plums ripened, they took the apples off the trees, and then they dug up the potatoes. Instead of sun, they now had clouds and rain, and the wind whistled around the eaves for many days. The year was coming to an end.

Thomas was no longer able to play in the garden all day and every day, sometimes he had to sit in his room with his toys. But when he got bored there, he would go up into the attic, and there among piles of kitchen things, suitcases full of odd-smelling clothes, bottles, vases, boxes and crates, and last year's Christmas decorations, he found no end of things to investigate and build and play with. He could undertake voyages of discovery up there, from Herr Schulz's carefully shovelled and raked piles of feed into the remotest darkest corners where there was an old rudder and old pictures facing the walls, and suitcases plastered over with all kinds of names.

There, in one corner, he found a little box with some strange hairy hemispheric shapes on wires, things whose use defied his imagination, though they did evoke some distant memory of cold and ice and twittering from somewhere in his past life. It was this vague memory that may have prompted him to pick up the box in his arms and carry it out with him. His shoes were filled with rye and powdered with groundnut dust, but he made it as far as the steps that led down into the brighter and warmer parts of the house.

The attic steps were steep, and a five-year-old had to keep hold of the handrail with one hand at least. But if he did that he couldn't keep hold of the box – and in his dilemma, Thomas threw it down the steps ahead of him.

Many things one puts down to naughtiness in children are in actual fact nothing but inexperience. If Thomas had anticipated the din the woody, hairy half-spheres would make on the stairs, then surely he would have thought of some other way of getting them down. As it was, he stood in consternation at the top of the stairs as his father came charging out of his study to one side, and his mother out of the kitchen to the other, imagining their little boy was lying in pieces on the landing. Whereas all it was was . . .

'Oh, it's the coconuts!' said Dete, a little irritably. 'Didn't you tell me they'd disappeared off the face of the earth, Zips?'

'And so they had,' retorted Herr Rogge. 'I turned the whole attic upside down looking for them. God only knows where they've sprung from now.'

'Ask you to put something away where you can find it, and this is what happens,' observed his wife, but at least it was sufficiently quiet so that Herr Rogge could affect not to have heard it.

'Thomas!' he called out. 'You're wearing light-coloured breeks, there's no point you trying to hide in the dark up there, I can see you. Climb down, you infernally noisy child, and tell us where you magicked those coconut shells from.'

Herr Rogge was apt to express himself a little fancifully, and one effect of this was that his son would often decline to reply to his appeals, but instead be silly. Hearing the word 'magicked', he twisted his features into something he thought might pass for the terrifying visage of a witch, and then he floated down the steps with a 'Whoo-whoo!' into his mother's skirts, and pinched her so hard she gave a scream.

It took quite some time for the resulting welter of scolding, whooping and gripping to abate, and the one party to learn that the coconuts had been in the corner over by the rudder –

Dete: 'Didn't I always think so!'

And Zips: 'Please tell me what you always thought! Nothing at all, to tell you the truth'

– and for the other to learn that these coconut shells had been in use the winter before last for feeding the birds.

'Then what did the birds have to eat last winter? Will you give the birds something to eat now, Papa? When is winter? Now or soon? Mama, what will you put inside the shells? Mama, why is there wire fixed onto the shells? Papa, what's coconut butter? Can you tell me how you make coconut butter, Papa?'

And so on, and so forth, till each parent fled into its respective domain, and Thomas stood all alone with the lost and found receptacles, so contentious a moment ago, and now so utterly disregarded by both the grown-ups.

But they were not lost again in the course of the autumn. For a while they lay around idly in the nursery, and during that while Thomas would pester his father with his questions: 'Papa, when are we going to feed the birds? Isn't it winter yet, Papa?' But then Thomas found some use for them, he turned them into containers for his toy store, filling one of them with dried peas, another with beans and a third with sweets – and then it was a torment for Dete to see how much good, expensive dry goods were needed to fill up half a coconut shell.

The last of the leaves had blown down from the trees, the garden was sodden, all the paths were squishy wet, and all the little boy's shoes were soaked through from jumping in puddles. Then the wind suddenly swung round from West to North to East, and at night – the nights were getting longer and longer – the sky was high, pitch-black, gleaming and sparkling with a thousand stars.

One morning, Tom's room was filled with a dazzling brightness as he was getting dressed, and his mother smilingly drew the curtains, and everything he could see was white! All white.

'Snow!' exclaimed Thomas. 'My sleigh!' yelled Thomas.

'We're going to start feeding the birds today,' announced his mother, but that was eclipsed by this pure, cool celestial surprise. With whoops of joy, Tom tumbled in the snow, somersaulted down slopes, tramped into deep drifts – was hauled inside amid cries of protest, clammy as a post in the woods and wet as a pig's snout. Was put into dry clothes – barely did his mother have a moment to attend to lunch, and he was outside again, whooping, cheering, exuberant: 'I tell you, the little fellow's beside himself!'

It wasn't until after his afternoon cup of cocoa – it was already getting dark again – that Tom had time and inclination to pay a call on the kitchen. Strange, enigmatic activity there! One of the maids, Isie, had a pile of old bacon rinds in front of her, and was jabbing little holes in them, and threading a piece of string through, and then tied the whole thing in a sort of necklace. Kati, the other, was at the stove, and was cooking something, and Mama had all the coconut shells in front of her, and was filling them out of a paper bag and Kati's frying pan.

Thomas had half a mind to tell them off for using 'his' shells without permission, but he got too wrapped up in watching his mother filling a porridge of hemp and sunflower and rape seeds and coconut butter, and the pale, transparent mixture was covered by a whitish skin, and finally set into a grey mass.

'Tomorrow morning we're going to put it out for the birds.'

'Tomorrow? Why not today, Mama?'

'It's already too dark, Tom. The little birds will all already be asleep.'

'But what have they had to eat today?'

More snow fell overnight, and they went from tree to tree through the deep drifts, hanging bacon rinds in one place and a coconut shell in another. The garden felt silent and empty, and the bright, snowy countryside seemed to go on for ever.

'Where have all the birds gone, Papa?' asked Thomas. 'I can't see one.'

And still they went on hanging. 'You'll see, Thomas!' And the old linden tree outside Tom's window was given the thickest bacon rinds, and not one but two coconut shells! There stood little Thomas, and sometimes he ran out into the garden too, but all it was was just some grown-up nonsense or other. 'There aren't any birds any more, just ravens.'

It was boring, and gliding down the hill to the lake on his sleigh was a thousand times more fun.

There was a cry, and Herr and Frau Rogge leaped out of bed. Little Tommy in his pyjamas stood by his window, pressing his nose against the glass, and crowed breathlessly: 'The finches . . . The greenfinches! Mama, Papa, the finches are back!'

He looked at his parents with shining eyes, with eyes full of the deep, mysterious light of joy, and then he looked out at the bird-feeder again. There were two greenfinches, hanging on the coconut shells, pecking and eating . . .

'Our greenfinch Mama! Our finch Papa!'

Bliss! A sheen from paradise. Bliss of a kind never experienced again.

Or – more bliss?

There's a flutter, a dart, round the corner of the stable. More finches. Thomas gets out of breath counting them: 'One, two, three, four, five, six – oh, Papa, the drownded birds are back! There's six of them! Oh, Papa, Mama, they didn't drowned at all, they've forgiven me, our greenfinches!'

Dete had no need to tap warningly on the shoulder of her husband – what is pedagogy? What is an untruth?

'That's right,' said Herr Rogge, and he cleared his throat. 'Our greenfinches are back – and they've come back to you.'

'Our drownded finches . . .' said the child, and he drew a deep breath, as though a mighty weight had been taken off his chest.

Food and Grub
(1945)

There was once a young man – not to put too fine a point on it, it was I, the author of these lines – who in his youth was condemned by doctors and his parents to go into agriculture because city life was deemed to be 'unsuitable' for his high-strung nerves. So it came about that for a dozen or so years, I parked my feet under the tables of various landowners; I'm afraid I can't say that they were always the most generous of hosts.

Good God, though, they were years of plenty, especially those before 1914, and a bit of food here or there couldn't really have mattered. But many of these people, most of them, in fact, were just mean, and to their wives it seemed to be a matter of honour not to let us have food that was grown on the farm, so that instead of good butter, they would smear our bread with the cheapest margarine, and they fed us on gruel that was sweetened not with sugar but with saccharin.

I remember a Christmas in the Neumark, on Christmas Eve we farm officials were invited to 'partake' at the boss's table. It was all very festive and cordial, peace on earth and goodwill to all men, as the celebrations would have it. But when I helped myself to a piece of breast when the platter went around, I caught the harsh words of the lady of the house, softened by no spirit of celebration: 'You might have taken the brown meat, you know! I put it on top specially for you, Herr Fallada!'

Another time I was a field inspector on Count Bibber's estates in Pomerania. It was a wonderful estate, seven manors and three small farms, the owner drove for over ten miles on his own land, a little despot. I lived in the stewards' housing on the main manor, and was fed along with the other officials by Fräulein Kannebier.

One morning I came in from the fields chilled to the bone – it was late autumn, and I was overseeing the plough teams. My breakfast is on the table, the usual two pieces of bread and sausage and a bottle of beer.

Before I could take a bite, my nose is warning me: this liver sausage reeks! Sadly, I push my plate away – I was very young at the time, and was constantly hungry – and I think: oh well, accidents happen. I drink my bottle of beer, and go back out on the fields.

The next morning it's the same deal: I'd got over the first time, but today's bread reminds me, the smell is the same.

In a rage, I pick up my plate and run into the kitchen. You wretch! I think. This is no accident, I think. I'm not going to let you walk all over me, I think. I can look after myself.

And: 'Fräulein Kannebier!' I say threateningly. 'This is the second day you've given me off sausage for my breakfast. I do proper work here, and I want proper food!'

'There's nothing wrong with that sausage!' she says, and looks at me insolently with her dark eyes. She has a fat, pale face, I can't stand the sight of her. I bet she eats everything she doesn't let me have, and she keeps everything from me she can!

'Smell this!' I shout, and I hold the plate under her nose. 'There, did you smell it!'

She takes a step back. 'There's nothing the matter with it!' she says. 'It's not even the least bit high!' she says. 'It's made right here on the estate,' she even says.

It doesn't seem like we can come to an agreement, neither of us will give an inch. I suggest that she give the delicious, home-slaughtered liver sausage to one of the others, and I'll make do with margarine, but she's not having that. After a while she starts getting heated, and she wants me out of her kitchen, but I refuse to give in. I'm on sixty marks per month, gross, and I can't afford to take myself out to breakfast on that. I want my regulation breakfast.

Finally, in the heat of the argument she lets slip the sentence: 'The countess personally instructed me to serve that liver sausage for the farm officials' breakfast!'

'Fräulein Kannebier!' I exclaim. 'I refuse to believe that. That's out of the question. The countess in person! No, it's all your doing, Fräulein Kannebier!'

'She did so order me to do that!' repeats Fräulein Kannebier, and turns her back on me. She evidently regrets having said it.

'I'll go and ask her then, shall I, the countess!' I say threateningly.

'Oh, suit yourself!' she says crossly. 'Just get out of my kitchen.'

A minute later, behold little Field Inspector Fallada trotting across the manor yard in the direction of the main house. He looks neither left nor right, and in front of him he is carrying the plate with the stinking liver sausage sandwiches. I'll show her! he thinks to himself.

I walk down the line of lindens across the park, up the drive and reach the entrance hall. The old major-domo Elias, whom I sometimes play skat with on Sunday afternoons, stares at me in wonder. 'What are you doing here?' he asks me.

'Elias!' I whisper like a conspirator. 'Do you know where the countess is?'

His look wanders between the plate in my hand and my face. 'Why do you want to know?' he asks me suspiciously.

'Never you mind!' I reply. 'Just tell me where to find her, everything else is none of your business.'

Elias has made his mind up. 'She's in the breakfast room that opens onto the terrace,' he whispers back. 'Straight on, then down the corridor till you get to the blue door. Mind, I never said a thing!'

'Not a thing!' I confirm. 'We haven't even seen each other. Bye!'

I stand in front of the blue door. By now, my heart has started to pound a little bit. But never mind, there's no going back on this. I knock and enter, but stay in the doorway.

This is no cosy little breakfast room, this is a vast hall where they are eating. One entire wall is lined with mirror-glass doors, the flower beds on the terrace provide little sprinkles of colour, the bright and dark clumps of ancient park trees – and in the distance the lake is sparkling away.

There they are sitting at breakfast, twenty, maybe thirty of them – the manor is always stuffed full of visitors. The gaudy peacetime uniforms of the officers, the dazzling dresses of the ladies. I see a sparkle of silver and crystal, there's a fabulous smell of freshly ground coffee, and a hundred other good things – and I'm standing in the doorway with my ponging liver sausage sandwiches. Another world, not for little field inspectors on sixty a month!

But it's too late to go back. The countess, young as she is, has straight away seen that something's amiss, and here she is standing in front of me. 'What brings you here, Herr Fallada?' she asks. 'Do you want to speak to the count? I'm afraid he's not here right now.'

I never supposed the countess knew of my existence, and by golly here she is even using my name! I am almost overcome. In spite of that, I say my piece as well as I can. 'Countess, this is the second time I've been given spoiled liver sausage for my breakfast.' I raise the plate ever so slightly in her direction. The countess glances at the sausage, and takes a step back. Oddly, I get the sense that countess and sausage have met before. 'The cook says you ordered the sausage expressly for us officials.'

'Oh, that wretched Kannebier woman!' cries the countess, and raises her eyes to the beautiful painted stucco ceiling. 'She really is too stupid! I told her to use the spoiled sausage for the farm workers, and here she is giving it to the officials!'

For a moment I stand there stunned. Then I say: 'Thank you very much, Countess!' Defeated, I slink back across the court. There really are two different worlds!

That evening, the count looks me up in my room and fires me

on the spot. He's even prepared to pay something for the pleasure of ridding himself of this Red troublemaker, who importuned the countess over the matter of his breakfast: he pays me an entire quarter's salary!

I held many posts during my agricultural period, and none of them for very long. But my shortest spell was on a big estate in Silesia: I worked there for just seven hours, and there too the issue was food.

This was in 1917. I was in Berlin working for a potato wholesaler and starving and freezing through the wretched turnip winter. In those circumstances, it was easy for Economic Councillor Reinlich to talk me into monitoring the progress of a strain of potato he had bred himself on his estate. I was deeply regretting having gone into the city from the country, where at least there was still bread and fruit and milk and potatoes – and not just turnips!

One evening, I clambered down from a hunting wagon that had picked me up from the station, I had reached my new sphere of operations. My boss, old Reinlich, was a good old fellow, a bachelor, by the way, corpulent, a bit deaf and a bit untidy – his standards of personal hygiene had little to do with his name.* He showed me to my ground-level room, it was all perfectly all right. 'Maybe you'd like to get moved in a bit. Supper's in half an hour.'

I had hardly washed when I heard the gong. Everything was very patriarchal here: at one end of the table sat the economic councillor, at the other his little wizened sister who ran the household. In between were the various officials: the field inspector, the farm administrator, the milk controller, the book-keeper, the cook. And in established patriarchal country fashion supper began with a flour soup which was spiced by some brownish-blackish clumps. Then there was bread and butter with cheese

* The word *reinlich* means 'clean' or 'sanitary'.

and sausage – yes, it was a good thing that I had come here, and I would stay a long time. No more turnips . . .

Supper was over, and the economic councillor said to his sister: 'I'm going to sit with Herr Fallada in the office for a while, and talk him through the record-keeping. Would you bring us a bottle of the second-best Mosel.'

Second-best Mosel and the prospect of something to smoke, it all sounded good, very good. Hang onto your hat, Fallada!

In comes the sister with the Mosel. The boss glowers up at her from under his spectacles. 'If I told you once,' he growls, 'I must have told you a hundred times to keep the lid of the flour bin shut! But no! The soup was full of mouse droppings again!'

Then I knew what the strangely spicy little brownish-blackish dumplings I had eaten were. And I thought: something that begins this shittily is only going to go on in the same vein. Knock the dust off your feet, Fallada, and hit the highway!

I listened with interest to everything the economic councillor told me about his remarkable potatoes, and smoked his cigars and drank his Mosel – all those, after all, were safe from contamination. Then, when I was back in my room, I waited quietly till everyone in the building was asleep. I lifted my two suitcases onto the window seat, clambered out and quietly went back the way I had come seven hours before in the hunting carriage. And as they were sitting down to breakfast on the estate – presumably with flour soup, with the same garnish – the train was already carrying me back to freezing, turnip-eating Berlin.

The economic councillor never got in touch. Perhaps he understood that there were people who drew the line at a bit of mouse dirt – I hope he did anyway.

The Good Meadow
(1946)

The village had never had enough grazing for its cattle – which wasn't helped when farmer Karwe sold his big meadow by the lake, and then not to a local, but to the owner of the Waldhof estate.

'What's he going to feed his six cows then?' they were asking in the village.

'He's supposed to have got clear eight thousand from the Waldhof, and none of us could have matched that,' they said.

'But it still ain't right,' they moaned. 'The lake meadow belongs to the village and not the estate, that's got enough land as it is.'

'Kurt and his old man are supposed to have practically come to blows over it,' they gossiped. 'The old man's gone mad, he said to Erwin Seiler in the pub, apparently.'

'Kurt needs to watch his lip,' they reckoned. 'If old Karwe loses his temper, young Kurt is on a hiding to nothing, in spite of his five-and-twenty years.'

Kurt was sitting under a cow, and milking into a bucket. One cow along, his sister Rosemarie was doing the same. Old Karwe was standing in the passage, pretending to be busy with something, but under his bushy grey brows he was glowering at his son. 'What's the matter with your milking today, Kurt?' he finally came out with. 'Then again, if you get plastered, then it's the poor beasts that have to pay.'

The son, with red boozy splotches in his face, made no reply.

'Why can't you act like a Christian, you flaming heathen, you!' scolded the old man. 'Can't you tell you're hurting Bianca?'

Again the son made no reply; but the cow Bianca turned her head in the direction of udder and milker, and mooed softly.

'Leave off!' yelled the old man suddenly. 'Get out of my byre!' he yelled still more loudly. 'You're a tormentor of animals.'

'And out of your farm and all, eh, Pa?' asked the son. 'Because I don't approve of you selling the lake meadow?' But he'd taken care to get up and step out into the passage.

'Keep it down, the pair of you,' said Rosemarie. 'Mum will hear you in bed, and worry.'

'You can start by shutting up, yourself!' Karwe growled at her. 'Without your womanly ways . . .' He stopped with a look at his son. 'I want to show you something in the orchard, Kurt,' he went on quite calmly. 'You finish the milking, Rose!'

'Then supper'll be late,' lamented the daughter. 'I can't do everything at once.'

'Who said anything about that?' replied her father, leading his son out of the cowshed.

In the orchard the old man stopped at the fence; his son stood a few feet away, leaning against the trunk of an apple tree. For a while they stood there in silence, the old man looking at his son, and the son looking at the fruit trees, the apples and pears bearing as much as he could remember. Even the Golden Noble apples, which were coming off a heavy yield last year, were full again; they hadn't taken a year off, as they usually did. 'But what use is it all?' thought the son, and probably he'd thought it out loud.

'No, Kurt,' confirmed the old man. 'It's no use being obstinate in the face of me and the world. It won't get the meadow back.'

'It's a shame,' Kurt insisted angrily. 'How could you make us a subject for gossip like that, Father?'

'The alternative would have been a worse shame, Kurt,' replied the old man.

The son spun round, stared at his father with round eyes. There was silence for a time. The father saw the son getting to grips with it, but declined to help him out.

Finally he asked quietly: 'Beese from Bergfeld?'

The father nodded slowly. 'That's right. He wants ten thousand as capital for his haberdashery, else he'll leave Rose on her own.'

'Let him!' exclaimed the son angrily. 'She'll find someone other than that wretched townie.'

'They'll marry in a fortnight, at least the child will be born in wedlock.' He saw the son turn pale under his tan. Farmer Karwe waited another moment, then he repeated: 'That's just the way it is!' and left his son alone in the orchard.

He took a few steps into it, stopped, looked round to check he was alone. Then he dropped heavily onto the grass, propped his head against a tree and thought: I feel like I've been sawn off at the knees.

He wanted to try and think of one thing at a time, he wanted to order his heart and mind, but everything was pell-mell: Beese the merchant from Bergfeld with the cunning yellow features and the dark, oil-gleaming hair as curly as a ram's. Then his sister, who had got involved with a character like that who didn't belong, an enigma, no attachments, an incomer. Someone who could have spent time in prison – and by the time you found out about it, it would be too late. And now he remembered how he had cleared the ditches in the lake meadow with his father, before and after winter. It had been hard, cold, wet work, but it hadn't felt hard to them, not for a moment; both of them, father and son, had relished the work. The meadow was a living thing for both of them: you had to look after it well, and then it would pay you back with a great yield. Last year, when no one in the village had any hay because of the drought, the lake meadow had yielded up three harvests! And now it was gone, it seemed they had cleared the ditches for others, it was no longer part of the Karwe farm.

The young man almost groaned with the pain of it. Again he looked around quickly, to see if someone wasn't listening, then he jumped up and ran off. He didn't run onto the village street, where they could all see him in his disgrace, he ran along the lakeside, clambering over the garden fences, and didn't stop running until he was in the lake meadow. He climbed over the rough board fence, he leaped across the wide ditch, he went as far as the corner where the reed roof was, that gave the cattle protection from sun and rain. There he sat down on the side of the trough and looked across the meadow, the Karwe meadow, his meadow . . .

Yes, there it was, it hadn't changed yet, it was still the same. And yet everything was different, it wasn't the Karwe meadow any more, it was a meadow on some rich person's country estate, one among many, not a shining individual jewel. You couldn't tell that it had changed. That was something else that Kurt couldn't understand: his father and his grandfather and his father before him and a generation before that, and himself as well, each of them a Karwe, they had put their work into the meadow. That was what had made it a good meadow, rewarding labour and love. It had become of a piece with the Karwes, barely separable from the hand that worked it or the heart that was attached to it. But now eighty blue banknotes had changed hands, and it was no longer anything to do with the Karwes – it was like selling a piece of your own heart, for God's sake! You couldn't do that!

No, Kurt couldn't understand it, this was a mystery he couldn't fathom, however he racked his brain. And with a sudden effort he pushed all these useless, tormenting thoughts away, and his whole fury settled on his sister: if only Rosemarie hadn't done what she had done, then Father wouldn't have sold the meadow, and everything would have remained as it should!

He sat there silent and tormented in the lean-to, and he didn't have the strength to get up, it really was as though his limbs had been severed. He would have happily gone to the pub, and maybe forgotten his tormenting thoughts in the chatter of the others, but he couldn't do that. Also, he needed to talk to Anneliese; they hadn't seen each other since the terrible news of the sale of the meadow. He hadn't kept their assignation: it was really important for him to talk to her now, and hear what she and her people thought about the sale, because he wasn't the same suitor as he had been before. But he couldn't go to Anneliese either, it was all he could do to sit here in his pain and rage and think about the lost meadow.

Then he noticed someone else on the meadow, it was the fat, red-faced inspector of the Waldhof estate. He was on horseback, and seemed to be enjoying riding back and forth over the meadow, galloping over the ditches. His horse's hooves threw up great clods of turf. So that was how they were going to treat his meadow!

After a while the inspector drew up alongside young Karwe, he patted the neck of his horse, and said: 'A bit of Bessemer slag and some potash will do wonders for this meadow!'

'The meadow's good enough without!' replied young Karwe. 'It's not acid.'

'Good enough for you farmers, maybe!' the inspector retorted. 'I'll get more out of it than you ever dreamed.'

'In good years, we had four mowings,' boasted Kurt. 'And you should have seen the grass, lovely thick swathes of it . . .'

'I know,' the inspector suddenly conceded. 'To begin with, the boss didn't want to pay as much as eight thousand. But I told him it was worth it, and it would have been worth ten.'

'Then how much would you be prepared to sell it for?' asked Kurt softly, and suddenly he could feel his heart beating. 'Twelve?'

'Sell it?' said the inspector mockingly. 'Sell the meadow?' He looked at the young man. 'You're probably not happy about your father selling it? You'd like to buy it back later on, isn't that right? Well, forget about that, son, this meadow won't be sold any time, it's part of the estate now!'

'But what if you were able to get twelve for it, or even fifteen?' Kurt Karwe persisted. 'Not that I could make you an actual offer or anything – Lord, it would take me a lifetime to get that much together! But at least so that I had a chance of getting the meadow back one day?' All of a sudden he had got rather talkative, strange for a quiet fellow.

The inspector could tell, and he felt almost sorry for the young man. 'Ach, Karwe,' he said finally, 'if you were to offer twenty, it wouldn't matter. What a big estate has, it keeps. It's gone. Your father for whatever reason let it go, and now it's gone for keeps, you understand?' The young man stared at him. He looked for a way out. 'You'll just have to sow serradilla everywhere,' he said. 'That way you'll have some feed. It used to be that a lot more serradilla was grown here in the village, you sell the seeds and keep the hay – you'll do fine.'

'Yes, I'm sure,' said Kurt Karwe mechanically, thinking about how his father had let the meadow go, for keeps. If it had been him, he wouldn't have bought Rosemarie a husband. Let her have her baby on her own, there would a big to-do about that at first, and then everyone would just get used to it and carry on. Whereas the meadow would always be missing from the farm, and that's all there was to it, always, as long as he lived. Father thought about these things the way the old people thought about them, and he was in charge. He, the son, just had to put up and shut up.

On the eve of the wedding, when Father counted out the money onto the table for his brother-in-law to be, he felt like walking out. Next door the drunken guests were carrying on. His brother-in-law Beese stood beside the table, his hands in his jacket pockets watching as Father laid the money out on the table. As though he saw sums like that every day of his life. Rosemarie stood next to Beese, her arm round his shoulder, her lips moving, as though she was counting along . . .

'Eight thousand five hundred!' old Karwe said finally, and put down the last bill. 'You'll have to wait a little for the balance, Erwin. It's a lot of money to raise from such a small farm, you understand.' His voice had a rare sound of begging.

Erwin Beese stood there impassive, hands in his pockets, and made no move to take the money off the table. He said: 'The sum we discussed was ten thousand, not eight and a half. You need to be serious in a transaction, especially a transaction like this. Eight and a half and patience isn't serious. All of me is getting married, I'm not waiting for a little bit to follow in the fullness of time. No, I'm afraid I need the remaining fifteen hundred, Father, everything as we agreed.'

'Livestock prices are hopeless right now, Erwin,' said the old man, imploringly. 'I'd have to lose another two cows. See,' he went on, and gestured to the money on the table, 'it's still an awful lot of money. I don't think there's ever been this much money on the table, and it's an old table, it's from my great-grandfather. You'll get the rest as soon as the butcher pays a bit better.'

'Whatever you arrange with the butcher is your affair, Father,' said Beese coldly. 'It's nothing to do with me. But when we discussed it, you said ten thousand, you said it, and so it must be. I need the money, I have put in hand a refurbishment of my shop, and ordered a lot of new stock – I must be serious with my suppliers, and so you have to be serious with me!'

'Give me four weeks!' begged farmer Karwe. 'Prices must surely have turned by then. Your suppliers won't all want to be paid at once. If I sold now, I'd be running the farm down. I've already run it down quite a bit for my boy, Erwin . . .'

Hearing his father begging like that, Kurt felt moved to speak, but Beese got in ahead of him. 'I have seen enough,' he said in his arrogant drone, 'and I can see you're not serious. You promised me ten thousand on my wedding day, Karwe, that was the deal that was struck between us. Isn't that right, Rosemarie?' It was the first time he had turned to his intended; thus far she had been an extra at the deal. 'Tell your father that was the arrangement, and that you want him to keep his word like a serious businessman.'

The girl didn't look at him, but neither did she look at her father or her brother. Nor did she take her arm off her husband's shoulder when she said, with a look at the money on the table:

'Yes, we agreed it should be ten thousand, and I want Father to keep his word to you!'

'You see!' crowed Erwin Beese. 'From the lips of your own daughter. And,' he went on, and took the girl's other hand between his, caressingly, 'and you know the state of your father's business. You can tell me yourself how to raise the fifteen hundred marks.'

The girl twisted under the eyes of the three men. 'You know very well, Rosemarie, that I'd have to slaughter the four best cows and probably the fat sow as well – we'd have nothing left! He's from the town, he doesn't know what it's like when all the animals are gone from a farm . . .'

'I'll buy the fat sow off you myself for whatever the butcher offers,' Beese put in hurriedly. 'Then we'll have something good to slaughter. Will it make good eating, your fat sow, Rosemarie?'

'Very good, Erwin. She weighs five hundredweight, and there's bacon on her as wide as my hand . . .'

'You see!' laughed Beese. 'We're reaching an accommodation, Father, the deal will work out for us both . . .'

'Beese,' put in the son suddenly, 'I'm thinking you need all this money to buy your stock, and here you are talking about getting a pig on the side, to slaughter.'

For a moment the smooth townie was confused, but soon he caught himself. 'But I'll be saving money that I'd otherwise be paying the butcher, and earning a bit!'

'And,' Kurt Karwe went on, 'I don't like your way of talking about your marriage to my sister. Is it Rosemarie you're marrying, or ten thousand marks? You keep going on about business, nothing but business – but marrying my sister isn't a business. You should count yourself lucky you're getting such a good wife!'

Beese twisted his mouth into a mocking scowl. 'I could have had as many good wives as I have fingers on my hand. If I'm standing here now, it's because she comes with ten thousand marks!'

Now it was the old man and his son who exchanged a look and understood each other, without a word. 'All right, you'll get the remaining fifteen hundred tomorrow morning, before the minister weds you, Erwin!' said old Karwe.

'That's what I call serious,' said Beese unctuously. 'And don't forget, I'm taking the fat sow in payment as well.'

'I don't recall anything being said about that in our agreement,' replied the old man. 'It was just the ten thousand.'

And so it was. So it began, and as it began so it went on, which is to say, not well. Rosemarie was one of those girls who, once married, almost completely lose touch with the parental home. She was content in her marriage, from time to time there was a little falling-out, because Beese was successful in more than business. But gradually she got used to that, just as she got used to the town, the children, the shop, the slowly growing respect she enjoyed on account of her husband's progress.

She sometimes saw her father and brother in town; to begin with she would ask eagerly how things were at home, but over time she stopped asking, because the replies didn't sound good, rather they sounded like an accusation in her ears.

In fact, the little farm never quite got over the haemorrhage that the wedding had brought about. The meadow was gone, the animals one by one came under the hammer, and while the old man and his son slaved away, there was no real progress. They were no longer proper farmers, they were cottars. And of course the marriage to Anneliese was off, her parents wouldn't allow their daughter to marry into such a poor farm. She married another farmer's son, and Kurt Karwe stayed at home with his father. The son couldn't help wondering if his father didn't regret selling the good meadow. He felt sorry for the old man, working himself to the bone, and to so little purpose. But the old man never mentioned the lake meadow, and Kurt, who still sometimes went there of an evening, never once saw his father there.

With that the years passed, people got on with their lives, and in the village they got used to thinking of the Karwes as cottars rather than productive farmers. Only young Karwe occasionally protested at this; the old man had stopped long since.

The old man was happy that his son, who wasn't a young man any more, finally did find a bride, an old spinster who brought an eight-year-old bastard into the marriage with her, but also a cow; he didn't say a word about any shame or disgrace. On the contrary, he bloomed; there were more children, and children are hope, children are the only real riches in this life.

A couple of years later, old Karwe went on, or rather he went out as a light goes out that has burned down to its last bit of wick. The evening of his death, Kurt Karwe went down to the meadow by the lake again. That was the only secret he had, not just from his wife, but from everyone, and the one person who might have guessed at it or understood it, well, he was gone now. Because for young Karwe it remained his meadow, the lake meadow, the good meadow – he had never given up on it, never accepted its loss.

As he sat there, he was no longer at odds with his father. His father had acted as he had to; he himself acted as it was in him to act, holding onto the good meadow against all reason and against all likelihood; it remained for him the Karwe meadow. For many years now he had watched employees from the large estate digging ditches there, spreading artificial fertilizer and mowing – and they had their hands full with the mowing. Oh, it had remained a good meadow, but for that very reason it had also remained his meadow, even if not many people even knew that the lake meadow on the estate had once been the Karwe meadow.

There is an old German saying: there are always grounds for hope, it just has to be the right hope. Germany went through some terrible years: warfare and other horrors that were worse than warfare. What had once been anguish was as light as a feather compared to the burdens that had to be borne now. Everything that had once existed broke down, but in this general breakdown something good and new came into being. The large landholders' estates were being broken up, and there was a commission sitting, and its members would often talk themselves into a lather.

But when they asked Karwe: 'What do you have to say? What do you want?' he simply answered: 'I just want to get my meadow back, the good meadow by the lake.'

That gave some of them pause, they didn't know what meadow he was calling his meadow, and usually a big quarrel started: he was asking for too much, they all needed pastureland.

But he remained stubborn, he wanted his meadow back, it had always belonged to the Karwes. And in the end he got his way. The evening came when he was sitting on the side of the trough under the rush roof, looking out at his meadow. No fat, red-faced inspector had the right any more to ride around on it, issuing silly advice about planting serradilla. The good meadow had been returned to the Karwes, and there was no more talk of cotting.

Almost twenty-five years had elapsed. Kurt Karwe hadn't been able to do much, only wait and hope and remain true to his ideal. And then, as though life had crossed out what it had done on that one awful evening, Rosemarie was back under his roof. The business had been destroyed in the war, the man disappeared, the children scattered; now the ageing woman was back home, helping a little, complaining a lot, everything was just the way it had been before.

No, not quite. The farm was still down by two cows. 'But I'll get them, see if I don't!' said young Karwe, whom people had long ago taken to calling old Karwe. 'You just see if I don't!' He felt very old, but full of wisdom and common sense, as though life was just beginning for him, as though he wasn't a mortal man. 'The meadow is back, and Rosemarie is back – surely I'll get the two cows as well!'

He went into the cowshed, to watch the women at milking. They didn't see him push a bit of hay into the rack in front of his favourites – hay from the good meadow.

Calendar Stories
(1946)

1 The Poor Neapolitan

This story happened many years ago in the Italian city of Naples; but it could – especially today – happen in any city in the world, especially Berlin.

A Neapolitan who was so poor that he had just one soldo in his pocket, and not the least prospect of acquiring any more, was so fed up with his misery that he decided to drown himself in the sea. On his way, he passed a stall where a man was selling roast cow-peas. With his last soldo the man bought himself a bagful, and continued on down to the sea, eating cow-peas out of the bag and spitting out the skins on the street.

As he did so, though, he had a sense of something tiptoeing after him. He looked, but he couldn't see anyone – perhaps on account of the gathering darkness, as night was falling. But when the rustling and shuffling continued, he spun round and saw a fat man creeping along behind him, collecting up the spat-out skins and eating them.

The Neapolitan came to a sudden halt and said to himself: 'What's this?! There I go, thinking of myself as the poorest of the poor, and here's someone who doesn't scruple to live off my trash! For him therefore, I'm not poor, I'm rich.' He had forgotten all about his decision to drown himself; he turned and walked back into the city, firmly resolved to look for work the next morning, and to find work too.

The moral: no one is so poor that he can't find someone even poorer. No one has so many worries that there isn't someone somewhere with even more worries. And bear this in mind as well: no situation is so hopeless that it can't be remedied by a courageous decision.

2 The Robbed Doctor

This is a story from Berlin in our time.

During his consulting hours, so to speak under his nose, a doctor in Berlin was robbed by a patient of the leather bag where he kept essential equipment for house visits, and certain irreplaceable medicines for emergency cases. The doctor was very angry at the wicked breach of trust on the part of someone coming to him for advice, but all his enquiries were unsuccessful: the bag was gone. The telephone rang, and the doctor was called away to the bedside of a gravely ill patient. Crossly and hurriedly he pulled what he could out of his stocks, and ran off.

By now, the thief had crept into the doctor's garden. So as not to be caught on the stairs with the bag under his arm, he had cunningly fastened it to a rope and lowered it out of the window while the doctor's attention was elsewhere, so that all he needed to do now was to cut the rope – or so he thought. Because when he got to the garden, he found someone else already doing just that. 'Hey!' he exclaimed. 'That's my bag!' To which the other thief replied cheekily, 'If that's the case, call someone in the house who can confirm that.'

After a bit of to-ing and fro-ing, the pair of them agreed to sell the bag and split the gains, and they set off for the black market. On their way they tried to guess what might be in the bag, and they agreed that, in view of the doctor's social position, the likelihood was that it would contain at least one or two packets of cigarettes and some money. Unable to contain their curiosity, they turned into an entrance and looked inside the bag. Imagine their disappointment when they found nothing but some well-used items of medical equipment and a few cardboard packages of medicine.

But there wasn't even time for the second thief to curse the first for such a worthless heist, because a policeman suddenly appeared and ordered them both to accompany him to the station. He had been watching their suspicious behaviour first on the street, and then through a window onto the passage. All their protests and assurances were unavailing, and the worthless stolen bag clearly indicated that they were thieves.

The doctor meanwhile was standing helplessly in front of a woman with a bad heart condition, whom he would dearly love to have helped with an injection. But he had neither syringe nor drugs. He despatched messengers, but they came back empty-handed: there was nothing in any of the nearby pharmacies. The doctor was on the point of leaving the patient to see what he could turn up himself when there was a knock at the door, and a policeman handed him his stolen bag. The name of the doctor on the inside of the bag had led him to the owner, from whose surgery he was redirected to the address of the patient.

The doctor hurried back to the patient's bedside and performed the injection, which afforded instant relief to the woman. He jammed his bag under his arm, and went straight off to his next patient.

The moral: even a valueless theft can do great harm – to others. And note further: any theft, great or small, puts you in jeopardy, and in the hands of others, who will be able to do with you what they like.

3 The Argument about the Fireworks

This story took place many years ago in a small Italian village.

A small village by the name of Positano had a particular reverence for two saints: Saint Vincent and Santa Maria of Positano.

Every year great celebrations were held in honour of those two patron saints: Saint Vincent's was in spring, once the last kernel of maize had been planted, and Santa Maria's in summer, when the first wheat was harvested.

Neither celebration would have been much to write home about, because the people of the village were wretchedly poor and lacked the wherewithal to stage any sort of celebration, were it not that – driven by their great poverty – the strongest boys and men of the village emigrated to America. In the rich new world they remembered their poor native village, and when they had saved a little money they would send it home, and usually with the express wish to support one of the two annual celebrations.

Now, it so happened one year that a sizeable sum of money from America, dedicated to a display of fireworks for Saint Vincent, arrived in Positano shortly after that saint's day had been celebrated. The village all but came to blows over what to do. Some were in favour of keeping back the money for next year's celebration, others wanted to use it for the forthcoming celebrations of Santa Maria.

People got more and more agitated about it, and they were close to fisticuffs, when the local priest came and said placatingly: 'My dear fellows, what are you doing! We can't possibly use the money for Santa Maria, because otherwise this strife might be perpetuated in heaven, and Saint Vincent would rightly accuse Mother Mary of Positano before the Almighty of doing him out of six hundred lire for fireworks. Equally we can't leave the money to lie for a full year, because the donor wanted it to be spent this year. So the only solution is to light some fireworks to Saint Vincent in the next few days, as a sort of belated celebration.'

This decision pleased all the villagers, not least because it allowed for a third feast in the village calendar. As arranged, the fireworks were set off, and there was nothing said of a charge brought by Santa Maria of Positano at a divine tribunal, to the effect that Saint Vincent had been fêted twice that year, and she herself only once.

The decision of the priest vis-à-vis celestial matters need not concern us here, who have our hands full with earthly affairs. But take this from it: one should not allow something that belongs to one to fall to another; there is an order in the things of this world that should not be meddled with.

4 Eighty Marks

This story happened about twenty years ago, in Berlin.

A young man who had just got his licence to practise as a doctor lacked the means to fit out a consulting room with all its expensive equipment. That led him to the conclusion that the best thing for him would be to take over the practice of a doctor who had moved away, or perhaps recently died. But how to come upon such a thing – and in the great city of Berlin?

At that time there were agencies that claimed to be able to find just about everything a man's heart could desire. Our young doctor turned to one such agency, and its owner, a young man like himself and, it appeared, also just setting out, assured him he knew of just the thing. Before giving him the address, however, he asked for an advance of eighty marks. The young doctor, who was a frugal sort, refused to pay the advance, and get a pig in a poke; he would only pay once he had seen the doctor's widow, and come to an agreement with her.

So the two of them argued – in a perfectly amicable way, let it be said – till the young doctor happened to exclaim: 'How do I know you have anything in mind at all, and aren't just after my eighty marks!'

Whereupon the agent, himself also heated, replied: 'I do have an address, and a very good one, and I'll tell you where it is, it's in Südende. But I won't tell you the name of the street until I've had your eighty marks!' Shortly afterwards, the two of them went their separate ways without agreement. Each one kept the thing that was his: the one his money, the other the address.

The young doctor, though, considered: there's not a lot of Südende, and I'm damned if I can't find the address myself, and save myself eighty marks in the process! So he took himself to that part of Berlin, and walked from street to street and from one set of premises to another, always asking whether anyone had heard of a local doctor dying or moving away. Already on the second day he was successful: he was told the address of a recently deceased doctor, and was quickly able to come to terms with his widow. He rejoiced that he had saved eighty marks, and thought a little contemptuously of the agent who had given himself away in the heat of the moment, and hence cost himself his fee.

Later on, once his practice was thriving, his contempt muted into a gentle regret that he had tricked the man of his fee. He even thought about sending the man the money anonymously, with an appropriate surcharge, but he didn't do anything. Much later, by which time he owned his own home in Südende, he forgot about the agent altogether and never thought about him at all. What was curious, though, was that all his life he kept an aversion to the sum of eighty marks; he would not buy anything at that price, nor would he issue a bill for that amount.

Years later, he was called to the bedside of a gravely ill patient, and each man failed to recognize the other – or, if you prefer, the doctor did not recognize the erstwhile agent, who over time had himself become a rich, if very sick man. The doctor treated his new patient with all his skill and with much sacrifice of time and attention, and finally he was able to save the man from almost certain death. Afterwards he sent him his bill, not excessive but substantial. Even though he had long been comfortably off, he couldn't help but relish each large sum of money that came in, and he made plans as to how to invest it. Because at the bottom of his heart he had remained the frugal man of yore, who was upset by each foolishly spent mark.

He was therefore astounded when, instead of the expected sum of money or cheque, he was sent a receipt, confirming the payment of eighty marks plus compound interest for information concerning a general practice. It took a while before it dawned on him what eighty marks were being referred to here, and that the agent had recognized in the celebrated doctor the young medical student who had once stood in his office. Now the doctor could easily have gone to law for the non-payment of his bill, but he was ashamed in front of the world and his patient, but most of all himself. So this once he renounced the large sum and crossed it from his records. But he wasn't quite able to cross it from his memory, and the older he got the more he regretted the excessive meanness of his youth.

The moral here is: it's never good to take advantage of someone, and any satisfaction from doing so will be short-lived. And note furthermore: one shouldn't think every person a fool, but excessive suspicion also brings harm – a little trust helps. And note finally: there is such a thing as excessive parsimony!

5 The Stolen Grey

This story happened not long ago in the Mark of Brandenburg.

A farmer, who had neither draught animals nor money, cast about to see where he might find a suitable horse. He found one finally in a fairly distant village, and one night he set off and stole the horse, a grey, from its stable.

While still in the forest, he dyed the horse black, and kept it in his own stable until the talk about the bold theft had died down. Then he took his black horse out of his stable and put him to work; he told his neighbour he had acquired him at a sale in the local county town.

One day, a stranger stood on his land, and stood there quite impassive, watching the farmer ploughing the stony ground. When the farmer had to stop to roll a large stone out of the furrow, the stranger lent him a hand, and said: 'That's a good team you've got there. But your black, it seems to me, is a little bit old for this sort of work.'

The farmer laughed and replied that the black was a young stallion not yet seven years old. The other disputed this, reached into the horse's mouth to check his age. Then he nodded and said: 'You were right. He's not yet seven years old – I can see it by the missing canine tooth. Just like my own grey, which was stolen.'

Thereupon neither man spoke for a while. The farmer was expecting accusations and had his avowals of innocence all ready. But no accusation followed; instead the other farmer finally said: 'Since you seem to like working with horses, you won't mind carrying some timber of mine out of the forest. Lord knows, I don't seem to be able to get around to it this year! I'm missing my grey, and am getting behindhand with everything. Well, at least you can help me with the timber. Here's the form for the wood!'

And the man was gone before the horse thief, the form for the timber in his hands, could say a word. He scratched his head, but finally decided to oblige the other fellow, happy to have got away so cheaply, because he was rather frightened of the law and of prison.

All spring and all summer he carted timber out of the forest with his horse for the other man, who seemed to own a lot there, and kept buying more. In the meantime, his own work was neglected, it had to be done roughly and hurriedly in the evenings and with a tired horse, and his business went downhill. Sometimes he felt like holding out against the other fellow, who had had much more from him than the worth of his grey, but in the manner of most thieves he was a coward, and didn't dare open his mouth.

Finally – it was autumn by now, and the last load of timber had been delivered to his yard – the robbed farmer said: 'There now, we're evens. Away with you and your black grey or your grey black and don't do it again!' The farmer went, but he could take no pleasure in his grey black, and sold it on as soon as an opportunity to do so presented itself.

The moral: however clever you think you are, someone else is always cleverer! And also: even the most profitable theft is bad business. It makes you poorer instead of richer, both inside and out.

6 The Three Drinking Companions

This is an old story, but it's always worth retelling; it's useful to everyone.

Once upon a time in Berlin, three men were sitting over strong drink and cards. They were all of them young and not long married, and hadn't yet given up their bachelor habit of meeting once a week for a drink. It had got late, and the landlord was making unmistakable signs of wanting to close, so they had to go, even though they would have liked to sit a while yet, wine-reddened faces and all.

As they went, one of them said he was in no particular hurry to get home. He wasn't looking forward to the reception he would get from his wife. The second chimed in: his wife too would have a go at him every time he stayed up late drinking, and for days afterwards would not only not have a kind word for him, but not even a decent meal.

The third laughed at their wine-loosened confessions, and sang the praises of his own wife, who never minded how drunk he was when he came home, was invariably sweet-natured and forgiving. And when his friends doubted that a wife could be so indulgent, he invited them to come home with him. Let them see for themselves what sort of welcome he had!

So they marched off to the home of this third of their group, who, on reaching his front door, wanted to show his drinking buddies how wild he could be: instead of ringing, he hammered at the door with his stick so hard that he smashed the little pane of glass.

In spite of that, his young wife opened the door with a happy smile, let him know how glad she was to see him home, and greeted his two companions as though there was nothing pleasanter for her than such drunken visits after midnight.

Her husband, however, roared at his wife to make them some coffee and bring them something to eat, and meanwhile set the schnapps bottle out on the table. That too the wife did with a good grace, while the husband went on drinking and bragging that he could do anything he liked without hearing an ill word. He didn't seem to notice how his two companions failed to keep pace with him, but sat in front of their glasses with long faces.

When the wife came back with coffee and a quickly assembled snack, the husband jumped up and scolded her for being a slow-coach, and shoved her out onto the corridor, then out of the flat altogether: she was to stand outside and wait till they were done, and not disturb them.

Now he thought he had shown his friends his full authority. But one of them stood up and called him a coarse brute, and too much was too much. If you were being scolded you had a right to stick up for yourself; but laying into pure love out of wanton excess struck him as low and cowardly. The other nodded in agreement, and the two of them left their friend, who was half-perplexed and half-embarrassed because the affair had ended so differently from how he had expected. Finally, shame prevailed in him, and from that hour forth he was never rough with his wife again, but learned to appreciate and be thankful for her love.

The second man was able to induce his young wife to give up her scolding, by desisting from drink. With the third man, though, everything remained as it was, the drinking and the scolding, either because his desire to better himself was just momentary, or because his wife was not willing to change.

Learn therefore: victories won by force are not lasting. Lasting victories are only obtained by love and patience and common sense. And learn this, wife: mere scolding just makes your husband's ears deaf; if you must scold, then scold lovingly!

7 *The Wise Shepherd*

This story happened a few years ago, in the province of Mecklenburg.

A recently married couple were deeply troubled when the wife, in the middle of the May of their love, began to sicken and pine. She would turn pale, then red, had less appetite than a sparrow, and often had melancholy moods – she had no idea why. After a time, they were afraid she was gravely ill from a lung condition.

Since they had neither friends nor relatives in the village, they didn't know where to go for help. She had never been to see a doctor in all her life, and she blushed furiously at the thought of undressing in front of a stranger. She felt her sickness as a kind of disgrace that she had kept concealed as long as possible from her husband, and wouldn't even admit it to her father, who lived in the house with them.

In her desperation, they hit upon a solution that struck them as promising. There was a wise shepherd whose praises were sung throughout the village and all over the surrounding countryside; he was said to be able to identify any illness from examining the patient's water, and to be able to prescribe draughts and tinctures against any malady. The husband was sent off to see the shepherd with a little bottle in his pocket.

He set off soon after breakfast, because he had a long way

ahead of him. As he approached his destination, he met others going to the same man, because this wise shepherd drew invalids as a flame draws moths. They all discussed their various afflictions and the great wisdom of the shepherd, which he had inherited from his father and his grandfather before him, and they didn't stop their talk when they came to the shepherd's house, which was most unshepherdlike, but stood there like a splendid villa. Chattering away among themselves, the fools failed to notice how relatives and helpers of the shepherd were among them, listening to their every word and quickly bearing it to the wise shepherd in support of his wisdom.

When our young husband finally stood trembling before the great man, and passed him his little flagon, he said with barely a look at it: 'This is the water of a woman in an interesting condition. There is nothing wrong with your wife, but she's going to have a baby!' With that he gave the young man a bottle containing some green syrup said to promote an easy birth, took ten marks for his trouble, and packed him off home.

How happy and relieved was the young husband when he trotted home. All his worries about a lung condition were taken from him, all he felt was pride that he was soon to be a father. His thoughts ran ahead of his feet, and he couldn't get back quickly enough to tell his wife the good news.

At last he was home. His wife was waiting for him at the garden gate, eager to hear his news. He took her inside, and proudly told her she need have no worries about anything, and she was having a baby. The young woman was just as delighted as he was, and they were just embracing in their happiness and good fortune when sudden loud laughter sundered them.

It was their respective father and father-in-law who, still laughing, said: 'And your wise shepherd was able to see that in the water in the little bottle?! Well, I'll admit it: I'd long been observing your secrecy, and was annoyed not to be taken into your confidence. So this morning I secretly switched the water in the bottle, and your wise shepherd managed to see that I, a man of sixty-eight, am shortly to bring a child into the world!' And the old man went off into another cackling peal of laughter.

The two young people had heard him, blushing and silent, but now the woman began to wail: she didn't know what the matter was with her, and maybe she did have a lung condition and wasn't long for this world. The father had to comfort her for a long time before she calmed down, and she didn't feel completely sure until she held her baby in her arms.

The moral: too much bashfulness can be foolish. And this too: not everyone whom people are pleased to call wise is wise.

8 *The Ladder in the Cherry Tree*

Here is another tale of the wise shepherd that happened a few years ago in Mecklenburg.

A farmer's son fell off his ladder while picking cherries, and broke his leg. The doctor from the local town set the leg in plaster; but because the farmer was a man who liked his little jokes, he took a bottle of his son's water and went with it to the wise shepherd, of whom it was said he could diagnose any illness by the water of the sufferer.

On the way he ran into acquaintances and told them blatheringly what a hard nut he was going to give the wise shepherd to crack, and how the little bottle would be a riddle for him.

When the farmer stood before the wise shepherd, the man had long ago been told what was coming. The shepherd pondered the little bottle thoughtfully for a long time, shook it, and finally said: 'This is the water of a young man who fell off a ladder while picking cherries, and has broken his leg.'

The farmer was greatly astonished by the wisdom of the shepherd, but wanted to make absolutely sure, and so he asked: 'Can you tell me, shepherd, how great was his fall?'

The wise shepherd gave the bottle another thoughtful shake, and then said: 'He fell from the eighth rung.'

'That's not true!' cried the farmer triumphantly. 'He fell from the fourteenth!'

'I see,' said the shepherd coolly. 'And did you bring me all the young man's water, farmer?'

'No,' the farmer had to admit. 'I had to leave some at home. It wouldn't all go in the bottle.'

'There!' said the shepherd. 'In the water you left at home are the remaining six rungs, which I can't see here.'

With that the farmer had to accept defeat, and he had all the laughers against him.

The moral: even a great rogue will find his master. And also: a quick-witted reply can achieve more than any amount of scheming.

9 The Parrot Feather

This story took place in the city of Berlin in our time.

A poor man in the city was thinking sorrowfully of the approaching sixth birthday of his young son, because he didn't know what he would give him as a present out of his small earnings, because everything was so expensive. He would like to send him something particularly nice, because the boy was living with his mother far away in the countryside, and he missed him very much.

Finally the man heard from colleagues at work that a certain shop was selling sweets at such and such a price. He also heard of a woman who knitted children's clothes for so and so much. He did his sums and did them again, and found that if he gave up smoking and generally tightened his belt, he would be able to send his son some sweets and knitted clothes in a few weeks.

In his pleasure, he sat down and wrote his son a birthday letter, announcing a parcel with presents. His mother was to read the letter to him. When the letter had been sent, he felt every bit as pleased with himself as though he had already mailed the parcel with the presents. Perhaps it was for that reason that he didn't economize as rigorously as he needed to, and that when he went to the shop the sweets had long since disappeared from sale, and when he went to the woman it turned out that she did indeed knit clothes, but only if she were given wool, which he didn't have.

Angrily the man went home. His wife had written to him that the boy was looking forward to the parcel from his father, and asking her ten times a day if it hadn't come yet. The man didn't know what to do. He had nothing to send, and didn't dare admit that he hadn't sent the parcel. Finally he calmed down: they would think the parcel had been lost in the post, and he spent his money on bread and cigarettes.

More time passed, and a letter came from his wife, asking whether he had really mailed the parcel. The boy was asking after it incessantly. The man didn't dare tell the truth; he wrote cursorily and not very nicely that of course the parcel had been sent. He wasn't responsible for the sluggish state of the post, and the parcel would arrive one day. Whereupon his wife replied that the boy was asking less often now, probably he had given up hope, and one day he would forget about it altogether.

The man felt ashamed when he read the letter, he for his part could certainly not forget the parcel. Shortly afterwards he found a gaudy parrot feather at his place of work. He picked it up and looked at it, and he saw that it wasn't a dyed feather for playing cowboys and Indians, but a genuine parrot feather, and he thought straight away how happy his son would be about this feather. At the most he would have seen pictures of parrots in picture books.

He hid the feather among his papers, and that evening he sat down and wrote his son another letter to go with the parrot feather. But while he was writing the letter, he went through a strange process. He had wanted to tell his son about parrots and what they look like and what they like to eat and how they learn to speak, but each time he wrote the German word *Papagei* he could hear his little son saying 'Papa'. He felt he was no longer a proper father deserving the name, but just someone unfairly laying claim to it: like a parrot who spouts things it doesn't understand at the wrong time for applause.

He left off the description of a parrot's life, and now told his son the truth about the parcel, and how it was almost entirely his own fault. Even though he could feel his confession humanizing the child's idolatrous view of its father, he felt a deep relief as he wrote, and this feeling only grew stronger when he sealed the envelope and posted the letter with the feather. He felt like someone who had been in prison for a long time who has finally decided to admit his guilt, and whose confession feels to him like an acquittal.

The actual acquittal came with the next letter from his wife, who told him how the boy's pleasure in the colourful feather had made him forget all about the parcel. The feather was so much nicer!

The moral: good intentions are not good actions. Don't plume yourself with intentions! And note also: no one is so strong that a sincere admission of guilt doesn't make him even stronger.

The Returning Soldier
(1946)

The sun warmed him on the bench in front of the house, the bench people sat on in the evenings after work, or on which the old people sat, who no longer worked anyway. And that's how it was with him, even though he was just twenty-six years old: he wasn't up to work any more, his father had chased him away!

How many times Erdmann Ziese had thought of the old house, the farm and the fields in the course of his long home-coming! He hadn't given much thought to his arm; he had got used to it being stiff at the elbow; something like that wouldn't keep him from working. Lots of men, lots and lots were a hundred times worse off than he was!

The doctors had examined his arm time and again; they saw no reason for the joint to be stiff. Every muscle and sinew seemed to be in good order. They had X-rayed it and irradiated it, they had strapped it to machines that were switched on and performed mechanical motions – he had screamed with pain. Yes, the arm would rather break than bend at the elbow; it was and remained stiff. The young assistant doctor had sent him away with the words: 'You'll be fine, Ziese, one day you'll be able to move your arm again. It'll happen just like that, and you won't even notice it.'

But that was just talk, to show how smart the doctors were with their skills. Erdmann Ziese wasn't impressed, and as I say, at that time he wasn't giving much thought to his arm anyway. Every day he was surrounded by dozens of cripples who were all a hundred times worse off than he was. He could work, of course he could, and he wanted to work. Work was the best thing in life. Work was maybe even better than Maria. Love was fine, love was terrific, nothing against it, to hold a girl, Maria, to hold her in your arms, to feel her soft lips, her breathing; dart a look up at her eyes which she kept closed when she was kissing – ah, lovely! Happiness and thrills, the sun and the stars, warmth, light – all that was what love was.

But you couldn't spend all day embracing and kissing. After a while you had enough, and you went and did your work, in which you took pleasure. Either you drew as straight a furrow as if someone had stood there with a ruler, or you chopped wood faster than anyone else. That was the way of it: life was work, or else it was nothing, and love came extra.

Out of some unclear feeling, perhaps simply because he was ashamed of it, Erdmann hadn't said anything about his crippled arm when he returned home. He hid his frailty so effectively that for a day and a half no one noticed it. But this morning, while chopping wood, his father had suddenly called out: 'What's the matter with your arm? Are you crippled or something?'

His father had put down his axe to watch his son chop and stack wood, and with his sharp eyes under the bushy brows had kept staring at his son's arm. Under such scrutiny, Erdmann worked clumsily. Finally, the father had jumped across to his son and had pulled and worked at the arm like a maniac. 'What's this?' he screamed. 'Can't you bend your arm? Not at all? Bloody brood, first they start a war that plunges the entire world into misfortune, and then they send us our children home crippled, just when we've begun to think they might be useful for a bit of work!'

He let go of his son's arm and glowered at him. Erdmann Ziese mumbled sheepishly: 'Oh, Papa, I can still do a lot of work with it. Think of the others . . .'

But his father cut him off. All his rage was levelled now against his son. 'Tell me what work you can do, cripple! You can eat soup and darn socks. Woman's work! I need a man on this farm – not something like you! Why didn't you tell me right away? Thought you could keep it hidden from your old man? Oh, get out of my sight! I don't want to see you out here again! I've got another useless mouth to feed!'

Those had been Father's words, hard, hurtful words, and unfair with it. Because Erdmann didn't feel as useless as his father made him out to be. But he couldn't hold it against him, Father was just like that. He had had to work too hard on the smallholding, surrounded by much larger farms that didn't even look after their soil properly and still seemed to flourish, while Father worked himself to the bone. That was what had made him so angry, the fact that the world was so unfair. It had to be the poor man who got his son back from the war with a bad arm! It was always the poor that had to bear the most! To a man like Father, that was enough to embitter him and make him unjust. No, there was nothing the matter with Father, even though he was difficult just now. But the son had other possibilities . . .

Erdmann sat nodding at these possibilities on the bench, filled his pipe, lit it and set off. He didn't want to sit around any longer on the lazy bench, playing the old-timer. Anyway, he needed to tell Maria how much his perspectives had worsened.

He had seen her go out with her people in the morning, the potato hoe over her shoulder, and accordingly he found her on her land above the lake, hoeing potatoes. Erdmann Ziese left himself time, first went across to his father's own potato patch and looked at it long and hard. Yes, they would have to hoe here soon as well. Suddenly a grievous feeling overcame him: he thought of how Father would have to hoe the ground alone with Mother, a big piece of field, and he surely wouldn't be finished till late at night. The son would be able to help, but he knew his father's obstinacy: he wouldn't allow him to touch a thing on the farm any more, his cripple of a son! With the Köllers, who had more potato land than the Zieses, there were five of them hoeing: father, mother, son and the two daughters, that was going some. Poor Father!

While Erdmann's thoughts were running like this, he had approached the Köllers' farm. He bade them the time of day, and quickly got into a conversation with the father about potatoes, and that it would soon be time for the hay harvest. They also discussed the rumour that the rich estate owners, who had all taken off into the West,* were now to have their land taken away from them, so that it might be distributed among the smaller farmers. But that was probably just talk; you could only hope that something so wonderful might come to pass, but it never would, not in this life!

'Ah, Erdmann, a poor man has to slave away the livelong day. There's never any joy for him. Poor he's born and poor he stays, and the rich hang onto their money. Well, you see it with your father every day. Now that he's got you back to help him, he could easily use another ten or twelve acres; as it is, he hardly has enough to feed his livestock through the winter. But it won't happen. Mark my words, Erdmann!'

Erdmann nodded his agreement. He didn't believe in land reform either, give or take the lame arm here and helping his father – no need for the Köllers to hear about that just yet, that only concerned his parents, and maybe Maria as well. But Maria, while the men were conversing, had stayed back with her hoe, and was now ten or twelve paces behind the others. Normally, old Köller might have given her a shout, but on this occasion he let her be. Nor was anything said when Erdmann didn't say anything, but hung back as well.

When he was alongside Maria, he hurriedly greeted her: 'Marie!' She nodded and smiled and said: 'It's good you're back,

---

* Millions of German civilians – not all of them rich, or landowners – fled west as the Russian forces advanced in 1945. Fallada, here writing for a Russian-managed East German publication, of course shows no sympathy for them. After 1989, estates were returned and modest compensation offered to the expropriated owners, where they could be found.

Erdmann, I'm pleased.' And he, out of his bitterness: 'Maybe it's not good at all, Marie, and you've no reason to be pleased! But we can talk about that tonight. Can you meet me at the old place at nine?' She just nodded and smiled, in spite of his grim reply. 'All right, then: nine o'clock!' he concluded and, more hurriedly: 'Get hoeing, Maria, I saw your father looking our way twice already!'

They parted, and when Erdmann turned back after three or four minutes, he saw the Köllers back in a line again: Maria had caught up. He nodded in satisfaction: that was the way a girl ought to be. Maria. Solid at work and true in love. But he would have to give up such thoughts. There was his wretched lame arm, a ridiculous appendage, like a turkey wing, good for nothing. It was because of that that his father said no, and the Köllers would say no, and probably Maria would say no as well. A girl in the prime of health, and a husband who was a cripple!

Among the others he hadn't been so conscious of it, but at home he felt it all the time, his father didn't have to treat him as contemptuously as he did the whole afternoon. He didn't say a word to his son, however much his wife implored him to do so, and when he saw Erdmann smoothing the dung heap, he simply took the pitchfork out of his hands and said: 'Stop that! I want no bodging on my farm!'

The afternoon was neverending, and Erdmann felt he was the most superfluous person in the world. Something had to happen, and he knew what: he would go to the city and find work there. Ideally with the post office, which was slowly up and running again. He would try and get a job as a rural postman; that would get him out of the city and into the fields, if he had to carry mail out to the villages. He could remember a postman with a bad arm, really with a withered arm. Muscular dystrophy, he said it was, but he had still been able to deliver letters! And there was nothing really wrong with his own arm, it was a healthy, strong man's arm, only it was a little stiff at the elbow – surely they would give him a job at the post office with that. And if they didn't, well, he was game for anything, he wasn't going to idle around on the farm and see his father's worried, angry face everywhere!

Over such thoughts, it did finally get to be evening, and Erdmann set off for the old beech tree on the lake, which was where they had met from the earliest times they were in love. They had met up there and only there during the brief furloughs he got in wartime, and even before the war, when they were still kids practically, and felt the first stirrings of love in their hearts. Back then they just sat quietly side by side, neither of them saying a word, and if one happened to brush against the other's hand, they would both tremble with a sudden blissful alarm. Later on in the war, he had taken her firmly in his arms, as though he meant never to let her go, never leave her, and he had never had enough of her kisses.

This time it was his resolve to talk to her seriously: it would be tantamount to theft if he accepted her tenderness without putting her in the picture. But she was there before him, and slipped easily into his arms, and when he felt her searching lips at his mouth, there was no hanging back possible, and he kissed her more hungrily than ever. 'Marie, my sweet Marie!' And: 'Erdmann! I can't believe you're back with me! I want to keep you for ever and ever!' And silence and more kisses.

Finally, however, once their immediate need was satisfied, they had sat down at the foot of the beech, the protectress of their love, and he had told her everything, about his arm and his angry father, and then of his decision to go into the city to try and become a postman.

She listened to it all practically in silence, only she had asked to see his arm, and how it really was stiff, and she couldn't bend it. But when he said: 'You can see for yourself, Marie, we have to break up. Your parents won't have it, and you're not made for a life in the city!' then she replied quickly and almost angrily: how could he talk like that! That showed he didn't love her properly, if he could give her up as easily as that. He just needed to show a bit of patience, his father would see sense eventually, and see that even with a lame arm he could do useful work. And if he still wanted to move to the city, that didn't bother her either. They would surely be able to rent a bit of land for a garden, and she would grow potatoes, so that she wouldn't be without her familiar work.

To this he objected that a marriage contracted against the wishes of both sets of parents would always oppress them, that she really wasn't cut out for city life – and so they got into an ever more heated quarrel. She was adamant that she didn't want to let him go, and he kept repeating that he was leaving this very night, and she shouldn't stand in his way. In between, they kept kissing – almost in spite of themselves – and probably they would have gone on like that all night if he hadn't put his foot down and said: 'All right, Marie, that's enough. I'm sticking to what I told you. I'm going to go the city, and we won't see each other again.'

With those words he slipped out of her arms, and stood apart from her, breathing hard, looking for her face in the dark, and waiting apprehensively for whatever she would say back to him.

In the end all she said was: 'Well, then kiss me goodbye, Erdmann!'

Happily he drew her powerfully into his arms and kissed her as he had never kissed her before, slowly and tenderly, as the sweetest and loveliest thing he had in all the world. Then – in the middle of kissing – he suddenly let her go, so that she almost fell over. In fright she uttered a little cry, but he ignored it, and just stood there, flexing his arm. He remembered the young assistant doctor who had told him: 'You won't even notice, but all at once you'll be able to move your arm!'

So that had been more than cheap words of comfort. Because when he was holding his sweetheart, he had suddenly noticed that she was in his arms, and he could move both his arms, perhaps had done for some time, without even noticing! He had held Maria tight, and his arm hadn't been stiff, and she hadn't noticed it either!

He stood there in bewilderment, flexing his arm this way and that, almost oblivious of Maria. He pulled down a beech twig, bent it and snapped it off, then he swished it through the air, and his arm behaved itself. His arm was all right again, he was no longer a cripple!

In the deep feeling of relief with which Erdmann Ziese made his discovery, there was mingled a sense of shame that he had been chosen by good fortune. He thought of his many comrades, the amputees, who would never mend as he had. What had he done to earn such luck? But then he thought that he had been prepared to go to the city, and leave his father's farm, and leave Maria, without a complaint. And it seemed to him that there must be some sort of solution for everyone, some sort of outcome, maybe not always a Maria, who insisted on staying with him, but some sort of contentment that lay in the tolerance of fate.

That thought diminished his sense of shame. Suddenly he saw Maria, standing in front of him in bewilderment, and he cried: 'My arm, see my arm! When I hugged you close, my arm was cured! Oh, Marie, how happy I am now that I can work on the farm, never to leave your side.'

And he threw down his beech twig, and pulled her to him again.

It was almost getting light when Erdmann finally returned to his parents' house. But it was a completely new Erdmann who came home: this was the first real homecoming! He knocked loudly on his parents' bedroom door, walked in without hesitating, switched the light on and went over to their bed. There he stood, while they – the one angry again, the other fearful – eyed him, and he called out: 'I won't be chased off the farm! I don't want to lead a scrounger's life! I want to work, just as Father does, but even harder, that's what I want!' And with each sentence he smashed his fist against the frame of the bed, so that it creaked and groaned.

The father supposed his son must be drunk, and was about to shout at him in renewed fury, when Erdmann went on: 'Yes, when there's something wrong, you see that right away, Father! But you haven't noticed that my arm's well again! And who made it well? It was Maria Köller! And we're getting married as soon as ever we can, whether you like it or not!'

With that he hit their bedframe once more, hard, and stalked out of the bedroom laughing happily, to lie down for a short nap before morning. In spite of the disturbance to their rest, the two oldsters were no less happy than their son, and all morning they tiptoed around their house, smiled to each other and said: 'Let him sleep, Erdmann! He'll sleep himself well! Thanks be to God that he came home in one piece! We've been lucky this once!'

That they would shortly be lucky again, when it came to the redistribution of the big estates, that was something they admittedly didn't yet know.

The Old Flame
(1946)

You ask me why I'm sitting here, an old lonely and embittered bachelor? Couldn't I have got myself a wife, like other men? And why is there no gossip about me?

Of course I could have married, and I was once the subject of gossip too. It's so long ago now that it's almost not true any more; the only one who knows about it still is me, and maybe Ria. But I don't think she remembers; I think she'll have forgotten long ago.

I called her Ria, that was my pet name for her. Her real name was Erika von Schütz, and her father owned a large estate in the east. They were both haughty characters, I often saw father and daughter riding past me, but they never returned the greeting of their poor inspector, who was fed on groats and skim milk in the officials' house, while they got through menus of God knows how many courses. I didn't mind them being haughty and seeing through me; at that time you took it for granted that people came in two kinds, rich and poor, and that being poor was actually a disgrace.

It's even possible I revered Erika von Schütz doubly on account of her haughtiness, she whom I thought of as Ria, and who made my heart skip a beat when I saw her from a distance. She seemed so utterly beyond me. Later on, after I'd been working on the estate for some time, she would sometimes use me as an errand boy: I had to walk her horse up and down, or deliver a note to a certain gentleman on another estate, and once I even had to stand guard outside the gazebo when she was in there with a gentleman, in case her father surprised them.

When she was forced to talk to me on such occasions, her face

226

took on such a disdainful, almost nauseated expression it was as though she was looking at a spider or some other foul creature. And for all that, I loved her – loved her with the whole force of my hot young heart, and each one of her contemptuously uttered words sounded like exquisite music in my ears. Once, on one such occasion, she surprisingly said to me: 'Do you know you're actually quite a presentable fellow, considering, Wrede?' And straight after that: 'But the maids will have told you that often enough! Now scram, get lost, stop staring at me! And I want a reply by four o'clock, have you got that?!'

And she swung her horse around so abruptly that its hindquarters almost knocked me over, and cantered off down a narrow path through the undergrowth, with the twigs whistling about her ears, but still scorning to bend her neck! This, by the way, was the only time she addressed me in any personal way, gave me to understand she had ever seen my face before. Otherwise she always acted as though she couldn't quite place me or remember my name. In anyone else such a pretence would have seemed foolish, but in her it seemed charming – mind you, I was helplessly in love with her. Often I would go to the stables late at night and bring her horse a piece of bread or some sugar, so as to do something for her every day.

One day I had a falling-out with her father, Herr Valdemar von Schütz, or rather, he fell out with me. I was said to have overpaid one of his workmen. He sacked me on the spot, he barely allowed me to spend the night on the estate. I was able to show him a moment later that he'd made a mistake, but he still thought it better we kept with the immediate dismissal.

'What I've once said holds. I don't care to have people working for me for a long time anyway; they get used to me, and that's no good. It's a new broom that sweeps properly. You can take the rest of your month's wage out of petty cash.' And with that he left me.

I was rather downcast; I hadn't any savings, and at that time jobs in the country were few and far between. When Ria phoned me shortly after, and asked me to run an errand for her in the park, I answered her insolently that I had no time for that. I had to close the books and pack my things, I was leaving! With that I hung up, and was happy for the first time to have shown her a bit of willpower, and not always have been her skivvy!

She didn't leave me feeling triumphant for long; fifteen minutes later she was in my room, watching my packing contemptuously, and sat down on the window seat. She tossed me a cigarette, lit another one, and said with infinite arrogance: 'What's got into you, Wrede? When I say go somewhere, you go, and when I say stay, you stay! So you're staying and you'll continue to be my go-between!' And she gave me a sneering smile.

Face to face with her like that, my courage almost disappeared; but I was able to tell her that it was difficult for me to obey both her father and herself. He had given me the sack, while she was telling me to stay!

'I see!' she said. 'Herr von Schütz was pleased to dismiss you? And the reason? Bound to be something involving a girl!'

I told her the reason.

'Is that it?' she asked, and looked at me thoughtfully. 'Of course it's difficult for you to find a way of going and staying. But not for me. I want you to be in the park at ten tonight, in the usual place, and have your case with you. It's possible I'll know of a post for you!'

I stammered a few words of thanks. But she cut me off. 'Bah!' she cried. 'Haven't you got ears? I said it's possible. It's also possible I'll leave you standing in the park all night, never to see me again. So I would say my goodbyes if I were you, to your girl-friends too!'

With those words her face took on the expression of disgust again. I told her I didn't have any, and that that was the truth. Ever since I first saw Ria, I had eyes for no other woman, all others might as well not exist so far as I was concerned. But she wasn't listening. She walked out of my room as if I didn't exist – yes, she brushed so close past me, I was forced to take a hurried step back. Then I was left to pack again on my own. I stubbed out the cigarette she had started and then tossed and put it in my wallet like a holy relic.

Of course I was careful not to say goodbye to anyone – it would have given rise to questions, what was I doing so late. At ten o'clock I was at the park, prepared to wait up half or even all the night. But luckily it wasn't that bad. I didn't see her in person, but her maid, an elderly, rather sharp-tongued woman, came along and led me into the manor house. On the ground floor there seemed to be a party in progress, all the windows were lit up. I could hear music and laughter, the bright clinking of glasses. I was taken up the dimly lit service staircase into the side wing of the first floor, into a little storage room, where discarded and broken furniture was left to gather dust. But I wasn't too disappointed by that, because I knew she lived in the same wing. I was braced for a long wait, but I was at least sure I would see her tonight. And anyway: even being under the same roof with her made me happy.

I sat for hours in that junk room, and dreamed of the bliss of seeing her come through the door. From time to time I went up to the window and looked out at the park at night. The nearest trees were lit from the light coming from the ground-floor rooms; the party was still in progress. But up in the sky, the stars had a festive glitter of their own, an everlasting light over us unfortunates. In these hours of waiting I learned what it meant to love. I lived in this waiting, which made me happy. I was expecting nothing but a few arrogant words and an errand, maybe with an address where I might apply for a new job.

But all that didn't concern me really. I was with her, in the same building, she would come to me in this very room! Oh, how lovely it is to be young and willing to love without the tormenting need to possess! Today I am an old man who has achieved much in his life, but if you ask me when I was happiest, my answer would be: during those hours of waiting in the manor house, when I hovered over my love as weightlessly as a water lily in a pond!

Finally, I fell asleep waiting, even youth needs a rest sometimes. I awoke to feel someone toying with my hair. An incredible feeling of bliss came over me. I sat up on the old chaise and stared at Ria in wonder. She was wearing a low-cut evening gown, her dazzling white bust and shoulders blinded me as though I had stared at the sun.

'Ah, Werner, Werner,' said Ria, with her fingers still in my hair. 'It's almost morning, and instead of waiting for me, you're asleep. I thought at least you truly loved me!'

I was so confused that I could think of nothing to say. She put both her arms around me and kissed me on the lips. She pulled me against her heaving bust, I smelled her sweet scent, under her kiss my senses almost perished . . . We clasped each other like two people drowning in the water, only accelerating their end. The waters of love closed over our heads!

After a while, she said: 'Come, let's eat!'

She took me to her bedroom. A table had been set for two, there was a bottle of wine in an ice bucket. Suddenly I was no longer a poor field inspector on skim milk groats, I was a great man. But it felt perfectly natural, nothing could surprise me really, after the great miracle of her loving me!

'Tuck in, Werner!' she said. 'No, you have to bump glasses with the bride first! The way you're looking at me – didn't you know I was getting engaged tonight?'

'Is it —?' I asked, and named the man I had taken so many letters to.

'No!' she shook her head. 'It's someone else. Someone you don't know. But it doesn't matter who it is – the hell with him!' And with that she hurled her glass against the mirror, sending the shards flying. 'Here's to the two of us – and *après nous le déluge!*'

So began the charmed days and nights in which I thought I was living in a dream or fairy story. Ria was utterly different, she seemed to live for me. No arrogant words any more, no wounding remarks. By day she was out a lot, often coming back only for a brief moment, to wake me with a kiss from my slumbers or dreams, and then running out again. Or we spent a quarter of an hour talking, never about our daily life, but about blessed South Sea islands, a *Robinsonade* for the pair of us, an end of the world that only we had survived.

We were the only two people in the world, and apart from her I only saw her elderly, sharp-tongued maid, who never said a word to me, but who tidied the room and ignored me. How long did our good fortune last? How would I know, my friend, I didn't count the days, everything seemed to merge into one until I had her in my arms again. A week, two weeks – does the summer count its roses? Oh, but I was happy, superhumanly happy. It was enough for a whole lifetime, as you see; I still rave about it like a schoolboy, even in spite of the bad ending!

One day, when I was crossing the landing to the bathroom, I suddenly saw Herr Valdemar von Schütz in front of me. I had stopped thinking of him; presumably he too would have forgotten all about me. For a moment he stood there like a goose in a thunderstorm, then in accordance with his nature he started shouting and screaming – probably he had seen me come out of his daughter's room. He waved his riding crop under my nose.

But straight away the elderly maid was on the scene. She begged him not to do anything to me. She freely admitted she had smuggled me into the manor house as her lover. She was only human, and it wouldn't happen again. Just so long as he didn't do anything to me, I would leave immediately . . .

I must admit, she was a remarkable old creature, unhesitatingly taking the fall for her mistress. She had to push her sentences into the short intervals of his yelling, but she did it very deftly. Very canny too was her repeated insistence that he not do anything to hurt me! That directed him towards the best way of venting his rage. A fiendishly clever woman. At last Herr von Schütz got the message. He drew the riding crop across my face in a slashing blow, so that the skin seemed to explode. Following that first blow came many others: a man discovers his appetite while eating. I was horsewhipped out of the house in best style. I took to my heels. He gave chase, and the whip whistled on my back.

Finally I got out of the house. On the terrace were the dogs, loafing. He went on whipping me, and sicced them onto me with a sharp hiss. Finally he stood and watched as I tried to fight them off with kicks and oaths, while trying to find my way out of the park. It must have been an extremely amusing sight, me trying to keep six or eight dogs at bay. There was one little dachshund in particular who kept getting under my guard and nipping me on the legs.

Herr von Schütz's humour was finally stirred too, and he started laughing loudly. And suddenly standing next to him was Ria, my beloved Ria who an hour or two before had lain in my arms, and now she was laughing, laughing heartily and uncomplicatedly at her lover in distress, yes, she was even siccing the dogs onto me: 'Gettim, Waldmann! Give it to him, Harras! Oh, poor Rex, that was a mean kick!'

And then she was laughing again. Her laugh was still ringing in my ears as I stood in the kitchen of one of the estate workers, cooling my cut and burning face in a wet cloth. I still had it in my ears weeks and months later; I can still hear it now we are both old, Ria and I.

Yes, she is still alive, as I happen to know. But I doubt if she ever thinks of her little interlude with Field Inspector Wrede. Perhaps her whole life is put together from such episodes. There are many women who never have a great experience, because they give themselves to a series of shifting trivialities.

I could have seen her later, Ria. It would only have taken a little help from my side, an invitation from an acquaintance, and we would have faced each other again: mistress and slave. But what would have been the point? I'm not one to poke around in old ashy embers in the hope of getting them to flame up again. Our fire won't ever burn as it did in our younger days. Anyway: I once experienced a great joy, everything subsequent can only be lesser. You can only love like that once in your life, so selflessly, so regardless of ego!

And further: you will admit, my friend, the experience was rather unsettling. For all the happiness I enjoyed, I was left with a deep suspicion of women. I was never able to persuade myself to place my heart in the hands of one of the moody, whimsical creatures again. So I remained alone, an old and lonely bachelor with a single experience of love in the course of a long life. Perhaps you won't understand me, but – it's the way I am! No one can escape their own skin – or wants to.

*

The speaker looked pensively at his glass of wine, raised it, and said: 'You were marvellous, Ria! Like a goddess you came down from the clouds to the delectation of a poor mortal! Then you returned to your Olympus!' He emptied his glass and threw it at the mirror: the shards fell tinkling to the ground. 'The hell with women!' he said.

Short Treatise on the Joys of Morphinism
(1925–30)

1

All of this happened in that first terrible time in Berlin when I was drowning in morphine.*

Things had gone okay for me for a few weeks, I had collared a big supply of benzene, which was the name we gave the stuff among ourselves, and that relieved me of the addict's worst fear, the fear of running out of drug. Then, as my supply dwindled away, my rate of consumption increased; what I had in mind, I suppose, was for once getting really full, with no half-measures, and then – a clean break. Sometime a different life would have to begin, and if I had some proper momentum I'd be able to see myself through the sudden stop. At least, I'd heard of others who had managed that way.

But when I woke up on the designated morning, staring into the void, I knew I had to have morphine at any price. My whole body was painfully jittery, my hands shook, I was full of a crazy thirst, not just in my mouth and throat, but in every cell of my body.

I picked up the telephone and called Wolf. I wanted to catch him off-guard, so, with a faltering voice, I croaked out: 'Have you got any benzene? Hurry! I'm dying!'

---

* An apt and suggestive echo of the beginning of Knut Hamsun's great first novel *Hunger* (1880), to which I have adapted my beginning. It goes (in Robert Bly's 1967 translation): 'All of this happened while I was walking around starving in Christiania – that strange city no one escapes from until it has left its mark on him . . .' The events Fallada describes happened – *más o menos* – in early 1919.

And fell back onto the pillows, groaning. A deep and solemn feeling of relief, an anticipation of the enjoyment to come, took the edge off my suffering: Wolf would come by car, I have the syringe in my hand – I can already feel the stab of the needle, and then life will be beautiful again.

The telephone trilled, and I heard Wolf saying: 'Why did you hang up so fast? I can't bring you any benzene, I haven't got any myself. I was going to go hunting for some.'

'One injection, Wolf, just one injection, otherwise I'm going to die.'

'But I told you I'm out.'

'You've got some left. I know you have.'

'I swear I don't.'

'I can tell by your voice that you've just had some. You sound full.'

'Last night at one a.m. was the last time.'

'Well, I've had none since eleven. Hurry, Wolf.'

'But it's no good. Tell you what, why don't you come with me. I've got a reliable pharmacy. Take a cab, we'll meet at the Alex* at nine.'

'And you're not going to stiff me? Swear!'

'Don't be silly, Hans! Nine o'clock at the Alex.'

I get up very slowly, getting dressed is incredibly hard, my joints are quivery and weak, the feeling of assurance is gone, my body doesn't believe I'm going to be able to resupply it.

I happen to look at the calendar, and see that today's an ill-starred day. That makes me sit down in my chair and have a little cry to myself. I'm suffering so badly, and I can sense I'm going to suffer much worse in the course of the day, and I feel so weak. Why can't I just die! But I've known the answer to that for a long time, it's because I'm too much of a coward, I'll have to

---

* The Alexanderplatz, heart of the eastern part of Berlin.

stick it out, I've got no alternative but to lie there prostrated and whimpering in front of fate, and beg it not to hurt me.

Then my landlady comes along and says something comforting to me, but I don't interrupt my crying for her, I just wave her away. But she's still talking, gradually I understand I'm being told that I burned holes in my bed last night again with cigarettes. I hand her some money, and since she leaves me alone, it must have been enough.

But I still don't go, even though it's nearly nine o'clock, I stare at the coffee I poured myself, and I think: caffeine is a poison that stimulates the heart. There are plenty of instances of people killing themselves with coffee, hundreds and thousands of them. Caffeine is a deadly poison, maybe almost as deadly as morphine. Why didn't it ever occur to me before: coffee is my friend!

And I gulp down one, two cups. I sit there for a minute, staring into space, and wait. I go on trying to kid myself, even though I know I've been deliberately trying to pull the wool over my eyes. Inevitably, my stomach refuses to keep even that watery coffee down. I can feel my whole body shake and a cold sweat come over me, I need to get up, I am shaken with cramps, and then sour bursts of bile. 'I'm going to die,' I whisper to myself, and stare into space.

A little later I've recovered to the degree that I can get up and take a few steps, and then I finish washing, go out on the street and hail a cab. Wolf's never early anyway.

2

I'm lucky, he's still waiting. I can see right away that he's hungry too, his pupils are dilated, his cheeks are sunken and his nose has some extra definition.

It turns out that he hasn't yet faked the prescriptions he needs to take to the pharmacy. Even though he was as jumpy as me, he couldn't settle to it at home. But he has his little valise with him and can show up in the pharmacy with a reasonable impersonation of a morphine addict just passing through the city on his way to a sanatorium. He's been round the block a few times, he knows better than to forge Berlin prescriptions that can be checked with a simple phone call.

We go into a post office, where we fill out a dozen prescriptions. We review the handwriting, and throw out three prescriptions that strike us as insufficiently doctorly-illegible.

Then we agree on the part of town where we're going to hunt. As Wolf's tame pharmacy is in the East, it makes sense to hunt there, even though the West in general has more going for it. The better-off class of person who lives in the West is more likely to be able to fund an expensive vice like morphinism than the working people in the East. The pharmacies in the West are already adjusting to their clientele.

We go by cab. Wolf has the driver pull over a little way from the nearest pharmacy and he hobbles off, looking sick and wretched. I lean back in the upholstery. Wolf has written Solution, and it'll take him fifteen minutes.

So I'll have benzene in fifteen minutes! High time too, my body is feeling weaker and weaker, I have these terrible pains in my stomach, which is crying out for its drug. I lean back, I shut my eyes, I try to think about how lovely it will be to have the needle in fifteen minutes. A matter of minutes, a few tiny tiny instants, really no time at all, and a deep and holy peace will flow into my joints, and life will be beautiful, and I will be able to dream about palaces and girls. They will all be mine, the most beautiful girls in the world, I'll just have to flash them a smile . . . Morphine makes it possible, I just close my eyes, and the whole world belongs to me.

What's keeping Wolf? How can it take them so long to brew up this bit of stuff? But I'm not going to complain, it's a good sign that he's not back right away, it means they really are making up the medicine. If he's back fast, it can only mean they've rejected the prescription. I'm going to have morphine in a minute! And I lay the syringe on the seat next to me, to have it ready.

Here's Wolf now. I can tell at a glance he hasn't got it. He tells the driver the next address, sits down next to me and shuts his eyes, and I notice he's panting, wiping the sweat off his brow with his hand.

'They're no human beings in there, they're beasts, they're filth! How can they inflict such suffering on innocent people? I had to plead with them not to call the cops.'

'I thought this was a tame pharmacy?'

'The old apothecary wasn't there, there was one of those young chaps instead. They're all so sharp they cut themselves, you know the type.'

'I can't keep going much longer, Wolf. Shouldn't we maybe call it quits, and check ourselves into an institution?'

'Do you think they'll give you any? You'll wind up in a padded cell and left to scream to your heart's content. Bobby hanged himself eight times one night from his bed-leg; in the end the warders left him till he was almost blue, so that it would take him a bit longer to get his strength up to do it again. But they still didn't give him any.'

The cab stops. Wolf tries again. While he's gone, I resolve to come off morphine by myself. If I am to rely on Wolf and his pharmacies, I'll never get my eight fixes a day.* I'll just have to lessen my dose, I can manage that. Only now, I need two or three fixes right off, just to get good and full.

Wolf is back already, gives the next address, and we set off.

'Nothing?'

'Nothing!'

It's looking bleak. And outside people are running around with their heads full of plans, looking forward to stuff, and there are flowers and girls and books and theatres. All of it doesn't exist

* Fallada wrote '80' in figures.

for me. I'm thinking that Berlin has hundreds of pharmacies, and every one of them has stacks of morphine, and I'm not getting any of it. I'm suffering, even though it would be so easy to make me happy, the pharmacist has only to turn a key . . . I don't mind paying, I'm happy to give him all the money I have.

Wolf moves on.

Suddenly it occurs to me that this repeated parking next to pharmacies must be making the driver wonder. What if he tells the police? I start a conversation with him, give him some rigmarole about the two of us being not exactly dentists but sort of dental technicians. And as such we aren't supplied with anaesthetics for pain-free extractions for our patients, we get prescriptions from dentists, and these prescriptions cost money. That's why we're going into all these pharmacies . . .

The driver keeps saying, yes, I see, and nodding his head. But there's something uncertain about his smile, so I remain suspicious of him and resolve to pay him off as soon as we can find a moment, only not right away because then he'll just go to the nearest policeman.

3

Wolf is back. 'Lose the car.'

My heart starts to beat. 'Did you get some then?'

'Lose the car.'

I pay the driver, and give him a ridiculous tip. Then: 'Have you got the stuff?'

'Like fun! Today's such a rotten fucked-up day none of these bastards is going to accept my prescription. We'd better go about it differently. I'll keep on with the pharmacies, and you go to a doctor and see if you can't steal some prescription forms.'

'Sorry, I can't do that. In my present state any doctor can tell at a glance that I'm a morphinist.'

'Well, let him. We just need the prescription forms.'

'And what will we do with them? If it says morphine, they just ring the doctor.'

'Then we'll take the midday train to Leipzig. Just be sure to take a good stack, enough to see us through a couple of weeks.'

'Okay, I'll give it a go. And where do we meet?'

'One o'clock at the Pschorr beer hall.'

'What if you get lucky before that?'

'I'll try and hook up with you sooner.'

'All right, then!'

'See you!'

I head off. It's not my first shot at a tour like this. I'm better at this game than Wolf because I am better-dressed and look more trustworthy. But today I'm in a pathetic state. I can't seem to walk properly; though I keep wiping my hands on my handkerchief, a minute later they're running with sweat again; and I have to yawn incessantly. This isn't going to work, I can tell already.

Passing a bar, I think a drink or two might help to settle me. But after one glass I need to get out, like before with the coffee my stomach is mutinying, I can't seem to keep anything down. Then I'm sitting on the grim bog, crying. As soon as I've recovered a little, I head off again.

The first doctor's I come to, the waiting room is chock-a-block. Panel-doctor, to make matters worse. They issue so few prescriptions to private patients that they usually keep the block of them inside their desks. I decide not even to try, and sneak out.

On the stairs I feel so ill, I need to sit down. I can't go on. I decide to lie here and wait for someone to find me and take me to the doctor. Who, out of sympathy, will give me an injection. At least that way I'll get faster service than if I sit in the waiting room for my turn.

Someone is coming up the stairs. I hurriedly get up, pass him, and go out onto the street. A few doors along I see another doctor's plate and I go up. He's not open for business for another fifteen minutes, fine, I'll go in and wait. I sit there all alone, looking through his magazines.

Suddenly I get an idea. I stand up and press my ear to the surgery door. Nothing. Very slowly I turn the doorknob, the door opens a crack, I peep in and I don't see anyone. Inch by inch I open the door, I creep on tiptoe into the surgery. There's the desk, and there in that wooden tray . . . I'm already reaching out my hand when I think I hear a noise, and I leap back into the waiting room and sit down.

No further noise, no one comes in, it was a mistake. But now I'm too demoralized to chance it a second time, I sit there idly, unable to do anything. The minutes pass, I could have emptied the desk, I could have had my pick of his medicine cupboard, but I don't dare; today just is an unlucky day.

Just keep still, Hans, and take your medicine.

4

The doctor half-opens the door and asks me in. I get up, enter the surgery, bow and give him my name. Suddenly all my hesitation and feebleness are fallen from me, I'm no longer a slimy dissolute something or other at the end of my rope, but a calm man of the world, expressing himself succinctly and effectively.

I know I'm making an excellent impression. I smile, I use a racy expression with the assuredness of someone in full control of his language, I throw in a little gesture and cross my legs to show off my silk socks.

The doctor sits opposite and keeps his eyes riveted on me.

I get to the point. I am just passing through Berlin and have a very painful abscess on my arm, would the Medical Councillor perhaps have the goodness to examine it, and see if it might be possible to lance it?

The doctor asks me to take my jacket off. I show him the

swollen, purple place on the inside of my forearm where pus is seething under the skin, ringed by dozens of puncture marks, from angry pink to brownish and almost healed.

He says: 'Are you a morphinist?'

'Used to be, Medical Councillor! Used to be! I'm in the withdrawal phase. The worst is behind me, Medical Councillor. Nine-tenths better.'

'Good. Very well, then I'll operate.'

Just that. Not another word. My serenity vanishes, I stand there pale and shaking, afraid of the knife which I know is going to hurt. The doctor has his back to me, is looking in a glass case for scalpel, pincers, swabs . . . I take one large soundless step on the carpet, my fingertips brush against paper, and –

'Be a good fellow, and just leave them where they are,' the doctor says curtly.

I'm reeling. I can see the city before my eyes, rushing by, where I am so all alone, victim to a despair that is like nothing else. I see the streets full of people going places, going to other people, only I am abandoned and washed up. A sob wells in my throat, forces my mouth open.

Suddenly my face is running with tears. I'm wailing: 'What shall I do? Oh, Medical Councillor, please can't you help me out, just one little jab?'

He's at my side, grasping my shoulder, he leads me back to the chair, he lays his hand across my forehead. 'Calm down, calm down, sir, we'll talk everything over. Help is at hand.'

My heart surges with gratitude, in a few seconds I will be released from this nameless torment and will receive my injection. The words tumble over one another, life is already getting easier, I will break myself of the habit, this will be my last, my very last injection, followed by no more. I swear. 'Can I have it now, please, right away? But it will have to be three per cent solution, and five mls, otherwise it won't have any effect.'

'I'm not giving you an injection. You have to get to the point where this life becomes so unendurable for you that you freely decide to institutionalize yourself.'

'I'll kill myself first.'

'No you won't. No morphinist will kill himself, except indirectly or inadvertently by overdose. He'd rather go through the most atrocious sufferings than give up the smallest chance of getting another injection. No, you won't kill yourself. But it's high time for you to go to an institution, if it's not already too late. Do you have money?'

'A little.'

'Enough to afford treatment in a private clinic?'

'Yes! But they won't give me any morphine there either!'

'You'll get some to start off with, then gradually less while they wean you onto something else, tranquillizers. Then one day you'll take a deep breath, and you'll be over it.'

I picture the bed-leg where the poor wretch kept trying to hang himself. The doctor's a canny bastard all right, trying to talk me into going, and then once I'm inside none of what he said will come to pass.

'Well,' says the doctor, 'what will you do, decide! If you agree to let me take you to a clinic right away, then I'll give you an injection first. Well?'

I look away, defeated. Yes, I will undertake to go through these sufferings, I agree to be cured. I nod my consent.

The doctor continues: 'It's important you understand I won't let myself be duped. After giving you the injection, I'll keep you locked up in the waiting room while I get myself ready. I'm not going to let you out of my sight, is that understood?'

Once more, I nod. All I'm thinking about is the injection which I'm going to get now, now . . . And then we get into some argy-bargy about the dose, which goes on for fully fifteen minutes, and in which we both lose our tempers. In the end, of course, the doctor comes out on top, and I am to get just two mls of three per cent solution.

He goes over to a cupboard, unlocks it and prepares the injection. I follow him, look over his shoulder at the labels on the ampoules to be certain I'm not going to be rooked. Then I sit down to wait. He injects me.

And now . . . I quickly get up, go into the waiting room and lie down on a sofa. I hear him lock the doors.

5

Ah . . .

There . . .

There it is again. Ain't life beautiful? A gentle, happy stream flows through my joints, in its wash all my nerves gently bob about like water plants in a clear lake. I see rose petals. And again I can appreciate the beauty of a single small tree in a backyard. Those petals again. Are those church bells? Yes, life is mild and holy. Those endless sunny Sundays when I used to work, before I decided I preferred death instead. Getting up at the crack of dawn, seeing the sun on the curtains and the sun in the leaves, and hearing bells and birdsong. Then the sound of a whistle, and across the little square with the feathery acacia trees comes my girl in her Sunday best. I'm thinking about you too, sweetheart, long-lost sweetheart, I have a new sweetheart, she's called Morphine. She's angry with me, she makes my life a misery, but she also rewards me more than I can fathom.

How limited you used to be, woman. I always reached past you and over you, I thought I'd reached you, but actually I was somewhere completely different . . . This girl, though, she gets under my skin. She fills my brain with clear, candescent light. I know now that everything is vanity, and the only reason I remain alive is for her intoxication. She lives inside me, I'm no longer a primitive beast so dependent on sex that even in exhaustion it thrashes about unappeased and wild in its yearning for the other, no, I'm sophisticated, man and woman in one, and the mystical union is celebrated at the point of a needle, there is my flawless beloved and my consummate lover, they're celebrating Whitsun together somewhere under the canopy of my scalp.

I feel like reading, I think I'll read the stupidest nonsense I can find in this doctor's waiting room, and a new dazzling sense will illuminate the high-flown bluestocking twaddle, one advertisement will smell like flowers, and in another I think I'll find the taste of fresh bread that my stomach can no longer . . . stomach. I feel like reading.

I open a book. There's a flyleaf, a smooth, white flyleaf, and that gives me pause: the cautious doctor has rubber-stamped his name, address and phone number on this white flyleaf. Don't worry, Mr Medical Councillor, it's not that I'm about to steal your book, I would just like to keep your flyleaf in my pocket for a keepsake. Because once it's been nicely trimmed by a good pair of scissors, it'll be indistinguishable from one of those long-desired prescription forms that are good for maybe fifty or a hundred happinesses. For today I'm laughing.

I'm beside myself. I lift my hand a little and then quickly let it fall again, so that the renewed rush of poison into it – briefly interrupted by my movement – can immediately affirm the presence of my possessive sweetheart. The effect of the injection isn't over yet, I can still take pleasure in my life. And for later, for later, I have the prescription.

Then I hear my doctor's footfall. Have I not committed myself to entering an institution? My sweetheart smiles, I'd forgotten all about that, but her mere being here with me means that nothing can stop me or force me to do anything. I am all alone in the world, I have no commitments, everything is vanity, only pleasure counts, only my beloved I must not betray.

And I think how rich and happy I am. Haven't I got enough money to buy my morphine? What do I need a woman for? Do I want for anything? I think of a book I have at home, a book by a Viennese author* who fell victim to a similar poison to me, I will read in it about his desperation and his fanatical faith in his poison, and I will smile and know that I am just as desperate and fanatical in the upholding of my own faith.

The doctor comes and unlocks the door. I take my feet off the sofa and slowly and cautiously sit upright, so as not to alarm the poison in me by a sudden movement. 'Are we ready, then, Medical Councillor?' and a cocky smile.

'Yes, we can go now.'

'But one more injection before we go, please, the drive will be at least an hour, and I can't last that long.'

'But my dear fellow, you're quite full.'

'I tell you, it's already wearing off. And when we're all alone together, I'm afraid I'll make a fuss. With another injection in me, I'll follow you meekly as a lamb.'

'Well, if you really think . . .'

He leads the way into his surgery. I follow in triumph. Little does he know me. He doesn't know that he could get me to do anything by dangling a syringe in front of me, but that when my sweetheart is on board I am strong and resolute.

I get my second injection, and then we leave. I walk down the stairs extremely cautiously. I can feel the good trickling in my body and the lovely, secret warmth. I have a thousand thoughts, because my brain is strong and free, it's the most resolute brain in the world.

There, the doctor opens the rear door of his car. I get in, and while he's starting the motor and getting settled and fussing with blankets, I open the other door and leap out, because my body is young and agile, and I go under in the crowd and disappear. And never clap eyes on the doctor again.

---

* Perhaps Leopold von Sacher-Masoch?

6

I knew I shouldn't go too far so as not to diminish the effect of the morphine by too vigorous movements. I looked at my watch, it was not quite noon. I thought of going straight to the Pschorr where I was going to meet Wolf later. But right away I realized that that was precisely the wrong thing to do. What if he was early too, he would see I had got some stuff, and then kiss goodbye to any chance of getting help from him, who was hard up himself.

Did I even have to see him at all? Hadn't I got a prescription form in my pocket that could be exchanged for loads of lovely shots? If I let Wolf have that, if I so much as indicate the existence of this piece of paper, then fully half those joys were as good as lost to me already. And I was hard up myself.

I am sitting on the nicely padded and sprung sofa of a wine bar, in front of me an ice bucket with a bottle of Rhine wine. I have the first glass already poured, lift it to my mouth and in deep draughts I inhale the nose of the wine. Then I quickly look aside to the waiter, see that he isn't looking, and empty the glass into the ice bucket. The alcohol would only fight with the morphine in my stomach and limit its effects, my only thought is to extend those effects for as long as possible. And I had to order something to be able to sit here unmolested.

Have I not delighted in the aroma of wine, as I delight in the girls in their Sunday best, even though I no longer desire them? The aroma, the girls, I'll put them in my dreams, where they won't disappoint me as they do in life with intoxication and sobriety.

I pour myself another glass and ask for a pen and ink. I fish the piece of paper out of my pocket and trim it to the size of a pre-scription block with my pocket knife. It's not quite right, it looks too wide to me. I cut off another strip, and now it's really much too narrow. An unusual format, where nothing about it is allowed to be unusual.

I begin to get annoyed with myself, I hold the paper aloft and look at it, put it back on the table and look at it again. 'Too narrow,' I mutter crossly, 'much too narrow,' and my irritation grows. I take the strip I just trimmed off it and press it against the sheet with my thumb, look again and see that the format was exactly right the first time.

I regret my impetuousness, why on earth didn't I wait for Wolf? What do I know about prescriptions anyway? He's the acknowledged expert! I reach for the pen and start to write. The glass is in the way, and I move it. It's still in the way. Oh, I really can't write like this. I reach out for the glass, and damned if I don't knock it over and spill it all over the prescription. The blue rubber-stamped ink blurs right away, all my hopes are quashed.

Discouraged and demoralized, I lean back. And then I suddenly understand what happened. The effect of the morphine is over, my body is hungering for more. And, abandoned by my sweetheart, of course I was incapable of doing so much as filling out a prescription.

I get up, pay and go to meet Wolf.

7

My God, how full Wolf is, how utterly unutterably replete! He's sitting there, half-horizontal, more sprawled than sat, barely capable of lifting an eyelid, dreaming and dreaming. I envy him his dreams, envy him every minute he spends in the blissful trammels of my darling, while I'm suffering inexpressibly.

'Well?' and from my wretched, collapsed gesture he reads the legend of my failure. He keeps it short. 'Hundred,' he says, 'hundred mls. Here you go, Hans. And be careful, don't overdo it, okay? So we get through the day.'

'Oh, two or three mls.'

'Fine,' he says, and he's off again. I go to the toilet, the precious stoppered bottle in my hand, I fill my five-ml syringe to the brim, and I'm happy again, I lean back.

And . . . and . . . I'm startled awake by a quiet rattling sound. The upset bottle is next to my extended arm, its contents all over the floor. Wolf! I think. After all his struggles today Wolf will murder me when he gets to hear.

But already I'm pouting defiantly, don't-carishly. Who's Wolf anyway? The associate of long morphine months, benzene hound, helper, helpee and in the end perfectly immaterial, just as everyone and everything is immaterial.

I hold the bottle against the light: there are maybe two or three mls left. I draw them up into my syringe and treat myself to a second helping, and my blood sings and surges, lightning flowers in my brain, my heart and my breath dance together.

The wide wild world! Wonderfully and uncomplicatedly pleasant when everyone is in it for himself, only out to sink his teeth into the other's flanks! Off quietly to the side the adventures that will befall me on street corners at night, the walks through cornfields where I can have my way with girls, the shuttered gates to pharmacies that I can break open, the money messengers I can waylay. And there are flowers with whorled petals, and shells that sound like the dying cry of a wild beast and then the wide rushing of the sea and the gulls dipping their wingtips in the brine, and the brown fishermen's sails and the sonorous sands.

I am everywhere, I am everything, I alone am the world and God. I create and forget, and all fades away. O my singing blood. Penetrate more deeply into me, princess, enchant me further.

And I fill the bottle up with water and hand it with my smiling thanks to Wolf, and he holds it up and says: 'Three? Looks more like five to me!'

And I say merely, 'Five.'

And we sit facing each other, dreaming, until he starts getting twitchy and says: 'I want to inject again,' and heads off.

And then I take my hat, sneak out of the bar and get into a cab, and the whining wheels take me a long way clear of his rage.

8

Then I got the crazy notion of trying coke. So far I'd only tried injecting it two or three times and seen right away what deadly stuff it was.

Flowery white Morphine is a gentle joy who makes her disciples happy. But cocaine is a red, rending beast, it tortures the body, it makes the world a wild, distorted, hateful place, knife tricks flash through its highs, blood flows, and for all that all you get from it are a few minutes of utter clarity of mind, a tying-together of remote ideas, a lucidity so dazzling that it hurts.

But I did it, and I got some cocaine from a waiter. I made up the solution, and I sent two or three injections into my body in a very short space of time. In those moments I saw the happiness of mankind. I no longer know in what guise it appeared to me, what mask it wore, all I know is that I was standing in the middle of my room, stammering: 'Joy, oh joy, I see it at last . . .'

But even as I'm speaking, I've lost the scene from my mind, I can't compel it any more, and each further injection I chase it with only makes me wilder, more furious, more demented. Pictures flash past me, bodies pile up on other bodies, individual letters in what I'm reading suddenly open their bellies, and I see they are really animals, secret, wily animals seething and swarming over the pages, pushing against each other, making strange word combinations, and I try to capture their meanings with my hand.

But then I see that I am talking to my landlady, I am trying to tell her I won't be wanting supper, in my mind I am forming the sentence, 'No, I'm not hungry tonight,' and I am perplexed to hear my mouth say, 'Yes, I am expecting Wolf later.' And then something infinitely quick happens that I don't understand, I am in a temper, single words get stranded in my memory: 'holes in the sheets – complaints – money – dishwater coffee', a wild fury boils up in me, and I leap at my landlady and grab her by the throat. I push her blonde bulk against the wall, her watery eyes are bulging out stupidly and offensively, her head makes a small, vulgar movement onto her right shoulder and she collapses in a soft pile, her sudden torpor pulling her clear of my hands.

For a second I am fully alert, and look around: I am sitting in some banal hotel room, a large, white featherbed is lying at the foot of the wall, where I was only now strangling my landlady. I know I am lost, totally and irrevocably lost if I can't avail myself of this one single moment of clarity to save myself. The only thing to subdue this crazed excitement of body and mind is morphine.

I race down the steps, barge a waiter aside, find myself outside, in a cab, going to the Pschorr.

In the car I inject myself again, I talk with wild gesturings, the driver keeps turning round to look at me, people in the street stop transfixed at the sight of me. I see all this, and I also see that a particle of my brain sees with perfect clarity, but that this one particle is helpless against the general craziness of my body and mind. I see it is madness to inject more, but I inject more.

At the Pschorr I ask for Wolf, I want to ask for him, my face is an uncontrollable paroxysm of muscles, I strive to speak the few words that my lucid particle up there has very slowly and distinctly prepared, only for my mouth to utter some wild drivel, and the waiter runs away, and I run out of the bar.

I chase over to Wolf's flat: no one home. I rush wildly through the city, here, there, continuing to inject myself, getting wilder all the time. My forearms are ballooning grotesquely, blood flows from the punctures over my shirtsleeves and cuffs, down over my hands. Madness towers menacingly above me, I giggle silently to myself as I think of a new plan to incinerate this ghastly city with its pointless pharmacies, to make it blaze like a spill of straw.

And I'm standing in a pharmacy, I'm screaming like a wild beast, I barge people aside, I smash a window pane, and suddenly they give me morphine, good, clear, white, flowery morphine.

Oh my sweet, now I am at peace again. I can feel the cocaine fleeing from it, there is still a little bit holding out at the top of my stomach like a burning thirst, and then that too is gone.

Several policemen lay their hands on my shoulders: 'You'd better come along with us.'

And I go with them, with very small, placid steps, so as not to alarm my princess, and I am blissful, because I know that I am alone with her and that nothing else matters.

And the long torture of withdrawal begins.

Three Years of Life
(1925–33)

1 The Test

One morning I awake from the deep oblivion that stood in for sleep in those days. And suddenly I know: this can't go on.

I swallow half a pint of cognac, something starts to stir in my brain, my hands are not shaking quite so badly, my stomach is working instead of merely hurting, but even so: this must end.

By and by it comes to me: today is Saturday, at eight o'clock I have to go into town, to the bank, to take out twelve thousand marks, pay in a couple of thousand somewhere else. After that I can take it easy, I don't need to be back here for thirty-six hours.

And while I drink the second half-pint, my brain formulates the following plan: I'll take plenty of spending money with me, five or six hundred marks. Once I get through them, I'll knock it off. If I bring the other money safely back from the bank, that will indicate a return to law-abiding decency.

Then the standard office morning, and I manage to keep up appearances, as I usually do. The usual small fears creep in: won't I have booze on my breath? Shouldn't I eat a piece of bread – for appearances?

An hour later the car drops me at the station. It's still trundling back out of the forecourt while I'm checking my pockets. Sure enough, I have forgotten the main purpose of my trip, the cheque for twelve thousand marks. I stop the car, we go back, the manager calls out some instruction to me, I hurry down to the safe and grab the cheque. 'All right, Pünder, let's go!'

And always at the back of my mind the thought: if I don't make the train, this (un)controlled experiment is off.

But I do make it, and no sooner am I sitting down than I feel a powerful thirst upon me again. Each station we stop at, I look to see if there isn't time for at least a quick one.

It's seven years now that I've been a slave to one substance or other, it's been morphine, cocaine, ether and alcohol. One unending round of sanatoriums, mental asylums and living 'in the community', albeit tethered to my addiction.

And with it, the constant struggle for money to buy the poison devil that's consuming me, the oh-so-clever false book-keeping to hoodwink the accountants, the constant act to keep anyone from noticing. Now I'm on my way into the city, at the cusp, maybe, of a new life.

At the bank everything goes smoothly, they know me there, I get the money, no problem. And in another bank I pay in fifteen hundred marks. That will help hide my traces if I need to flee – after all, what fraudster would set aside some of his ill-gotten gains to pay his boss's bills?

After that I'm free, and take a stroll through the city. The harbour sparkles blue in the sun, people swill this way and that, talking, laughing – but my feet know where to go: they take me to the row of brothels down near the waterfront. They know me there too, and the news spreads like wildfire: Hannes is in town.

Eventually, while they're next door whooping it up, squabbling, showing off, crying, whatever, over champagne – my champagne – I go to the bathroom and count up what money I have left, and I see I've already eaten into the twelve thousand. I've failed the test.

I walk out on the street, to the station. More train rattle. My flight begins. Hamburg. Most of the day asleep. At night to St Pauli. The following morning I fly to Berlin. Let them come for me. After that, Munich, Leipzig, Dresden, Cologne.

Always the same scenario: the poison won't let me go. I am

unable to eat at all. Sleep – what passes for sleep – is a vividly tormenting blackout.

Back in Berlin again. What am I doing there? What am I doing anywhere? I meet a girl I used to see. Maybe this time. I put my arm around her, pull her to me, and she says, ever so gently, but she says it: 'You're a drinker, aren't you? Aren't you a drinker?'

2 Unless You Like Porridge!

Detectives are always saying how difficult it is to apprehend a villain. My own experiences suggest the opposite: how difficult it is to get yourself arrested.

I walk into the police station at Berlin-Zoo.* 'I'd like you to arrest me, please.'

'Why? On what grounds?'

'Because a week ago, in Neustadt, I stole twelve thousand marks from accounts, and that's on top of taking money for my own use over a number of years and disguising it by false accounting – well, that should do to be getting on with! So, arrest me!'

'What's your name?'

'Hans Fallada, from Neustadt.'

The lieutenant or whatever he is takes a long look at me. 'Well now, wait a minute. I take it you're telling me the truth here?'

'Of course. What would be the point of lying . . . ?'

He goes into the other room. The only other civilians at the station besides me are a woman in floods of tears over a boy who's been nabbed for pickpocketing and a rowdy drunk who claims he's been robbed of some money. A sergeant is attempting to pacify him, but he gets angrier and angrier, till the man

---

* In former times, one of the main Berlin railway stations, and close to the fleshpots of the West End of the city.

questioning me turns towards him – and just then the crying woman whispers in my direction: 'Get out of here while you can, you melvin! Unless you like porridge!'

And everything goes on, the questioning, the crying, the muttering of the drunk, while I consider what 'melvin' and 'porridge' might mean. Eventually I will have three years in which to learn that a 'melvin' is a fool, and that 'porridge' is criminal slang for doing time.

The lieutenant comes back. 'They're not looking for you. I suggest you go home and sleep it off.'

'But I just told you I've stolen twelve thousand marks . . .'

'Just you and your drunken stories get out of here. Or do you want me to have you thrown out?'

'But someone must have reported . . .'

'Not a word about it on our list of open investigations. Now will you cut along, we've got work to do here.'

'It's not exactly a pittance, twelve thousand . . .'

'I'm going to count to three – one, two . . .'

'In Neustadt, I . . .'

'Three! Right. Scharf, Blunck, throw this drunken idiot out of here!'

So I go.

3 Flying Squad

Three hours later – by now it's one in the morning – I'm standing in the Rotes Schloss* on the Alex outside the door marked 'Flying Squad'. I knock and enter.

There are a dozen or so men seated round a big table. Some of them are reading, some are talking, most are smoking, and all

---

* 'Red château', jocular name for the police HQ on the Alexanderplatz, the third largest structure in Berlin when it was built in 1890.

of them are looking bored. I walk up to them and say: 'I'd like to be arrested, please. I've embezzled twenty or thirty thousand marks.'

They all turn towards me and take me in. Then, apparently spontaneously, without looking at each other, they seem to come to some consensus. They go back to reading the paper, chatting, smoking, being bored, and only one of them, with a straggly grey moustache, says to me: 'I think you must have had a few too many.'

Don't explain, I think, and I say: 'You know, sometimes you need a drink to get your courage up.'

'True enough,' he agrees, looks at me again, and then asks me for name, address, type of crime. My answers seem to satisfy him, because he says to one of the others: 'Willi, will you go through the wanted list for me.'

'I'm not on it.'

'Oh? What makes you so sure? Do you think Count Totz is happy to let you have thirty thousand of his marks?'

I tell him what happened with the police at the station.

'Well, sit here a minute then.' And he and Willi both go next door.

I sit there on my own, not bothered by anyone. I get up, stretch my legs, fish a cigarette out of my pocket, the last one, and light it. Take a couple more steps, till I'm standing by the door. I look round: they're all still reading, drowsing, bored.

I push the door open, not especially cautiously, just the way anyone might open a door, and stand out in the passage. The door shuts after me, I walk on, I'm out on the pavement, no one stops me. And then I turn and go back inside.

The grey moustache returns. 'I've just called our boys at the Zoo. It seems you really did put in an appearance there.'

For the second time, everyone turns and stares at me. The fact that I was truthful, and that I am presenting myself for arrest a second time, is enough, it seems, to change me from a pig-headed drunk wasting police time to a subject of interest. I am brought a chair, a packet of cigarettes is put out on the table, they want to take a statement from me.

But first of all it's: 'Empty your pockets on the table!'

I do so. Predictably, it's my purse and my wallet that provoke the most interest. Then consternation: 'Is that all the money you have?'

There are seven marks twenty pfennigs lying on the table.

'So that's why you've come to us! Because you've run out of ideas!'

Interest in me is gone again, the cigarettes are taken away ('you've smoked enough for the next few years'), the statement is taken in next to no time, and by two o'clock I'm in the cell, duly arrested.

4 Bedbugs

My first sense on awakening is that I must still be dreaming. Right in front of my eyes, so close that they seem monstrously large, are two broad, brownish, armoured insects. My head jerks back, I feel a horrible itching on my face and arms and I think: bedbugs.

So far I've only ever seen them on posters for insect powder, but the light that falls through the opaque glass in the cell door puts it beyond doubt: bedbugs. I squash them. They leave big bloodstains on the coverlet. After that I see the blackish-brown stains on the walls in a new light. These are no stray individuals, these are the advance guard of a considerable army with which I will have to get to grips.

My first feeling is indignation. They can be as rigorous as they like in prison, with rules against everything under the sun, but bedbugs surely aren't on any legitimate roster of penalties. I'm going to complain about this in the morning.

I go back to sleep, but it's not long before I'm woken by a new stabbing pain. The bedbugs are back. I try and sleep once or twice more, but in the end I'm driven to get up, crawl into my clothes and walk up and down, waiting for it to get light.

The second the key turns in the lock, I make my report: 'There are bedbugs here!'

'Bedbugs, eh?' comes a return question. 'Your predecessor never complained about them. Tell the duty officer, and he'll give you something.'

Since I don't know who the duty officer is, I repeat my complaint each time someone opens the door, maybe twenty times. I'm not given any insect powder. When it's dark again, and the place is quiet, I bang dementedly on the door. An indignant voice outside gruffs: 'Shut up in there! What's the matter?'

'Where's my insecticide!'

'Tell them tomorrow when they unlock the door. And now pipe down, or else I'll have you put in a punishment cell.'

'I want a different cell then.'

'They're all full,' and the fellow shuffles off. I spend another night pacing up and down, livid, freezing.

The next morning I make my indignant report.

'Oh, you and your bedbugs! You obviously weren't ever in the trenches!' But I am given my insecticide. A trusty comes along with a white, acrid fluid in a spittoon, with a brush to apply it. 'There you are. Now keep your cell nice and clean, and paint this on against the bedbugs. That'll keep you out of trouble.'

I'm on my own again. And I've got a job to do. I strip the bed and inspect the mattress and bolster. In some little crannies there are five or six of them, and I smoosh them before they can run off. Full-grown, they are reddish-brown, the little ones are a sort of whitish-yellow aspic colour. Then there's the pallet itself. I pull out the cross-struts, paint everything out, drive the brush deep into the cracks. They flee. I slaughter them. I want a decent night's sleep at last.

I go to bed early, so as to be nice and sharp for when my case comes up. I am awakened by the now familiar stabbing pain, followed immediately by itching. My day's work seems to have been in vain, the bedbugs are out in force.

The worst of it is that for some reason there is no light on in my cell tonight. I begin to wonder if the itching couldn't be some figment of my imagination. Then I happen to catch one on my face, and another taking a walk up my leg. I sniff them to make sure. The smell of bedbugs isn't one you'd ever mistake for anything else. It's a sweetish smell – synaesthetes would call it green – oddly like grass. During my test, I'm put in mind of Flaubert, who found this bedbug smell so arousing on Rustschuk Hanem.*

It's extraordinary how much those bedbugs get on my nerves. All day I spent seeing the flat brown and whitish forms wherever I looked. Even when I was writing, they seemed to crawl up the inside of the pen. In the desert of prison life, those beasts take on a significance that alarms me. I'm wondering: am I sure they're not a hallucination on my part?

I remember that I sometimes used to feel a similar itchiness when I was outside, if I hadn't drunk any alcohol the previous night. Admittedly, I didn't find bite marks all over my arms and legs when that was the case. But then I remember that a hysteric is capable of 'thinking' a tumour, for instance, with such suggestiveness that it will appear the next day. What if something like that is the case with me?

Vainly I try to comfort myself by saying I've seen the shapes of the bedbugs myself. But what if this 'seeing' is a form of hallucination? Vainly I remind myself of the appearance of two prize examples on my bolster that left spectacular bloodstains. I can

* Properly Kuchuk Hanem, an Egyptian prostitute, his exploits with whom Flaubert proudly related to his friend Louise Colet in 1851. The exotic combination of bedbugs and sandalwood prompted Flaubert to the Baudelairean exclamation: 'I want there to be a bitterness in everything . . .'

still see them emerging from a crack in my pallet between wood and iron, while I was daubing it with paint. I see them sitting in the pleats of my sea-grass mattress.

But the only way this would add up to proof would be if someone else had seen it with me. And the warder expressly said: 'Your predecessor never complained about them.' I can't imagine a human being stoically enduring being nibbled like that.

Next thing. When they brought me the solution, a warder with the trusty, I showed them my right forearm, an astonishing sight, studded with literally dozens of bite marks. They both looked past it as if it wasn't anything. Well . . .

And this afternoon, while I was writing, I felt a tickling on my neck, grabbed at it and felt the creature disappear under my shirt. I tore off my shirt – I was sitting there in my shirtsleeves – and surely I must have found the thing if it did exist: I found nothing.

While I was writing, two or three of the bite marks appeared spontaneously on the inside of my left arm, with which I was holding the paper. How is it possible that I fail to see a bedbug on my bare arm, which is in plain view as I'm sitting writing: enter bedbug, bedbug do its business, exit bedbug? – It can't have been bedbugs, then, but . . .

Better I get up and pace for the rest of the night. I'm going slightly potty. In fact I don't see why a doctor doesn't come and examine me. Aren't you supposed to be given a physical examination when you're booked? Those are the rules. The ones that are honoured in the breach, as the saying goes.

5 I Get My Hearing

From hour to hour, from day to day I'm waiting for something to happen. Nothing does. Sometimes, when I'm tired of reading the same newspaper stories on my toilet paper, and chasing bedbugs, and pacing up and down the cell, I imagine I've been forgotten.

But no, they don't forget about you here. Just everything takes its own sweet time. On the fifth day, my cell door is abruptly unlocked. A man stands there in civvies. 'Come with me, Fallada.'

Corridors, doors, I find myself in a room with a couple of officials in a part of the building that isn't prison. On one table is my suitcase. So they've traced my hotel, that's clever of them.

'Fallada, is that your name? Did you sign this?'

'Yes, that's my statement.'

'Well, Count Totz has sent a telegram. They thought you must have had an accident.'

'Yes,' I say.

'Took the opportunity to do a runner, did you? But then, once the money's spent, the little mama's boy wants to crawl into his safe little hole.'

'Yes,' I say.

'Do you stand by what's in your statement?'

'Yes,' I say.

'The first time you've done anything like this?'

'Yes,' I say.

'It shows.'

'He's had a real change of nature,' says the second official, who thus far had studied me in silence. 'Did you buy those clothes with the money you stole?'

'Yes,' I say.

'Right, you'd better take them off then. They're not yours.'

The two of them stand there and watch as I undress.

'There. Now put on the stuff in the suitcase. I take it that's yours?'

'Yes,' I say.

I get dressed.

'That suit's pretty new too. Did you buy that with the stolen money too?'

'I must have been wearing something when I left.'

'Who knows. Maybe some old rags you chucked in a ditch.'

'Yes,' I say.

'Now get a move on. Pack the things away. I should tell you the hotel wants to press charges for non-payment of your room.'

'That's good,' I say.

'What do you mean by that?'

'I want a stiff sentence. I intend to come off the sauce while I'm inside.'

The two men burst into hysterical laughter. 'No fears there! You'll have more than enough time!'

'Do you think this is a sanatorium or something?'

Then they look at me for a while in silence.

'You're not reckoning on getting out under paragraph 51, are you?'

'Quite the contrary,' I say.

'Quite the contrary – I like that. Because I promise, if you do, you'll be in for it. Have you ever spent time in the insane wing of a prison?'

'Naa,' I say.

'They dish it out a bit,' he says meaningly. 'Not something a little mama's boy would like.'

'Don't try and intimidate me. And I want to talk to a lawyer.'

'Why don't you send him a visiting card then?'

'I have the right to see a lawyer within twenty-four hours of being arrested. I've been here for over a hundred.'

'If counting hours is your thing, you'll have your hands full for the next something years. Okay, get back to your palace! Hang on, the hat goes in the suitcase.'

'But I didn't buy it with stolen money.'

'It's brand new.'

'Sometimes I buy myself new stuff, you know.'

'Whatever. Back to your cell.'

6 Chuntering

I spent six months and five days in remand prison. All during that time, I expected every day to be taken to an examining magistrate, or at the very least to be presented with the charges against me. Not a bit of it.

During those six months I was in three prisons and more than twenty different cells. Of course I always thought the change of address betokened some progress in my case. Again, not a bit of it.

But I had time, time aplenty. And I used it the way most remand prisoners use their time, for introspection. For that typical remand sickness of moaning or chuntering.

I was soon pretty advanced. For the first four weeks it was the bedbugs that dominated my thoughts and actions. No one outside can imagine the extent of my phobia. How many days and nights I spent, shaking with rage, running round my cell, suddenly pulling my bed apart, going through everything in a demented quest for the creatures, spotting them on the sheets, the floor, in cracks in the floorboards. How they gave me the slip, resurfaced, made mock of me. There was no doctor to help me against my fear of them, exacerbated of course by the symptoms of alcohol withdrawal.

Then I was put in a different prison, and the bedbug phobia abated. Only to be replaced by other fears. In the yard, where we had our half-hour's exercise every day, there was a push-button with the word 'alarm'. Every exercise time I fought with myself not to push it, to see what would happen. Then there was cell-cleaning furore, in which I would scour the lino floor of the cell for hours on end, slamming it with the bristle brush till it shone. Completely wiped out, I would then crouch on my stool hugging my legs against my chest so that my feet didn't spoil the sheen. Till I spotted some corner that wasn't quite as brilliant as the rest, and I would start all over again.

Others had different troubles. For a long time I had a cellmate, a former officer of justice, who was accused of having tipped off a suspect that he was about to be arrested. This man forgot about his family, his own situation, the approaching hearing, over the obsession with getting the remand system abolished.

His was a particularly grave case: everything that looked self-evident and reasonable and set in stone to him, professionally, looked so radically different to him once he was behind bars himself. Now remand looked to him like criminal madness.

The ideas that took possession of this once-sensible man and to which he tried with endless submissions to convert attorneys, judges and ministers were absurdly childish. For instance, in place of remand prison, a permanent stamp on the right hand of a person awaiting proceedings. While they might be able to conceal it in general by the wearing of gloves, it was to be instituted that no long-distance tickets were to be sold without the buyer showing his right hand to the official at the desk to prove that it was unstamped.

For a time I had another neighbour whose obsession was that there was 'no paragraph' that met his case. To begin with, I didn't see what he was getting at, and because of our continuous invigilation it wasn't easy to have a proper conversation with a cellmate either. Finally it dawned on me that he meant that his crime was covered by no paragraph of the penal code. He went to see the examining magistrate almost every day, and must have brought the man to the edge of madness himself with his impertinence and stupidity and the bee in his bonnet. I still recall his version of one of their interviews:

Magistrate: Where did you first meet Scharf?

Petersen: I was staying in the Brandenburger Hof, where he liked to drink a beer of an evening.

Magistrate: And that's when you sold him the wood?

Petersen: No, I never sold him any wood.

Magistrate: Come on, man, tell the truth.

Petersen: That is the truth.

Magistrate: But you knew he dealt in wood?

Petersen: Only at Christmas, when everything was out in the open. That's when he asked me to sign the purchase agreement.

Magistrate: Yes. On the wood that you'd sold him.

Petersen: No, because I shagged his wife. But there's no paragraph against that.

Magistrate: Oh, don't you start that again! Sergeant, take the man away.

Of course a paragraph was finally found that met the case, and Petersen was taken down for a long time for illegal dealing in wood. The night after the sentence, he was put in a rubber cell. He couldn't get over the fact that there was a paragraph for him.

The most widespread condition of course is 'chuntering' – talking incessantly about your case. It's only human that in the eyes of the person concerned the most minor incident becomes a monstrous case to be laid out before every official and every fellow inmate. For a long time I was put with an elementary schoolteacher who was accused of having falsified a bond, a typical family story. The man didn't tire of telling anyone and everyone his story. When he had driven the people around him so demented by dint of his incessant repetitions that they no longer listened, he clambered up to the cell window with the help of a table and stool so he could see the wall on the other side of the yard. Then he would bang and shout till a face popped up at a window opposite, and in seconds flat he would tell the fellow 'the whole story'.

The teacher received regular visits from the marshal, as he was called in prison slang, in other words he had the stool and table taken away to stop him clambering up to the window. Nothing seemed to make any difference, even the furious official was given a report on the latest state of the case, the man would jam his foot in the cell door and go rabbiting on and on.

I ran into the teacher later on in prison proper, and he was still talking about his case. Shortly after his release he shot his wife and himself, even though financially they weren't that badly off. Probably he never got over the fact that he couldn't get an appeal going in his case, and saw that to people on the outside his case was a matter of complete indifference.

Then there is a great section of people who don't survive separation from their families, their wives, their children. Especially at the beginning of remand, it's almost always extraordinarily difficult to get to see your family. As a result, the prisoner gets the idea he's been abandoned and despised, there are the most frightful breakdowns ranging from silent crying to wild tantrums. Nothing makes the least difference. It's almost unheard of for a doctor to take an interest. In the eyes of the officials, 'chuntering' is just something that happens during remand.

I have a grim memory of quite a decent official saying to a complete basket case who was crying for his wife all the time: 'There, there, don't take it so hard. Once you've been with us for a year, you'll have adjusted quite nicely, and in the end you wouldn't want it any other way.'

The production of individuals who at the end of a year might *want* things to be different but are incapable of living any other way because they are mentally ill is one of the greatest drawbacks of prison.

7 Robinson Crusoe in Prison

The man entering prison for the first time is like Robinson Crusoe caught in a storm and fetching up on his desert island. None of the gifts and attributes he has developed in his life outside are any use to him inside, in fact they will probably be a hindrance. He has to start again. If he wants to have a bearable existence he will have to forget what he knew, and take a leaf from Crusoe's book.

For instance, how to get a light without matches or a lighter. In my first few days I managed to get hold of a bit of tobacco, but no amount of cunning, no pleas, no begging could procure me matches, which seemed to be an extremely rare item.

One evening found me sitting pretty disconsolately in my cell, with four or five hand-rolled cigarettes in front of me, crazy for a smoke, but stuck for a light. I jumped to my feet. My predecessor must have known my plight, he must have had some solution, maybe he had left some matches hidden somewhere.

I embarked on a systematic search of my cell. Miracles exist, you just have to want them badly enough. On the top of the lampshade just under the ceiling, only reachable if you piled the chair on top of the table, I finally found these three things: a steel triangular file, a long piece of wood with an embrasure cut into it and, jammed into it and secured with twine, a piece of flint. And finally a tin can with some scorched lint.

Steel, flint and tinder – here was Robinson's fire-making equipment, I was saved. I stuck a cigarette between my lips, put the tin can with the tinder on the table and set myself to strike sparks. I got the steel to glow, but there were no sparks. I struck and struck for all I was worth, sweat ran down my brow, maybe I struck two or three sparks but they died before they could catch on the tinder.

It got dark, still I was striking away. It was night, and I was striking. There was no fire. The cigarette in my mouth was half chewed-up, and that was how I found the secret – not of striking a light, not tonight, that took a few more evenings' practice, but at least of chewing tobacco.

The hidden meaning of certain phrases that are still used outside, though they have long lost their original sense, became apparent. In one prison there was the custom of only allowing inmates one jug of fresh water every twenty-four hours. Habituated to two issues of water a day, I had poured away my dirty water and had no fresh. I would have liked to wash my hands, but as the saying goes: you shouldn't pour away your dirty water before you have fresh.

We were given bread in the morning and evening, in the form of a sturdy half-pound wedge. In the mornings you cut it up into slices for yourself, but you couldn't do that at night: there was a nonsensical rule that said inmates had to leave knife and fork outside the cell door in the evening in a cloth bag. That left you sitting in front of a great lump of bread which, try as you might, you couldn't wrap your mouth around to bite. You had no option but to revert to the biblical action: you broke bread.

But all these plain, simple actions that you learned were only external indications of a wholly new world. You had wound up in a type of existence where you could look to no one else for anything, only yourself. The more you cut yourself off, the more certain you could be of being left in peace; the more you looked to help from others – warders, officials, lawyers – the deeper the difficulties you were storing up for yourself in future.

8 Chicanery of One Sort or Another

As a rule, the new bod coming into prison for the first time has no other wish than to be left in peace. If he's not a fool, he will realize soon enough that every wish he expresses – even the most natural and obvious – will lead to him being taken by any official, great or small, for a troublemaker. He cuts his cloth accordingly and tries to keep to a minimum his contact with Messrs Guard, Senior Guard, or beyond them the galactic multitudes of master machinists, foremen, overseers, secretaries, inspectors, chief inspectors and governors.

But there are times when he will have a wish to express. His arrest has come precipitately, he wants to write a letter home, to vest power of attorney in someone, to request that something or other be sent to him. Very well. He asks for leave to write a letter.

The first thing he is told is that he is only allowed to express such a wish at one particular time of day, unlocking time.

He masters his impatience and the next morning asks to be allowed to write a letter. His wish is noted, and if he is very lucky he will be given a printed letter form as early as that afternoon, complete with a letterhead bearing his name, details, cell number and designation: remand prisoner. He would like to get a piece of letter paper without this perfectly superfluous letterhead on it that does not concern the addressee and that seems, moreover, to find him guilty before he has even received sentence; but to get one he would have to ask specially. If the request is approved he must, if he has money, get it bought on his behalf; if not, he will have to use the unlovely paper to write to some friend or other, and ask him to send some proper letter paper. Then, in one or two weeks, if all goes well, he will be in a position to write his urgent letter.

Then he sees on the letter form that he is only allowed to write along the lines, not between them, not on the edge of the paper; that he will have to get by on four sides of small octavo, that larger formats will as a rule not be authorized; that he will have to be as brief as possible, and other such ridiculous stipulations.

Perhaps his money was confiscated when he was taken in; then he will have little chance of actually mailing his letter, once completed. For a first letter, the state is supposed to bear the postage, but often that tends to be 'forgotten'. Or his letter is impounded. Then either he will be informed of this – a mere four weeks later, and all the while he's been consumed with impatience for a reply – or else, in the interest of the case against him, he will not be told at all. Both are possible, and he won't know which it is.

Among the stipulations that come with the letterhead there is one missing, the most important: that the remand prisoner is not allowed to write anything about his 'case'. This condition, which is unwritten, merely observed in practice, prevents him from writing to his friends or next of kin about the reason for his arrest, the reason for writing.

Take another example: he has got something to smoke, say a visitor has left him some cigarettes. But the visitor failed to take account of the fact that his friend is in prison, he didn't think to bring matches as well. If the prisoner brought money with him into prison, then he's in reasonably good shape, he just needs to wait for the day of the week to come round when he is allowed to express wishes. Then matches will be bought for him with his money and, a mere three to nine days after the wish presented itself, he will already be able to indulge it.

If he has no money, though, he will have to take the route of deceit, using trusties, who are the inmates who swab the corridors and dole out food. He will have to pay the asking rate. When I was still green in prison, three matches set you back one cigarette.

Of course he then runs the risk of being shopped to the authorities, with his tobacco seized and his smoking privileges withdrawn because he has shown himself unworthy, he has broken the good and holy law of the prison edicts.

Another helpful stipulation has it that the prisoner, unless he is sick, may not lie on his bed during the day. By day the bed has to be folded up against the wall. You are only ill if a doctor has declared you to be ill. If you're ill, but haven't yet seen a doctor – and in some prisons he only does his rounds once or twice a week – then you are not allowed to lie down. If you do, punishments threaten, and scenes are made.

Of course all these difficulties – and they are legion – are only there for the novice. The experienced inmate, who has been through the remand process a few times, will know the ropes. He will keep his complaints to an absolute minimum. The way he keeps his cell, receives his meals, talks to the trusties, answers the warders, all identify the old jailbird whom no guard would want to mess with – he wouldn't want the aggravation.

It's the new inmate who has to deal with the onerousness of

prison. More than that: he is often victim to the whims of the guards, who are badly paid, nervous, stressed-out people at the best of times, and who don't mind taking out their frustration on a helpless victim. I can recall one especially shaming instance of this.

The only variation in the endless days of the remand prisoners is the exercise hour. Then they are let out into the fresh air for half an hour where, three paces apart, they make the familiar rounds of the yard. Talking, of course, is prohibited, but everyone, of course, talks. Anyone caught talking gets yelled at, and if he repeats the offence he will be taken out of line and made to pace back and forth all by himself, along some distant wall. That's the rule anyway, but even in my first few days I witnessed an exception.

Ahead of me was a scrawny little Jew, a dentist, I heard, who had failed to pay some tax and had been sentenced to prison, then paid up – but was arrested before the payment was put through. Now he was in prison, and vainly trying to get information through to his wife as to what office she should go to with proof of payment. He was doing time for a misdemeanour he had, albeit tardily, atoned for, and with every day he saw his small practice dwindling further and was helpless while the authorities took him for both money and penalty.

Of course he was incredibly agitated, pleased to have found a listener, and was chattering away. He wasn't even particularly indiscreet about it; five or six paces in front of each guard he would fall silent, and begin again after that little kowtow. But a fat moustached guard took against him, probably because he was a Jew – most prison officials, as ex-NCOs, are anti-Semites – and he got yelled at.

For the next two or three circuits he kept still, but then he couldn't manage it any more, he had to say a couple more words, and once again they spotted him. He was made to step out of line, caught a torrent of abuse and was taken back to his cell and lost the rest of his time off.

The following morning. My man is walking ahead of me, as

before, with lowered head, visibly resolved not to say a word. But that's not going to help him, the other side is every bit as determined to yell at him again. 'You were talking to the man behind you. I warned you yesterday,' and so on and so forth.

The dentist tries to protest, but they haul him off. The following morning the same rigmarole. 'Next time you'll land up in a punishment cell!'

He's the sergeant's bunny, as the phrase goes, and we watch him go, pale, trembling with fury and humiliatingly bawled-out.

I never saw him again. I hope he managed to get through his remaining ten or twelve days. But I'm afraid he looked to me like a suicide candidate, one of those who, for all the talk of 'humane' treatment, just don't get on in prison.

9 Tobacco

When I was arrested that September night and taken to my cell, I was filled with a consuming thirst for alcohol. I had had nothing to drink for five or six hours, and I thought I was simply going to die unless I got some alcohol. I could hardly wait for morning, to see a doctor. But when morning finally came with its dishwater coffee and hunk of dry bread, I didn't ask to see the doctor. Somehow the new environment had stung me to resistance. I didn't want any alcohol any more, I wanted a long sentence where I could finally and lastingly break the habit.

And that's what I did. In all my time in prison I hardly missed alcohol, and I feel so completely cured now that I am happy to drink the odd glass of beer or wine in company, but alcohol as such has quite lost its appeal to me. I get on better without it.

Instead I suffered a different craving, from the very first day: a hunger for tobacco. It's barely comprehensible to me that I got over a serious addiction with hardly any trouble, but never got to grips with the other, lesser one. Perhaps it's that I saved all my will-power for the fight against alcohol, perhaps it's that my fellow inmates all had the same trouble as I did. The cry for tobacco is the universal cry from every prison, every jail, every penal establishment, and the desire for it is what drives all those hidden swindles that always manage to get the better of the surveillance systems in prison. All the passing-on of messages, the trading in money, in clothes, in food and soap – all those are just ancillaries compared to the overwhelming business of tobacco.

When I was delivered to my cell, I didn't have even one cigarette with me. Morning came, the hunger for nicotine came, and the first words I addressed a fellow inmate, a blue-uniformed trusty, were: 'Psst, mate, could you spare a drag?'

I had waited for a moment when the guard was unlocking the cell next to mine, but the trusty gestured dismissively, I wasn't getting anything. Each time they opened my door I would try and cadge a drag, and the gestures of the trusties turned to mockery, open ridicule. They pointed me out to the guards as the one who was desperate for a smoke. I saw I wasn't going to get any help from them. Either they had nothing themselves, or they wouldn't give it up without something in return – and at that time I had no idea what I had to offer them.

Those first days in the Alex I met no one, there was no exercise, and I would have been destroyed by my nicotine addiction if, in the course of going through my pockets, I hadn't found a couple of mouthpieces. I ripped a long bristle out of the broom and pushed it through the mouthpiece. When I pulled it out the other end, it was coated with the thick brown precipitate of tobacco. It tasted as bitter as bile, but it was so good, so good that my whole body enjoyed the sticky mess and calmed down a little.

Even then I was cautious enough to remind myself that the residue in the two mouthpieces wouldn't last for ever. And since there was no way of knowing when I would next get tobacco, I restricted my intake to one of those nicotine-tipped bristles every three or four hours.

Then there was my interrogation by the police, which at least had the virtue of bringing almost fifty cigarettes into my possession. When I had to change, I managed to pick two packs of cigarettes and a box of matches out of my valise and smuggle them into my underpants. How good it felt when I was back in my cell, filling my lungs with fragrant smoke, past and future were equally unimportant compared to that instant's joy: prison wasn't at all bad if it allowed you such pleasures.

But what are fifty cigarettes to a serious smoker! They were used up long before I left the Alex, even though I took out the filters and rolled up the leftover tobacco in newspaper to smoke. I was soon back on my bristles and mouthpieces.

Then I was removed to Moabit, and on the way I was allowed to smoke all I wanted. There were twenty or thirty of us in the 'green August',* all of us excited by the prospect of change. Most of us, along with our personal effects, had been given our smokes for the move. All of it was going to have to be surrendered when we arrived in Moabit, so we lit up with divine calm and doled out cigarettes with blithe assurance.

I stuffed what I was given – which was no small amount – up my trouser legs into my socks and, in spite of the jeering of the others, I was able to convey the contraband into Moabit. It was in flagrant violation of the administrative rules, but those rules are framed in such a way that a prisoner has no option but to breach them. The system ensured that one became a comrade to one's fellow inmates, united with them in opposition to a system that was petty, vindictive and stupid.

In Moabit things were better for me, there was the exercise hour, there was association, and almost every day there were at least of couple of fag-ends that I could roll up into a festive cigarette for the end of the week. And if everything went pear-shaped

---

* A paddy-wagon, like the (in German) better-known *grüne Minna*.

I would resort to snaffling dog-ends, a dangerous and exciting sport that I could play every exercise hour.

It was like this: the yard where we had our exercise was used before us by those exalted individuals, the serious criminals. Unlike us small fry, they weren't released in a swarm of thirty or forty to shamble round and round under the supervision of three or four guards; no, they went out singly, or at most three or four at a time, under strict guard and (this was enforced, just about) in silence.

These exalted personages were of course allowed to smoke – which we could only do in our cells – and they had the wherewithal too. And since they had no reason to economize, they tossed the ends in the yard. It was these butts that we now collected up, snaffled them, which is to say picked them up casually, as it were *en passant*, as if there was something the matter with your shoe or pulling up a sock. The orbit was invariably soon picked clean, but there were still those butts that were outside the ring, in the proximity of the guards.

And then it was a matter of the enterprise and discretion and sheer need of the individual. The very hardest ones were left till last. When we gathered to troop off back to our cells, there was often a little barging, and you might be able to take two or three steps to the side to reach the precious half-inch of tobacco. And the happiness you felt when you'd snaffled five or six dog-ends! That was an entire cigarette. A day with a cigarette was good, and a day with nothing was bad, it was that simple.

But here too some guards showed their meanness. They made a note of the collectors and waited calmly till the end of exercise, then called you, told you to empty out your pockets onto the ground. Not content with that, they sometimes told you to trample the ends into the ground, lest someone else try and pick them up. A scene like that would leave you seething with fury, harbouring fantasies of revenge and mocking the pious twaddle of the regulations that blathered on about reforming characters. I'd like to see anyone reform on such treatment.

But there was a weapon you could use even against the guards: you simply put the ends you found in your mouth. They were safe there, and in the form of chewing tobacco they lasted much longer. And that was how, in spite of my initial revulsion, I learned to chew tobacco.

10 *The Sentence*

The big day in the life of any remand prisoner is of course his day in court. Before he finally enters the anonymity of blue or brown gear, and for a greater or lesser time, there is this day which is all about him. Judges, prosecutors, lay assessors, defending counsel, the onlookers in the public gallery, the series of witnesses: they all remind him of his life outside. He is allowed to talk about himself, once again he has a character, everyone is talking about him, thinking about him. And then there's the prospect of the struggle for those who have some hope of being acquitted.

On that March day, there were three of us awaiting trial. We were introduced in the presence of the warden, we were dressed, we got given our civilian clothes back. Oh, the feeling of a proper suit, after your baggy prison gear!

In the last few weeks, ever since I'd known the date of my hearing, I had one grave worry: in the time I'd spent in my own clothes in the Alex and in Moabit, my white stiff collar had turned black. An appeal to have it washed at my expense in time for the hearing was turned down. 'Don't worry, we'll provide you with a scarf.'

Now, I really didn't want to show up in front of people who had known me in my past life in a blue-chequered prison scarf. But I wasn't a complete novice at this stage either. I got hold of my trusty, informed him of the size and shape of the collar, and from some corner of the prison, from a man I never saw, and through a whole chain of middlemen, I was given exactly the collar I wanted: pristine white. It wasn't the cheapest collar in the world, it set me back two packets of tobacco and three rolls of chewing tobacco. But I got it, just like you can get anything you want in prison if you can pay for it.

In the 'green August' I made the acquaintance of my two fellows, a young man of twenty and an old and steady-looking fifty-year-old. Both were quite convinced they would be acquitted, they were completely innocent. The young fellow, a cobbler's apprentice, was charged with having broken into seltzer booths and tobacconists' kiosks, the older man, a master butcher, with having duped several people with worthless IOUs. I seemed to be the only one who was expecting a conviction, and I got pitying smiles for not having lied about my case.

'You've got to lie. If they put a witness up against you, you've got to deny you've ever seen him. At the very least you'll get a lighter sentence.'

'If we only knew if the judge had a good breakfast.'

'It's all a matter of that. And if his old lady cut him some slack in bed.'

'I'm first up,' said the butcher. 'Hope to God I don't get Jürss! Jürss always gives a stiff sentence.'

'Oh, that's nothing. In Reichenbach we had a judge who was permanently pissed. Once by accident he sentenced a witness instead of an accused. There was nothing to be done about it. A sentence stands . . .'

'Now hang on a minute . . .'

Animated debate as to whether that was even possible.

We reach the holding cell of the court. A bare room, with just a bench along one wall. The walls themselves covered with scribbles. The butcher runs up and down. 'If only I knew how much time I had left. I need to have a shit . . .'

'Wait a bit,' I suggest. 'When you're brought in, tell the guard.'

'I can't wait. I'm desperate. I need a shit.'

We bang on the iron-reinforced door. The long corridor outside echoes with it. No one comes. When we turn around, we see the butcher has unbuttoned his trousers. He is squatting down in the corner.

'Wait!' I yell. 'Not on the bare floor! Here's a newspaper.'

I barely manage to push it under him. Already he's squittering and farting away. The butcher has gone deathly pale. He keeps mumbling: 'I hope he's had a proper breakfast! If only he's had a hearty breakfast!'

The cobbler and I exchange glances. Finally the stream dries up. The paper is bundled up and pushed, not very successfully, into the air vent. The stink is godawful.

'You are scared, aren't you,' says the cobbler provokingly. 'It's nice of you to share that with us, and all.'

The butcher says nothing, glowers, runs back and forth, pale, mumbling.

'I thought you were innocent,' I say. 'You're going to be acquitted?'

'What if he hasn't had a good breakfast?' he mumbles. 'Oh my God, what do I do then? What do I do?'

Finally the guard comes. 'All right, Rudszki, your turn. Oh, Jesus Christ, the smell in here!'

'Couldn't you, er, unlock the window?'

'The window stays locked at all times.'

Svenda, a Dream Fragment; or,
My Worries
(1944)

I must have known Svenda in earlier times, but my memories of her are indistinct, like the shadows of the clouds that lie over our lakes even on sunny days. My first clear memory of her is climbing a wide flight of oak stairs, with nice old-fashioned low risers, straight up to a double door, which instead of a wooden panel at its heart had clear glass panes. It's like the French windows in my house, only bigger and not so pretty, with ugly decorative brass and coloured glass details in the corners.

The other side of the clear glass panes I see Svenda standing looking blankly at me, with her dark curls tumbling to her shoulders. I stand on the top step for a moment, we look at each other in silence. Then I put my hand on the doorknob. Svenda shakes her head. Then suddenly I remember something I'd forgotten, namely that I may never set foot here again, because I have made a proposal to Svenda and been turned down, that only awful things took place here, I can't remember them except vaguely, like the shadows of those clouds that hang over our lakes on sunny days.

I turn and go slowly down the stairs. I walk through the streets of the town, I leave the town and find myself in open country. I walk slowly on and on. I am approaching a railway line, the crossing-gate is just coming down, the monotonous ringing of a bell announces that a train is coming through. On a little rise the other side of the tracks is the crossing-keeper's house. I lean against the top of the gate and crane round to it. There are yellow and pink hollyhocks blooming round it. A little girl steps out, with the red flag in her hand. Dark curls tumble round her shoulders, it could almost be Svenda but I know it isn't Svenda. I know the little girl's name, but it won't come to me. And while the train is clattering and rattling between us, I remember that I offered myself here too, and was turned down as well. Slowly I turn away, and wander back in the direction of town, whose rooftops, lit by the sun, seem to hang over the tops of the fields.

I am standing in a large, unevenly paved market square, and have just purchased three horses. They are incredibly big. How will I be able to feed them? I wonder. Suddenly I recognize them, they are the ancient nags of our drunken publican. And all of a sudden there he is too, laughing in my direction, unshaven and unwashed as ever, the corners of his mouth stained with tobacco juice. I head into town from the market place, the horses, out of harness, follow me, one of them has my bag with my cigarettes looped over its hindquarters. One of them is particularly devoted to me, he keeps nuzzling me under the arm, making me step aside. I'm a little afraid he might tread on my sore right foot with his great hooves.

I stop in front of a large house. I walk in and ask if Frau St. is in. No, she's left – but a room has been made ready for me. I go up to wash, but am told I have to eat right away. I sit down at a long table, opposite me is a general. He is dressed in a linen summer suit, but I know he's a general anyway. He is of unsound mind, and hates me. He has a small, red face and stares at me with bloodshot eyes. The dishes are served very quickly, and there is no change of plates, we have white boiled turbot, pike tails in runny aspic, haddock in mustard sauce – I am shown the huge menu, and see that today is meatless. For pudding there is a large, marbled ice *bombe*. I help myself to a big piece, and put it on my already crowded plate. The piece of ice *bombe* starts to melt right away, it dribbles over the edge of my plate, my whole plate is overflowing. I spread my legs and let it trickle down between them. I look round hurriedly; the bloodshot eyes of the crazed general are levelled at me, the whole table is eyeing me silently and grimly. Between my legs, the runnel from my plate continues to drip on the floor.

It occurs to me that I have forgotten to take my cigarettes back from my horse, I don't have anything to smoke. I go to the window and open it. The horses are gone, I know I will never see them again. I have nothing to smoke. I survey the area round the Kaiser Wilhelm Gedächtniskirche. The church is burned down, the surrounding buildings are in ruins, the streets are choked with rubble. There is no one out in them. It is war after all, I say to myself, Berlin is in ruins. Even the building from whose third-floor window I am now looking has been hit and torn apart by a bomb. I myself saw the ruins, back when I was on business in Berlin. A strange feeling creeps over me. I am my own ghost, I think.

Then I spot a cigarette machine on the wall. I start fiddling with it to get a packet of cigarettes out of it. 'Don't you know there's a war on,' says somebody behind me. 'Those are all dummy packs.' But at the top I see a compartment with a flat door that I open easily enough. This compartment is also full of dummy packs, but behind them I find four packets of tobacco. The tax labels have been torn off them. It's lucky I've managed to find some tobacco, I think, because I remember that nurse H. has a lot of cigarettes for me, but only one opened packet of tobacco. I leave two marks in the compartment in exchange for a packet of tobacco.

Night has fallen, the arc lamps are burning over the dead stations, no trains are running, I am running away from my father. I know he is dead, but he has come back to call me to account for what I did to my mother. There is nothing alarming about my father, he looks well, the little goatee that I remember as white is now brown, he is striding rapidly down the street next to the rails, looking for me. I myself am running away along the line. The line has been bombed, but they have put out great sequences of duckboards along which I half-run, half-fly. My father is long since out of sight; when the line starts to climb, I know it's time to turn off, and then my father will never find me.

I step into a gateway, and ring a bell on a very dark panel. A white-haired lady in a black dress with a fine white lace trim opens the door, and greets me as a stand-in for the master of the house who is away on travels. I ask her to set aside two downstairs rooms for my work, and one for my secretary, but she declines in no uncertain terms; I would have to make do with some rooms upstairs. In the big downstairs room with its upholstered furniture, the reddish flowers on yellow cretonne, my secretary is waiting. I hired her in a bar, a very tall, very beautiful woman, taller than me. At the time she was heavily powdered, now the powder has been washed off, and I can see two anchors tattooed on her pale cheeks. This woman could almost be my wife, that's how much she resembles her, she wears the same wide blue trousers that my wife wears with the appliquéd anchor, and their faces are practically identical too – but for those two little tattoos. I am very disappointed. At least I will be able to dictate to her.

Once again I am climbing the wide, easy oak staircase leading up to the glazed double door behind which Svenda stood. I am very sad, because I know there is no more hope for me. My feet are dragging, my heart is heavy. When I look up I see Svenda looking at me through the glass door. I pass through the door and walk up to her. She does nothing but look at me; there is no expression in her eyes, neither refusal nor desire, neither fear nor question.

I pick her up in my arms, and carry her into her flat. The doors open silently in front of me, as I carry the motionless woman through them. A pallid, unearthly light that doesn't come from outside fills the rooms. I am standing in front of a massive ornamental bed, over which a great canopy drops in dark pleats. The bed looks very white and cold. As I lay Svenda down on it, her clothes unpetal and silently fall to the ground like yellow roses.

I lay Svenda down naked on the cold, white bed, she lies there, her body is even whiter than the sheets, her curls are black on the pillow. She looks at me unblinkingly, without love and without anger. I knew her once before, I was rejected, painful things took place, my memories are as vague as the shadows of the clouds on the lakes at home. I lean down over Svend . . .

Looking for My Father
(1944)

No, Your Honour, I didn't steal my father's bicycle, as I stand here; may I fall down dead on the spot if that's a lie. Let me tell you what really happened, you won't want to sentence an innocent now, will you, Your Honour. But it seems no one wants to let me have my say. My stepmother says: 'You're a thief, off to prison with you.' My father won't talk to me, and leaves the room as soon as I open my mouth. The policeman comes and gets me, doesn't listen to me: 'Shut your mouth, you miscreant, you stole that bike, don't waste your breath!' No one wants to listen to me. But you'll maybe let me talk, Your Honour, half an hour is all I'm asking, and what's half an hour when I'm to go to prison for many months?!

Well, Your Honour, here goes, I'll sit down if I may. A cigarette would be good, but I know there's no chance of that, because I'm only fourteen and you're the judge and I'm meant to have respect for you. Though in actual fact I don't. You look so adorable with your white hair; if we were outside, I'd offer you a ciggie right away. I've always smoked, ever since I was nine years old.

Don't tell me I've been cheeky again! I really didn't mean to be. People are always saying I'm cheeky, but I don't know the meaning of the word. I was always this way, I can't be any different, I don't mean anything by it. You've got to be able to talk to someone, ain't you – that's what talking's for.

Sure, Your Honour, I'll make a start, in fact I'm already well on the way. My mother, she's from Polack country in East Prussia, but I'm no Polack myself, even if my name is Stachoviak, Felix Stachoviak. My father, he was a good German, by the name of König, I'll tell you about him when I get to him.

A dodgy gentleman told me once that Felix meant 'fortunate one'; well, in that case my mother chose the wrong name, because I've never had the least bit of luck in my life, or else I wouldn't be standing here, would I? By the way, I'm a Catholic – but I don't believe in anything, I'm enlightened. No, not that way, Your Honour, of course I'm enlightened about the birds and the bees and that, too, have been for a long time, but I was meaning religion-wise. Don't laugh at me, Your Honour, my life and liberty's at stake. If you laugh at me, how can I talk to you?

My mother used to go out on the big estates with the reaping gangs, every year she was some place different, some years she was on two or three different estates. That depended on the work that was available, and on the men that were available too. Each job she has, she looks out a new man for herself, and each one I have to address as Father. But I knew that my proper father's name was König, and that he was a foreman. An aunt told me that once, that I spent a couple of months with; at the time I was five years old, and my mum was in prison over some robbery. I remember that time very well, Your Honour, my mum was a good-looking woman who was never stuck for a man, I tell you. Generally she would go for the foremen because they were better paid, and we children had some benefit from that too. One time my mum went out with an inspector, but that German bastard was meaner than any Galician reaper, and she got him into so much trouble that he lost his job. We laughed.

But even now, Your Honour, when my mum's getting on and isn't so hot any more, she's got a way about her that makes men crazy, especially when there's been drink taken. And she gets them to toe her line, she's really good at that, Your Honour, you know, I have to admit it if I do say so myself, not just for a night or so, she's not like that. But she's got flaws too, I do admit that, even though I am her son. She can't bear to be in the same place, even though it's got everything going for it, she's always wanting to move on. She's got ants in the pants, Your Honour, she's not capable of sitting somewhere quietly. And then she doesn't want to get married neither, my mother could have got married a dozen times, thrifty reapers, widowers with their own furniture and all, but not Mum, not for all the tea in China!

'Brunka,' one bloke said to her once, 'Brunka, I beg you! You'll get everything in your name, the furniture and the two cows and the five sheep and the chickens . . . Only don't leave me, Brunka, I need you, I gotta have you . . .'

'Do one,' was all Mum said. 'You're getting on. What good is your furniture if you're an old man? I need a young fellow who makes me warm, all I get in bed with you is your cold feet!' And so we moved on again. And Mum was never careful neither, just about every year she got knocked up, it didn't seem to bother her. All day long grubbing up sugar beets, which is about the hardest work there is, and then in the night she gave birth, and at seven the next morning she's back out in the fields, with the beets again. Giving birth wasn't a job to her. 'It keeps me healthy!' she laughed. And there's something else I have to say too, Your Honour: Mum was no slouch when it came to getting rid of her kids either. She always managed to palm them off on some man, not one of them stayed with her, excepting me.

I've got brothers and sisters all over, I don't even remember the places we lived in, and how many of them there are, and where they are neither. The fact that I got to stay with Mum is probably down to the fact that she lived with my old man König the longest time, and had two kids with him and all, which was me and then my sister Sophie. When Mum split with König, they divvied us up between them, and I went with her, and Sophie went to Father.

I didn't like being all alone with Mum all the time, I wouldn't have minded having a few of my brothers and sisters with us. And nor did I get on with the father that Mum was with now, and having to call him Father too, he was just seven years older than I was, so he was just twenty-one, and he didn't work neither, he drank and played cards and visited the girls of the reapers in their cots, and Mum just had to earn, and it was never enough for him. I often told Mum to get rid of him, but she wouldn't take my advice, but swore and hit me and told me to work as well. But I wasn't so stupid as that, work was just invented for fools, as you must know too, Your Honour, else you wouldn't of become a judge, woodjer!

I preferred hanging around out of doors, fishing or laying traps for hares and deer, and if I caught something, I would sell it on to some Polack in return for a carton or two of cigarettes, and sometimes money as well. Then I would go along with my sweetheart to the pub and pick up a soda water bottle full of schnapps, and we would crawl off to a haybarn and get drunk together and sleep it off. When I crawled home the following afternoon, Mother would yell at me and bang pots and pans around. But I didn't care, I was used to her yelling and her beatings, the main thing was she gave me some proper dinner. And that she always did, once she had blown her top. With Mum, you just needed to have a thick skin, then you could get whatever you wanted out of her. And a thick skin is something I've got, Your Honour, you bet your boots I have. I've been through as much as an oldster, you won't frighten me!

Back then, we were living on an estate called Glasow, and my mother and my newest father, that young feller I was telling you about, they told me that once I was through with school, at Eastertime, I was to go with them to Holy Communion in Paderborn and then be apprenticed to a master craftsman. Of course I never went to school much, the teachers were always happy to see the back of me, but I picked up reading and writing anyhow. The doctor in remand prison is bonkers if he thinks I'm educationally subnormal – I've got more wits about me than he does. I'd like to see him make his way all alone in the world like me, with a leaky pair of pants and not so much as a shilling in my pocket, and the cops after me, as I'm about to tell you, Your Honour. If I'm dimwitted at all, then so is my mum and so is every woman I've had, because I know more'n all of them, and it was always me what had to read them the paper, because God knows they weren't able to do it for themselves.

Might I have a cigarette after all, Your Honour? I'll pay you back once I'm out, promise. And you will let me out, because I didn't pinch that bike, may lightning strike me!

You serious, Your Honour? Well, I'll try not to take it amiss. I understand, you're worried about losing your job, and if I had such a cushy one as you, then I'd hang onto it too for all I was worth, and not give anyone else a look-in!

All right, all right, I'll go on. Where was I? Oh yeah, they'd just claimed that I was to go and do some apprenticeship in Paderborn, after Easter. But I'd been listening at doors, and so I knew I was a burden on them, and I was onto them, and Mum had been to talk to the social worker, and at Easter I was going to an institution in Paderborn, that's what they actually had me marked down for. Only I was careful not to let on, and I played the dummy and that I believed them. But I wasn't going to go into one of those places where you just get cuffed all day long, and get given piss-and-water soup, and hear bad words and sent out on a life of crime.

I thought a lot about my König father, and wrote a letter to my aunt in Zurow, asking if she had an address for him. And after a while, I gets a reply from her which I didn't really expect, and I learn that my father is in Thurow, which is in Mecklenburg, and is a foreman. And I might as well go see him, because blood was thicker than water and he'd surely take me in. That made me happy, and I let Mum and her feller talk all they wanted. I was just waiting for an opportunity to take a bit of food on board and some money, because it was winter, end of January, and it was bitter cold, and I didn't want to run away empty-handed. But there was nothing in the house, every day my father took Mum for every penny she had, and I didn't dare go in the woods neither, because the gamekeeper said he would give me a load of buck-shot up the arse if he saw me there again.

Well, my mother had got in the habit of stealing from about Christmas on, because she was never able to get enough money to keep my father happy. One time she took me with her; she wanted me to climb down the cellar of a dairy and pass the pats of butter to her. My father had been along the night before and loosened the window bars. Anyway, I smelled a rat, I was convinced Mum was angling to get me caught, so I refused to go down, she had to do it, while I stayed outside and she passes me the butter. It all went tickety-boo, and I picked up five marks from her, which I drank away with my girlfriend. That was the night we happened to set fire to the haybarn we were sleeping in, with our cigarettes, not meaning to, Your Honour, just because we was so drunk. We managed to escape though, and no one suspected us neither, because in the ashes of the barn they found the charred remains of an old tramp, and so they said: stands to reason it was him. And there's every chance the old feller liked a smoke, Your Honour.

Why are you always writing stuff down, Your Honour? There's no call for it. This is all old stuff that no one can prove against me anyway, if it comes to it I'll deny everything on oath, and anyway it was in another province, not here in Mecklenburg, so it's none of your beeswax! You know, you don't scare me, Your Honour, I know my rights, and the bicycle which is your concern, I didn't steal that, as I'm about to explain, Your Honour!

A day or two after this, my mum comes along again and says I'm to go and do another job with her tonight, this time a grocery. I didn't fancy it, so I take the afternoon off, and hole up with my girl, so they couldn't find me that night. That proved I was sharper than the rest of them, because that was the night my mum got herself caught, and they beat her up before shoving her in the pen. And they came for my father and all – I just happened to be out at the time, or maybe they'd of taken me in as well. The next morning, when I come home, it was all empty and deserted, and I thought to myself: the time has come, my son, for you to clear off and look for your natural father! Before I went I turned the whole place upside down, but I couldn't find more than just a couple of spuds and a crust of bread. Of her rags, there was nothing that would have fetched a mark piece from an old Jew, that was what my newest father had reduced Mum to!

I set off. I knew I had to make for Sternberg and then Güstrow, that's what the map at school said. It was a long way, and it was very cold, it had snowed and it looked like there was a lot more to come. I had nothing but rags on, but that didn't matter to me. I wanted to find my father and my sister, I wanted to live in a proper family and become a proper person. That's the truth, Your Honour, I'll swear it on the blood of Christ.

I had plenty of cigarettes, and at noon I begged for food, and got some too, a good ladleful of pea soup with potatoes and bacon fat, and in return for that I was supposed to chop some wood. I followed the fat geezer out into his yard, and I started chopping, and chopped well while he was watching. But before long it got to be too cold for him, and he went back indoors. I was going to run off, but I thought: take a little look and see if there's not something here you can lift. I opened the kitchen door, and there was no one in the kitchen, I heard them next door in the dining room, gassing. In the table drawer I found two marks and thirty-five pfennigs, and on the table there was half a side of bacon that they'd cut some off of for the peas, and I put that in a rucksack that was hanging on a hook. I picked up a knife and a spoon as well, there wasn't any bread, worse luck, but then I could afford to buy bread now. I was on my way out when I spotted a pair of nice leather workboots. They'd do me better than my wooden clogs, and I pulled them on right away. They were on the big side, but I thought I could stuff some straw into them to make up.

Then I scarpered, and at the end of the village I hid in the woods in a place from where I could see the street. And that was smart of me again, because not fifteen minutes later they came down the road looking for me, with a dog and all. They couldn't find me though, because there were so many footprints at the entrance to the village they couldn't see which were mine.

I didn't move off till evening, and on this whole trip, which took sixteen days, I got to say I was lucky all the time, no constable nabbed me, I always had enough to eat and drink and smoke, and I didn't get through my money neither. One time I went into a pub to get a bottle of beer. I stood at the bar for ages, and no one came. Quietly I pushed open the door to the back room, and there was the fat barman sprawled on the sofa snoring away for all he was worth. I didn't hang around, but stashed all the schnapps into my bag as would go; and I emptied out the till too, but there weren't more'n a couple of marks there. The barman woke up and almost caught me in the act, but I nipped round the front of the bar in time, and ordered a pint of beer. I paid him for it out of his own change, and I spent the whole afternoon sniggering to myself about the fat sleepyhead! He must have cursed me afterwards. I went off into the woods with my schnapps and found a foresters' hut. There I called a rest day, which I'd deserved too, Your Honour, and I washed out my throat with schnapps, I tell yer!

The next morning I wake up with a mighty appetite, I reckon it must have been the drink, and thought I had to have roast goose. For some reason I was dead set on roast goose that day, Your Honour! Then I slunk back into the village and I heard some cackling coming from a shed not far from the woods. I had such a hunger on me that I couldn't wait for it to get dark. First I dug up a pit of spuds, and carried some back out to my hut. I found some dry wood too, I was dead set on making myself a feast! To keep going, I took the occasional nip from a bottle, I still had plenty left. In the afternoon – it wasn't even beginning to get dark – I headed for the coop. I really was a bit crazy, because

I didn't pay any mind to the racket they was making, I just waded in, and sawed the head off the biggest one with my chopping knife, and tucked the carcass under my arm, and ran off into the woods – and there were the people already running out of their houses.

I ran and ran, always away from my hut, in a big loop round the village. Once they got pretty close to me, and I thought: uh-oh, Felix, you've had your chips! Then I couldn't think of any other way of getting out of it than dropping the goose, and that delayed them while I got away. And I ran and ran some more, and sure enough, because I'd been running in a circle, I soon found myself back in the village. It was all dark and snowy and deserted, they were all off looking for me in the woods. I went straight back into the shed and killed another goose, and carried it back to my hut. It was far too dark by now, and snowing too hard for the people to have gone on looking for me. I roasted the goose on a stake over my fire, and baked some potatoes in the hot embers – I don't think anything ever tasted so good in my life as that feast in the woods, Your Honour! I ate so much that I almost overslept the next morning, which would have been serious, because in their rage they would probably have kicked me to death, the stupid village farmers!

But I just managed to get away, and I continued on till I got to Brüel in Mecklenburg. At that point I stopped thieving, because I was getting close to my old man, and I didn't want to disgrace him right away. And I wanted to turn over a new leaf anyway. I didn't need to go thieving, because I had enough of everything and could carry on as I was for a long time. Between Brüel and Warin it suddenly started chucking it down, but it was still freezing, so the road was a sheet of black ice. I slipped over in the middle of the road, and at that moment a car came along. The driver saw me fall over, and I was just barely able to roll out of the way. He drove on another ten yards and stopped. He asked me where I was heading, and I said, 'Just into town.' He took me as far as the Neukloster turn-off. Again, it was bitterly cold, I walked on, and came to Zurow, where my aunt lived with her husband who was a Polack. When I opened the door and called in 'Anyone by the name of Gramatzki live here?' my aunt threw herself round my neck and cried: 'Felix, where have you sprung from? Do you remember when you were little and used to drink the ends of all the beer bottles?'

She recognized me straight away, even though it was almost ten years since I'd lived with her. I had a great reception and a bang-up dinner. I gave them all the stuff I still had on me: my Polack uncle got the schnapps and the cigarettes, and my aunt got the foodstuffs, including the half a side of bacon that I still had. She was well pleased with me, and that night I was allowed to sleep in the same bed as my twelve-year-old cousin. My aunt went off laughing: 'Don't try anything, will you, anyway, you're not old enough!' Nor was I contemplating anything of the kind, my cousin's flat as a board anyway. But the next morning my Polack uncle flew at me and hit me and chased me out of the house for trying it on. I'd just gone out to use the privy before breakfast when my cousin started crying and telling lots of untruths about me. But that wasn't the reason my uncle threw me out, it was because they'd already taken everything off me that I had, and now they were too mean to even give me breakfast. I would have gone without lies and beatings, Your Honour, I've got my pride.

I walked back to Neukloster, and hung around all day. I found a nice-looking villa that looked the part – I couldn't very well show up at my real father's empty-handed! That would have been a disgrace. In the afternoon I went out begging, I got plenty to eat, and I managed to lift a cook's purse, but that only had a mark in it. I spent the night in a barn that had hardly any straw left in it, and it was so cold I couldn't hardly sleep. But then I finally got to sleep, and almost missed the moment; by the time I got to the villa, it was already starting to get light, and there was a light on over the kitchen. I wondered for a moment whether I should risk it, but I didn't feel like hanging around Neukloster for another day.

So I climbed in through the laundry window, and everything went as smoothly as I could have wished for. I took my time breaking open the desk with a crowbar I found in the toolbox in the kitchen, while I listened to the cook tramping about overhead. She already had her shoes on. I looted over a hundred marks, a few delicacies, some nice stockings and put ready some cigars, a camera and some clothes on the landing for me to pick up on my way out, while I went looking for a suitcase. My rucksack was already stuffed, my pockets too. Unfortunately, when the cook came down the stairs, her eye lit on the things I'd put by, and then the light in the room, and she started screaming. I hurried out of the window. The engineer fired some buckshot after me out of the window, and I could hear it whistling past my ear, but not one bit hit me. I'd had to leave all the things I'd put by, which was a pity, but I'd done all right; I wasn't going to my father as a poor destitute.

I sat down in the train and rode via Warin and Blankenberg back to Brüel. From there I walked the two miles to Thurow where my natural father lives as a foreman. I open the door in the reapers' accommodation and see a thirteen-year-old girl on a sofa, a nine-year-old on a chair, and a bony woman of thirty-nine or forty doing some sewing. I ask: 'Am I right here for König?' even though the reapers downstairs had already told me this was his place.

The woman looks at me and says unfriendly-like: 'Yes! What do you want with him?'

I says: 'Then I expect you're my sister,' and I walk up to the girl and give her a smacker on the mouth. Sophie was very pretty, and she had a lot more about her than my cousin, if you know what I mean.

'I see,' says the woman, 'then I suppose you're Felix Stachoviak?'

'That's right,' I say.

'I always expected you'd turn up sometime. Where's your mother?'

'Mum's in choky, and she won't be getting out any time soon,' I reply. 'Where's Dad?'

'He's in the bedroom next door,' says my sister Sophie. I went in, and there lay my father on the bed, fully dressed, gawping up at me. He'd probably just woken up.

'Here you are, old fellow, have a ciggy,' I say, and I hold out the pack. He stared at me stupidly for a while longer, but when I started to laugh, then he laughed too.

'So you're Felix,' he says at last, and helps himself to one of my cigarettes. 'How's yer mum?'

I told him. He seemed to feel bad about her having come to such a pass. Then when we both went into the parlour, there was my stepmother already unpacking my rucksack what I'd put down there. That did not suit me at all. I had wanted to do my own unpacking and distributing. My sister and little half-sister was watching on, I had packed some really high-class undies. 'This is all stolen loot!' cried my stepmother furiously.

My father didn't seem to think that was so bad. He laughed. 'Well, Felix,' he asks, 'where d'you collar this little load?'

'Mum gave it me to take to you,' I said.

Father laughed again and gave me a saucy wink, I'd just told him Mum was in choky. 'Well, then everything's fine,' said Dad. 'Is that schnapps in that bottle?'

'That's cognac, Father,' I said. 'Shouldn't we all drink a toast?'

'Nothing's fine!' cried my stepmother again, she seemed to be a bit of a harpy. 'There's even a name-tag sewn into these smalls. What's that say? Grahl – is your name Grahl then?'

'No, but we had a teacher by that name in the village,' I quickly put in. 'She died, and Mum bought her effects, and lots more.'

'So what's the problem,' said Father. 'Let's all drink to Felix here!' We did so, but my stepmother didn't want to join in, and she wouldn't let me little half-sister drink either. My proper sister did. And she got to keep all the smalls I'd picked up, again stepmother and half-sister didn't want none. My father got stuck into the schnapps, and I heard my parents arguing long into the night in the bedroom. My two sisters were in with them. I was on the sofa in the parlour. What they were quarrelling over was me. My stepmother wanted my father to send me packing right away, and my father refused. 'Let him stay at least until his mother gets out of prison.'

But my stepmother wasn't having that, she said she'd rather leave the house herself than have me stay a moment longer. I was a thief and would only make trouble. Suddenly my father started laughing and fooling around with my stepmother. First I heard her scold him furiously, he was no better than his son, but gradually she give in, and I could go to sleep with an easy mind about my immediate future.

To begin with, the following day didn't look good at all. My father had gone off to work early, and I was left in the hands of my stepmother, who was constantly having a go at me. I had to wash under her supervision, with her claiming I hadn't washed properly for at least four weeks, which wasn't true at all, because I had, before I left home. Then I had to carry in wood, scrub the steps, clean the pigsty – in a word she was on at me all morning. When she caught me having a quiet puff in the corner of the pigsty, she confiscated all my cigarettes. The minute my sisters got back from school, though, there was dinner on the table, and dinner was good, I have to say that for my stepmother, my mother's cooking wasn't a patch on hers. After dinner, my stepmother went out to work on the estate herself, she seemed to be dead keen on money. My sister was supposed to go to Brüel and do the shopping, and I was to chop wood in the yard, and my half-sister was to do her homework and get supper ready.

I saw my stepmother out, then my sister. I let her go for a bit, and then I set off after her. First, she was alarmed, but then I told her I didn't take orders from my stepmother, and it wasn't her fault if I happened to be going to Brüel as well. On the way there I told her lots of stuff about my free and easy life at home, and suggested going back to live with our real mother. We would have a much better life than under the eyes of her stepmother. Sophie promised to think about it.

In the shops in Brüel there was quite a bustling scene, Sophie König was well known, and so no one kept an eye out for me. I was able to fill my pockets and by the end I had acquired more than Sophie had managed to buy. Since I still had plenty of money from my visit to the villa outside Neukloster, I bought a bottle of sticky liqueur and some cigarettes at a pub, and we set off home.

Once there, we didn't go indoors where our half-sister would have cramped our style, we went up to the hayloft. There I give Sophie some liqueur, and then I unpacked my treasures, sweets and biscuits, and a silk shawl for her, and apples and nuts and a little grater. I gave them all to her. First she tried to refuse, because it was stolen goods, but then I explained to her that people had equal rights, and that it was unfair that one man like the merchant had a lot, and I had nothing. She understood that. We emptied the whole bottle of liqueur, and kissed a lot, and I told her what a pretty girl she was, and I'd be sure to find her a good-looking swain in Glasow. She promised me she would run away from here, and go to Glasow to be with Mum and me.

Once the sticky liqueur was gone, we went over to the reapers' lodgings. It was almost dark by now, and my stepmother was home. I was none the worse for the bit of drink I'd had, but my stepmother saw from my sister what was going off, and she started a terrible racket. And then when she saw the presents, her fury knew no bounds. She beat my sister and would of beaten me, if I hadn't fought her off. For my fourteen years I'm pretty strong. She swore she would tell my father everything, and I would have to leave tonight. When she wouldn't leave off, I told her to kiss my arse, and walked out.

I met my old man coming off work, and invited him to a drink. We turned into a pub, and I bought him schnapps and beer and good cigars, so that I had to lead him home by the arm. Even so, we managed to tumble a couple of times into the roadside ditch which was full of snow. The old man thought that was mighty funny. At home my stepmother got stuck into him right away, and demanded that he chase me off that same evening. But my father wasn't up to much any more, first he just laughed, then he dropped onto his bed, and was asleep on the spot. Then, in a towering rage, my stepmother dressed herself and her daughter and left the house. She wrote a note to the old man that she wasn't coming back until I was out of the house. No sooner was she out of the house than I tossed the note in the fire. Sophie and I had a jolly evening of it, and I went to the pub for more liquor.

When my father woke up the following morning, he couldn't remember anything, and was just surprised to find his wife and daughter gone. Sophie and I pretended we didn't know anything, and then it was time for Dad to go to work. I persuaded Sophie to cut school, and we hung around in the village and in Brüel all day. Sophie told me she liked that sort of life a lot, and that she would really like to go to Glasow with me. I persuaded her to wait a couple of days, there were some provisions here that needed finishing off.

We made my father a good supper out of the last of the supplies in the larder, and I stepped out for schnapps and cigars from the pub, but he didn't seem to enjoy it. He had heard from the people under us in the tenement about why my stepmother was gone, and was a bit upset about it. He didn't tell me in so many words to get lost, but I could see he was looking at me differently. I was a pain.

In the morning Dad told me: 'Felix, hop on my bike and go to Brüel, and then take the train to your aunt in Zurow, and check if your stepmother's there. Then come back and tell me.'

Now, Your Honour, listen carefully, we're getting to the point. I swung myself onto his bicycle and rode to Brüel, and left the bike at the left luggage counter. Then I took the train to Neukloster via Blankenberg and Warin, and went to Zurow on foot. I didn't go directly to my aunt's, mind, because I'd been there not long before, I went into the pub and asked around if a woman with a nine-year-old girl had showed up in the village. No, they hadn't.

I spent the night in Zurow, and the next day I went back the same way. When I got to Brüel, I go to pick up the bike at the station, I go through all my pockets, but I must have lost the chit. I say as much to the man on the counter, and describe the bike to him, but he says, no, he can't do anything. I'm to come back in the evening, when his colleague will be there who took receipt of the bike from me. He'll probably remember me. So I walk to Thurow, and who do I find as I get in the door, but my stepmother and her little girl. But she's like she's never seen me before, and she won't say a word to me, and my half-sister doesn't say a word either.

I didn't care at all, though, it was no skin off my nose, just that my sister Sophie was sitting in a corner crying, that bugged me. I asked her what she was crying about, but she didn't want to say, or she couldn't, because my stepmother was watching her the whole time.

In the evening, Dad came back, he knew his wife was back, she must have got in the night before. I told him I'd lost the receipt for the bike, and I had to go to the left luggage counter because the other official would be there. Then my father said: 'Well, I suppose I'd better go with you.' And took down his cap. I noticed him flashing a wink at my stepmother. I thought it was just because now he was going to send me home. That was fine by me anyway, I didn't like it in Thurow any more, only I wanted to take Sophie with me. But that wasn't on, not that night, maybe I could try it the next day.

When we got to Brüel, my old man said: 'The other day, you stood me a drink, Felix. Well today it's my turn to buy you one.'

So we sat down in a pub and we had a few. Then my father made as if he had to go talk to a wheelwright, and I believed him and all, in fact he went up to the police. When he came back he said: 'All right, Felix, let's get to the railway station.' I'd had a good bit to drink by now, and wanted to buy him one, but all at once my dad's in a hurry. We get to the station, and I don't even notice that there's a policeman standing by the left luggage counter, I've blundered into a trap. Admittedly, I never thought a father could be so mean to his own son. I recognized the man at the left luggage right away, but he claimed he'd never seen me. We described the bicycle to him, and he went looking for it, but there was no bike answering to that description. Then my old man König said at the top of his voice: 'Now, admit it, Felix, you stole the bike and flogged it.'

'No,' I says to him. 'I swear I handed it in here, and if it's no longer there, then it's because someone's found the ticket and collected it.' At that my father just laughed, and said: 'Constable, please! You've heard our whole exchange, now I hand you over this lad; I wash my hands of him.' And the constable puts the bracelets on me, and my father walked out and didn't even shake hands or say good night.

Now, think about it if you will, Your Honour! I've confessed to a whole lot of jobs I had no need to tell you about, and actually wasn't going to when I started, and there are some offences in Mecklenburg among them that you can lock me up for, and I'm not about to deny them either – but why wouldn't I own up to the theft of a lousy bicycle? See, I didn't steal it, and I want to be acquitted on that charge, so that my father can stand there in shame for getting his innocent son hauled off to prison for something he didn't do! I've every right to ask that, and I know what's right, Your Honour, and that's why I want you to acquit me on this charge! Because I've got my honour too, and that won't permit me to rob my own father, whereas my father, he's got no honour, because he's perfectly able it seems to get his innocent son hauled off to prison.

Now, if you had a cigarette for me, Your Honour, I promise I won't smoke it till after lock-up, so you won't get into trouble on account of me. No one's got in trouble on my account. I've given you so many good charges against myself, that'll make you popular with your superiors for getting all that out of me, even if I did tell them all to you freely.

No? Well, never mind. But I'll tell you this, Your Honour, don't go by anything I said to you because I don't know nuffink about nuffink, I just made up the whole bang shoot to get you to give me a cigarette, and if you won't, then I got no option but to deny it all. Not just the bicycle, which I was denying anyway. Everything else as well. The lot. The whole flaming lot.

Note on Sources

Dates of First Publication

The Wedding Ring: 'Der Trauring' in *Die große Welt*, vol. 2 (1925) 17 [August], pp. 113–19.

Passion: 'Länge der Leidenschaft' in Hans Fallada, *Gesammelte Erzählungen* (Reinbek bei Hamburg: Rowohlt, 1967), pp. 99–114.

Tales from the Underworld: 'Gauner-Geschichten' in Hans Fallada, *Märchen und Geschichten*, edited by Günter Caspar (Berlin and Weimar: Aufbau-Verlag, 1985), pp. 38–46.

Farmers in the Revenue Office: 'Bauernkäuze auf dem Finanzamt' in *Berliner Montagspost*, 4 May 1931.

Kubsch and His Allotment: 'Kubsch und seine Parzelle' in *Berliner Montagspost*, 1 June 1931.

Mother Lives on Her Pension: 'Mutter lebt von ihrer Rente' in *Berliner Montagspost*, 29 June 1931.

A Burglar's Dreams Are of His Cell: 'Einbrecher träumt von der Zelle' in *Berliner Montagspost*, 13 July 1931.

Why Do You Wear a Cheap Watch?: 'Warum trägst du eine Nickeluhr?' in *Berliner Montagspost*, 10 August 1931.

On the Lam: 'Ein Mensch auf der Flucht' in *Uhu*, vol. 7 (1931) 12 [September], pp. 43–51.

I Get a Job: 'Ich bekomme Arbeit' in *Die Tat*, vol. 24 (1932) 9 [December], pp. 778–86.

A Bad Night: 'Eine schlimme Nacht' in *Münchner Illustrierte Presse*, 20 December 1931, pp. 1616–18.

The Open Door: 'Die offene Tür' in *Die grüne Post*, 3 January 1932.

War Monument or Urinal?: 'Das Groß-Stankmal' in *Der Querschnitt*, vol. 12 (1932) 2 [February], pp. 117–23.

Happiness and Woe: 'Fröhlichkeit und Traurigkeit' in *Frankfurter Zeitung und Handelsblatt*, 2 February 1932.

With Measuring Tape and Watering Can: 'Mit Metermaß und Gießkanne' *Uhu*, vol. 8 (1932) 10 [July], pp. 25–34.

The Lucky Beggar: 'Der Bettler, der Glück bringt' in *Berliner Montagspost*, 13 June 1932.

Just Like Thirty Years Ago: 'Wie vor dreißig Jahren' in *Die grüne Post*, 27 November 1932.

Fifty Marks and a Merry Christmas: 'Fünfzig Mark und ein fröhliches Weihnachtsfest' in *Uhu*, vol. 9 (1932) 3 [December], pp. 28–38 and 104–6.

The Good Pasture on the Right: 'Gute Krüseliner Wiese rechts' in *Berliner Morgenpost*, 27 October 1934.

The Missing Greenfinches: 'Die verlorenen Grünfinken' in *Die Dame*, vol. 62 (1935) 25 [December], pp. 36–8 and 92–7.

Food and Grub: 'Essen und Fraß' in *Nacht-Express*, 23 December 1945.

The Good Meadow: 'Die gute Wiese' in *Tägliche Rundschau*, 16 June 1946.

Calendar Stories: 'Kalendergeschichten 1–3' in *Tägliche Rundschau*, 27 June 1946; 'Kalendergeschichten 4–5' in *Tägliche Rundschau*, 30 June 1946; 'Kalendergeschichten 6–9' in *Tägliche Rundschau*, 28 July 1946.

The Returning Soldier: 'Der Heimkehrer' in *Tägliche Rundschau*, 14 July 1946.

The Old Flame: 'Alte Feuerstätten' in *Tägliche Rundschau*, 3 November 1946.

Short Treatise on the Joys of Morphinism: 'Sachlicher Bericht über das Glück, ein Morphinist zu sein' in Hans Fallada, *Drei Jahre kein Mensch. Erlebtes. Erfahrenes. Erfundenes. Geschichten aus dem Nachlaß 1929–1944*, edited by Günter Caspar (Berlin: Aufbau-Verlag, 1997), pp. 5–24.

Three Years of Life: 'Drei Jahre kein Mensch' in Hans Fallada, *Drei Jahre kein Mensch. Erlebtes. Erfahrenes. Erfundenes. Geschichten aus dem Nachlaß 1929–1944*, edited by Günter Caspar (Berlin: Aufbau-Verlag, 1997), pp. 25–53.

Svenda, a Dream Fragment; *or*, My Worries: 'Svenda, ein Traumtorso oder Meine Sorgen' in Hans Fallada, *Drei Jahre kein Mensch. Erlebtes.*

Erfahrenes. Erfundenes. Geschichten aus dem Nachlaß 1929–1944, edited by Günter Caspar (Berlin: Aufbau-Verlag, 1997), pp. 109–13.

Looking for My Father: 'Ich suche den Vater' in Hans Fallada, *Drei Jahre kein Mensch. Erlebtes. Erfahrenes. Erfundenes. Geschichten aus dem Nachlaß 1929–1944*, edited by Günter Caspar (Berlin: Aufbau-Verlag, 1997), pp. 114–34.

PENGUIN MODERN CLASSICS

ALONE IN BERLIN
HANS FALLADA

'A truly great book .. an utterly gripping thriller' Justin Cartwright, *Sunday Telegraph*

Berlin, 1940, and the city is filled with fear. At the house on 55 Jablonski Strasse, its various occupants try to live under Nazi rule in their different ways: the bullying Hitler loyalists the Persickes, the retired judge Fromm and the unassuming couple Otto and Anna Quangel. Then the Quangels receive the news that their beloved son has been killed fighting in France. Shocked out of their quiet existence, they begin a silent campaign of defiance, and a deadly game of cat and mouse develops between the Quangels and the ambitious Gestapo inspector Escherich. When petty criminals Kluge and Borkhausen also become involved, deception, betrayal and murder ensue, tightening the noose around the Quangels' necks ...

'Fallada's great novel, beautifully translated by the poet Michael Hofmann, evokes the daily horror of life under the Third Reich, where the venom of Nazism seeped into the very pores of society, poisoning every aspect of existence. It is a story of resistence, sly humour and hope' Ben Macintyre, *The Times*

'[*Alone in Berlin*] has something of the horror of Conrad, the madness of Dostoyevsky and the chilling menace of Capote's *In Cold Blood*' Roger Cohen, *New York Times*

PENGUIN MODERN CLASSICS

A SMALL TOWN IN GERMANY
JOHN LE CARRÉ

West Germany, a simmering cauldron of radical protests, has produced a new danger to Britain: Karfeld, menacing leader of the opposition. At the same time Leo Harting, a Second Secretary in the British Embassy, has gone missing — along with more than forty Confidential embassy files. Alan Turner of the Foreign Office must travel to Bonn to recover them, facing riots, Nazi secrets and the delicate machinations of an unstable Europe in the throes of the Cold War.

As Turner gets closer to the truth of Harting's disappearance, he will discover that the face of International relations — and the attentions of the British Ministry itself — is uglier that he could possibly have imagined.

'Exciting, compulsively readable and brilliantly plotted' *The New York Times*

Contemporary ... Provocative ... Outrageous ...
Prophetic ... Groundbreaking ... Funny ... Disturbing ...
Different ... Moving ... Revolutionary ... Inspiring ...
Subversive ... Life-changing ...

What makes a modern classic?

At Penguin Classics our mission has always been to make the best
books ever written available to everyone. And that also means
constantly redefining and refreshing exactly what makes a 'classic'.
That's where Modern Classics come in. Since 1961 they have been an
organic, ever-growing and ever-evolving list of books from the last
hundred (or so) years that we believe will continue to be read over and
over again.

They could be books that have inspired political dissent, such as
Animal Farm. Some, like *Lolita* or *A Clockwork Orange*, may have
caused shock and outrage. Many have led to great films, from *In Cold
Blood* to *One Flew Over the Cuckoo's Nest*. They have broken down
barriers – whether social, sexual, or, in the case of *Ulysses*, the
boundaries of language itself. And they might – like *Goldfinger* or
Scoop – just be pure classic escapism. Whatever the reason, Penguin
Modern Classics continue to inspire, entertain and enlighten millions
of readers everywhere.

'No publisher has had more influence on reading habits than Penguin'
Independent

'Penguins provided a crash course in world literature'
Guardian

The best books ever written

PENGUIN 🐧 CLASSICS

SINCE 1946

Find out more at www.penguinclassics.com